CLOSING
CEREMONIES

Novels by Harold King

PARADIGM RED
FOUR DAYS
THE TASKMASTER
CLOSING CEREMONIES

CLOSING CEREMONIES

Harold King

Coward, McCann & Geoghegan
New York

Lines from "Lili Marlene" © copyright by Edward B. Marks Music Corporation. Used by permission.

Lines from *Adolf Hitler* by John Toland, copyright © 1976 by John Toland. Reprinted by permission of Doubleday & Co.

Library of Congress Cataloging in Publication Data

King, Harold, date.
    Closing ceremonies.

    I. Title.
PZ4.K52165C1   1979   [PS3561.I476]   813'.5'4   79-10582
ISBN 0-698-10950-3

Printed in the United States of America

*For Brian
and Jack—
mentors,
professionals
and friends.*

The opening ceremonies on August 1 were
blessed by a clear blue sky. That afternoon
Hitler led the parade to the stadium down
the Via Triumphalis. His car, followed by
a long caravan, proceeded slowly down the
ten-mile boulevard, protected from the
crowds by 40,000 Brownshirts and other guards.
When the procession reached the stadium
Hitler, in the simplest uniform, and two
Olympic officials strode forward. They
marched through the tunnel into the world's
largest stadium to be greeted by a brassy
voluntary from thirty trumpets.

—John Toland, *Adolf Hitler*

The most important thing in the
Olympic Games is not to win
but to take part, just as the most
important thing in life is not
the triumph but the struggle.
The essential thing is not to
have conquered but to have
fought well.
—The Olympic Creed

OPENING CEREMONIES

1

The hacienda was ahead, maybe fifty meters.

"When we rush it, wait at the fence." That's what he'd been told.

Aaron lay on his stomach in a muddy depression near some thorny Paraguayan bush, praying to God the Uzi machine gun he clutched beside him in the darkness was on safe. The night sounds of insects were all around, and twice in the last few minutes he had felt something light on the crown of his black beret.

He hated bugs. Any sort of bug. But Abe had told him not to move. With a sudden swift gesture, he had told them all to get down. Abe, Aaron told himself, knew what he was doing. He had been telling himself that again and again since they had climbed out of the wretchedly cramped boat from the slimy waters where the Paraguay and Apa rivers converge in Boqueron Province opposite Brazil's western border. He'd been telling himself that since they marched out of the marsh onto the scrubland and half-walked, half-crawled these last hundred meters to this muddy, buggy spot. Abe knew what he was doing. What wasn't clear to Aaron at the moment was what on earth had possessed him to be here too. Abe was the professional. And the other two, Hill and McDermit. They were the experts. So what was he doing here?

"Practical experience, kid," Abe had said, grinning his devilish grin. At the time, back in his Georgetown apartment with ice clinking in his bourbon and the stereo purring a soft Sinatra, it had sounded like a reasonable way to make five thousand dollars. "It's a simple pickup," he remembered Abe saying matter-of-factly. Everything Abe said was matter-of-fact. "I'm taking three men. It'll be easy money, kid, a piece of cake. Believe me, the danger will be minimal." He believed Abe. He'd always believed Abe. Honest Abe.

So why was he here, lying in a dark Paraguayan mudhole, the target of a cloud of killer bugs?

Because you don't distrust your older brother. That was Abe's First Law. And Abraham Sullivan Miller was a person you listened to. At least he was if you happened to be Aaron Kyle Miller. Up to now, it had been a law that had served him well. The week after they buried their parents was when Aaron learned his first lesson. Aaron was fourteen and Abe was a man, that December in 1962. He came to live with his brother in Virginia and went to a private boarding school. Abe paid for that because there was nothing in their father's army chaplain estate except a De Soto station wagon and a five-thousand-dollar insurance policy, and it took that to lay them both to rest in Portsmouth, Ohio. High school in the mid-sixties was when he learned Abe's Second Law. Aaron hadn't exactly known what his brother did. Abe would be around for a while, not keeping any particular hours, and then sometimes be gone for weeks at a time. When he asked, he learned: You don't answer dumb questions. So, Aaron quit asking. He understood dumb questions. Like, why did the Miller brothers have Jewish names if they weren't Jews? To the son of a Methodist army chaplain whose name was Joseph and the grandson and great-grandson of Daniel and Joshua Miller, *that* was a dumb question. Did anybody ever ask if Abe Lincoln was Jewish?

After the University of Maryland and a stint with the Coast

Guard, he landed a civilian job with the Defense Department in 1973. "Evaluation of Program Analysis Section" was another way of saying contingency planning. If the Soviets stage a war games exercise at Gdánsk, what would the NATO reaction be at the Northern European Command in the United Kingdom? It had been a guessing game of colored blocks and computer printouts. *Had* was the operative word here. This was 1976. Watergate was behind us, if you could believe an unelected President. What wasn't behind us was an ever spiraling inflation rate and the need to dig out from recession brought on by the Republicans, if you could believe the Democrats. This bicentennial year was also an election year and if it was difficult for incumbents, it was murder for non-Civil Service types. The Defense Department was in the midst of another cleansing. "Evaluation of Program Analysis Section" was also another way of saying unemployment. They would contact him again for reemployment in December (after the elections). That was when Aaron called his big brother and got this offer of a trip to South America. He also learned Abe's Third Law. You take what you can get.

Something touched Aaron's ear.

He'd been squinting intently at the hacienda, trying to concentrate on the light filtering through the shuttered windows, on what was inside, trying to avoid thinking about what was out here, flying around in the dark.

"When I signal down," Abe's words came back to him, "I mean down *flat still* and I don't care if you're knee deep in toad shit. Down is down like a rock. Frozen."

Aaron was frozen. A scared, sweaty rock. An insect moved along the fold of his beret and onto the prickly hairs at the back of his neck, its sticky legs feeling the clammy skin around his sweat-soaked collar. Bugs are not carnivorous, he told himself again and again.

"Go!" Abe's voice cut through the darkness. "Now."

The sudden command startled him. The shadowy figures rose up from the ground around him, and Aaron was suddenly gripped with a new fear. Run low. Stay close to Abe. Hold the Uzi with both hands.

From somewhere behind the hacienda came the sound of goats or sheep moving in a corral. The smell grew stronger the nearer they came. And they came fast. Hill and McDermit were already past the fence. They moved incredibly quickly. And without a sound. Abe hit the patio just as Aaron was climbing the fence.

The sentry had moved to a corner of the mud-caked patio to take a piss. He was a short, fat man with a shabby mustache and he'd left his ancient rifle propped against a chair. His brown shirt was dingy in the dim light, but there was no mistaking the emblem on the wrinkled armband—a hand-drawn swastika inside a white circle.

Abe had the moves of a cat. He was across the patio like a blurred image. The sentry's face registered ignorant surprise, his hands still groping in his trousers, until Abe's tap against his head with the butt of the Uzi dropped him. Then Abe crashed inside. There was a machine-gun burst, and from Aaron's position at the fence he saw roof shingles dance violently from the impact.

For several minutes there was nothing. Then loud voices speaking in Spanish that told Aaron nothing except that there were frightened men inside. McDermit came out on the patio to haul the dazed sentry inside.

Aaron began to feel foolish. The initial flush of fear was gone. He wanted to be involved now. But Abe had told him to wait at the fence until he called. So Aaron waited.

A Guarani Indian awakened the German at his place in the mountains. There was some trouble at the hacienda down in the scrublands. They had seen four men with guns who came from the river.

It was of no particular concern to him, except that the Montoneros were getting bolder these days and raiding Indian settlements for food. The Guarani was afraid. The man they called the German in the village of Bela Vista dressed and slid a Luger into his waistband. He would have a look, he told the Guarani.

The German had known the hacienda was more than a shep farm because herdsmen do not flaunt armbands or receive visitors in long black Mercedes limousines. He had known other things too, but his interest in their secrets did not move him to investigate further. Until now.

The German had seen the rag-tag operation of the Peronist guerrillas before. But this did not sound like bandits. Montoneros would not come from the river. This had the markings of professionals who knew what they were after. He knew this would come one day. He had prepared himself for it. The German left his place in the mountains. He moved swiftly and quietly through the brush. Night stalking suited him.

A big familiar figure stood in the frame of the shattered door. "All right, kid. Time to go to work."

There were maybe a dozen of them lined up against the wall, hands on their heads, frightened faces. McDermit and Hill stood off to the side with their weapons at waist level.

"Hold your weapon up," Abe commanded sharply as Aaron entered the room. "The idea is to terrify the fuckers."

The place smelled of sweat and stale cigars. Something had been left to burn on the stove in the corner.

"Which one is it?" Aaron asked in a conspiratorial whisper.

Abe cast hard eyes across the faces of the prisoners. "Let's find out, shall we, little brother?"

"Abe, c'mon . . . not here." It was difficult enough having your older brother take special precautions for your safety—even for a piece of cake—but announcing it was worse.

As Abe moved to each of the men against the wall, Aaron got his first glimpse of himself in the shards of a shattered mirror that hung from a knotted twine beside the door. Gritty, streaked-black face, white eyes below a dark beret. Muddy dungarees and canvas jungle boots and a stubby, ugly machine gun. *He looked like a goddamn commando.* He straightened up, holding the Uzi level like McDermit and Hill as he realized that's exactly what he was. Theoretically.

"This one."

Aaron turned back to see his brother roughly pull a frail-looking old man in white pajamas out of the line.

"This is the one," Abe repeated pitilessly.

The man studied Aaron's brother with eyes that were unafraid. "If you are Montoneros, you make a big mistake."

Abe nodded at Aaron. "He speaks English." To the man in pajamas he said, "We are not bandits." He smiled his grim smile and Aaron knew immediately that the old man had better watch his step. "We came here for you. Erik Semmler." The last was in a dead tone.

The man paled. His glance touched Aaron as it swept quickly around at the other men with the machine guns, at the faces of men without compassion. "Señor, I—I am Manuel Suarez."

"No," Abe said coldly. "You're Erik Semmler—Herr *Hauptsturmfuehrer*. And you're taking a little trip with us. Someone didn't forget you."

"Suarez!" he blurted. "I am Suarez! I am Manuel Suarez!"

"Sure you are." Abe unbuttoned his shirt and slid out a small manila folder. From it he held up a photograph for the man to see. The man pictured was younger then, dressed in an SS captain's uniform. He was standing tall and arrogant beside a cart full of eyeglass frames. Thousands of them. "And this is Manuel Suarez?"

Beads of perspiration stood out on his face and his pajamas clung to his sweaty body. "No, no . . ."

Abe handed the folder to Aaron. "Read it to him."

"You are Erik Franz Semmler," Aaron said, reading from a sheet of paper. "Born April 26, 1915, in Altmünster, Austria. You are the accused—"

"*Nooo!*"

Aaron stopped, blinked, glanced at Abe. "Read it," Abe repeated.

"You are the accused," Aaron went on, "charged with the murder of no less than 400,000 men, women and children—"

"No, no—you are Jews! You cannot do this! This is Paraguay, you cannot—"

Abe stepped up, slapped him once, very hard. The frail old

man reeled back, stunned, suddenly silent. His eyes were red now and teary. The menace was gone.

Aaron stared at him a long moment, then looked back to his paper. "Of no less than 400,000 in the death camps of Buchenwald in 1943 and 1944 in your capacity as deputy commandant." He looked up from the page. "These are the charges against you."

"No! Please, you cannot . . ."

"Yes, I can, Herr Semmler." Abe stepped forward again.

"It was Eicke . . . and Stangl. Not me. I was only a soldier. It was not me!" Semmler stepped back. "What will you do with me?"

"You remember Eichmann," Abe said. He smiled as he moved.

"No—" Semmler said to the man coming toward him. "No!" He tried to move away. "Wait—wait! We must speak in private. I . . . I have money."

"You won't need it."

"I have—"

"You have nothing," Abe said in a tired voice. "Nothing."

"You want Nazis? I can give you Nazis." Semmler was desperate now. The menace had crept back into his eyes. There was only one bargaining commodity left.

Abe seated himself on the edge of a table and shook out a cigarette from a pack. "Take the others outside, Mac," he ordered, "and deal with them." McDermit and Hill herded them out onto the patio. Abe cupped the lighter in his hand and lit the cigarette. When he snapped the lid shut, Semmler jumped. "They're always ready to make deals," he said to Aaron, nodding at the little man in the soiled pajamas.

"Yes, yes," Semmler replied eagerly. "We shall make a deal. I can—"

"Not interested," Abe said. He did not look at Semmler. "Who is worth the deputy commandant of Buchenwald, kid?"

Aaron shook his head.

"Mengele," Semmler answered.

Abe shook his head. "Semmler, Semmler, you underrate your own value." He hopped down from the table. "Let's go."

Abe slung his Uzi over his shoulder and started toward the door.

"*Wait!*" Semmler lunged after Abe and fell to his knees. "There is something else. I can give you something else! I can give you . . . I can give you Martin Bormann."

"Bormann is dead."

". . . and . . . and . . ."

Abe glanced back at Aaron. "Get him off his knees. We're leaving."

Semmler began to laugh, slowly at first, and shaking his head until he was almost hysterical. "You Jews . . . you are still so stupid. *So stupid!* You come all the way here for little Semmler and do not know what you have found. You learn nothing. You see nothing!"

Aaron crossed angrily to Semmler and hauled him up by the front of his pajamas. "We found you." He was learning initiative. Abe's kind.

"I am nothing." Semmler's breath stank. "You do not know what I can give you."

"What?" Aaron demanded.

"Something you could never dream of."

"Bormann is dead, kid." Abe snuffed out the cigarette. "Don't let yourself get conned."

"Yes," Semmler said quickly, "and Himmler. And Heydrich . . . others. It is curious, the mind of a Jew. Interesting, I think." Semmler's expression soured. "The stinking corpses of a million Jews brought you here, I think, yes? Is it not true Auschwitz is a monument today? We do not forget those things that are left behind to remind or inspire us. Or do you Jews reserve that for yourselves only?"

"What are you selling, Semmler?" Aaron said.

"I can give you something of great importance—greater than Martin Bormann alive. And you give something of importance to me." Semmler sank to his knees again.

"We let you go?" Aaron asked.

"Forget it, kid. We've got a long walk ahead."

"For you it would be the bargain worth a thousand Semmlers," said the former *Hauptsturmfuehrer*, concentrating on Aaron. "Besides, I will die only one time and it will be done." He wiped his sleeve across his face. "I can do what I say . . . I promise you."

Aaron said nothing, only stared at the old man in white pajamas. A man who in another time had annihilated hundreds of thousands simply by signing his name.

"There is a place near here," Semmler said to fill the pause. "A sacred place. It is called *das Reichsgrabgewoelbe* . . . Mausoleum of the Reich. Bormann is there. And Himmler and Heydrich and several more. Skorzeny. And also Goebbels. It is a very splendid place with much—"

"Goebbels was burned in the bunker . . . they doused his body with gasoline." Abe was getting impatient. "C'mon, kid."

"Yes, that is exactly so. But I can tell you—on this fact I have intimate knowledge—a corpse cannot be totally destroyed by fire." Semmler arched his eyebrows as if to emphasize his observation. "Enough remained that could be saved."

Aaron looked suddenly at his brother. "A crypt?"

Abe shrugged, then smiled. "You want a souvenir, kid?"

"If it's what he says it is, maybe it's worth a look." Aaron tried not to sound excited.

Abraham Miller rubbed his jawline thoughtfully. "We got what we came for. Let's not push our luck."

"Abe . . . if he's telling the truth . . ." Aaron glanced back at Semmler. "Where is this mausoleum?"

"Near. Very near." The old man's smile exuded confidence.

"Abe?" Aaron said, watching his brother. Abe was the professional.

For a long time the elder Miller was quiet. Finally he moved to where Semmler was kneeling on the floor and forced the old man down with his foot across his neck. "My kid brother never dealt with assholes like you. If this is a con . . ." He pressed his boot down.

"Truth!" the old man choked out. "I swear it!"

Abe removed his foot. Semmler struggled to his knees, coughing. Abe leaned down close to his face. He slipped a knife from its sheath and touched it to Semmler's nose. "I'll cut out your fucking eyes if you're lying, old man." He said it low, barely a whisper. Aaron was suddenly caught in the net of fear his brother cast. He'd never seen him this intent, this deadly. He knew he meant exactly what he said. Now, so did Semmler.

"Truth," Semmler repeated fearfully.

"Show me."

"And afterwards?" the old man said. "Our deal?"

"Show me first," Abe said, sheathing the knife.

Semmler smiled. "My pleasure."

The place was exactly as Semmler had described it, an abandoned rock quarry with half a dozen dilapidated buildings.

They drove an old Ford pickup from the hacienda and the old man sat between Abe and Aaron. Hill rode in the back and McDermit was left to finish up at the hacienda.

When Hill signaled that the place was deserted, Abe shoved the old man out of the truck and Aaron walked behind him with the muzzle of his Uzi against Semmler's ribs.

"You people are very efficient," Semmler said over his shoulder. "But I think you are too apprehensive. I told you there was no one here. You can trust me."

"Sure, kid," Abe said. "Just don't let him offer to show you the showers."

Semmler led them to a mine tunnel entrance. Tacked on the crossbeam was a sign warning against rotted timbers and cave-ins. Inside, Aaron could see broken beams and mounds of rubble from a collapsed wall.

"Now what?"

"It's your show, kid," Abe said. "I'm just along to keep you company." Aaron looked at Semmler. "Well?"

"Ingenious, isn't it?" In the faint light Aaron could see the old man smiling. "Actually, this was purposely constructed to discourage curious children if they happened to wander to so remote a place. This is a shell of reinforced concrete. The

Fuehrerbunker was not this solidly constructed."

"This isn't a tour, Semmler." Abe's voice was hard.

"Behind the beam, there on your left. A switch. It will admit us."

Aaron found it with his free hand, a weatherproof toggle switch inside a protective cover plate. When he flipped the toggle there was a whir of distant motor and a moment later a section of the opposite wall, two battered, rotted beams, opened. Behind it was a cement passageway, lit with green-shaded bulbs.

They waited at the tunnel entrance until Hill returned from the passageway.

"Jesus, Abe, I don't believe it."

"What have we got here?" Abe said.

"A fucking nightmare. Take a look. Three levels down. You won't believe it."

Hill was instructed to wait at the entrance. "Stay behind me, kid," Abe said, then prodded Semmler ahead of him into the passage and down the stairs. At the bottom was a small wall-papered foyer with a walnut stand beside an ornately carved door. A leather-bound guest book lay open on the stand.

"Take a look at this, Aaron," Abe said. The last visitor had been only four months ago. Aaron saw the name.

Dr. Josef Mengele.

Abe glanced down the page list of names. "He's been here more than once. Others, too. Look there." He pointed out another name. "Bormann." The date beside the name was July 1974.

Abe looked angrily at the old man. "What the hell *is* this place?"

"There is more," Semmler said.

They stepped into a marble gallery—the size and grandeur made Aaron suck in his breath. The ceiling must have been twenty-five feet high and the hall ran at least fifty yards. The left side of the gallery was a continuous colonnade of marble stucco window wells twenty feet high with enormous Nazi flags hung in the inserts instead of windows. Between them, gilded wall sconces of bronze lighted the way with a low incandescence that emphasized the massive scale of the place. The wall opposite the colonnade held three imposing portals, each with huge double mahogany paneled doors recessed in marble. The center portal was flanked by decorative seventeenth-century Gobelin tapestries suspended on the walls. Below them, padded high-back chairs were set around low dark wood pedestal tables. Above the lintel was a crested shield with the initials A.H. in relief.

"You could turn a goddamn truck around in here," Abe said.

"Welcome to the Long Hall of the Reich Chancellery," Semmler offered boastfully.

"Chancellery?"

"A scale facsimile of the Berlin original." Semmler smiled. "The Fuehrer's study is just through there." He pointed to the central portal.

Aaron looked down the length of the gallery. Semmler pushed open the double doors. Inside was opulence on the same grand scale, a massive space surrounded by dark red marble walls and brown ebony wainscoting. At one end of the room was a broad fireplace let into the wall with a large sitting area before it. At the other end a long, wide rosewood desk stood in the middle of an oriental rug and behind it, a tufted leather chair. The desk top was clear except for a large blotter, a bronze lamp and a black narrow-handled telephone.

"The furnishings of the Fuehrer's study were crated and shipped here by Herr Bormann himself." Semmler walked to the center of the room. "It is as if the Fuehrer could walk in at any moment with Reich Marshal Goering and Dr. Goebbels at his side."

"Not bloodly likely," Abe said. He walked to the desk, opened drawers, tested the phone. He glanced at Aaron. "Dead."

"A decoration only," Semmler said.

"But it keeps the illusion alive, eh, *Herr Hauptsturm-fuehrer?*" Abe put his foot on the leather chair. As Semmler's mouth opened to object, he kicked the chair over backward.

"What kind of fucking crazy funhouse is this!"

Semmler took an angry step forward, but stopped suddenly at the pressure of the muzzle of Aaron's weapon in his back.

"Bormann built it," the former vice commandant said after a moment. "And the *Oberkomitee*. It is more than an illusion."

"It's a goddamn *shrine*," Abe said, glancing around the room.

Semmler smiled enigmatically. "No, no. The shrine is through there." He nodded toward a set of doors behind the desk.

"There's more?" Aaron said.

"Much more."

The little man led the way to an adjacent room that was at once ghastly and magnificent.

Paneled walls of polished oak and mahogany were covered with portraits and enlarged photographs of Hitler and his inner circle. There were pictures of Goebbels and Himmler sitting together in the garden at Berghof, sipping drinks with Eva; Heydrich with a group of Brownshirters; Goering with a slender young woman in front of the Chancellery; a portrait of Eichmann in SS uniform waving at the camera; and scores of pictures of Hitler at work or relaxing. One small frame held a grainy blowup of Blondi, the Fuehrer's dog. The room was filled with tables and glass cases of Reich memorabilia; medals, buckles, knives, badges, emblems, pistols, rifles and swastikas, hundreds of them—metal, cloth, braided, on music stands, armbands, posters. Aaron was dumbstruck.

"An impressive collection, wouldn't you say?"

Abe shoved the old man down to the polished marble floor so hard that Semmler slid against the wall. "Shut up!"

The displays were arranged neatly in long rows of showcase tables. At the end of the rows were manikins in the dress uniforms of each branch of the Wehrmacht. Two rows near the center were headed by models dressed in the formal uniform of Himmler's rank, *SS Reichsfuehrer*, and the black regalia of a Gestapo *Obersturmbannfuehrer*. The centermost row was reserved for personal items of Hitler. His birth certificate encased in glass. Sketches by him. An Iron Cross, 2nd class, from World War I. Boots. A tie. Gloves. A pair of glasses. A Walther pistol beside a photo of his mother as a young woman. Other things. Last on the row was a rubber comb next to a lock of hair.

"This is depravity," Aaron said. He started at the lines of pictures covering the walls.

Semmler, his arms still tied behind his back, worked his way up to his feet. "Look in there." He nodded toward a door beneath a large portrait of Hitler. "In there is something for you to see."

Abe nodded for Aaron to go ahead.

He moved slowly to the door, hesitating a moment before opening it. He was totally unprepared for what he found. The room was bathed in a red hue. Indirect lighting from recesses in the twenty-foot ceiling highlighted dozens of Nazi flags suspended on the walls like drapes. In the middle of the wall opposite the entrance was a giant photographic enlargement, almost a mural, of a Nuremberg party rally. A hundred thousand German soldiers in precise unbroken ranks held out their arms in the familiar salute to the figure on the elevated platform. Aaron felt himself shudder. He could almost hear the *"Sieg Heil."*

The room held perhaps twenty sarcophagi on marble bases. Each was engraved with a name and below each name was etched in stone the Reich symbol of an eagle, its talons clutching a swastika. He walked among them, touching the polished surfaces as if to confirm the reality of what he saw.

REINHARD HEYDRICH. HEINRICH HIMMLER. MARTIN BORMANN. JOSEPH GOEBBELS. OTTO SKORZENY. THEODOR EICKE.

The shock was not in reading the names. The shock was knowing they were in this room. The short rows of sepulchers were symmetrically arranged to provide space for more.

From the door, he heard the old man call him. "I told you it would be worth your while. I told you that. Look there, at the front. It will entrance you."

He moved toward a large altarlike platform shrouded with two large flags. At the edge, he looked down into a lighted glass-encased well lined with black velvet. In the center was a gold cinerary urn. On its top was a wreathed swastika. But no name. They could not put a name on this shrine, as if a deity needed none. Aaron could only stare at the inscription.

Der Fuehrer.

"Sweet Jesus!"

"What do you make of it, kid?" Abe said. "Museum?"

"More than that."

"Much more," Semmler said. "No Jew has ever seen this place."

"And still hasn't," Aaron replied angrily.

"Go to the truck," Abe said. "Bring all the gasoline you can carry."

"Gasoline?" Semmler said dully.

Abe nodded. "There's a twenty-gallon can on the truck. As quick as you can."

"Right," Aaron said.

"What are you doing?" Semmler said quickly.

"We're going to have a bonfire."

"Burn the *Reichsgrabgewoelbe*?"

"Clever, isn't it?" Abe said, resting the Uzi on his hip. "Our own private Holocaust."

"You cannot—"

"Watch me."

"Then you will let me go?" The old man was sweating again.

Aaron looked at Abe. His brother smiled.

"No." Abe had a smile that could kill.

"No!"

"Yes, I think you have it now." The professional glanced at his younger brother. "Lubetkin would be very disappointed if we didn't bring back his buddy from Buchenwald."

"You gave your word!" Semmler rasped.

"Yes," Abe said after a moment. "That's exactly what I did, isn't it?" To Aaron he said, "Now get the gasoline, kid."

Aaron splashed the contents of the gasoline can in each of

the rooms as Abe placed the plastic in the walls and along the colonnade. Aaron brought another can and emptied it. Before they were finished the place smelled like a filling station.

When he heard the click of the cocking arm, Aaron was with Abe setting a charge at the base of a pillar and suddenly wondered what had happened to Semmler. Too late.

"Streicher was right. You Jews *are* a stupid breed." The voice behind them was resonant with contempt. The old man had lost his whine. When Aaron turned back, Semmler was standing beside the heavy door leading to the gallery. His wrists were no longer tied. In one hand he held a 9 mm Luger from one of the displays. In the other, an SS dagger. Abe glanced at Aaron. "I told you to watch him!"

"Sorry, Abe, I—"

"Shit, kid." He didn't seem half as frightened as Aaron was.

"You thought I was an old woman?" Semmler said. He moved laterally, taking care not to have any great distance between them or too short a distance. Semmler knew how to handle the weapon he'd found. He held it in the correct assault fashion: arm cocked at the elbow, knees bent, body leaning slightly forward. He might have taken the same lessons from Abe. Aaron remembered from Abe's briefing that the Luger was not terribly useful as a field weapon, its effective range was less than forty meters. An academic point, now he was well within killing radius. But Semmler probably had never shot a man face-to-face. His style was from behind. From less than a foot. At the base of the skull.

"Don't move, Jews. Do not make an attempt to unsling your weapons."

"I'm sorry, Abe, I should've been watching . . ."

"Silence!" Semmler motioned for Aaron to drop the gasoline can.

Aaron did exactly that, but Abe held his hands out from his body at waist level. "This will get you nothing, Semmler," Abe said.

"Silence! You tricked me, Jew."

"He's going to be disappointed," Abe said, "when he finds out we aren't Jews."

Semmler pointed the Luger between them, unsure of which to concentrate on.

"You can't shoot us both, you know," Aaron's brother said. "One of us, but not both. Either way, you'll lose." His voice was incredibly calm. "Just put down the—"

"Silence!"

He continued to move to his left slowly, a small figure moving before the red tapestry of flags. Semmler nodded toward the ceiling. "Look there. A closed-circuit camera. At this moment we are being recorded."

Aaron looked up to see the recessed cavity and the black camera lens.

"And how do you suppose they'll figure we got down here?" Abe taunted. "We sure didn't know about this place. Someone brought us here. What do you think, kid?"

Aaron was too frightened to think. "Right," he said in a strained voice.

Semmler wiped the sweat from his forehead. "You said you would release me!"

"Where would you go now?" Abe said.

Suddenly the lights from the gallery through the doorway went out. A moment later a pistol exploded. Semmler's face registered surprise. He staggered a step forward, the Luger dropped from his hand and he half-turned in the doorway. A spot on the back of his white pajamas was stained red and spreading quickly. Semmler's eyes widened. He was looking back into the gallery, his mouth gaping, then quickly trying to work.

"*Kettenhund! Nein! Ketten—*"

He raised his hands as if to stop the slug that ripped open his throat.

Abe was down instantly behind the sarcophagus marked HEYDRICH. He flicked off the safety on the Uzi. It had happened so fast, so violently, Aaron was still rooted to the spot, staring at Semmler's body, watching the blood collect in a pool beside his chest. "Jesus."

"Kid, for Chrissakes, get down!"

But Aaron lacked his brother's instincts. He'd never seen

this kind of death. Death was a closed casket, not a crumpled, oozing body on a tile floor.

"Aaron!"

"He's dead," Aaron said stupidly. He looked toward the darkened doorway. "Who . . ."

"*Get down!*"

Aaron crouched behind a sarcophagus. "Who's out there, Abe? Isn't Hill—"

"Hill doesn't have a Luger," Abe's voice came back. "Stay down."

"But, then—"

"We have uninvited company."

Aaron took a deep breath, rested his head against the cool wood of Eicke's sarcophagus. "Jesus."

For several seconds there was silence.

"Kid?"

"Yeah?"

"When I say go, I want you to let loose at that doorway."

Aaron swallowed. "Shoot at it?"

"Yes, asshole . . . Christ!"

Aaron nodded to himself. "Okay. Okay. Say when."

"And keep your goddamn head down."

"I will, Abe." He damned sure would. Aaron clicked the Uzi safety off the lock S position to A. "Okay." He gripped the weapon with both hands.

"Now!"

Aaron held the submachine gun up and squeezed the trigger. Hell broke loose in his hands. The area above the door and beside it exploded from the impact. He could hear glass breaking behind him, but he kept up the rain of bullets until the last round was ejected and the bolt slammed shut. When it was over, he dropped back behind the sarcophagus, sweaty, scared and pleased with himself. He'd destroyed an empty doorway.

"Abe?"

"You didn't have to use the whole goddamn clip, kid. Stick in another and, remember, short bursts. We'll get out of here yet."

"If you say so." Aaron ejected the empty clip, inserted a full one. The smell of spent gunpowder was in his clothes.

"Just remember Abe's First Law."

"I don't see anybody," Aaron said.

"Don't look for trouble. Stay down."

"I heard glass breaking." Aaron sat back on his heels. He couldn't see Abe or anything else except the ends of sarcophagi. "Was that you?" he called out.

A hand touched his shoulder and his heart nearly stopped. He turned to see his big brother grinning. "Yeah, me." Abe handed him the gold urn from the showcase. "A souvenir, kid."

Aaron looked at him with amazement. Abe shrugged. "It seemed like the thing to do."

"So what now?" Aaron said, holding the urn under his arm.

"I'll create a diversion." He held up the plastic detonator. "There's enough c-4 at the end of this to bring down a mountain. And we got gas for a nice little fire and smoke-screen." Abe pulled a folder of matches from his pocket. "Leave the Uzi, you won't need it. Just hold onto that thing." The urn. "When I say go, you head for the door to the museum."

"But, what about—"

"I'm going to be right on your ass, kid. Got it?"

Aaron nodded.

Abe took up a kneeling position, holding the submachine gun pointed toward the ceiling. "In a situation like this, getting out is the important thing. Noise helps." He patted Aaron on the shoulder. "Get ready." Abe grinned. "See you topside." He turned and lit the matches, tossed them out across the floor where a gas can was lying on its side in a puddle of fuel. It ignited with a burst of flame, fire spreading quickly along the trail of gasoline, licking up the huge, billowing flags. Then he began firing randomly around the room. The large mural collapsed first, crashing into a heap behind the wreathed swastikas. Flags started dropping into the mounting flames. Suddenly, the whole chamber was burning.

"Go!"

Aaron started running for his life, the urn cradled under his arm, cool against his sweaty ribs. He ran zigzag between the tombs, splashing through the burning gasoline, sucking for breath against the smoke. There was shooting behind him, the sounds of mahogany being ripped and splintered by Abe's short, measured bursts. Covering fire from his big brother. Aaron wanted it to be over. He was running, his canvas boots soaked with gasoline and smoldering. He wanted to be back with Sinatra and the security of his overpriced apartment and the unemployment and the Washington *Post*, his favorite chair and all the rest. *He wanted this to be over*, but first he had to get to the door.

At the passageway he stopped, chest heaving, and looked back. Abe was coming. He was running low, crouched, the Uzi and the detonator timer in one hand, and playing out a coil of wire with the other. He was grinning. Only Abe would grin in a flaming underground Nazi Chancellery.

Aaron turned and started to run for the study. He had a flashing glimpse of burning SS manikins at the end of the display cases. But only a glimpse. Because he hadn't taken three good running strides when he ran into the German.

Aaron saw his face clearly. They'd slammed together shoulder to shoulder and in the instant of time it took him to fall to the floor, Aaron saw his angry face, scowling, illuminated by the flames. And he saw the Luger in his hand. Somehow he'd circled back around the gallery, through the study, to here. Aaron watched the finger tighten on the trigger. This was the place he would die, he realized, in a puddle of gasoline and blood, and there was nothing he could do about it.

Then he heard Abe's voice, loud, enraged, as he burst through the door. The Luger adjusted reflexively with a twist of the wrist, fired. And again.

Abe took the blasts full in the chest. The impact staggered him but his momentum propelled him forward and his huge arm, swinging up with the detonator timer, caught his assailant square at the temple and he went down, the Luger sliding across the floor as he crashed into a display table. For several moments, Abe just stood there like a great bewildered bear. Then he dropped forward to his knees. The Uzi slid off his shoulder. His face was as blankly surprised as Semmler's had been when he turned lazily toward Aaron.

"Abe!" Aaron screamed and caught his brother in his arms as he fell.

"Detonator . . ." Abe's mouth was full of blood.

Aaron held his hand over the massive chest, felt the hemorrhaging wound. The fire had spread to the next room. Flames were already licking the ceiling. "Oh, Jesus! God, Abe!"

". . . twist detonator . . ." Abe gripped Aaron's shoulder. "Take the urn . . ."

Aaron tried to stop the blood pouring from Abe's wound. "Christ!" Tears clouded his eyes. "Abe!" The grip on his shoulder tightened.

"Get out, kid."

"No!"

The fire was raging in the doorway. The plastic eyelets on Aaron's boots were beginning to blister.

"No choice." Abe grinned bloodily. "Gotta move ass, kid."

"Abe!"

His eyes fluttered. "Go . . ." Aaron wiped Abe's mouth with his sleeve. "Go, now . . . sorry about this . . . really . . ."

Tears streaked Aaron's blackened face.

Abraham Sullivan Miller said, "Abe's Fourth Law," with a grim smile. "No regrets." Then the breath went out of him, and he was gone.

"You sons of bitches!" Aaron screamed into the fire, rocking on his heels with his brother's corpse. "You god-damn, fucking bastards!"

Part of the ceiling collapsed in a corner. Aaron sheltered Abe's face from the flying cinders. Then he knew he *had* to go. He found the detonator, twisted the timer switch and grabbed the urn. He was crying when he folded Abe's arms across his chest. And then he was running. For an instant he thought he saw Abe's executioner move, but there wasn't time to be sure.

The Fuehrer's study was filling with choking smoke and the oriental rug was blazing as he passed through. He stumbled to the portal and out into the hall of the gallery. The detonator timer had a thirty-second delay and there were precious few seconds left before a mountain would crash down into this goddamn hole.

He held the urn to his side and ran for the exit, twenty yards away, racing down the wide marble hallway. A gasoline-saturated flag dropped burning from a colonnade window and hung on a sconce. He could hear the echo of his footsteps pounding in his head as he ran. Ten yards from the exit passage. Then he heard the sprinting footsteps of someone behind him, long strides of a big man accelerating, closing the gap. Aaron hit the door when the first explosion cratered the far end of the gallery. He was halfway up the passageway, taking two and three steps at a time, when the second explosion rocked the mineshaft, bouncing off the narrow walls, loosening rocks and cracking the concrete bunker. Another blast knocked him down at the mouth of the mine. When he got to his hands and knees he was suddenly staring into the unseeing eyes of John Hill. He was sitting against a rock, his Uzi across his lap, his throat cut.

Aaron was in the truck, pumping the starter, when the succeeding explosions rumbled up from the ground like the sound of a distant surf. In the side mirror he could see smoke belching out the shaft entrance, then a figure darted out. There wasn't time to wait to see who it was. The truck's engine finally spurted into life and lurched forward.

The old Ford truck bounced wildly on the rough, rutted road, speeding crazily for the villa, headlights on full. What remained of the hacienda was only a smoldering ruin. Aaron searched for McDermit almost an hour before he found his body in the ravine beside a dirt road, a bullet in the brain. The executioner had been here too.

It was dawn before Aaron started back into the jungle. One man returning instead of five. One man running, whose fear had turned to anger and anger to rage. He moved quickly, the Uzi strapped across his back. The tears were gone. There was a driving purpose to his life that had not been there before. Under his arm, wrapped in an oily dropcloth and tied with a web belt, he carried the thing that he would make them pay for. And they would pay for it. For Abe.

Aaron would make his own laws now. Aaron Kyle Miller. Because nothing else mattered. Because Abe was dead under a hundred tons of rock in a dirty Paraguayan mine. They would pay.

Aaron knew what he was doing.

2

The São Paulo sun had been up more than an hour by the time Alfred Strausser stirred sleepily beneath satin bed sheets. The brown-eyed Guarani Indian girl he'd found selling programs at the Teatro Municipal was kneading him gently from a kneeling position learned the night before. Strausser came awake slowly, with a pleasureable awareness of the girl's dexterity. She was the best he'd had in months. Last night had been perfect, he remembered. It was not easy for an old man to find someone with the right aptitudes.

Strausser watched her work. He loved to watch. Her deft fingers rolled and pulled at him, urging him on. It wouldn't be long now.

He sighed and the girl smiled without looking up. She pulled back the sheet so he could see better. Ah, oh, yes, this one learned quickly. She was wonderful. Not like so many he'd found. This one didn't talk, which was a blessing. So many of them felt obliged to talk. Not that Strausser didn't know the language—he'd been here long enough for that—but talking was not what had brought them here, to his big house.

Besides, talking tended to break his concentration.

Strausser watched her. She was doing wonderfully well. Her fingers slipped over him easily now, cupped together, getting stronger, rising with the moment. Strausser was responding to her efforts. Slowly, but he definitely was responding. Not like the false alarms he'd had before. This time something was happening. This was another real one, like last night. She really was excellent.

Strausser watched her bend down to him, touching him with her breasts, then holding him in them, pulling gently. Something extra. He admired initiative, inventiveness. She began to rock ever so slightly, forward and back, forward and back, until Strausser felt himself caught up in the rhythm. Her long dark hair dipped up and down along the wide expanse of his belly. He knew this was going to be a real one, no doubt about it. He could see she knew it too.

She smiled, exposing an upper row of beautifully white teeth. Strausser wished she would not smile. He didn't like a lot of teeth on them. But he couldn't have everything. He chose them for their mouths—small, full-lipped. It never occurred to him until it was too late to check their teeth.

She bent over him. He felt the moistness of soft full lips and the tentative, probing tongue. Absolutely no doubt about it now, this was going to be a real one. She moved slightly for a better position, helping him adjust tired, aging legs.

Strausser closed his eyes. "Yes, that's it, my lovely." His hands were in her hair, pushing, pulling. *Oh, yes. Wunderbar!* She was struggling some, but that was to be expected. No letting go now. *My, my, yes.* This girl was the best! The real thing! Strausser panted, dry-mouthed and realized what a treasure he'd found. He would not recommend her to anyone. He would keep her. Let Mengele and Mueller find their own.

It was nearly noon when Strausser finally left his bed. The girl was asleep. Exhausted. Strausser smiled. He felt invigorated. He showered, slipped into a robe and house shoes and padded across the house to the south wing. The stone veranda was bright with the midday sun. Below, his gardener sweated busily with clippers over a sculptured hedge. When Strausser seated himself at the garden table his man brought him a chilled glass of orange juice, a newspaper and his spectacles.

"Several calls this morning, sir. The Doktor. Urgent business he said, sir."

Strausser nodded, as if not to be bothered. His man left and when he returned he set a telephone beside the empty glass.

"The Doktor, Herr Strausser."

"Yes, yes," Strausser said impatiently. He waved him away. After so wonderful a night, this was not the way to begin a new day. Business, always business with Mengele.

"Guten Morgen, Josef," Strausser said brightly.

"Christ, Alfred, are you finally up?"

Strausser sighed. Mengele is upset. Mengele is always upset.

"I've been calling for hours. I am at Concepcion and I have been calling you for hours. Do you never answer urgent messages?"

"I do not take messages in bed," Strausser said firmly.

"From me?" Mengele demanded. "You have some bitch there, haven't you, Alfred? You've been screwing some bitch there while I've been here calling you!"

"What are you doing in Concepcion, Josef?" Strausser asked politely. It was the only way to handle the Doktor. "I thought you were in Tucuman with the sugar-cane mission this week."

"I was," Mengele said. "This morning. That's why I'm calling. There is a crisis."

The Committee had decided long ago that there was no need in using code words or code names because they only made it all the more confusing. Not that they weren't careful about their movements and at times even secretive, but Eichmann had taught them that hiding was not the answer. Besides, enormously wealthy men did not need to hide. Safety was assured in the knowledge that men could be bought. That, and the fact that they'd not been inconvenienced by the threat of criminal proceedings since 1967 when Franz Stangl had been deported to Germany. The consensus seemed to be that the Nazis still on some wanted list would eventually die if they hadn't already. The Israelis had their hands full these days just trying to survive. The world had other, more important things to consider than a handful of aging Nazis. The Reich was dead. Thirty years dead. The world need not be tormented with yet another trial.

So when Mengele spoke of crisis, Strausser was not concerned. There was a time, in the early days, in the fifties, even in the early sixties, when "crisis" was used to mean danger. But not now. The only crisis Strausser faced today was whether he could find the right girl to breathe life into his fading masculinity.

"Did you not hear me, Strausser?" Mengele said.

"Yes, I heard." Strausser held up his empty juice glass and motioned to his man to refill it. "You should come to São Paulo, Josef. There is no crisis here, I promise you." He thought briefly of telling the Doktor about the girl, but dismissed the idea. Mengele was too rough with his girls.

"*Dummkopf!* I tell you of trouble and you speak of sunning in Brazil!"

"Josef—"

"Semmler is dead."

"Dead?" Strausser repeated dully.

"Executed."

Strausser came up in his chair. "What?"

"Maybe now you will take an interest, eh, Strausser?"

"Semmler . . . how? When?"

"*Who* is important," Mengele said. "And where. A Jew. . . I saw it all on videotape."

"You saw it?"

"It was in the *Reichsgrabgewoelbe.* Strausser, the Chancellery . . . it, it is destroyed!"

Strausser was on his feet; his eyes wide with dread.

"Did you hear, Strausser?"

"A Jew!" Strausser stammered. "In the Chancellery?"

"I went there this morning as soon as I heard. It is burned. They . . . the swines used petrol. It is destroyed. It is all destroyed. . . ."

"*Ach, Gott!*"

". . . all burned. And the Jews—the pig Jews!—they took it."

"Took?"

"They stole it," Mengele said. His voice trailed off and Strausser strained to hear. "They broke into the glass . . ."

"NO!"

"*Sie haben die Fuehrerurne gestolen!*"

"*Mein Gott!*"

"We will make them pay, Herr Strausser. The Jews will pay for this day!"

Strausser bit down on his fist so as not to cry out again. *Der Fuehrer! Yes, they will pay. They will!* Strausser's eyes moved restlessly, glancing everywhere, calculating. "I will call a meeting of the Committee."

"Of course," Mengele said.

"You must come at once. I will call the others."

"Immediately, *mein Feldherr.*"

It was a lifetime ago that Strausser had been called that. SS *Gruppenfuehrer* Alfred Strausser then. The remembrance touched emotion deep inside him. Mengele was right, after all. Something would be done. Allegiance to the Fuehrer demanded action.

"We will not allow this desecration." Strausser spoke into the telephone. He was barely aware that Mengele listened on the line. "It cannot be allowed," he said. "There will be retribution."

"I leave now," he heard Mengele say.

"Yes, yes. Now, immediately." Strausser was thinking of the Jews, the filthy swine who committed this sacrilege. They would pay. He remembered the old hatred, felt it. Before he hung up Strausser gave the old salutation. It was as if it had not been more than a generation. It came easily.

"Heil Hitler."

3

Aaron was in Santiago by noon. Between planes in Mexico City he made a call, collect, then flew nonstop to Dulles International. He carried no luggage except for the gray canvas bag. He did not check it through at the airport, but stashed it under his seat like a briefcase.

Henry met him in the passenger lounge as he stepped off the plane. Henry Nickelson was a large man, bigger even than Abe, but not as muscular or agile. His bushy eyebrows hid sad brown eyes. For all his size, he was more George than Lenny, though he could smile in a way that would panic a longshoreman. He wore a wide-brimmed panama, and nobody called him fat. Except Abe.

Henry lit the last cigarette from his pack. Aaron guessed he'd been waiting for hours.

"No luggage?"

"No," Aaron said.

He nodded at Aaron's bag. "That's it?"

"It's enough."

"Where's Abe, kid?"

41

Aaron swung around quickly. "Don't call me that."

Henry's eyes narrowed. "When you called from Mexico you said there was trouble. What happened? Where's Abe?"

Aaron couldn't bring himself to say it. "Abe's . . . Abe's not coming," Aaron said quickly. "Is Lubetkin waiting?"

"Of course." They were outside. Aaron waved for a cab. "Never mind, I have a car," Henry said. He pointed with his cigarette to a blue Olds. "Over there. He's coming on a different flight, Abe is?"

"No."

"No?"

"Semmler's dead."

"Dead?"

Aaron nodded, avoiding Henry's eyes. "They're all dead."

Henry stopped short, a cigarette ash dropped down the front of his huge bulk. "Christ, kid. Where's Abe?"

Aaron looked at him, said nothing.

"Oh, Jesus Christ," the fat man said quietly. He tossed the cigarette away as if it had suddenly lost its taste. "How, Aaron? What happened down there?"

"Death happened."

"Aaron . . ."

Aaron held up the canvas bag. "And this happened."

"What's that?"

"You wouldn't believe it." Aaron slid into the Olds. "Take me to Lubetkin."

They drove to Virginia, an estate near the Loop. Henry stopped once in Alexandria for cigarettes and smoked six of them, one after another, lighting each one from a previous butt. His nervousness was irritating because it was contagious. Aaron concentrated on watching the countryside pass by—tried to. Lubetkin was on his mind, and Abe. And something or someone named *Kettenhund*. He rested a hand on the canvas case beside him as if to protect it from sliding off the seat. Aaron answered Henry's probing noncommittally, his face showing nothing, not concern, not trepidation.

It wasn't that Henry didn't have a right to know. He would learn it all soon enough. But Lubetkin should be told first. After a while Henry stopped asking questions and they drove in silence. Aaron tried to imagine how Lubetkin would react and what the consequences might be. Henry only smoked.

He was waiting in the library, a room not large but dominated by bookshelves and pictures. Aaron had been there maybe half a dozen times before, but always in the evening. Each time he had felt odd about attending strategy sessions on the finer points of kidnapping and paramilitary methods in a room so femininely delicate in decor. The late Mrs. Lubetkin's parlor, Lubetkin had called it when Aaron was there with Abe the first time with his maps and charts. The walls between white enamel shelves were papered in light blue pinstripes and the chairs seemed too small. Aaron imagined she must have been a petite woman, fragile and lovely, who cared for small things. Lubetkin's handshake was firm but quick, as if he were embarrassed by the custom or disliked personal contact. He was short, small-boned with white bushy hair and a gravelly voice. Not all of his old-country habits had been Americanized. He still "received" guests in the library. A living anachronism, Aaron thought, who had lived—survived—beyond his time. There was no mistaking him for an old man. One might credit him with more than his seventy-one years, but anyone who suspected senility in this old man made a foolish mistake. His soul was driven by a fiery quest for vengeance.

The son of a German consul, Emil Erich Lubetkin was born in London in 1906. Aaron had checked him out and to his surprise found him listed in Who's Who. Lubetkin had followed the family tradition and entered the German diplomatic service after finishing school at Oxford. His family was of the old German aristocracy dating back to Bismarck. In the late 1920s he was posted to the German embassy in London, thanks to some string-pulling on his father's part, and by 1931 was transferred to the embassy in Washington. It was the next year, while he was home visiting his father who'd recently retired, that Lubetkin attended his first NSDAP rally in Düsseldorf where Adolf Hitler addressed Rhineland industrialists. When Hitler was appointed chancellor in 1933 after Von Schleicher's resignation, Lubetkin was reassigned to London. Shortly afterward his father, who had been against the Nazi regime since the Reichstag elections, was arrested as a dissident. The following year he was sent to the concentration camp at Buchenwald for protective custody. Lubetkin worked for months to have his father freed. When he was released, in the spring of 1935, the elder Lubetkin was a haggard, spent old man who lived only another four months. Lubetkin had thought his father was mistaken, thought Hitler was moving Germany forward. He believed in him—until the invasion of Poland. He returned to Germany and entered the Foreign Department of the *Oberkommando der Wehrmacht,* which later was the center of a resistance movement against Hitler of which Lubetkin was a dedicated member. For years during the war the movement tried desperately to remove Hitler from power. Finally in 1944, after the July twentieth bomb plot, Lubetkin was betrayed to the Gestapo, arrested and taken to Ploetzensee Prison in Berlin to await execution. Only a bribe and the confused course of the war stalled his execution, and he was sent instead to the concentration camp at Sachsenhausen as a political prisoner. After three months he was transferred to Buchenwald where his father had been ten years before. Only now the camp was not simply a place of internment. It was a Nazi death camp, and for seven months until the camp was liberated by the Allies in April 1945, Lubetkin witnessed the deaths of tens of thousands of Jews.

After the war, with his family dead or missing, Lubetkin emigrated to the United States. With what remained of his family's money he opened law offices in New York. Over the years he had prospered and by the early 1970s his firm had branches in New York, Seattle, San Francisco and Boston. He was sixty-eight years old, retired and extremely wealthy when he began hunting Nazi criminals who'd escaped punishment. All his energies were now devoted to that task. His early successes resulted in the extradition of a number of death camp guards and Gestapo henchmen. Lubetkin had grown impatient with the lengthy extradition proceedings and finally decided to recruit men, not necessarily Jews, to track down war criminals. Semmler was the first Nazi of relative importance he had located. And now it looked as though the mission had gone sour.

"Sit, Aaron," Lubetkin said, indicating one of the small chairs. "Tell me what went wrong." The old man seated himself in his chair beside a low table crowded with pipes in a wide tobacco-stained dish. Lubetkin's voice was not harsh, but his eyes were intent on Aaron.

"My brother is dead," Aaron said. He was surprised how easily he could say it. He placed the bag on the floor near his feet. Lubetkin nodded as if he'd prepared himself for bad news. "Hill and McDermit too."

"And Semmler?"

"Dead," Aaron said. "They're all dead . . . murdered."

"And only you survived?"

"My brother was very protective, Mr. Lubetkin."

"Yes, of course." The old man apologized with his hands. "I'm sorry, my boy. Your brother was a friend. I know how you must feel."

"I doubt it," Aaron replied coldly. "And don't call me boy."

Lubetkin looked up sharply. He frowned.

"Abe died because I didn't know the rules," Aaron said. "I do now. The whole plan went bad because I . . . I . . ." He stared at his hands. "What happened was my fault."

"What *did* happen?" Lubetkin's voice was cold. He fixed his eyes on Aaron with a hard stare. "I want to know exactly why these men are dead."

Aaron lifted the bag and let it drop near the old man's feet. "They died for this," he said. He got up, walked to the window. It was getting dark. A pair of robins perched on the edge of a planter outside in the light from the house. He remembered Abe laughing in his apartment when Aaron tried to insert the clip in the submachine gun upside down. *I think the CIA could use you, kid.*

Aaron stared at the robins, blinking back the tears.

"What is it?"

"A souvenir," Aaron said slowly from the window. "Open it." He turned back toward the room. Lubetkin glanced questioningly at Henry. The big man shrugged. "Go on, open it."

Lubetkin bent to the bag, pulled it into his lap. Carefully and gently, he extracted the bundle from inside.

Henry watched curiously as Lubetkin untied the belt and unfolded the wrapping cloth. The urn's highly polished surface glinted in the reflected light. "An ossuary?"

"A funeral urn," Aaron said. "From the Reich." He walked back to his chair.

"Interesting," Lubetkin replied curtly, "but . . ."

"Turn it over. There's an inscription."

Lubetkin pivoted the vessel on its base, found the engraving. When he spoke, it was a whisper. "My God." He held it with new awareness between frail, trembling hands. His eyes were wide, stunned. "Can this be?"

"It *is*."

"But where . . . where did you . . ." He couldn't take his eyes off it.

Aaron took his seat. "Now I'll tell you about Paraguay."

He told them everything. About Semmler. About the *Reichsgrabgewoelbe*. About McDermit and Hill. And about the executioner Semmler in his last breath of life called *Kettenhund*. But mostly he spoke of Abe.

Lubetkin did not interrupt. He chose one of the pipes from the dish and puffed on it thoughtfully until Aaron had finished. Aaron had expected some sort of reaction when he described the mausoleum, its contents, but Lubetkin offered none.

When he was finished, he drank a glass of water. Henry had not moved from his crossed-arms pose, leaning against the edge of the desk. Lubetkin spoke first.

"Incredible." He shook his head and ran his fingers lightly through the white hair. He did not appear even slightly sad, as if there was no more sadness left in him, as if sadness was an emotion for other men who had not endured what he had. "Incredible." He set the pipe in the dish. "Isn't it? For these men to have such power, such wealth, even now?"

Aaron shrugged. It wasn't a question he could answer.

Lubetkin studied the urn carefully as if it was the key to some central mystery. "The rest was destroyed?"

"I've already told you," Aaron retorted.

"Yes, yes, but again, please," Lubetkin said impatiently. "This could be very important."

Aaron sighed. "It was destroyed . . . burned. The explosives should have brought a mountain down on it."

"Why did you save this . . ." the old man couldn't find the words. ". . . this piece?"

"It seemed like the thing to do." Abe had said that.

"And you say there was a surveillance camera?"

"It *looked* like a surveillance camera."

"So they saw you take it? They saw you burn their temple and take the prize of the collection."

"Whoever 'they' is," Aaron said. "The German saw me. I expect he was a German. The *Kettenhund*. The one who shot Abe." The muscles in Aaron's jaw tightened.

"*Kettenhund*. Do you know what that is, Aaron?"

"A name."

Lubetkin frowned. He stared past Aaron as if he suddenly recalled some grim memory. "Yes, but not a surname. During the war there was a special paratrooper group attached to the Ninth SS Panzers. I knew about them through my work in the Wehrmacht High Command. Schellenberg's Section VII." When he returned his glance to Aaron, the old man's eyes were bleak. "They were an elite band of commandos. Some of them worked with Skorzeny in the rescue of Mussolini in the Abruzzi Appenines. Some worked on the planning of Eisenhower's kidnap in the Ardennes in 1944, though it never came off. A good many were assigned to Operation Grief— Germans dressed as G.I.s behind the Allied lines during the counteroffensive to create havoc."

Aaron nodded, engrossed.

"They were known as *Die Kettenhunde* . . . the chain dogs," Lubetkin said. "An extremely vicious breed. I think you ran into one."

"He hasn't lost his teeth."

"Skorzeny founded a secret organization called *Die Spinne* —the Spider—which helped several hundred SS to escape from Germany. This man may have been one. Probably on some dictator's staff. Advisory capacity. Peron's, perhaps."

"I don't care what he calls himself," Aaron said. "I'm going to find him."

"I think running into him once should be enough," Lubetkin said. He sat forward in his chair. "Quite enough."

"You can think what you like."

"I see." The old man selected another pipe from the stand. He took his time to fill the bowl and light it. When he looked at Aaron again it was without sympathy. "You botched the job with Semmler. You yourself admit that it was through your own incompetence that four men are dead, including your brother. I tell you the man who killed your brother was a trained assassin. And despite all that, you say you want to go back?" Lubetkin shook his head. "I find that the height of stupidity, Mr. Miller."

"Look," Aaron snapped, rising from his chair, "I don't—"

"You're an amateur," Lubetkin interrupted. "You don't know the first thing about stalking another man."

"I'll learn," Aaron said.

"And what do you know about killing?"

"I'll learn that too."

"I don't think you have the stuff for it," Lubetkin said with a hard look. "You aren't like your brother. I think he would be the first to point that deficiency out to you." Lubetkin stared grimly at Aaron. "If he weren't dead."

"You son of a bitch!"

"Realities," Lubetkin said. "You must face realities. Your loss is my loss also."

"He would do the same for me!" Aaron exclaimed defensively. "Abe would do exactly the same! He would track the bastard."

"Yes, I'm sure he would," Lubetkin agreed.

"Then what's the difference?"

"The difference," Henry said from his place beside the desk, "is that you aren't Abe." The fat man had not participated in the discussion because he had no part in it. Until now. He moved a chair to the edge of the rug between Aaron and the old man.

"Abe would not have come back here until he'd found the fucker who killed his kid brother. And he would never have left you behind. Never. Not even if he had to dig up a hundred tons of rock. You aren't your brother, Aaron."

Aaron found himself staring at his hands. "Well, it doesn't matter, does it? He's dead. I *am* going to find the one who murdered him." He looked up at the fat man. "That's it."

"Then you're going to need a crash course in staying alive. I know something about that."

"The complete commando course in three easy lessons?" Aaron said sarcastically.

"There won't be anything easy about it," Henry said. "Not if what you intend to do is stalk and kill a man. Can you spare a month?"

"A month?" Aaron shook his head. "No—a month is too long."

Henry shook his head skeptically.

"Are you really serious? You'd train me?"

"It'd take a month to do it right."

"It'll take a week—that's as long as I'm willing to wait."

Henry looked at the ceiling.

"Deal?" Aaron asked.

"It would take a week just to find a place to work out. A range. Trees. A place where we can work without being interrupted."

"Here," Lubetkin said from around his pipe. "If you really mean to do it. You can use the grounds here." He nodded toward the urn. "But I think first we must make a decision about this."

Aaron shook his head. "It doesn't mean anything to me."

"I don't think you realize. You are too young and you have

not experienced certain things." Lubetkin's mouth hinted at a smile. "The way you described this shrine—the extremes they went to protect it, to hide it—you've stripped them of something irreplaceable."

Aaron glanced at the old man but said nothing.

Lubetkin went on. "The elaborate and painstaking effort exhibited is proof that a camaraderie of powerful ex-Nazis still exists. A fraternity of old men. Still loyal to the Reich."

"That's not my concern," Aaron said. "I'm not a Nazi hunter."

The old man looked at him for several moments, then shook his head. "You cannot understand, Aaron. These men once conspired to conquer the world. They are old men now, forced into hiding, but still influential and vindictive. Their common disease is an unfailing allegiance to one man whose dreams were their dreams. Hitler. The Fuehrer was cheated of his rightful destiny, betrayed, they believe, not by them, but by a racial principle that could not be crammed down the world's throat and that ultimately choked the Reich to death. The Fuehrer will always be a god to them, and they cannot allow his martyrdom to go uncelebrated."

Lubetkin nodded toward the urn. "Now that we have this, we must use it to the best advantage. This situation must be unbearable for them. It makes me curious. You might also be interested. It may be a solution to your own troubles." He nodded. "Yes, it makes me very curious."

"About what?" Aaron said.

Lubetkin did not bother to look away from the urn. He smiled at his own reflection. "About how badly they want it back."

4

The telephone awakened Linka immediately. His apartment was dark except for the small lamp beside his chair.

"Yes?" The phone was slightly cool on his ear, but he was alert now.

"Ira, this is Eliahu. You're to go to Ben Gurion Airport. Now. A ticket is waiting at the El Al counter."

"Zadok called?"

"I'll say he did. From Chile. Listen, you'll have to hurry. We're sending a brief profile to you at the airport. It should be in the ticket envelope when you pick it up."

"Where am I going?"

"The United States. Washington National."

"Lubetkin, is it?"

"He's really done it this time, Ira."

"They made the pickup, did they?"

"What?"

"Semmler." Linka sighed. "This is a secure line. You can tell me. Did they pick up Semmler?"

"No . . . bigger. Much bigger, Ira. One more thing, this

assignment is unofficial. You are not from the Shin Beth. Understood?"

"No," Linka said.

"Damn it, Ira—look, the profile will explain."

"What happened in Paraguay?"

"Semmler is dead," Eliahu said quickly. "The Americans found something. Something . . . big. Enormously important."

"Semmler is dead?"

"Ira, will you please hang up and leave? You are ready to leave?"

"Yes, I've been ready since you called this morning. What did the Americans find that was so important?"

"Ira!"

"What did they find?" Linka said firmly.

"A tomb. A Nazi museum and tomb. Some sort of underground cavern. They were all in it."

"They?"

"Bormann, Heydrich, Himmler, Goebbels . . . Hitler . . ."

"Hitler!"

"The American in command destroyed it all . . . except Hitler. It's an urn, Ira. They destroyed the place and stole the urn. Will you leave now, Ira? Will you please go?"

Linka did not answer. He hung up the phone. He was at Ben Gurion Airport in less than thirty minutes.

5

The *Oberkomitee* met in emergency session. Officially, if a secret organization can be called that, it was known as the *Oberkomitee der Kameradschaften*, High Committee of the Brotherhood.

Bormann headed it until he died.

Now it was Strausser.

"The filthy Jews should be hung until they rot . . . down to the last filthy one of them," Mengele was saying. He was drunk, or nearly. It had been going this way for hours and Strausser's dining room smelled of stale nicotine. Strata of cigarette smoke brooded over the long oval table, diffusing the light of the chandelier like a hazy sunset.

They were all there.

Strausser had stopped listening to them long ago. The bickering of old men. Soon enough they would wear themselves out. Then he would put forward his plan. The tired sagging faces before him were red with age and frustration. And anger. And not a little fear. Strausser understood that. What tried his patience were the sweeping threats and promises of unsurpassed vengeance that he knew were no more potent than the air.

Mengele would castrate or mark for "special experimentation" every Hebrew and Jew lover.

Heinrich Mueller would simply shoot them all one by one. Personally. With his own rusty pistol that was even now hidden away somewhere in Brazil. Quite a feat for a man barely able to stand, soon to celebrate his seventy-sixth birthday.

Walter Helldorf would gas the entire Mideast. As a lesson.

Otto Gluck, figurehead of the now defunct rescue organization, would lead legions of former SS men against them in a final, glorious, Panzer assault.

Gerhard Westrick would fire-bomb the world. At least the Jewish world. He didn't explain, but then he had drunk nearly as much as Mengele.

For another hour it went this way. There were arguments. Helldorf threatened Gluck. Mueller and Mengele nearly came to blows with their canes. Tired, frustrated old men. Westrick, the fat one, had had his measure of wine and was valiantly struggling to stay awake.

It was Mengele, the businessman, who finally laid the matter before Strausser.

"Alfred, Alfred, we accomplish nothing!" Herr Doktor's eyes were watery, from smoke or exhaustion, Strausser could not tell. "We must *do* something."

"Agreed." Strausser looked at the faces. He was surrounded by weariness. Now was the time to lead them. To command.

"If you are finished bickering like old washerwomen . . ."

"You are the *Präsident,* Herr Strausser," Gluck said defensively. "You have offered nothing here."

"Only when you will hear me."

Mueller raised his hands in a gesture of acknowledgment. "So? Now we listen."

Strausser nodded at Westrick. "Someone wake Gerhard . . . so I do not repeat myself."

"You have a plan, *Feldherr?*"

"The Jews have designed a plot against us," Strausser said. "Mine is a countermeasure."

"Countermeasure, Herr Strausser?" Mueller, the old Gestapo chief, sat forward attentively. "Explain, please."

"The days of the *Sturmtruppen* are over, gentlemen," Strausser began. "However distasteful it may be, the truth is we cannot mount any sort of military operation."

Mengele bristled, started to object, but Mueller shot him a forbidding glance. "Go on, Herr Strausser," Mueller said. "We are listening."

"If we accept my appraisal, then we must also accept that all of our comrades who are prepared or capable of striking back at these Jews are known or wanted outside the restricted boundaries of South American countries. None of them could track down the thieves without looking behind them for fear of being arrested as war criminals."

"So we will hire an outsider," Helldorf said. "We have money. We have plenty of money."

"True," Strausser said. "But consider this. If we pay an outsider—and for this job it would mean a considerable sum—even if it were paid half on agreement and the balance on delivery, we have no guarantee. It would be easy for such a man to take our money and do nothing. We could not pursue him. We could send someone after him and another after him. . . . Do you see, gentlemen? We could wind up throwing money away and never retrieving it or *Der Fuehrer's Urne*."

"Then we are lost," Westrick cried, awake for the moment.

"This you call a plan," Gluck said angrily.

"*Moment, bitte,*" Mueller said. "There is more, Herr Strausser?"

"Yes, Heinrich. But first we must be made aware of our restrictions. Then there is the matter of settling on the main objective."

"We'll make the Jew bastards pay." It was Mengele, Mengele of the single mind.

"I believe not," Strausser said. "I believe our objective is the return of our property. No more."

"But . . . but . . . the Jew . . ." Mengele was on his feet, so full of rage he could not speak.

"Sit down, Josef," Strausser commanded. "What are we? Are we the Reich? Are we millions of soldiers poised to strike down our enemies? Are we squadrons of Luftwaffe? Are we divisions of Panzers? No! We are six old men."

"We are the *Oberkomitee!*" Helldorf shouted proudly.

"We are six old men," Strausser repeated firmly, "responsible to oversee a financial empire that was founded on SS treasures smuggled here by Bormann."

"*Heil* Bormann!" Westrick shouted, not to be outdone by Helldorf.

"We cannot jeopardize that responsibility. Bormann reorganized the structure of power with emphasis not on a new *Nationalsozialismus,* but on a different course. His efforts have made the *Kameradschaft* a corporate giant in South America and made us millionaires. We are businessmen, influential, powerful, but within certain limits. We must remember our relationship with the Vatican is a delicate one. But, we have protection here. We are comfortable. Do not think for a moment that that security would last for a blink of an eye if we should initiate some reckless killing spree. The Jews, the world, would turn on us and there would be nothing."

"Then, Herr Strausser, do you suggest we *plead* with these Jews to return what is ours?" Mueller asked sarcastically. "Would you offer them money? Do you think they stole it and destroyed the Chancellery so they could sell it back?"

"It does not concern me *why* they took it, Heinrich. Only that they give it back."

"And if they have already destroyed it," Gluck said. "What then?"

"I think they have not. Why go to so much trouble to take it. If the intent was to destroy it, they could have left it behind with the rest."

"How do we persuade them to return it?" Mueller said. "I will not beg a Jew."

"We will beg no one," Strausser said. "We will demand."

"Demand, Herr Strausser?" Mueller said. "How? With what?"

"I think we will threaten them," Strausser said, smiling mischievously. "I think we will threaten the life of a Jew they hold dear."

"Impossible!" Westrick retorted. "You just said—"

"I said we cannot start a killing spree. It would be suicide for us. But that is a deed completed. The world would rush in like avenging fools, after us and the smoking pistol. But I speak of a cocked pistol, pointed at the Jew's head. The world could care less for threats. But not the Jews. They know what they have taken. They know what it is worth to us. They know they must submit."

Mueller nodded. "An interesting plan, Alfred. But to make it work we must be prepared to mount an offensive. Someone must be found to carry this cocked pistol of yours. Even the Jews would not heed an empty threat. So we are back where we begin. There is not a man we can send who would be trusted to guarantee the threat."

Strausser smiled. "But there is a man. He exists and he does not exist."

"Strausser!" Mengele said angrily. "Are we down to riddles? If you have a plan, let us hear it."

"Yes," Mueller said. "Please."

"Forgive my melodramatics, gentlemen," Strausser said. "As you might suspect there is a mass of detail to be worked out. You all know the man I speak of. But what I wish to know now is if you each agree to my proposal."

"There is an alternative?" Gluck asked.

Strausser shook his head. "I think not."

The other five men looked at each other. After a moment, Mueller spoke for all of them.

"We are agreed. Who is this man we are to rest our hopes on?"

"He worked for a branch of your Gestapo, Heinrich. Otto, your ODESSA brought him out of hiding from Italy to safe refuge in Brazil. He was a friend of SS-Standartenfuehrer Skorzeny, the hero of the Reich. He was a Hitler Youth. In 1936 he won the first gold medal for Germany at the Berlin Olympics, personally honored by Der Fuehrer in his private box. That was his beginning, actually. Der Fuehrer took an instant liking to him. Adolf gave him his identity. After the Games he was so impressed with this youth that he had the boy change his name. Symbol of the new Reich.

Deutschlaender of the Third Reich. You remember the posters."

"Yes, yes," Gluck said excitedly. "He was called . . . he was called . . ."

"Reichmann." It was Mueller who remembered. "Eduard Reichmann."

"Man of the Reich," Helldorf said. "I recall him now."

"A perfect model of the new Reich," Mengele said. "Our best. Yes, Alfred, yes. A good choice. A good Aryan. A good German."

"His goodness is not why Herr Strausser has selected him," Mueller said. He bowed his head slightly toward Strausser. The former Gestapo chief smiled knowingly. "Herr Reichmann was good at many things. An accomplished assassin."

"Exactly so." Strausser beamed.

"But where is he now?" Westrick asked.

"Reichmann is here."

"Here?"

Strausser nodded. "Here in Paraguay. He was always a loner. He has not changed. I am told he lives a hermit's existence . . . near Bela Vista. His personal agony is that he failed his Fuehrer."

"Failed?" said Gluck.

"Reichmann the boy—the man—was not one to accept idly his Fuehrer's charge. He *was* the 'Man of the Reich.' His dream goes unfulfilled."

"I congratulate you, Herr Strausser," Mueller said. "It is a brilliant scheme."

"Brilliant?" Westrick said dully.

"Reichmann will do it for nothing," said Mengele, impressed.

"He will agree to this?" Helldorf asked. "To repay his debt to the Fuehrer?"

Strausser nodded his assurance. "Of course. We need only ask."

"But *can* he do it?" Gluck wondered. "It is one thing to be dedicated—another to be capable. These accomplishments you speak of—they were a long time ago. How old is he now? Can he—"

"He is Reichmann!" Strausser exploded. "In all the world there was only one. The Aryan. The model for all Deutschland. The Fuehrer created him. He believes it. Do you think such a man would ever forget that?"

"But . . ." Gluck hesitated.

"Do not concern yourself as to his capabilities, Otto," Mueller said. "I think he has already demonstrated his aptitude. Has he not, Herr Strausser?"

Strausser raised his eyebrows. "You recognized him, then?"

"I only just realized," the Gestapo chief said.

"What are you talking about?" Helldorf frowned.

"You saw him," Strausser replied. "You all saw him. On the tape of the closed-circuit replay of the shooting in the Chancellory. He killed the traitor Semmler. And the big Jew."

"*That* was Reichmann!" said Gluck, surprised.

"And I think the incident guarantees Reichmann's steadfast devotion to the task we shall put to him." Mueller offered something of a smile.

"How so?" Westrick said.

"Because, my dear Gerhard," Mueller said, "one of them got away from him. The one with the urn."

Strausser rose. "We shall meet again tomorrow. I will have Reichmann report to me and then I will bring him before this *Oberkomitee*."

"And then?" Helldorf said.

Strausser glanced at Mueller, then at Helldorf. "And then we shall unleash this chain dog on the Jews." The thought made him smile. "The *Kettenhund* returns."

6

It rained in Paris until nearly noon.

The overcast skies broke up slowly, letting the sun shine through. It made for a hot, muggy afternoon. The Champs-Elysées was still wet and steamy as Rafai Jamil entered the Hotel Claridge. His appointment with the chief of the Popular Front for the Liberation of Palestine was to be at quarter past the hour. Jamil was not late.

"Good day to you, Rafai," the Palestinian said. His familiar bearded face was relaxed, his smile reassuring. They sat together in the main suite. Two silent bodyguards were near the door.

"You were wounded in the mountains east of Beirut," said the Palestinian with interest. "Last month. How does it mend?"

"It was in early May," Jamil corrected. "Healed now. I have been waiting in Paris for new orders." If Rafai Jamil was impatient, he did not let it show.

"You are repaired and rested and ready for action, then?"

Jamil nodded.

"Good, Rafai, good. You have enjoyed your respite here in Paris?"

Jamil was quiet a moment before answering. "It rains too much."

The Palestinian smiled. "A sign of your restlessness. Good. Good, because there is something I wish you to do."

Jamil nodded.

"An agent for the Shin Beth is in the United States. He was leader of a commando raiding party at Entebbe"—Jamil's eyes flickered with interest and a quiet rage at the mention of the Kampala airfield—"who led a team of commandos secretly from the Kenyan border earlier in the day to guide the rescue planes in and cut the airfield's communications links and radar system. He is a great favorite of the Israeli general Shomron." The Palestinian paused a moment to fit a cigarette into its holder, light it, his eyes on Jamil. "It is this same man who is this afternoon in Washington on a mission for Israel. Which brings me to the reason I asked to meet with you, Rafai." He exhaled and waved a hand to disperse the smoke from his cigarette as if there should be no barrier between him and the man Rafai Jamil. "I want you to go there. Follow him as closely as his own shadow. It is important, Rafai. It is the reason I chose you—that, and because this man was an instrument against our brothers at Entebbe. A justice of poetry, I think it is called."

Jamil didn't know anything about poetry. He did know about what the newspapers were calling the great raid at Entebbe and the heroes the press made of the Israelis who cut down his comrades with submachine guns. Had he not been convalescing in Paris, he would have been there. Jamil had known Wilfried Böse, leader of the hijacking team. They were not friends but knew each other, as friendships were rare in the business of terrorism. Böse had simply made a mistake that cost him his life. Had it been him instead of Böse, Jamil thought, the Jews would be counting bodies not blessings and the great raid would have ended differently.

Jamil lifted his head to see the Palestinian. "I am grateful for your consideration, *Yahid*."

The Palestinian nodded his pleasure, then hunched forward in his seat. "I have been informed, through sources in South America, that a group of Americans raided a villa there. It belonged to what remains of the Nazi hierarchy of World War Two. The Americans took something of great importance. I believe this Israeli will contact these Americans and try to persuade them to give up what they have taken." He inhaled deeply from his cigarette. "I wish that he not be successful."

"Name?" Jamil said.

"Linka. Ira Linka."

"The Americans," Jamil said slowly, "they are a government group? CIA?"

The Palestinian shook his head. "No." He smiled. "Amateurs. Mercenaries financed by an old immigrant German and led by a young American soldier of fortune."

"A curious mix."

"Perhaps. But no more so than our own organization. This assignment may not sound so important to you, an Abou Moussa commando—"

"It is not for me to question," Jamil said.

"The struggle goes hard, Rafai," the Palestinian went on. "The progress we enjoyed in the April elections of the Israeli-occupied West Bank has been upset in recent months with the setback of Jumblat and the leftist-Moslem alliance in Beirut. There is resistance from the Arab League. There is renewed pressure since last month's death of the American ambassador. Syrian tanks advance deep into Lebanon. The plan to exchange Palestinian prisoners for the airbus hostages ended in disaster at Entebbe." He let the ash from his cigarette fall into a small bowl. "It goes hard." The Palestinian shrugged his heavy shoulders in a tired sigh. "That is why we must advance on every front. The Israelis are the darlings of the world's eye today because of this rescue. They think they have won a major victory. They—forgive me, Rafai, I digress. It is important, especially now, to thwart them at every mission they undertake. This is why you are to do this thing. We must continue to be the thorn in their sides, even such small irritations as this."

"I understand."

"You will be responsible for this Israeli in the United States. I do not wish him to be successful in his mission." He pinched the cigarette from the holder and stubbed it out in the bowl. "You are ready?"

Jamil's eyes glanced up to the tall french windows of the balcony. Outside the overcast skies had closed together, shutting out the sun. There would be rain again before evening. He looked back to the Palestinian. "When do I leave?"

7

It was not possible, absolutely not possible for one man to hurt, to ache, to feel so much misery as Aaron did at this precise moment. But it was possible and the living proof was squinting back at him from the mirror over the marble sink Aaron clung to for support.

Twenty-four hours ago he could stand up without help. But, then, twenty-four hours ago he hadn't been through a day of so-called training with a sadist. Up at six, run half a mile before breakfast. Breakfast, he called it! Four eggs, poached; a steak; trimmed toast, dry; and milk. Milk! Protein was the ticket, Henry had said yesterday. Coffee was poison. Sugar was taboo, at least for now. Must work on stamina and fitness. And this from the fat man who drank more than his measure of the poison, sticky with mounds of sugar added.

Twenty-four hours ago Aaron was only irritated with his tutor. Twenty-four hours ago was just the prelude to a deep and abiding hatred. That was before the running, the calisthenics, the salt tablets, the running, the calisthenics, the orange juice, the rope climbing, the steak and salad lunch, the running.

And during the breaks, instruction on knives and footwork.

Never weave with a blade. Weight forward on the toes, feet apart and balanced. Eyes on your opponent's eyes. Blade flat to the ground, never perpendicular. Belly, heart and throat, those are the targets. Always.

Then more calisthenics. And more running. And more instruction. Henry was a master of the killing arts. He was an encyclopedia on the style and technique of death throws and blows.

Calisthenics. Running. Unarmed combat. *Never break a man's neck from the rear with your bare hands. Use a weapon even if it's a stick. Smash the windpipe if your opponent is straight on, with an open hand, fingers rigid. A kick in the groin might incapacitate—if it's a man, if you're quick enough and if he doesn't kick you first. But these are killing blows we're considering here. Unless he comes at you in some kind of faggot hustle with his balls dangling like grapes in a sack, don't waste time kicking. Chances are, you run into a character like that, he doesn't want to hurt you anyway. Remember, your feet are your balance. There are only certain masters who are any good with their feet as weapons. You aren't going to be one of them. The man who comes at me with his feet, unless it's Bruce Lee, is going to be handed his leg back to him from the knee. Right. Now, strangleholds. Never try it from anywhere but behind. . . .*

Small arms. *The most devastating weapon is small caliber, like a .22. It ricochets off bone and pierces vital organs. One .22 in the rib cage can rattle around like a pinball and never exit, but the little bugger's been through everything from sternum to asshole. The heavy artillery is for shock impact. A .45 or magnum will knock a 250-pound man off his feet at twenty yards.*

By 6 P.M., after the last half-mile run, Aaron had survived. Of course, Henry didn't run, do the sit-ups and squat thrusts or climb a single rope. He watched the running from the gazebo, counted off each excruciating sit-up with a cigarette from a shaded hammock. His only physical exertion came during the hand-to-hand instruction when he demonstrated amazing agility for so fat a teacher, dropping Aaron time after time, and all the while smiling his complacent smile. Henry didn't even sweat much.

"Thought you were in good shape, didn't you?" he'd said with a smirk at the end of the first day.

"I *am* in shape," Aaron panted. When he'd had a job he played tennis three times a week.

"How do you feel?"

"Tired . . . exhausted, then," he said, answering Henry's raised eyebrows. "Christ, a decathlonist couldn't keep up this pace."

"Killing a professional soldier on his own turf isn't one of a decathlonist's events."

Aaron dragged himself out of the afternoon sun and sank into a patio chair opposite Henry in the shaded gazebo. "I want to kill the bastard—use a gun, not run him to death."

"There's always the unexpected," Henry said. "It's not like you have a street address. You'll have to find him in unfamiliar terrain. You don't even have a name, just a recollection of what he looks like. You think he won't remember you?"

Aaron sighed. "Okay, okay."

Henry got up. "I'll be back tomorrow at six sharp." He smiled at Aaron. "Actually, you're in better condition than I expected."

"That's encouragement, right?"

"Tomorrow, then. Three-quarter mile first thing."

"What!"

"And two miles by the time we're finished."

"Jesus, Henry, I don't need more running. I'm fit enough."

"Oh?"

Aaron stared at himself in the mirror. Today, he needn't remind himself, was the second day—and Henry was wrong. Aaron didn't know what possessed him to get out of bed. He was paralyzed. Nothing didn't hurt. Even his hair was sore where he'd gripped it for sit-ups. It took all his concentration to shave and most all his strength. He held the razor with one hand and held himself up with the other and cursed the fat man throughout.

Abe was the runner in the family, the athlete. Aaron had vague recollections of watching his big brother playing football in high school. Abe Miller may have been the best high school quarterback in the school's history, but all Aaron remembered clearly about those late fall afternoons in Ohio was the cold. It got very cold in October and November for six-year-old younger brothers at football games. But enduring the cold was a small price to pay to watch Abe. Abe was the best. There wasn't anything Abe couldn't do. If he was a gifted athlete, he was also smart. Oh, he was no genius, but he was cunning and possessed a sardonic wit and was generally wiser than he let on. It was Abe who recognized in his little brother an appreciation of words and a faculty for grasping abstract ideas. He was, Aaron remembered himself, a bookish kid. But that all changed with the accident. When Captain Joseph Sullivan Miller and his wife, Martha, slid across an icy road into the path of a mail truck three days before Christmas 1962, his life and life-style underwent a drastic change. Aaron was a puny kid then. Abe changed that. Aaron read too much for a kid about to enter puberty. Abe changed that. Aaron depended on others to make his decisions. Abe changed that, too, but it took longer. Aaron was not so much a self-made as he was an Abe-made man.

That's when he first learned about running. "Your head's okay, kid, it's your body that needs work," Abe had told him shortly after he'd moved in. And if Abe said it was so, it was so. "If you can't swim, run." Words from the almighty. So Aaron ran. He didn't like it from the beginning, but he ran. He ran with his brother in the mornings before school. He jogged in the evenings after supper. He hated it, the monotony, the long stretches in the park, but he did it because Abe told him to. After the first year he'd gained fifteen pounds, added two inches to his chest and grown an inch and a half. Before he graduated from high school he actually *looked* like Abe's brother.

Aaron wiped the residue of shaving cream from the face

that looked back at him in the mirror. There was a re-
semblance all right. Abe was there, in that face. His gray eyes
were brown now, his hair a little less curly, the line of his jaw
not quite so pronounced—but he was there. Henry was only
partially right when he said Aaron wasn't his brother. He
wasn't Abe, but the spirit was there. He carried his big
brother's soul and that's all that mattered. It's what motivated
him to endure Henry's torture. Abe. Abe. Abe. *Oh, Abe!*

Aaron dressed in a clean sweatsuit. Lubetkin and his
servants would be still asleep when he went downstairs. The
first rays of dawn greeted him as he jogged back to the
Lubetkin mansion from his lonely and painful half-mile run.
Henry was waiting too, sitting in a wicker chair on the patio.

"You're learning discipline," the fat man said with a grin.
"That's good."

Aaron wiped the sweat from his face with a towel. "I had a
good teacher once." His shoulders and calves ached unmer-
cifully, but he wasn't about to admit it. Not to Henry.

"You still want to go on, then?" Henry raised an eyebrow.
"After yesterday?"

"It wasn't so bad."

"No?"

Aaron studied his face. "No."

Henry nodded to himself. "Good." He lit a cigarette and
tossed the match back over his shoulder. "Today will be
worse."

There had been less running and more instruction. Fire-
arms. Stalking techniques. Tricks with wires and explosives.
Hand-to-hand. And he had been as bad with it all as he was
the first day except it hurt more when he fell. Henry was
torment personified. He seemed to enjoy it. By the end of the
day Aaron ached in more places than he knew he had.

"How's the fit tennis player?"

Aaron glanced belligerently at the fat man and said nothing.

"You're doing very well, considering," Henry said.

"Considering what—that I'm still alive?" He rubbed his
aching shoulder with a leaden arm.

"Tomorrow will be better. Some of your muscles will rebel for days—but from now on each day will be better than the last."

"That's exactly what I wanted to hear."

"Have you been eating everything at dinner? I gave Lubetkin's cook a special menu."

Aaron scowled. "Yes, Mummy. It takes an hour to get it all down."

"Good. And you're sleeping well?"

"I don't know what keeps my head up out of my dinner plate."

"Good," Henry replied, smiling again. "Good."

It was his favorite word for days.

Aaron fell asleep in the bathtub, letting his punished muscles float numbly in the warm water. It had been three days now. Three battering, miserable days. It had to end soon. The agony *had* to subside. He wasn't sure how much longer he could go on. He had nightmares. In the last one, he wrestled a big brown bear that wore track shoes.

By the time he was up and dressed, he was nearly late for dinner, even if he wasn't hungry. Lubetkin, despite pleas to the contrary, insisted they dress which, in Aaron's case, meant a corduroy sports coat and a gray tie. Dinner was served promptly at eight. It seemed like midnight.

He came down the stairs carefully, feeling his way along the banister. The last thing he needed in his condition was to fall down and injure something else, if there was anything left. When he entered the dining room he smelled the roast and immediately got a headache. Lubetkin was across the room holding a brandy decanter. Aaron was startled when he saw the girl. She was standing with her back to him, admiring a painting.

"You're late," the old man said as he poured a measure of brandy.

"Sorry," Aaron said. He wasn't, but it was all the energy he had for words.

The girl turned, acknowledging his presence with a smile.

"We are three for dinner this evening." Lubetkin handed him a crystal snifter of brandy before he could decline it. Brandy wasn't on his training diet. "Aaron, I'd like you to meet Emma Diels." He handed her a glass. "This is the man I've been talking about, Emma."

"Nice to meet you, Mr. Miller," she said. She was twenty-five, no more than thirty, Aaron thought. Her accent was French and her hair was short and wavy in the European style. Aaron wondered if she traveled a great deal.

"My pleasure," he said. Aaron had always despised introductions. He was especially uncomfortable when required to shake a woman's hand. He hadn't the knack for it—like Abe had—particularly with liberated women. It always seemed a contest for the firmer grip. Luckily, she only nodded.

"I've asked Emma to dinner for a special reason," Lubetkin said. "We've corresponded on several occasions but this is our first face-to-face meeting." The old man raised his glass to her. "And let me say, my dear, you are as lovely as you are competent in your avocation."

Emma acknowledged his compliment shyly. "Thank you, Mr. Lubetkin. If I had known you were so gracious I would have come sooner."

Aaron felt like a playgoer who'd missed the first act. He raised his glass, following Lubetkin's lead, without understanding why.

"Emma was in New York for a few days," Lubetkin said. "She was kind enough to come down before flying home."

Aaron nodded. "Where is home, Miss . . . sorry,"—he reddened—"I'm not very good with names."

"Diels," she said.

"Miss Diels."

"Please call me Emma," she said. "I have an apartment in Paris, but I seem never to be there."

So, she does travel. Aaron nodded again. He felt foolish.

"Have you ever heard of Miss Diels?" Lubetkin asked.

Aaron shook his head. "No." He glanced at her, shrugged. "Sorry."

"She's very good in her work," the old man went on. "That's why I asked her to come. I wanted you to meet."

Aaron wondered if she might be an actress. She was a strikingly beautiful woman. He found himself staring at her.

"Mr. Lubetkin tells me you've just been in South America," she said.

Aaron looked sharply at Lubetkin. The old man seemed unconcerned. "Only briefly," Aaron replied.

"Have you known Mr. Lubetkin long?"

"Not long. And you?"

"A few years. We correspond. We're pen pals, in a sense."

Something amused Lubetkin. He coughed, nearly spilled his brandy.

"Look, I've had a very hard day," Aaron said suddenly. "What is all this?"

"I'm sorry, Mr. Miller." She set down her drink. "This isn't very fair, Mr. Lubetkin, really."

"What isn't?" Aaron said.

"Emma is one of my trusted allies," the old man admitted, setting his snifter beside the decanter. It left Aaron holding the last glass, unsipped, with nowhere to put it. He felt incredibly silly.

"She has been a valuable contact for me in Europe," Lubetkin added.

Aaron listened but he wasn't following. "I'm sorry, I don't know who you are." If Aaron hated introductions he hated apologizing even more.

"I'm a widow," she said, her smile beginning to fade. "I have dual citizenship in France and West Germany. I was an orphan in Germany and I married a French national who died four years ago in an automobile crash outside Lyons." Her large brown eyes were steady on Aaron. "But none of that will be as interesting to you as what I do, at least, what I've done since my husband was killed. I spent thirty days in jail for striking a German official in Cologne. And four months for attempting to kidnap a German banker named Kurt Lischka to France."

Lischka. Somewhere he'd heard the name.

"We share a common determination, Aaron," she said quietly but with unmistakable bitterness. "I'm a hunter. I search for the SS. Nazis. One of them killed my husband."

For a long while Aaron said nothing. Then he drank the brandy, all of it at once.

Dinner was visibly awkward. The topic was Nazis. Mostly, Aaron listened. Lubetkin was one to talk when he was uneasy or felt others around him were. Emma would fill in details— the old man's topic included her and the work accomplished by her dead husband—though she appeared embarrassed whenever he made an especially complimentary remark about her. He also talked about Aaron, for her benefit, but these were short asides as if he was trying to be polite, to include everyone in the discussion.

She was born, apparently, in Cologne, according to Lubetkin. No one knew for sure since she was left there on the doorstep of an American commander, a colonel with the Occupational force. The American authorities suspected she was the result of a liaison between a local fräulein and a G.I., but it was never established legally. She was adopted by an American Special Services officer and his German bride, a sensitive and gentle couple in their mid-forties. Her mother was a German schoolmistress and music teacher who'd fled the Reich to Paris after the first book burnings. After two years when her father's army hitch was up, they moved to Holyoke, Massachusetts, where he ran a small weekly newspaper. When he died in 1961, mother and daughter returned to Paris.

Emma was a graceful and intelligent woman with an abiding appreciation of the arts when she met Jean-Paul Delouette, a young attorney whose father was a member of the Maquis during the German occupation of France and was captured and murdered by the Gestapo. Her education in the history of the SS began with their courtship. Delouette was a member of a postwar Maquis organization known as Le Trident. Made up of French, Germans and Dutch, the group searched for Nazis in hiding. Their record had been impressive but not without its failures. Four years after their marriage, Emma had worked devotedly with Delouette to bring back to France scores of SS killers and Gestapo criminals, many of whom had escaped or who had never been tried by postwar military tribunals in Germany. But France did not forget. Some of the most notorious criminals are free in Germany, Lubetkin was quick to point out, though they have been condemned *in absentia* by trials in France. Kurt Lischka was one, at that time a banker in Cologne, but in 1943 a member of the SS, accused of authorizing the deportation of more than one hundred thousand French Jews to Nazi death camps.

Emma was in Bolivia, tracking Klaus Barbie, "the Butcher of Lyons," who'd murdered Jean Moulin, the legendary Resistance hero, and sent thousands of children of Lyons to die in extermination camps, when Delouette was killed in a fiery car crash southeast of Paris. The *Trident* was convinced his death was retribution for exposing Klaus Altmann, the prosperous La Paz businessman, as the war criminal SS-*Obersturmfuehrer* Barbie. The Jews, the Maquis, the victims of the Reich did not forget, Emma said, but neither did the Nazis. Jean-Paul was dead. It was proof enough.

"So, you see, Aaron, Emma is a dedicated woman," Lubetkin was saying. "Tenacious. She is one of several who helped me track down Semmler's whereabouts, just as I have helped her on occasions." He nodded, smiled proudly.

They were all still in the dining room, Lubetkin at the head of the long table and his guests seated on either side of him. The dishes had been cleared away and the trio sat together sipping a superb port. Henry would have had his hide. Alcohol was strictly prohibited. But to hell with Henry.

Lubetkin had fired up his pipe and Emma, with her long slender fingers, had produced a pack of slim cigarettes with flowers on the cover.

"You haven't said much, Aaron," she said. "Is this ancient history so boring for you?"

Aaron shook his head. "Not at all. I guess I didn't realize what big business it was, I mean, searching for Nazis."

"I wouldn't have thought you to be a man to belittle our work."

"It isn't that. But there's a difference between a job and an obsession."

Emma nodded. "*Touché.* And I can actually understand a

cavalier attitude from someone who hasn't suffered at the hands of these animals."

Aaron glanced at Lubetkin who for once was quiet. The old man just sat there puffing. Aaron said, "I'm not Jewish, either."

"Is that supposed to be a requirement?" she said.

"I thought so."

"Jean-Paul wasn't Jewish. Most of the children of Lyons who died in extermination camps were not. Mr. Lubetkin—"

"Yes, all right," Aaron said quickly.

"You're looking for a Nazi."

"I'm looking for a murderer."

"Oh?" She shook a cigarette from the pack, lit it with a small Cartier lighter, rolled her head back, exhaled. "There's a difference?"

"Yes."

"What?"

"I don't care that he was a Nazi or an SS or Gestapo," Aaron said firmly. "I don't care about ODESSA or The Spider. I'm sorry for the children of Lyons. But the war had been over five years before I was even born. I can't take on the responsibility of another generation's guilt or vengeance or whatever you call it. Life's too short to hunt other men's criminals. It sickens me to read what the Nazis did to the six million. But my target is a single man. The man who killed my brother. I'm going to find him and kill him. If you want to help me, which is why I suspect Lubetkin brought you down here, then, fine. But you'd better understand it from my point of view. Finding the urn was a mistake. I wasn't even *looking* for the goddamn thing! I've got one thing in mind. Revenge, simply that."

Aaron had talked himself out. He took a long swallow of wine and felt slightly dizzy for a moment. The ache in his head returned. He hadn't been this angry for a long time and he wasn't sure why. Wine and brandy perhaps. Probably it was frustration. Or apologizing. Aaron looked at her and she stared back.

"Are you finished, Mr. Miller?" She didn't blink.

"Yes, I'm finished."

"I have a question."

Aaron sighed. "Just one?"

"Just one. What urn are you talking about?"

Aaron frowned, glanced at Lubetkin.

The old man took another puff, leaned forward. "Yes, well, actually I haven't told Emma about that yet, Aaron."

"For Chrissakes!"

"I thought I should leave it to you. It belongs to you."

"Me!"

"You discovered it." Lubetkin let his gaze rest on Emma a moment. When he looked back to Aaron he also relit his pipe. "And it may be the key to finding your *Kettenhund*."

"I'm sorry," Emma said, "but I seem to be missing something here."

"What *did* you tell her?" Aaron demanded.

"Only that you went to Paraguay for Semmler."

"And?"

Lubetkin shrugged. "And that he died."

Aaron glanced slowly at the girl. "I didn't kill him. I probably should have, but I didn't."

"Oh?" It didn't seem to matter to her what circumstances led to the death of a Nazi extermination camp commandant, only that he was dead.

"Look, Lubetkin, I don't know what this game is, but—"

The old man silenced him with a wave of his hand. "We can help each other," Lubetkin said. "There is a puzzle to piece together here and we can solve it." He set the pipe down beside his wine glass and sat forward. "I want to bring as many Nazi criminals as I can out of hiding in the time I have left. Miss Diels is an expert on the SS in Germany and France and in South America. She found Klaus Barbie."

Aaron shook his head. "You keep forgetting. I don't care."

"But you do care about one of them, Aaron. The German. The *Kettenhund*. Which brings us to your part in this."

"I don't have a part!"

"The urn," Lubetkin said softly. "It is the key. You can find this man—we all will find those we seek because it is the key. We—forgive me, you—have a great treasure of theirs. It puts us in an extraordinary bargaining position, gives us a leverage that no one—*no one*—has ever held before."

"If it wouldn't be too much trouble," Emma Diels said, "would someone please tell me what you two are talking about?"

Aaron sighed. "Our host has the eccentric notion that we can be led to an organization in South America run by the former bosses of the late great Third Reich through something I found. Actually, something I took."

"We already know, at least suspect, there is such an organization," the girl said. "But no one's been able to penetrate it."

"Mr. Lubetkin thinks we can now. I don't mean *we* ... someone. Don't you?"

The old man nodded. He didn't smile but his expression was confident. "Yes, I do. Aaron unlocked the door with his discovery. I think, working together, we can track them down."

She looked back at Aaron questioningly. "What did you find?"

"An urn," Aaron said. "Made of solid gold, apparently."

"The urn, of course, is not important in and of itself," Lubetkin said quickly. "What is important is its contents. Substantially important to us. Precious to them, I believe. Priceless."

"What is?"

"Not what, my dear," the old man said. "Who."

"Please, gentlemen, please," Emma pleaded. She turned to Aaron. "What did you find, Mr. Miller?"

"Hitler." Aaron nodded. "Adolf Hitler. Enshrined in an urn like an evil genie in a lamp. That's what I found. That's what Lubetkin wants to bargain with."

"Hitler!" The girl spoke the name suddenly; surprise mixed with an almost hypnotic terror of something endlessly deadly. *"You found Hitler!"*

Less than a half mile from the Virginia estate a rented Ford Maverick was parked under a large oak tree, hidden in the dark. Its driver was no more than two hundred meters from the main house, lying prone on a small rise.

With his binoculars he had an unobstructed view of the dining room and the dinner guests inside. He'd been here for several hours. The telescopic lens of the camera beside him on the grass had already captured the images of the three inside.

He already knew the old man, though they had never met. The file on Emil Erich Lubetkin was as thick as a telephone book. The American was a new face. But seeing the girl surprised him. No one had briefed him that she was involved in this. He knew Emma Diels. They'd met in 1972 after the terrorists had struck in Munich. He'd taken her to dinner in Haifa. He'd known her husband.

What was she doing here?

For another quarter hour he waited. Watched. When the taxi arrived, he noted the license as she got in. He would find out what she was doing with the old man and the American.

He found the taxi northbound on Telegraph Road and followed it into Alexandria until it discharged its passenger at the Ramada Inn on North Fairfax. Ira Linka watched as Emma entered the lobby and walked to the west wing. He was concerned for her. He wondered how much of the old man's scheme she was party to, if she was party to any of it. Linka sat in the parking lot for several minutes and decided not to contact her tonight. Time enough for that later. If the situation warranted. If the situation changed.

Linka did not notice the headlights of the sedan flick on in another part of the lot as he pulled the Maverick on to the boulevard. The same headlights that had followed him from Virginia. The same headlights that followed him now.

Saturday.

By 9 P.M. the *Oberkomitee* had gathered. They dressed to befit the occasion; summer suits, shirts open at the collar. Gluck and Helldorf wore their *Reichsorden*—SS service medals—above the right breast pocket. Mueller had pinned an armband to the sleeve of his finely pressed suit. Mengele sported a new cane.

Strausser had had the long dining table cleared. Six chairs were arranged on one side of the table facing a single chair—Reichmann's place—in the center of the room. The table's centerpiece was a small metal-wreathed swastika in the middle of a red felt blotter. It was all very much like a military tribunal chamber.

When Strausser entered there was a suppressed excitement about him. He hurried to the others.

"Reichmann is here," Strausser announced. "If the *Oberkomitee* will please take the seats I have provided, we shall proceed."

Mueller sat at the far left. "Very impressive, Herr Strausser.

Congratulations on your preparations. There is dignity here."

Gluck agreed. "It makes the blood run hot with the old memories. The Reich lives!"

Strausser executed a smart bow, accepting the praise. "It is important, members of the *Oberkomitee*, that we impress upon our guest the significance of his summons. I have taken the liberty today of briefing Herr—excuse me—*Schutzstaffel* Major Reichmann of our problem and our strategy for its solution."

"He understands the gravity of the situation?" Mueller asked. "The outrage?"

"Yes."

"And the plan?" Westrick hunched forward on his elbows. He looked rather like an old Hermann Goering; his fat, splotchy cheeks reminders of the once-jolly *Reichsmarschall*. Tonight he did not smile. "Did you explain his part in our plan?"

"To a certain degree, Gerhard. There are many details left to be decided."

Mengele nodded impatiently. "Yes, yes. Then let us get to our business. I am ready to meet Herr Reichmann."

"*Major* Reichmann, *bitte*," Strausser corrected. "I think it important to our purpose that we remember he was a member of the Waffen-SS—our finest soldiers. Not only that, he was one of Skorzeny's group of hand-picked *Kettenhunde*. The fiercest, the most elite, the most highly regarded fighting unit of the entire war. The generals Eisenhower and Montgomery made specific references to its superiority as a combat force. It is important that we instill in him the fervor of that distinction for this special mission." Strausser paused to take a breath. He was proud of this moment. There was a sense of accomplishment. The *Oberkomitee* was doing something more than balancing ledger sheets or accounting for cement mixers. "It is to that end, gentlemen," Strausser continued, "that I have attempted to make our guest feel that he is part of us. You will not meet a former SS *Soldat*, forced into hiding like so many others. You will meet SS-*Sturmbannfuehrer* Eduard Reichmann!"

Strausser stepped back to the double doors of the dining-room entrance, opened them with a flourish. The moment was not lost on the *Oberkomitee,* as its chairman knew it would not be. The members seated behind the table were struck dumb as if the figure at the door were some vision out of a long-forgotten past.

Reichmann.

He wore the black uniform of the *Allgemeine-SS,* magnificently in order. Black cap with its silver death's head *totenkopfver* insignia. Black tunic with black leather buttons and black tie. Black breeches. Black jackboots polished to high luster. The three plaited silver threads on the shoulder tabs identified his rank: *SS-Sturmbannfuehrer.* A dozen ribbons lined the top breast pocket over a *Reichsorden.* Proof of valor if there had been any doubt. The Kuban campaign. Lapland. Demyansk. Iron Cross 1st and 2nd. *Winterschlacht Mosten.* Narvik. Bronze and gold war service crosses. And at his throat, between the collars of his tunic, hung the *Ritterkreuz* from a black and red ribbon; the Knight's Cross of the Iron Cross with silver oak leaves and swords. The uniform fit splendidly. Tall, blond, lean, Reichmann *was* the Man of the Reich. Here was the Aryan every German soldier was taught to be. Here.

Reichmann.

Strausser cleared his throat. "Gentlemen of the *Oberkomitee,* Major Reichmann."

Reichmann walked directly to the table. His blue eyes were clear, alert to every movement. He towered over the old men sitting before him.

Mueller spoke first. He rose, raised his arm. "Heil Hitler!" The former head of the Gestapo was caught up in the moment, forgetting it was the subordinate who initiated the salute. The others at the table rose together as if marionettes on the same string, uttered the oath. Reichmann responded in kind.

"Please sit here, Major," Strausser said, indicating the single chair. "There is much to be discussed."

9

"First, I think we should get acquainted, Major," Strausser said, moving to his place at the table between Mueller and Mengele.

Reichmann followed him with his eyes. He sat very still in the chair provided him, the cap tucked under one arm, hands resting gently on his thighs. He revealed neither mood nor character. Only his eyes moved. Cool blue eyes. They flicked from one member of the *Oberkomitee* to another, pausing briefly on each as if recording vital statistics. Reichmann, it was plain to see, was not awed or intimidated by the assembly before him.

"Feel free to smoke, if you like," Strausser said amiably, settling in his place. "We want you to be comfortable here."

"I do not smoke, Herr Direktor," Reichmann said.

Westrick, poised to strike a match to one of his large cigars, hesitated a moment, then blew it out and set the cigar to one side. He remembered vaguely that the Fuehrer did not smoke either.

Mengele leaned forward. "Major, you understand the outrage committed against us? You have been briefed on the general strategy we intend to initiate?"

"Yes, Herr Doktor."

"And you agree to carry out our plan? You understand, Major, we must be sure we have the right man for the job."

"Josef!" Strausser was angry. "We have already discussed the Major's qualifications."

Mengele shook his head. "I would like to hear from Major Reichmann. It is on his shoulders that the success or failure of this mission depends." Mengele turned to Reichmann. "You understand my concern, Herr Reichmann?"

"*Major!*" Strausser retorted. "It is *Major* Reichmann!"

"I think," Reichmann interjected, "that it is not my former rank that is important here, but my former specialization." The blond German sat forward slightly. "Specifically, my capabilities as commando and assassin. I will not try to assure you with a list of similar assignments I have accomplished in recent years because there are none. Since 1950 I have lived in several South American countries. Like many others I was brought here to escape the criminal proceedings pending against me, initiated by Allied tribunals. Unlike many others I have not offered my services as an enforcer to the several dictatorships that actively sought such professionals. Therefore, I am not known to agencies like Interpol who have at least a file dossier on every SS man in South America. The weakness of the computer generation is its own dependence on bureaucracy to survive. If a man does not appear on someone's computer tape with a number after his name, that man does not exist. So I do not exist. As to my capabilities, you have only my war record and my presence here to recommend me for the job. In either case, I think you have no other choice."

There was silence in the room as the *Oberkomitee* exchanged glances. Reichmann stared at Strausser for a response.

Strausser cleared his throat. "Yes, well, thank you, Major. Have you another question, Josef?"

Mengele shook his head.

"Major Reichmann," Mueller said, startling Strausser. "You remember me?"

"You are Heinrich Mueller. *Gruppenfuehrer.* Chief of the Gestapo. Subordinate to *Obergruppenfuehrer* Heinrich Heydrich until his murder by Czech infiltrators. You were assumed killed by a Russian tank platoon near the Lehrter railway station in Berlin on the morning of May 1, 1945, attempting to escape from the Chancellery. We met once. At the ceremony of *Standartenfuehrer* Skorzeny's awarding of the Knight's Cross." Reichmann nodded. His blue eyes were intent on the old Gestapo chief. "Yes, Herr Mueller, I remember you."

"The occasion was also a happy one for you, Major," Mueller said, trying a smile. He nodded at the German's decoration between the collars of his tunic. "That *Ritterkreuz.* Is that not the same Knight's Cross with oak leaves and swords awarded you that same day?"

For a few seconds Reichmann stared at Mueller. "It was not so happy. It was December 1944. Patton's tanks were on the Ruhr."

"Yes," Mueller said, withdrawing the smile.

Reichmann's eyes found Strausser. "Herr Direktor. Let us be frank. You know who I am. I know who you are. For varied reasons we need each other. Ultimately our goals are the same. Recover the property that was stolen. I am here to offer my services. I ask nothing in return."

"Surely, Major," Helldorf began, "we can—"

"Nothing." Reichmann's cold stare communicated he meant exactly that.

Gluck raised an eyebrow. "Is it that you feel responsible, Major, that the Jew escaped from the Chancellery?"

"No."

"But he *did* escape!" It was Mengele. Mengele, always looking to place the guilt.

"He did," Reichmann replied. "But only him." His eyes snapped back to Strausser. "Security was inadequate. If I did not live near a village of Maca's I would not have been informed of the strangers who raided the villa and I would not have followed them to the quarry. I had never seen the chambers below ground—having never been invited—so I did not know there was a separate passageway other than the main entrance. I do not feel responsible that he escaped. In any case it is not important."

Mengele half rose from his seat. "Not important!"

"I cannot change what is past. I can only assume the duty I see ahead."

Mengele started to respond, but Strausser silenced him with a gesture. "The plan we have agreed upon here could be dangerous, Major."

"*Your* plan will not work," the German said with a touch of malice. "I am experienced in such work. You must trust *my* judgment."

"Must?" Gluck squinted through his glasses.

"To be successful," Reichmann said. "If I am to pose the proper threat it must be clear to the Jews that I alone am responsible. In the *Kettenhund* detachment I made my own plans, organized my own strategy. It will be the same now. I have studied your proposal. The weaknesses in it are obvious. They are access, deadline and target."

The German fell silent, waiting.

Strausser looked sideways at Mueller, then Mengele. Down the table Helldorf shrugged. Gluck and Westrick only stared stupidly. Finally, Strausser nodded at Reichmann. "What changes would you make in our plan?"

"Eliminate the defects," Reichmann offered cruelly. "Concentrate on the offensive. First, as to access. I will answer to no one." He paused, glancing at the faces for a sign of objection. Mengele frowned briefly but said nothing. "It is critical," Reichmann went on, "that a mission of this sort have no weak links. Therefore, there will be no continuing line of communication between us once I begin. You will not be able to contact me. If you control my movements, then you are subject to assault. If, however, you make it clear that I am on my own, then I become inaccessible and you remain safe from retaliation. I will contact you for word of the urn's return. When it does, I will have served my purpose."

Strausser nodded. He glanced at Mueller who nodded back. "Yes, good," the Direktor of the *Oberkomitee* said. "It sounds better already."

"Second," the perfect German said, "is the matter of deadline. It would not do that they *promise* to return the property. It must be handed over. I will not accept an excuse that it be left somewhere for you to find it. That course leaves open too many avenues for double cross. They may say they put it somewhere and someone else found it, expunging their own responsibility. No, it must be handed over. But any such agreement must be heightened by the threat. To say we will take direct action unless it is turned over requires a deadline. So you will supply a date. If the urn has not been recovered by that date, tell them an assassination will take place."

Helldorf held up a finger. "What date? Not tomorrow? How long can we wait?"

"Soon," Reichmann said. "You cannot afford to allow them time to hatch another plot and I cannot afford to trust my luck too long with forged or stolen passports and identity papers. I suggest two weeks."

"Two weeks," said Gluck, closing his eyes, "that would be . . ."

"The first of the month," Reichmann helped.

"That is enough time?" Strausser asked.

"Just enough," the SS major said. "I have given it some thought."

Strausser clasped his hands together. A gesture of finality. "Done."

"Last is the consideration of target," Reichmann said. "The victim-to-be. The most important element of the scheme."

"I have some thoughts on that, Major," Mengele began.

"Keep them," Reichmann said quickly.

"What?"

"None of you will know who I have selected."

"What!" shouted Mengele, rising from his seat. "What bargaining power is that if we cannot tell these swine who among them we have chosen for execution?"

"The very best." For the first time the Aryan smiled. "How

will they know whom to protect? They cannot hide a victim they cannot identify. With this plan no one will know where to expect a strike. Or against whom. It is a very workable conception, gentlemen. The victim need not be a Jew. It may be anyone. The American President or Secretary of State. A prime minister. A party chairman. Anyone. Make that clear and the threat is a hundred times more effective. Failure to comply with your demands places the blame for the consequences squarely on their heads." Reichmann glanced at each of the faces. "It will work. I guarantee it."

Mueller slapped his hand down hard against the table. "Brilliant! Brilliant, *Sturmbannfuehrer!*" The old Gestapo chief nodded vigorously. "It *will* work!"

Strausser too nodded. The faces around him were all smiling, approving of the deal. But he studied the man in the chair opposite them who was sitting there, as before, without expression.

"Major Reichmann." Strausser watched the cool blue eyes. "I have the impression that there is a certain friction in the air between us."

"Do you?"

"Why is that?"

The Aryan studied them all a moment. "Perhaps, Herr Strausser, it is because I find you contemptible. All of you."

The smiles evaporated. The room was suddenly still.

"Why is that?" the Direktor repeated. He held up his hand to silence the rage before it could be articulated by Mengele. Mengele, the shortsighted one.

"I do not trust you." He did not raise his voice. There was no need. "I do not trust you as *der Fuehrer* did not trust you. He was abandoned by his generals, by his inner circle of friends. *His* military decisions were sound, contrary to the popular view today. Early in the war *his* assessments of enemy strengths and weaknesses were strategically correct. It was only after relying on incompetent political hacks that *he* was forced to wildly deviate from sensible war campaigns. It destroyed him. I hold you and your breed responsible. That is why it will be by *my* design that he is returned. Make no mistake. *I* will succeed. On my terms."

Strausser took a long heavy breath. "If you feel that way, why bother with us?" He tried to contain himself. "Why not go out on your own?"

"Unavoidable necessity," Reichmann said. "We need each other. You have no one else to turn to whom you can trust."

"Trust!" shouted Mengele who could not contain himself. "You think we can trust you? After this!"

"Absolutely, You have to, don't you?"

"Tell me why," Strausser continued, oblivious to Mengele's outburst, "you need us."

Reichmann rose, preferring to look down at them. "I am the victim of my own anonymity. No one knows me. Who would take seriously a threat from Eduard Reichmann? No one. Our common objective is the same. Recover the Fuehrer's urn. For that I need the prestige of your names, your organization to back the threat. I am no one. My rage means nothing. But you gentlemen . . . who in the world would dare to predict what you might do?" The Man of the Reich offered the slightest hint of a smile. "You are crazy Nazis."

"I don't like it." Mengele was white with rage. "He insults the *Oberkomitee*. He insults me!"

Strausser raised a hand to calm the Doktor, but watched Reichmann. "You don't have to like it, Josef. The Major is right, after all. He knows he is right and we know it. As he said, there *is* no other choice."

"Then it is agreed?" Reichmann stood perfectly erect before them in his magnificent black *Allgemeine-SS* uniform; a vision of Aryan strength before the old men of the shattered Reich. The *Ritterkreuz* at his throat, its oak leaves and swords, glittered in the reflected light.

Strausser did not bother to look at the other faces. "Agreed."

"There will be expenses."

"Of course. I will give you an authorization for our Swiss account—"

"Cash," Reichmann said. "I cannot depend on a Swiss bank account. It could be a clue to my whereabouts."

Strausser nodded. "Cash then. How much?"

"Enough that I remain independent."

"A hundred thousand dollars?"

Reichmann indicated approval. "The unused balance to be returned, of course."

"Of course."

"I suggest that you all go to a place where you feel secure, just as a precaution," Reichmann said before Strausser could object. "You should remain together at a place where I can contact you easily."

"Bariloche," Strausser said. "The Argentine Andes. We have a resort there. *Das Adlernest.*"

"Go there. You will hear from me. Contact the Jews. A telegram will do. Identify yourselves and make the demand. Be sure it is understood what consequences will result if they do not comply. Then wait."

"And where will you be, Major?"

"It is not important for you to know where I am. Send the telegram as soon as you are together at the Argentine resort. You will hear from me in three days."

"What will you do?"

"I *am* the threat, Herr Strausser," Reichmann said softly. "I will make my presence known. Just follow my instructions and by the first day of the month it will all be done."

Strausser nodded tiredly. "You enjoy this, Major? Taunting old men?"

"Perhaps not as much as you think."

"Some day, Major Reichmann, you will be an old man."

"Some day?" The *Kettenhund* considered it a moment. "Some day, indeed."

10

The weekend had been like no other Aaron had ever endured. Henry had been a fastidious taskmaster. He was always prompt. The exercise began at six sharp. A brief rain shower Saturday afternoon did nothing to alter Henry's schedule. "There is always the unexpected," the fat man said from the protection of the gazebo. Aaron ran the mile and a quarter through the mud.

By Sunday, the fifth day, Aaron was up at five forty-five and ready for Henry's day of pain. He'd been right about one thing. The aches and soreness were less than yesterday. And yesterday less than the day before. Aaron could feel himself getting stronger, though he kept it to himself lest Henry take it as a sign of overconfidence. There was a new hardness to his calves and biceps, and his thighs took on a muscular tone he hadn't had since high school. He could breathe without opening his mouth when he ran and wasn't slowing to a jog the last hundred meters. Not a marathon contender by any means, but he wasn't quite so annoyed at Henry's caustically calling him "the athlete" anymore. With the growing strength he was also learning agility, and the other instructional phases of Henry's crash course were coming easier. The fat man was throwing him not as often as before. At the end of a session, Henry actually perspired. It was a sign.

But Henry's involvement in his tutoring was only a part of the curriculum. When Henry was finished, Lubetkin and Emma took over. Since the war, Lubetkin had compiled probably the most complete and detailed private collection of dossiers on Nazi fugitives in existence. The old man's den was a veritable archive of information on so-called war criminals.

"You cannot search for a man you do not know," Emma had said the first evening after dinner. "You must have an idea of the kind of soldier he was. The *Kettenhunde* were a special breed . . . with a special motivation. You must understand that motivation." She had spoken with the determination of one who knew. "Perhaps . . . perhaps we will find a photograph in this collection—" she had gestured at the long rows of binders in the bookshelves "—and there will be a name to put with a face."

So Aaron Miller's education began. *The history of the Third Reich started officially in January 1933 . . .*

Aaron's vow of revenge had now touched three others, if for different reasons, and a pact was born. Lubetkin gave his house staff an indefinite holiday with pay including (to Henry's chagrin) Geraldine, the cook, and the estate was transformed into a research headquarters and commando training center. Emma took one of the five upstairs bedrooms to be nearer the work. The old man became, in his way, chief cook and archivist. Henry was the only commuter, arriving at the estate at dawn and returning to the city at dusk.

The strategy proceeded on four fronts. Lubetkin provided the research material—seventeen volumes containing twenty thousand names and beside each a crime and cross reference to other volumes, another two hundred looseleaf binders of photos, vital statistics, last known aliases, capsule biographies. Emma served as Reich educator and decipherer of the massive Nazi collection. If the German's photo was there, she would find it. Henry continued in his role as tutor. But from the beginning the unspoken understanding had been that Aaron was to be the instrument of the plan to ultimately track down the *Kettenhund*. He alone. It was a curious foursome against an all-but-known adversary and the odds were against them. But Aaron was convinced he could change the odds. He *would* change them. He was going to change a lot of things. Like Abe did.

Lubetkin went to bed at ten, an hour past his usual time. He and Emma had spent the hours after dinner preparing the Reich material for Aaron at his next day's session while Aaron studied photographs of SS officers known to be associated with the divisions from which the *Kettenhund* corps was drawn.

It was a long, laborious process. When the old man suggested they finish for the night, Aaron welcomed the chance to rest his eyes. Faces were beginning to look alike. He went to his room, showered and put his tired body to bed. But he could not sleep. He lay awake, staring at the ceiling, only seeing the face of the German. Finally, he got up, slipped into a robe and headed back to the study. *No use,* he thought, *wasting time trying to fight for sleep.*

When he entered the study, Emma was sitting in an old-fashioned cotton nightgown in front of the television with several dossiers in her lap.

"What are you doing up?" she said.

"Couldn't sleep."

Emma nodded. "The same. I thought I'd watch the news and . . . as long as I'm up . . ." she indicated the files.

"You're dedicated, I'll say that for you," Aaron said.

"And what do you intend to do?"

He smiled. "Well, as long as I'm up—"

"You should be asleep."

"In a few minutes." He switched on the desk lamp and sat down. "I'll just go through a few more photos."

A few minutes became half an hour, then an hour. Emma

slid the files she'd been scrutinizing to the end table beside
the sofa and got up slowly. She stretched her back, then
gathered a stack of binders marked "Reich Photos: SS" from
the desk where Aaron studied grainy blowups by lamplight.
She sank into the chair across the desk. Her hair had come
undone. She propped her head on her hands, elbows on the
desk.

"It's late, Aaron."

He grunted. The photos before him were reproductions of
faded SS identity cards. He had to hold them in the light to
get a clear image of the faces.

Emma yawned, glanced at her watch. "It's very late." She
looked at him. "Aaron?"

"Five minutes," he said without looking up.

She nodded, stretched her neck. Across the room the
television was still on, but without sound. She hadn't the
energy to turn it off. "You won't be able to walk a mile and a
half tomorrow, much less run—" another yawn had to be
suppressed "—unless you get some sleep."

"In a minute."

"Henry isn't very forgiving," she said. Her eyelids were
fluttering.

Aaron didn't hear. He was nearly through the W's. *Allgemeine-SS.* The overall body of the SS composed of full-time,
part-time, active, inactive and honorary members. *Wels,
Werfel, Wessel, Wever, Wirmer, Witzleben* . . . Hundreds of
faces set in the same background, the same confident expression. Ageless faces. Aaron turned the pages of the binder,
searching for the one that would fit the image he carried in his
head . . . *Wolff, Wolke, Wolzek, Wulff, Wunsche, Wurst,
Wyche* . . . and there were still the general SS files and the
Waffen SS . . . *Yago, Yeager* . . .

Several minutes later Aaron rubbed his eyes, focused them
on something across the room. Emma was asleep, her head
resting on folded arms like a schoolgirl. He stared at her for
some time, blinking back the tiredness, and wondered again
why she should devote her life to tracking other men's
criminals. A beautiful, intelligent woman like Emma should

have other less morbid interests. It occurred to him that he might not have given the subject another thought had Emma been a man. Possibly. Nevertheless, she had been helpful. Well, then, more than that. She *did* know what she was doing and perhaps that was what bothered him most: She had taken the time to involve herself in this hunt. And for what? Old and aging Nazis, whatever their crimes, were of no more concern to him than the atrocities attributed to the Russian tsars. They belonged to a different age. It was not for one generation to pass judgment on another except in a historical context. This was a new time with different problems. This was . . .

Aaron yawned. He stretched out his arms and suddenly realized how desperately tired he was. He got up slowly from his chair. He could tackle questions of morality another time. Tomorrow he would start again, to search for Abe's killer, to find a face among so many. There was such a long way to go.

He came around the desk to Emma. When he tried to rouse her, she did not respond. He got her to her feet, but she leaned against him for support, draping her arms around his neck and mumbling incoherently.

"Emma, time for bed."

She laid her head against his chest. ". . . mmmm-hmmm . . ."

"Emma?" She began to slide back down toward her chair. Aaron grabbed her around the waist. "Emma?" She slumped against him. "Damn!"

He gathered her up in his arms, stooped to switch off the lamp and very nearly dropped her. "Damn." Emma snuggled into the crook of his neck, hugging him in her sleep. And he carried her upstairs to her room just that way, aware of her softness, the sweet smell of her, her vulnerability, but without the inclination or the strength to do anything about it. She was much more than simply a hunter of Nazis, he was suddenly realizing.

He set her gently on the bed and started to draw her arms away from his neck when she resisted, tightening her hold. Emma, frowning in her sleep, tugged at him, mumbling. "Mmmm, Jean-Paul . . . no, stay . . ."

Aaron shook his head in the darkness. "I'm not—" He pulled her arms away, but she clung to his hands.

"Jean-Paul . . ."

He should have left her downstairs, Aaron chided himself. What was he doing carrying a woman around in the middle of the night? He stroked her hair and whispered, "Go to sleep now." Then he took her hand away and started to move. Emma woke with a start, reaching for him, grabbing his arm.

"Don't leave, Jean-Paul. *Please!*" Her eyes were open, pleading, staring up at Aaron. Suddenly she was awake—consciously awake—and it took her a moment to realize where she was. She loosened her grip. Her hand went to her lips. "Oh."

Aaron felt very foolish, leaning over her. He bent down and kissed her gently. It was the most absurd thing he'd ever done, but it was suddenly the thing he most wanted to do. She returned his kiss and her arms came around him and he slid into the bed beside her. He touched her face, her neck, the loose nightgown that covered the warmth of her breasts. He untied the string at its neck and slipped his hand inside. Emma responded eagerly. She moved hungrily under him, moaning softly at the touch of his fingers. She parted her legs and reached for him. Aaron pushed the hem of her nightgown up past her waist. She moved her hips under the gentle prodding of his hand. She pulled him to her and for a moment he hesitated.

"I'm not Jean-Paul," he said. Emma moaned softly with her eyes closed.

"Please," she said.

Aaron started to object. "I'm not—" She pulled his face to hers and kissed him deeply, then arched her back and hips to meet him, drawing him into her with the action of her thighs, and the argument was over.

Aaron lay with his head on the pillow and Emma snuggled against his chest. He was serenely content and absolutely exhausted. His physical exertion over these last several days had now reached a milestone of sorts.

Eventually he said, "Are you awake?"

She stirred beside him. "Yes."

"I feel like I ought to explain," Aaron said. "I'm just not sure what to say."

"You? I've been lying here wondering what you must think of me."

"I'd think that was pretty obvious."

"No, I mean . . . I don't usually fall into bed with the first man who comes along."

Aaron turned on his side to see her face. He smiled. "How do you usually do it?"

"I'm not apologizing, Aaron. It—it just happened. Let's not analyze it, okay?"

"You're not embarrassed!"

"No, not for the fact of it. I—this isn't the time to give you reasons."

"You called me Jean-Paul."

Emma glanced at him quickly. "Did I? I don't remember. I'm sorry."

"You were asleep."

She nodded. "Oh."

"Has it been that long for you?"

She lay her head back on his chest. "I don't think that's really any of your concern." She stared at him a few moments. "But I'm going to tell you anyway. This may happen again. I don't want you to have any doubts about why." Emma stared at the ceiling. "Jean-Paul was—" she tried to find the right words "—a kind man. I'm afraid Mr. Lubetkin described a rather fanciful picture of us. It wasn't quite so romantic. Our relationship wasn't based on the usual thing."

"What's the usual thing?"

"Love, I suppose I mean. Romantic involvement. We did respect one another a great deal." She didn't look at him. As she spoke she seemed conscious of her hands only, turning the ring on her finger around and around. "When Father died, we moved back to Paris. Le Monde did a story on Mother and me. You know—'Displaced German war bride returns to France with daughter after Yank husband dies.' A good bit of it was about me . . . adopted orphan. Jean-Paul came to see us. He'd seen the article. That's how it began. I didn't know what he did then, I mean, about the war criminals. Mother was having some trouble with selling the newspaper back in the States—something about capital gains and divesting property rights—and Jean-Paul helped there. He came to be very helpful to us. And through it all he gradually explained his mission—what he thought was his mission, I suppose—and I was introduced to my responsibility." She glanced over at Aaron quickly, then back at the ceiling. "It wasn't rash, on my part, if that's what you're thinking. There are war criminals still at large. Men and women who did terrible things during the war who have never been faced with their crimes. I worked with Jean-Paul for nearly a year before he asked to marry me. We'd traveled a lot together and he suggested that in the interest of propriety we wed. Oh, I'm not explaining this very well at all. It wasn't as businesslike as it sounds. But Jean-Paul never made any conjugal demands. It wasn't that kind of relationship. I respected him enormously and he . . . I suppose he felt responsible for me." She was silent a long while.

"I'm sorry he died," Aaron said.

"Jean-Paul might have been different," she said quietly. "He might have been someone I cared more for. He could be tender, but there wasn't room enough for that. He was diseased with hate . . . an extension of his father's guilt. He thought he had to finish his father's work." She turned her face toward him. "In that way, you're very much like him."

"I don't think it's quite the same," Aaron said. "Not at all."

Emma's breasts heaved with a short sigh. "No, of course not. You're just searching for the man who murdered your brother. It isn't the same at all." She rested her head on his chest again. "In any case, I wanted you to know about Jean-Paul. What happened tonight, it—it just happened."

Aaron stroked her hair. "It may happen again. You're a remarkably beautiful woman, you know."

"I don't think beauty or remarkableness has anything to do with the satisfaction of lovemaking. The act satisfies itself."

"Is that all it was for you?"

"It's all I want it to be," Emma said softly. "I don't want you to be confused about me. If we make love again . . ." She paused a moment. "When we make love again, it will be for the pleasure of the moment. Nothing can come of it."

"You're so sure?"

"Yes," she said. "I'm sure."

They lay together without speaking for several minutes. She was not an uncomplicated woman, this Emma Diels, Aaron thought. Not uncomplicated at all. After a while, he caught himself dozing. He started to move even though his body rebelled.

"I think I'd better go," he said softly into her hair. He touched her face and was surprised to find the tears.

"Please . . . stay," Emma said. She clung to him. "It's been so long—so long."

Aaron cupped her head between his hands and kissed her cheeks. "I don't think you're so tough as you think you are."

"Hold me," she said. "Just hold me, Aaron, please." She kissed him gently and said, "Analyze me tomorrow, but just hold me tonight."

And he did, close to him, until exhaustion overtook them both and they slept entwined in each other's arms.

The television droned on in the quiet of the empty study. A news program recapped highlights of another drama begun earlier that day. The television camera that had recorded the pageantry, now played it back.

Nine thousand athletes from ninety-four nations marched into the stadium greeted by martial music and the boisterous cheers of seventy thousand spectators. Lord Killanin of Ireland, president of the International Olympic Committee, spoke to the throng. Next were a few words from Roger Rouseau, president of the Organizing Committee. Then, finally, Her Majesty, dressed in pink, with Prince Philip, Duke of Edinburgh, at her side, uttered the sixteen prescribed words.

Folk dancers celebrated the moment. Cannons boomed in salute. From the west entrance, two teen-aged athletes, the last members of a relay that started in Greece, came running onto the track, each carrying a torch. They ran across the infield, between two rows of red-suited guards, up the stairs of the huge platform and touched their flames to the dish-shaped structure. A giant flame ignited. The seventy thousand spectators clamored their satisfaction with a resounding roar. Three hundred white doves took flight in a frenzied moment of freedom.

The Olympic Games of Montreal, celebrating the XXI Olympiad of the modern era, were on.

The Palestinian scanned the bulk of intelligence reports. They were filled with discouraging news. The situation in Beirut remained unchanged. The liberation forces seemed stymied on all fronts. A despondent mood prevailed within the movement and the scandalous attack at Entebbe was the cause. The success of the Israeli commandos, in spite of the fool Amin, had been a devastating setback. Somehow he must reverse the present tendency toward despair. He must think of something.

He came across the Tel Aviv report. More bad news on the political front. The Americans were calling them heroes. Everyone applauding the daring rescue. The only glimmer of good news was an addendum to the Tel Aviv file. Early fragmented reports suggested the Israelis were still greatly concerned with the business in South America. There was something more developing than a simple theft here. Luckily, he had had the foresight to assign Jamil to that task. Perhaps there was a way to use this Nazi relic to his advantage against the Jews.

Perhaps.

He would think about that.

*   *   *

At the same time in a São Paulo hotel room, a blond German packed a small kit. Nothing in it indicated that he might travel a great distance or be gone a long while.

That afternoon he'd spent several hours in the library, and when he was finished he'd paid a visit to an office on the Rua de Abril and placed a long distance phone call. The man he spoke to was pleasant, jolly and obliging. By the time he'd returned to his room in the early evening, a small package was waiting on the dresser. Inside were a passport, identity papers and a bundle of American one hundred-dollar bills.

The cash went into the kit. The passport and papers he slid into the breast pocket of his new suit. At the airport he paid cash for a one-way ticket to Lisbon. The customs officer, a gray man with a thin mustache, greeted him with a tired smile. He leafed briefly through the passport and returned it.

"Have you anything to declare, señor?"

The German nodded, handing over his kit. "American currency. One hundred thousand dollars."

The Brazilian looked up in surprise. "*Cash*, señor?"

"Yes."

"It is much money to carry," the customs officer said, inspecting the kit, touching the paper bands around the bundles of bills. "You are not frightened?"

"Damned right," the German responded apprehensively. "The usual courier is on company leave up in Brasilia. Broke his foot mountain climbing. You'd think the company would have two couriers, but, no." He leaned closer to the inspector. "Not even bonded, you know." The German shook his head with a look of dread. "I'll be happy to have this done soon enough, don't you see. At least in Lisbon someone can take it off my hands."

"So much money," the customs man said again, handing the German a declaration sheet. "Should you not have a briefcase and handcuffs, señor?"

The blond man hurriedly filled in the spaces of the form. "And let everybody know I'm a courier? Not damn likely! Too many in this business get killed, as it is. I'm not advertising. I heard about a courier in Santiago . . . carried one of those things. They cut off his hand." He handed the form back to the inspector.

"I think that is only in the movies, señor." The inspector was losing interest. Behind the German an elderly couple was approaching the customs counter. They had four large pieces of luggage and a heavy trunk on a cart. He viewed the prospect of digging into the baggage with relish. "Thank you, señor." He handed a carbon copy of the declaration over. "Have a pleasant flight."

The German nodded.

The Man of the Reich sat near a window in the first-class section. He reclined his seat slightly to watch men below on the pavement loading baggage in the light from the airport terminal. For most of the day a tune had been caught in his head and, as he sat by the window, he remembered the words. It was the German soldier's song of a boy and the love he left behind. He hadn't thought of it in thirty years, but perhaps now, now he was heading home, now that old memories stirred, it seemed appropriate.

Underneath the lantern by the barracks gate,
Darling I remember the way you used to wait:
'Twas there that you whispered tenderly that you love me,
You'd always be my Lili of the Lamplight,
My own Lili Marlene.

Reichmann watched until the runway slid gracefully away below him, then snapped off the overhead light. He should sleep. He would be traveling a lot in the days to come. He closed his eyes and thought of the lover's song and of the *Oberkomitee* and smiled to himself in the dark.

It begins.

THE
GAMES

11

The telegram was first received by Lieutenant Hannah Zadok of the Israeli State Department early Monday morning. She immediately reported it to her superior, Captain Uri Gorin, who delivered it to the office of the prime minister.

Captain Gorin was slightly out of breath as he stood before the minister's aide. An overhead fan was turning in the small office.

"Major Cady, an incredible telegram!"

"Get your breath, Uri," the aide said, sorting through the morning mail. He waited a moment, sitting back in his chair. "Now, what is this exciting correspondence?"

"A threat, Major Cady."

The aide sighed as if threats were routine order of business on hot Monday mornings. "Oh?"

"I'd better read it to you," Gorin said. He unfolded the message from the envelope. "It is routed to Prime Minister Rabin. From Argentina."

"Argentina?" The aide looked puzzled.

"Yes, sir. *Oberkomitee der Kameradschaften.*"

"*Kameradschaft?*" Major Cady's expression went suddenly blank, then angry. "Look here, Uri, I'm in no mood for jokes this morning."

"I'm not joking. It's from San Carlos de Bariloche, Argentina. I verified it myself. It's—no, no, let me read it." Gorin looked down at the paper in his hands. "The message begins, quote, You know what you have done. If our property is not returned by one August the Zionists will be responsible for the penalties that we most assuredly shall exact. At this moment an agent of our employ, independent of our control, is ready to act. No head of state is safe against our rage. Make no mistake as to this warning or its demand. Our determination is as firmly resolved as destiny itself. Heil Hitler." Gorin looked up. "Unquote."

"Heil Hitler?"

"That's what it says."

"Crazies," the aide said. "Someone's putting you on, Uri."

"Someone from Argentina," the captain said without smiling. "I've confirmed the place of origin, Major. It *is* from Bariloche. This message went out from a resort hotel there at 11:48 P.M., Sunday local time. I can't vouch for what's in it, but the message is real enough."

The aide shook his head. "A bad joke. Someone with a very sick sense of humor—"

"There are six signers." Gorin looked back at the paper. "Alfred Strausser, Walter Helldorf, Heinrich Mueller—"

"Mueller!"

"Joseph Mengele, Otto Gluck, Gerhard Westrick." The captain looked up again.

"Let me see that." Gorin handed it over, Cady studied it, reading it twice. "These men are dead."

The captain nodded. "Yes, sir."

"Mueller was killed in Berlin. By the Russians. Helldorf too. We know Gluck ran ODESSA in the fifties, but he died of cancer in seventy-one." He stared at Gorin. "They're supposed to be dead!"

Gorin nodded again. "It *could* be a bad joke, sir."

"Yes, yes," said the aide impatiently. "But . . ." He studied the list of signers again. "Strausser, the leader of the Reich Office East Ministry, the Nazi party leader who set up the Wannsee Conference, the architect of the Warsaw ghettos." Cady recited the names as if remembering a brutal history lesson. "Helldorf, Eichmann's commanding officer in the Reich Central Office of Jewish Emigration. Mueller—" he stared at the name as if it had some personal connotation— "head of Gestapo. Mengele, the White Angel of Death at Auschwitz. Gluck, cousin of Richard Bluecks, chief of the concentration camp inspectorate. Westrick, Goebbels' minister of Reich propaganda." He sighed, staring grimly across the desk at nothing.

"Sir?" the captain said, making his presence known. "Sir, *is* it a joke?"

"Thank you, Captain Gorin," the aide said after a moment. "That will be all."

"But, Major Cady—"

"That will be *all*," the major said, coming around his desk with the message. He moved to the door, stood beside it with his hand on the knob. "I don't want you to mention this to anyone. See that whoever has knowledge of this cable keeps his mouth shut. From this moment it is classified top secret. Do you understand?"

"Yes, sir."

"It may be only some crackpot drunk with nothing better to do."

"What do *you* think, Major?" Gorin asked stiffly.

Cady said nothing, opened the door. "Thank you again."

When the captain had left, the aide dialed his telephone, drumming a pencil against the desk calendar. He circled the day's date, July 18, and drew a line to the first Sunday in August where he made a question mark. He spoke quickly to the prime minister, then read the message. When he'd finished there was a long pause while he listened.

"That's all it says, Prime Minister . . . I don't know what it means. It just says 'You know what you have done.' I don't have any idea what it's about."

Cady listened, made notes on his telephone pad. "Call the

Defense Minister, yes, I have it. Ten o'clock this morning in your office. I'll send this message to you immediately. *Shalom.*"

Cady sank into his chair. He held the paper up against the light, shook his head. "Terrorists, Syrian tanks, Idi Amin . . . now this."

There were those in the government who did know what the message meant. A short debate was held and a decision reached. They had dealt with threats before. Those who knew contacted their man in Washington.

It was time for Ira Linka to move.

The intelligence dispatch from Tel Aviv had arrived much later in Paris than was usual. But it was an unusually good piece of intelligence and the Palestinian's eyes danced gleefully over the printed news as he read it a second and third time to be sure it was true.

The Israelis were frantic. The Nazis had commissioned one of their own to slip out of South America on a killing mission. There would be an assassination unless the property of the Germans was returned.

The Palestinian was beside himself with joy. The great Allah, may his name be blessed, had guided his hand. The urn, the Nazi relic, would be the Jews' undoing. He would see that Rafai Jamil received instructions immediately. Here was the means to undo all that the Jews had accomplished since the Entebbe fiasco. Now they could suffer humiliation as he had suffered. The urn would *not* be returned. Let the German assassin carry out the threat. Let the blame be on the Jews' heads.

But the dispatch also cited a caution. It was not a significant matter, observed the Palestinian, in light of the greater news. It was a minor concern that could be dealt with summarily. He would see to that.

A man was hunting the German for personal reasons. A

man who had nothing to do with the Jews. An expendable man, the Palestinian decided.

A man named Aaron Miller.

In another city, Rafai Jamil listened attentively. The transatlantic telephone connection was not the best, but he recognized the voice of the Palestinian.

"So you see, Rafai," he was saying, "it was fortunate that I put you on the trail of this Israeli. A man of his station, in Washington . . . it will be he who goes to collect this priceless object from the old man."

If Jamil wasn't quite sure what the Nazis in South America had to do with the movement to liberate his homeland, he didn't reveal his ignorance. If the Palestinian was pleased that he, Jamil, might in some small way further their common cause with his presence in the American capital then it was satisfaction enough.

"You have been watching the Israeli discreetly, Rafai?" asked the Palestinian.

"Yes."

"Good," the voice from Paris said delightedly. "My information tells me he will soon be contacting the old man. Wherever he goes, you shall be nearby. Your instructions are to wait until he has the object, as he surely will. It is important to the struggle that you be successful in this, Rafai. It could be as important as the purpose of the taking of the French airbus from Athens. Perhaps more important."

"I am your instrument," Jamil said. "What are my orders?"

"Take the urn," said the Palestinian. "Use whatever means are available to you, but you *must* possess the urn. Whatever the cost. When you have it, guard it with your life."

"Should I bring it to Paris?"

"No. Once you have it in your possession, go to ground. It would be too risky to travel here. Go into hiding. It is not to leave your sight. The Israelis will turn the world over to find you, but you will not be found. You understand, Rafai?"

"Yes. I will disappear."

"Excellent, yes, you will vanish. But I must be able to

contact you." There was a long pause, then: "You shall call me once a day at noon. Once each day."

"Why not destroy the urn?"

The Palestinian came back quickly. "No, Rafai! It serves no useful purpose destroyed. We will return it to the Zionists *after* the deadline; after the assassination. Then we shall expose to the world that they had it the whole time. Do you see? No, we must not destroy the Nazi relic."

"As you command," Jamil said. "Are there any instructions as to the Israeli? What shall I do about him?"

"Whatever pleases you. He does not matter once you have the urn."

Jamil smiled to himself. He couldn't be happier. He knew exactly what would please him.

Emma sipped coffee at the file-strewn desk in the study and stared through the glass-paned doors that led to the patio and the gardens beyond. Aaron and Henry were grappling in the sun on a large canvas mat like contestants in a martial arts demonstration. In the midst of it, Henry would stop, make some point with an animated gesture and Aaron would nod resignedly, take up a new position and start again. It had been going on this way for hours. It was already nearly noon, Emma had been up since eight organizing files for Aaron's evening session, and she was almost bleary-eyed from her part in it. His enduring determination was at once awe-inspiring and a source of frustration to her. She'd never seen a man work so hard and learn so quickly. In their sessions together his mind was like a sponge retaining every drop of information she offered—that, after eight and ten hours of Henry's physical punishment. *What drove a man so?*

The more she watched him—his chest heaving through the sweat-soaked T-shirt, grunting with each practiced blow of his tutor—the more she was aware of her part in his metamorphosis. Acutely aware. And her awareness was beginning to translate itself into an inexplicable concern for him. It was as if she was contributing to the making of a single-minded machine that was without feeling or sensitivity—that she was helping to create a hardened, resilient soldier whose real identity was being replaced by pieces and ideals of others. Of course, it wasn't true. He was who he was whatever her influence. And, anyway, it was what he wanted, wasn't it? *Wasn't it?*

Emma sipped again at the coffee and suddenly frowned. It had gone stone cold. She set the cup aside. How long had she been daydreaming? She returned to the file in front of her, chiding herself for the lapse of concentration. It was childish for one night's lovemaking to cloud her own purpose. He had made his choice and she had nothing to do with that. Whatever he did he did without added encouragement from her. Still, the doubt lingered.

When next she glanced up, Aaron was off, jogging toward the far fence with a towel around his neck. It was the signal the morning's workout was over. Without thinking why, Emma got up from the desk and joined Henry in the shade of the patio.

She stood at the edge of the terrace watching Aaron, as Henry settled into the middle of the porch swing. "How's he doing?"

The swing creaked under the weight of the fat man. "Not bad."

Emma turned. "Really, how's he doing?"

Henry mopped his forehead with a handkerchief. "Actually—I wouldn't tell *him* this—he is about as fit as a man can be. Aaron wasn't as out of shape as I led him to believe. Any other man would have quit long before now."

"So why—"

"I thought there was a chance to discourage him," Henry said impatiently. Emma noticed the rings of perspiration around his collar and under his arms. "I didn't judge his chances of going up against a professional as even worthy of consideration."

"And now?"

Henry shrugged. "Oh, he's physically fit enough, his coordination is good. He responds well to instruction. He's an excellent student . . . eager, aggressive and all that, but, still . . ."

"You don't think he's ready?"

"It isn't a question of being ready. Aaron is as quick and agile as his brother was in his prime, but it isn't simply a matter of coordination and muscle tone." Henry sighed, dabbing the handkerchief under his neck. "I can teach him the mechanics, even technique, but I can't teach him instinct. That's something you have or you don't have. Abe had it."

"And Aaron doesn't?"

"I don't know. Not even he knows. And he won't until he's forced into a situation where he has to use it."

Emma frowned. "But all this, this training . . ."

"It means nothing," Henry said, "without an ingrained desire like a reflex. I don't mean he hasn't learned anything. He has, and faster than I expected. I would not like to be a mugger in some dark alley who tried to make Aaron his target. He's ready for that kind of confrontation. Self-defense is actually triggered by fear. But the kind of instinct I'm talking about transcends fear. Killing a man, I mean. Just knowing *what* to do isn't enough."

"What is?" Emma stared at him. "I mean, what if he doesn't have what you say?"

"Against a pro?" Henry shook his head. "He won't last ten seconds."

Emma looked back across the field. Aaron was rounding the fence, heading back to the house. He ran with strong, graceful strides. She could see the muscles in his legs glisten through the sweat. "Then what makes him do it?" she asked in a voice that was barely a whisper.

"You'd have to have known Abe," Henry replied.

"I think I'd rather have known Aaron." She watched him for a few moments more, until she could see his face plainly. It was set with grim determination, like a schoolboy out to prove himself worthy of his father's expectations. Or a brother's. Suddenly, she saw it wasn't they who were transforming him. He was transforming himself and it sent a shiver through her spine to realize whom he was making himself into.

12

The Israeli ambassador to Spain stepped from his car to the cobblestoned street in Madrid. The rain had been heavy for several minutes, and as it slackened, he fought the umbrella open and dashed for the side door of the embassy.

The ambassador was annoyed that his driver had reported in ill this morning. He was more annoyed, however, that he had decided to drive his own car through this muck of rain. He knew he could have waited for another driver but he was in the habit of arriving at the embassy early every day and there was absolutely no telling when a car would be around for him.

He was across the street, desperately trying to hold the umbrella upright, walking beside the stone wall that surrounded the embassy, when he was suddenly thrown against it, his face slammed into the wet, gritty fortification. His glasses shattered, broken at the bridge of the nose, and fell away. He tasted the warm, sweet flavor of blood as it trickled down from his nose, mixed with the wetness from the stones in the wall. Someone had wrenched his arm back, twisting it terribly behind him. An arm around his neck brought him up on his toes.

"Say nothing."

With terrifying strength, someone swung the ambassador around, almost lifted him from his feet. The voice was still behind him, softly urging.

"Watch your automobile, Herr Ambassador."

One moment it was there, parked against the curb behind a three-year-old British Wolseley, half a block away. The next instant it was gone, or nearly. The blast had come from the rear, near the petrol tank. The explosion disintegrated the rear half of the car, blew the roof cartwheeling into the air, then crashing down to the pavement. In an instant, before his terrified eyes, the ambassador's car was a fiery wreck.

"You could easily be dead at this moment, Ambassador." The voice behind him displayed no emotion.

"Please, I—"

The grip around his neck tightened. The ambassador's head suddenly arched back up. He stared wide-eyed at dark clouds. Rain pelted his face. He gasped for breath.

"Say nothing. Listen."

The ambassador's toes barely touched the ground. The hands of the voice behind him had the strength of ten.

"You will report this incident immediately to Tel Aviv. Understand what I say, Ambassador. I am the threat. I am the *Kettenhund*."

The ambassador tried to blink the rain from his eyes. The pain in his shoulder was excruciating. But he listened.

"If the urn is not returned by the deadline, an assassination will take place. I will see to it. But not you, Ambassador. No one so trivial. Perhaps a prime minister. A president. Someone worthy. Do not attempt to reach the *Oberkomitee* or I will strike. I promise you. Deliver the message."

Suddenly the ambassador was on his hands and knees in the street. He gasped heavily for air and finally got to his feet. His face was bloodied. He found the broken pieces of his glasses near the curb. When he looked up two boys were striking at the smoldering fire that was once his automobile.

He glanced around terrified. But there was no one there. Only the rain and the smell of burning tires.

Later, when asked to describe his attacker, the ambassador could say nothing. He saw nothing. There was only the memory of the horrible calmness in the voice.

Nothing more.

The binoculars held on the man in running shorts as he circled the fence at the far end of the estate. He seemed to run with less exertion now, long legs stretching out, arms high, face relaxed. The lenses followed him as he leaped a patio chair and walked to the garden gazebo. The man in the big hat handed him a towel. The girl was there too and the old man. They walked together to a picnic table set for four.

Ira Linka left his shaded spot on the hillside and walked the quarter mile back to his car where he'd parked it on an abandoned dirt road. He drove to a service station on the interstate and made a call to a number printed on a card in his wallet.

"Willson-Ives Real Estate, may I help you?"

"Linka," he said, glancing out the booth's glass partition at a small boy dashing from a car to the station's rest room. "Update."

"It's about time, Ira," the voice on the phone rattled. "We've been waiting hours."

"I'm here now. What is it?"

"Their threat is real." The man's voice was anxious, in a hurry to explain. An ambassador had been beaten up. His automobile blown to bits in a street in Madrid in broad daylight. They meant business. It was a warning. There would not be another. Linka must go to Lubetkin. Quickly.

They must have the urn.

13

Emma let him in, or rather, she was at the door when he came in.

"Where's Lubetkin?"

Emma studied him with surprise. "Ira Linka . . . Isn't it? We met—"

"Yes," Linka said shortly. He was looking past her, searching for the hall that led to the patio in back. "I have to talk to Lubetkin." He glanced down at her. "To all of you. The game's over."

"I must have it," Linka said. "I must have the urn."

They were in Lubetkin's study. Emma had moved the stacks of dossiers from the sofa and set them beside the television on the floor. She and Henry were in opposite corners of the sofa, SS files between them, photos spilling out of folders. The old man sat in his usual chair, sucking gently on his favorite pipe. Aaron, a sweatshirt draped around his shoulders, leaned against a bookcase. They formed an L and Linka paced back

114

and forth between them in front of the desk where Aaron studied at night. Emma had called them in from the garden where Aaron had been working out strangleholds on Henry. There hadn't been much of an introduction. Linka did all the talking. He seemed to know who everybody else was, and after he let them know who he was he went straight to his business.

"It is absolutely vital," Linka was saying, "that I have that urn."

Lubetkin withdrew the pipe from his mouth. "Urn?" He glanced questioningly at the others. "What urn?"

Aaron nearly laughed. The old man should have been on the stage.

"You know what I'm talking about," Linka retorted. He looked at Emma. "You all know exactly what I'm talking about. Paraguay."

Lubetkin's blank stare indicated nothing. He was very good at this, Aaron realized.

"We know about the expedition you sent to South America to get it." The Israeli's glance took in Aaron. "We know Abraham Miller led it. We know only one man returned." He was staring at Aaron. "You. With the urn."

Aaron came away from the bookcase, arms unfolding, slightly surprised.

"I'm sorry about your brother." Linka gave a little sigh. "But what you're doing—all of you—it can't work."

Aaron looked at Emma, Henry. They said nothing. "What can't?" Aaron said.

"I've been watching." He gestured toward the south. "From out there. It doesn't take a genius to figure out what's going on. One of you has got it in his head to go back." He was looking directly at Aaron.

"You seem to know a lot about what we plan to do," Aaron said.

"Do you think groups like yours are not carefully watched?" Linka said angrily. "We've known about Mr. Lubetkin's interest in Nazis from the time he wrote his first letter to the bureau at Yad Yesham. Miss Diels belongs to a

European group. There are small energetic bands all over the world tracking ex-Nazis. Few are successful." He began pacing again. "Last year a group of South American Jews went into the Brazilian river country on a tip that they would find Martin Bormann. Their bodies turned up two months later floating in the Paraná. I wouldn't make the same mistake twice, if I were you. But you can do what you want. Our only interest is the urn." He stopped, looked back at Lubetkin. "The one you sent Miller after."

"You are mistaken, Mr. Linka." The old man put the pipe aside. "I sponsored a group to locate and bring back a certain Erik Semmler: SS deputy camp commandant at Buchenwald concentration camp in 1943 and 1944. He escaped from an Allied internment hospital after the war and followed the same route as hundreds of other SS men to Buenos Aires. From there he disappeared." Lubetkin stared hard at the Israeli agent. "I found him. I decided to have him brought back to justice. Much the same as your people found Eichmann."

"We appreciate your efforts," Linka said. "The people of Israel applaud your dedication in seeking out a criminal against humanity. But that is not the issue here. I—"

"It is the issue I have concerned myself with for more than thirty years!" cried the old man. "It was not Jews only who suffered in the concentration camps. Slavs, gypsies. Germans, too. Yes." He shook his head. "Political prisoners, so-called. I was one, my family. Friends. I can understand the slaughter too because I was there. At Buchenwald. So do not tell me what is the issue. To me Semmler was the issue."

"And now he's dead." Linka's glance touched on Aaron quickly.

"Unfortunately," Lubetkin said sadly. He looked at Linka. "Not that he is dead, but that we who suffered could not face him before the world."

"Revenge?" said Linka.

"It is what your people call it?"

Linka shook his head. "No. That's what it is, but we don't

call it that. I believe there is such a thing as just vengeance."
He was quiet a moment, they all were, then he remembered
his mission. "It is not important . . . no, *to me* it is not
important why you went to Paraguay. What is important is
that you came back with something quite extraordinary."

"*I* came back," Aaron said, quietly waiting for the Israeli to
get to the point. "Whatever happened in Paraguay was my
responsibility."

"You brought the urn here?"

Lubetkin started to object, but Aaron waved him off.
"Everyone seems to know about it, Mr. Lubetkin. No point in
denying." He faced Linka. "Yes, I brought it here."

"The urn is safe then?" Linka said anxiously.

"Perfectly." Aaron glanced at Lubetkin who nodded, began
the process of refilling his pipe. "You've told us that you must
have it, now explain why."

"To give it back."

Aaron stared at him, surprised. They all did. Even Henry
was caught off-balance.

"Give it back!" said Aaron finally. "Why!"

"You don't know what you've started, Miller. You've
stirred up a hornet's nest. Those Nazis . . . those old men . . .
they want it back. They've threatened us. Lives are at stake."

"Threatened you?"

"Israel. Jews. Zionists. Us."

Aaron shook his head. "Jesus, I took the goddamn thing."

"They don't know that. Look, Miller, as far as they're
concerned this little raid of yours was planned and executed
by Jews. They believe we stole their precious urn. Their
paranoia hasn't changed. Now they've retaliated the only way
they know how. An attack against Israel, at least the threat of
one. One of their soldiers is out there somewhere prepared to
assassinate someone unless we—the Jews—return the urn."

Aaron crossed his arms. "You believe that?"

"Yes, I believe it. The Defense Minister believes it. The
Prime Minister believes it. Mostly the ambassador to Spain
believes it because this chain-dog soldier of theirs personally

blew up his car in front of his eyes half a block from the embassy in Madrid. I think he's crazy, but I do believe he means what he says."

"And what is that?"

"Someone will die if the urn is not returned by August first. Someone, not necessarily a Jew. He threatened your President. He's said in no uncertain terms that any head of state might be a target. That's why *we* have to see it is returned. *You* took it, but *I* have to see that the crazy bastards get it back." Linka's anger had risen to rage level. "I don't like it, Miller, but there it is."

"Chain dog," Aaron said calmly. "You called him a chain dog."

"The assassin?" Linka nodded. "That's what he called himself. When he had our Spanish ambassador by the throat, whispering in his ear. 'I am the chain dog,' he said. Or whatever the German translation—"

"*Kettenhund*," Aaron cut in sharply. His pulse quickened. "Did he say *Kettenhund*?"

"Yes, as a matter of fact. What's so—"

Aaron turned quickly to Lubetkin. "It's him!"

The old man shrugged. "Possibly."

"Not 'possibly.' It's him."

"Aaron—"

"Who else! Hell, they can't have a regiment of the sons of bitches down there."

"Excuse me," Linka said, "but just who is it you're talking about?"

"The man who killed Aaron's brother," Emma volunteered from her place in the corner. "He was called by that name— *Kettenhund*."

"It's what we're doing here," Henry said. "Aaron's going to track him down and . . . deal with him." He lifted his large shoulders and let them drop. "In our own ways we are assisting him."

Linka spun around to face Aaron. "You're crazy, Miller. You're all crazy. Deal with him!" He made a face as if the idea was too ludicrous to imagine. "The man who ambushed the

Spanish ambassador was no ordinary thug. This is a professional and he knows what he's doing. It isn't a game of dominoes those old men are playing. They mean what they say. And they mean to assassinate a major figure if they don't get the urn back." His stare fell on Lubetkin.

Lubetkin shrugged. "It is not mine to give." He was already tired. "The urn belongs to the man who found it." He looked at Aaron.

"Well, Miller?"

"I want to know about this assassin," Aaron said. "You say he'll kill someone if the urn isn't returned?"

"That's right."

"Returned to whom?"

"That doesn't concern you," Linka said.

Aaron shook his head. "You're mistaken. It concerns me because I have it."

"Good God, Miller—"

"Who is supposed to take possession?" Aaron snapped. "This chain dog?"

Linka exhaled through his teeth. "Yes. We return it to him and he backs off. Nobody gets hurt." He glowered at Aaron. "And that's the way we want it, Miller."

Aaron glanced at Emma, then nodded to himself. "Tell you what." He turned to the Israeli. "We'll compromise. You get the urn if I get the German."

"Forget it," Linka exploded.

"How badly do you want the urn?"

"The only way you could even get close to this man is if you came along when—" Linka stopped short. His eyes widened.

"That's right," Aaron said. "I want to go." He smiled.

"You're a crazy bastard, Miller. You really are."

"All the same . . ." Aaron shrugged.

"Why would you want to take such a risk?" Linka shook his head. "It doesn't make sense."

"You didn't know my brother," Aaron said. He would have said more, but it would have defied Abe's Second Law.

*　　*　　*

The dark sedan waited in the shadows of late dusk. When the Jew's car swung onto the road from the gravel entrance to the big house, Rafai Jamil nudged his driver awake. When the car started, the Bedouin in the back seat was up, the Soviet machine pistol like a toy in his hand. Jamil told him to wait. They drove without headlights until they met the interstate. The Jew's car was easy to follow.

14

The back seat of Linka's Mustang seemed a terribly small space, Emma thought. Her legs were crunched up behind the driver's seat and what room was left was taken up by Henry's bulk beside her. She disliked riding in the back of two-door cars because there was no way to get out quickly and sitting cramped up like this with a driver who couldn't go fast enough didn't make her any more comfortable.

No one had spoken since they left Lubetkin's. It was just as well, she thought. Aaron had forced the Israeli into a situation that he had no alternative but to accept. There was no mistaking Linka's mood. She could see his eyes in the rear-view mirror as he glanced up to speed past a car. Frustrated and angry. And Aaron sat stoically in the front passenger seat, staring straight ahead, but there was a new wariness about him, a renewed determination, that was frightening. She had thought she was beginning to know him, to understand him for himself. The days they had worked together proved, at least to her, that he was something more than just the brother of Abe Miller. Whether he realized it or not, there was nothing wrong with being simply Aaron Miller. He had a sensitivity that was not limited to lovemaking. Circumstances had rendered him vulnerable, a private vulnerability she understood and shared. Perhaps that was what drew her to him. They had been, in their own ways, beginning to share a common strength in each other's loss. The first night they spent together had demonstrated that. Then, suddenly, everything had changed. Like a recurring nightmare, she was frightened all over again. Just when she thought it would be different, that in Aaron's convalescence she would find her own, he changed. And it was frightening because she had allowed herself to care for him. It was terrifying because she had seen it before. Jean-Paul. The nightmare returned.

Emma jumped with a start in the darkness of the back seat when Henry leaned forward suddenly. "Right at Washington Circle," he directed. "K Street."

Emma glanced outside. They had just passed over the Arlington Memorial Bridge. The Lincoln Memorial loomed up before them, majestically lighted, as Linka guided the car on the cloverleaf around it.

The Israeli grunted with a nod at Henry. He looked over at Aaron. "Tell me, Miller, what did you do before you hunted professional assassins?"

Oh, God. Emma looked at the ceiling.

"Paperwork," she heard Aaron reply in a subdued voice. "A government paper pusher . . . before my section was pared down. I was one of the parees."

"So you decided to go to South America?"

Aaron said nothing.

"Why don't you just drive, Ira," Emma said.

Linka glanced up to see her in the mirror. "You mean it isn't any of my business?"

"That, too."

"What on earth brought you into this, Emma?" asked the Israeli in the mirror. "I thought after Jean-Paul . . ."

"She isn't involved anymore." Aaron turned to face the man from Tel Aviv. "Just me now."

"You and the chain dog," Linka replied. He lit a cigarette.

"You really don't care about the urn, do you, Miller?"

Aaron shook his head.

"Why is that? Don't you realize how important it is?"

"No," Aaron said. "Not a pot of ashes." He looked gravely at the Israeli and Emma saw in his face a bleak malevolence. "The German, I take seriously. He killed four men. One was my brother." He turned back to the window.

Leave him alone, Emma wanted to scream. *Just leave him alone.*

"You must have known there were risks," Linka said.

Emma sat up from her cramped place in the back, leaning on the front seat. "Look, Ira, why don't you—"

"Nobody was supposed to die," Aaron said, staring through the passenger window. "Just get Erik Semmler and bring him back."

The car turned onto K Street. "A simple kidnapping." Linka shook his head as if he knew of such things. "You'll learn that nothing that requires violence is ever simple." He glanced up at the mirror. "Isn't it so, Emma?"

"I wouldn't know," she snapped.

"What about you, Nickelson?"

"I wasn't there," Henry said from the shadows beside Emma.

"Maybe not Paraguay," Linka observed, "but somewhere. I've been watching you, remember? It doesn't take a genius to recognize an old pro."

The seat beside Emma creaked as Henry adjusted his position. "Are we back to that?"

"But I'm right. What was it, CIA? Mercenary?"

The fat man did not reply. After a moment, Aaron said, "He worked with Abe, when he was in it. Abe called him the best."

"Your brother had a big mouth," Henry said.

"So why did you quit?" Linka asked.

He's baiting everyone, Emma thought. She started to say something when Henry covered her wrist with his huge hand. He shook his head. "Mozambique," Henry said. "Seventy-three. Frag in the kidney and spleen . . . upset the hormones.

Wouldn't have recognized me then." He shrugged and smiled without remorse. "Two eighty-five now. But it sells antiques, the image."

"Antiques?" Linka frowned.

The big man responded by directing his smile at Emma. "It's what I do when I'm not watching the athlete run." He pointed to a large stone building. "Stop here."

Emma was surprised to find it was an old house and small. The place was full of art works of one kind or another; paintings, rubbings, sculpture, antiques, bric-a-brac—hanging, stacked, piled everywhere. It certainly was a change of scenery from the orderliness of Lubetkin's mansion. It wasn't so dirty as dusty. If a woman had been here, Emma judged by the decor, it wasn't evident.

"Have a seat," Henry said with a sweeping gesture when they were in the parlor.

"We're not staying," Linka said. "I'm just here for the merchandise." He glanced around the room. "Who keeps it when you're not here?"

"I didn't get rich like this paying employees."

The Israeli's eyes widened in astonishment. "You didn't leave it here unguarded!"

"We told you it was safe," Aaron said. "It's safe."

He seemed amused, Emma thought. The Israeli didn't notice.

"I could have picked the ancient lock on that door with my eyes closed," Linka shouted.

"Henry has his own alarm system."

The fat man nodded. "Actually, there isn't anything that valuable to anyone except dealers or buyers. Oh, an original Nussbaum and a Rumbelow print, perhaps, but my clientele isn't the sort to—"

"Great," Linka interrupted. "Can we get on with it?"

Henry sighed, nodded. "This way." He led the way to a back room, a door strung with beads on a string that clinked together as they passed through. He flicked on the lights. The windowless room was much like the parlor. A dozen tables were stacked with boxes, crates littered the floor. Frames were stacked against the walls and a hundred doodads were crowded together along a counter at the far end. Beside a large oriental brass lamp, leaning against a stack of books, was the urn, its gold surface gleaming.

Emma caught her breath when she saw it. "God, what an ugly thing."

"Ugly?" Henry shook his head. "My dear girl, that may be many things, but ugly—"

"The swastika," she said.

"Oh, yes, that."

"Then you won't mind if I take it off your hands." Linka started toward it. He'd taken half a dozen steps when the room was suddenly filled with a short boiling growl. It was dreadful, low and menacing. Emma glanced down. Less than six feet from Linka, behind a crate of colored bottles and poised to lunge, was the biggest German shepherd she'd ever seen. Its teeth were exposed in a snarl that froze Linka to the spot.

"My God!"

Henry laughed. "I'd like you to meet part of my old team. This is Chester."

"Call him off!" Linka said shallowly.

"I want you to understand the urn is safe here," Henry said.

"All right, all right, it's safe." Linka stood with one foot before him like a dance student learning a new step.

"Turn to your right now," the fat man said. "Slowly."

Linka obeyed. When he moved, his eyes widened. Emma looked at the same moment. At Linka's feet, with snapping yellow teeth and deadly eyes, was a pure white Alaskan husky.

"And Sasha here is the other part," Henry added. "She's slightly more ill-tempered, being a bitch."

Linka's hands hung motionless at his sides. "I said all right. You made your point."

Henry glanced at Aaron, smiled. He snapped his fingers and both dogs responded immediately by sitting back on their haunches, tails wagging, eyes alert.

"Come, my beauties," the fat man commanded. The dogs

came, panting happily, licking Henry's large face as he kneeled and grabbed them playfully around their necks. "Aren't they lovely?"

"Beautiful," Emma said. She glanced at Linka.

He wiped his forehead, let out a breath. "Wonderful."

"I think you spoil them, Henry," Aaron said, bending down to the shepherd.

"Best team I ever worked with," Henry said, smiling at Emma. "Chester and his girl Sasha could sniff out the smell of armaments a mile off."

"They're beautiful animals, Henry," Emma said.

"Just terrific," Linka retorted. "Now—"

Aaron nodded. "Yes, now. Take it."

Henry wrapped the urn in the parlor with crate cloth and tied it together with nylon cord. "There. One Maltese Falcon, ready to travel."

Linka took it, a wary eye on the shepherd that had moved beside him.

"Who will be handing it over?" Aaron asked.

"I don't know definitely." The Israeli frowned when the husky opened her mouth wide from her place on a small oriental rug near the door. But it was only a yawn. "I expect it will be me. There will be further instructions when I report to the embassy, but I'm the logical choice."

"You and Aaron," Emma offered. She turned to Aaron. "If it has to be."

Aaron nodded. "It does."

Suddenly she didn't want him to leave. An emotion deep inside her would not be suppressed. Maybe she'd misjudged his commitment. Maybe there was a way to persuade him to reconsider. It was a fantasy, what he was trying to do. A man with a boy's face. Emma touched his arm.

"Aaron, I . . . Maybe you should think this over . . . maybe you—"

"No," Aaron said.

"But, Aaron—"

"It's not for you to judge," Aaron snapped. He looked at Linka. "Shall we go?"

Emma stood with Henry at the door, the dogs sitting at their feet, the light from the house silhouetting them against the dark, as Aaron and Linka walked toward the car. Suddenly Chester's ears perked and he stood. Then the husky was up too, whining. For an instant, Emma stared blankly at the watchdogs, then jerked her eyes toward Henry. The fat man sensed it too. He was frowning, looking out into the darkness. When she followed his glance, she saw Aaron and the Israeli were no more than ten feet from the curb. The shepherd's whine turned into a deep growl. Then Emma saw the sedan parked across the street. She saw the two figures inside, saw the doors open, then recognized what they held in their hands.

Oh, God! "Aaron!"

The tranquil night exploded with the deadly raking fire of semiautomatic machine guns—lightning bursts from two weapons. Emma felt the weight of Henry's hand shove her down. For a moment she lost sight of the men on the lawn, then she saw Aaron—he was already on the ground rolling, but the Israeli was trying to run for it, crouched low, heading for the tall shrubs that flanked the house. Henry hit the floor when the windows beside the door shattered, spilling antiques backward into the parlor. The dogs were wild, barking, straining to attack against Henry's grasp on their collars.

"Down, Chester! Get down, Sasha!"

Aaron had rolled against a car parked behind the Mustang and was pinned down by the gunman who fired there, flattening the tires, shattering the windshield. Emma could make out two figures, both in ski masks, shooting from the hip, advancing across the street. Linka had fallen, the turf around him popping up in divots from impacting slugs as he tried to get to his feet. He clutched the bundle he was carrying against his chest.

It took Emma several seconds to realize that Aaron was the one in danger. The gunmen were doing their level best not to hit the Israeli. Linka had the urn. It was suddenly clear to her that these assailants did not want the urn damaged. But Aaron had nothing. *He* was expendable. And they were halfway across the street before she realized it. "Let them go!" she screamed at Henry. "Let the dogs go!"

Henry released them. "Go!" Henry yelled. "Go to Aaron!"

The dogs responded as if they had done this a hundred times before. Chester was off in a blur, circling left, in a dead run to the flank. Sasha, faster, took the shortest route—head on—unafraid, sixty pounds of rage. She bounded onto the hood of the car and catapulted herself straight into the gunman on the right.

Chester hit the other a second later, knocking the weapon away, teeth flashing, clawing for his face.

Henry was off the front stoop, running, after a fashion, toward Linka who was almost to the shrubs. Emma was running too, but toward Aaron.

"Get down!" Aaron screamed. When she reached him, beside the car, he pushed her roughly down against the curb. "Stay there!" Then Aaron was up, galloping after Linka.

A figure stepped out from behind the hedge. He wasn't wearing a ski mask. Emma watched as Linka tried to stop. The man brought the pistol up and seemed to smile.

"For Böse," he said, "and my other comrades." He fired three times at point-blank range, and Aaron dove into the damp grass. Linka dropped the urn, fell sideways. Henry fell to the ground when he saw Jamil raise the pistol toward him.

The Palestinian grabbed the bundle and fired twice more before disappearing back into the hedge. A few moments later Chester and Sasha were bounding past Linka, searching for the intruder. There was another pistol shot, and another. The barking stopped. By the time Emma reached Linka, Aaron was already there, ripping open the Israeli's shirt.

"Son of a bitch!" Aaron cursed.

Emma panted heavily as she knelt beside him. "Is he dead?"

"Get out of here!" Aaron snapped.

A car started. Aaron twisted around to see the sedan with the gunmen speed off down the street.

Henry trotted over. "They're gone. They took the urn."

"Get her out of here, Henry." Aaron took the Mustang keys

from Linka's hand and shoved them toward Emma. "Go to Lubetkin's and wait."

Emma didn't move. She could only stare at the blood on Linka's chest.

"Damnit, Emma, will you get away from here!"

"Aaron, I—"

"Just do what I tell you—please, goddamnit! We're going to have half the Washington police here in twenty seconds."

Henry pulled her gently to her feet. "He's right for a change, Emma. You'd better go."

"But—"

"Quickly," Henry said.

Aaron watched her go. Then he jerked his head toward the house. "Call an ambulance, Henry. Quick."

The fat man started off. The German shepherd returned through the shrubs and Henry looked up quickly for the husky. He whistled, but only the shepherd was there, whining, awaiting another command.

"Henry!" Aaron was wrapping Linka's wounds, trying to stop the bleeding. "Move!"

Henry's eyes searched the darkness, then he started for the house. "Bastards," he said, running toward the light. Chester was at his side. "Bastards."

"He took the urn," Linka cried through his pain. "He took—"

"Shut up!"

"Miller, you have to get it back." The Israeli's face was turning gray.

"Don't talk, you want to bleed to death?"

A blue and white patrol car stopped in the street. Aaron yelled for help.

"You have to—"

"Yeah," Aaron said.

"They were PLO." Linka's breathing was shallow, strained.

"Shit."

"You have to get it back, Miller." A whisper. A sticky hand grasped Aaron's arm. "You will. Please."

The cops were running toward them now, guns out.

"Aaron?" The Israeli's grip tightened.

"Yeah, right."

Linka coughed blood. "Remember, you gave your word." The shirt was soaked. Blood dripped on Aaron's shoe.

"Okay, shut up now."

Linka's eyes rolled back and he exhaled a long sigh as the two cops ran to them. Aaron got to his feet.

"Get an ambulance here! Fast!"

The older cop held his gun on Miller, glanced at the man bleeding on the lawn.

"C'mon, he's bleeding to death!" Aaron demanded.

The cop nodded to his partner who dashed back toward the street. "All right, buddy," the cop said, "what's going on here?"

Aaron knelt down again next to Linka. "A war," he said softly. "A war just started."

15

Reichmann's train arrived in Vienna shortly before noon. He had a leisurely lunch at a *Gaststaette* near the Danube and spent another hour in the library of the Landstrasse District. He then rode streetcars to the Hotel Sacher where he took a room with a view of the world-famous Vienna State Opera House. After a long bath and a change of clothes, the German walked to an address just off Schwarzenbergstrasse. He took the elevator to the third floor where he found the number he'd written on a slip of paper from the directory. He rang and waited.

After a time he heard the shuffling footsteps of someone managing an artificial leg.

"*Ja?*" Through the door the voice sounded tired, old.

"Herr Rudel, *bitte*," the German said.

"*Wer ist da?*"

"It is Reichmann, Herr Rudel. Eduard Reichmann."

"*Wer?*"

"The Fifth Panzer Division," Reichmann said. "Wiking. I

am Reichmann, comrade of *Standartenfuehrer* Skorzeny . . .
Die Spinne."

For a moment there was no response, then the German
heard a bolt slide; the door opened slightly. He had a glimpse
of the man behind the door; the dark eyes, receding hair,
dimpled chin. It was he, older now of course, but the same
man. Once the most celebrated hero of the Reich, winner of
the only Knight's Cross of the Iron Cross with golden oak
leaves, swords and diamonds ever awarded. The figure behind the door looked out dubiously. *"Bist du denn wirklich
Reichmann?"*

The German nodded. "Yes, my colonel. I am Reichmann."

The door closed, the chain released, then opened again.
"Herein!"

Reichmann entered and was immediately surprised at the
size of the flat. It was not large or elegant but rather quite
plain. The windows offered a view of a *Stadtpark* to the west,
certainly attractive, but the place was not at all what he'd
expected to see. Rudel wore a housecoat and slippers and
moved with the sure control of a man who had mastered the
mechanics of walking on an artificial limb. He indicated a
chair for Reichmann, then sat on a pastel-colored divan.

"You look like Reichmann," the old Luftwaffe hero said in
German. He studied his visitor a moment, then nodded. "Yes,
very much. I wouldn't know absolutely, of course, we only
met once or twice. You do look very much like what I would
expect. Perhaps not as old as I might have thought." He shook
a cigarette from a pack in his breast pocket and took his time
to light it. "Why would a man who says he is Reichmann
suddenly come to see me in Austria?"

"First, you must be convinced that I am who I say," the
German said.

"How do you propose to convince me?"

"I am from—"

"No, no," Rudel said impatiently, waving his cigarette.
"These facts, these vital statistics, *everyone* knows them these
days who can read a book." He took a long drag from the
cigarette. "Anyway, why should I care if you are
Reichmann?"

"I am from the Mato Grosso region of Brazil where it approaches the river Paraguay, Herr Colonel," Reichmann continued undaunted. "I came to be there because of the *Kameradschaft*—the rescue organization you yourself founded. During the aftermath of the war, it was Bauer and Niermann who supplied me with an identity certificate as a stateless and displaced person from the Vatican's Refugee Bureau, good to Syria and Argentina. I went to Argentina."

Rudel listened, slightly intrigued. "It is widely known that the Catholic Church of Rome issued thousands of such certificates and that an unknown number of them went to fugitives from the revenging Allied powers." Rudel sucked deeply on the cigarette. "It was a matter of Christian love for fellowmen on the part of the Church that the certificates were issued."

"The Catholic Church has never been so humanitarian-minded," Reichmann said indifferently. "I heard of but never met the Monsignor Giovanni Montini, then Deputy Secretary of State of the Vatican, who with other Church authorities helped save the flowers of the Reich in similar *Christian* efforts." Reichmann smiled. "The Monsignor must have done something right. They call him Pope Paul VI today."

"Is this why you have come here," Rudel asked, "to give me lessons in Church history?"

"I am working for the *Oberkomitee*," the German said, holding his stare on his host. "Of the *Kameradschaft*."

"I have nothing to do with that group anymore," Rudel said. "It is no longer the rescue organization that I set out to make. It has accomplished that end. Now it is something else entirely. Anyway, that also is widely known."

"Not so widely, I think, Herr Colonel."

"If you are working for them you must have met them?" Rudel eased back into the divan. "Is Martin Bormann resting easily these days?"

"Herr Bormann is resting permanently," Reichmann said. "Do not try to fool me with clever tricks. I have met the entire *Oberkomitee*. Four days ago."

"Then you would know their names, eh?" said the man

who had received the highest Reich award from Hitler himself. "Don't tell me you have forgotten them."

"Strausser and Mueller," Reichmann said. "Mengele and Gluck. Westrick and Helldorf."

Rudel stiffened, his eyes were suddenly alert. "You do know!"

"I am Eduard Reichmann, my colonel. I fought with the Fifth SS Panzer Division under the badge of the *Wiking*—the rounded swastika on a sculpted shield. I was a *Kettenhund* under *Standartenfuehrer* Otto Skorzeny. For thirty years I have lived in the wilderness of Brazil. Now I have been called back to do a duty that is not worthy of those who would employ me." Reichmann stared hard at Rudel. "I've come to Vienna for good purpose. I need your help."

Rudel made *Melange mit Schlag* and set it on the table between them. He spoke of the old days; sinking the battleship *Marat*, his exploits in the air against tanks, being shot down by the Russians, escaping, and finally the flight that ended in his losing his right leg. The old warrior seemed to come alive as if the retelling of the six most glorious years in his life made up for the other fifty-four. Hans-Ulrich Rudel was the hero of the Luftwaffe. He was the man credited with 2,530 operations, 532 tank kills and with sinking a British cruiser and battleship. With Skorzeny they might have been the three greatest heroes the world had ever known, if the war had gone differently. Rudel the pilot. Skorzeny the adventurer. Reichmann the soldier.

If the war had gone differently.

Reichmann remembered the *Oberkomitee* and what it represented. Old men. Remnants of the most powerful empire since the Roman legions under Sulla. And now the most precious artifact of their age taken. It was never clearer to Reichmann than now that only three men were worthy to reclaim their legacy and revenge the outrage. But Skorzeny was dead. Rudel limped about on one good leg and boasted of his achievements in a low voice behind closed doors in the privacy of his Vienna apartment. If ever there was a choice, time and age had reduced it by two. The job fell to Reichmann. Clearly. Absolutely. Finally. If Strausser and the others were fools they at least were correct about one thing. It was destiny that brought Reichmann to the Fuehrer's attention so many years ago, when he was not Reichmann but a schoolboy from Heidelberg and a gifted athlete. It was the Fuehrer's foresight that created him and instilled in him the dream of the Reich. Reichmann considered it. Though the dream was gone the legacy remained. It was destiny calling again. This time, Reichmann thought, it would be he discharging a debt too long unpaid.

The German sipped his golden coffee as Rudel talked. Finally, Rudel lit another cigarette and said, "I think I bore you with my old stories, Eduard. You have listened patiently and graciously and I thank you for that. Now I think you have other business to discuss. How may I be of service?"

The German set down his cup. "First, tell me, what is your opinion of the men of the *Oberkomitee?*"

"Strausser, Mueller . . ." Rudel shook his head. "Politicians, clever and ruthless men. They were a different kind. We did not share the same goals. They were like little Bormanns . . . scheming, yet hiding behind, using the Fuehrer." He shrugged. "I do not think much of them."

"But they took over your *Kameradschaft.*"

"Bormann did that. Anyway, it was not useful as a rescue organization after so many years. Bormann translated it into a financial empire."

"On Reich money?"

"There was that, yes. But there was also Bormann's secret treasury." Rudel flicked away an ash, squinted as if the subject was distasteful. "Booty from the *Konzentrationslager* . . . jewelry, rings, gold . . ." He avoided Reichmann's eyes. "The Jews."

"Yes," Reichmann said, "the dead Jews."

"Bormann's treasury," Rudel added quickly. "My *Kameradschaft* was supported by different sources."

"Exactly why I am here, Herr Colonel."

"Money?"

"No. I am on a mission to recover a precious item that was stolen. But my movements may be somewhat restricted if I maintain only one identity. It is a weakness I cannot afford to let continue."

"You need new identity papers?"

"And passports. I would like three separate identities. You created the greatest underground railroad ever devised. There must be contacts at your disposal still prepared to do the work."

"For a price, yes. They are in a position to regard their expertise as expensive."

"Of course," Reichmann said.

"It will take some time, Eduard."

"I will need one within the week. The others can wait a reasonable time. But I cannot wait long."

"Three false passports and an assortment of personal papers. Yes, it can be arranged."

"Only two will be faked," Reichmann said. He took a slip of paper from his pocket and slid it across the coffee table. "The third passport should bear this name. It is legitimate."

Rudel glanced at the name, looked sharply up at Reichmann. "But, Eduard, this name is—"

"Can it be done?"

"Anything can be done, but do you really want to use this?"

"It is necessary for my purpose."

Rudel nodded, shrugged. "As you wish."

"Excellent."

"You understand that no identity paper, no matter how professionally prepared, will stand the test of scrutiny. At best it is an expedient. The longer you use forged papers, the greater is the likelihood of your discovery."

"I will only be using them at customs and for hotels. No single set will be used more than a few days."

"Good, I can arrange it quickly. You will need to supply, of course, the photos of yourself."

"Yes."

"I shall make an appointment for you with—"

"Three, Herr Colonel."

"Three?"

"Three sets of papers, three forgers."

"But, Eduard, the man I know can do all these papers for you. It would be far simpler and less expensive."

"Three," Reichmann said. "It *would* be simpler. However, it has been my experience that if the authorities trace one set of papers to the forger, then all sets have been compromised."

"But if you only use them for a short time each . . .?"

"One can never take too many precautions, Herr Colonel. I will require three forgers. You can arrange it?"

Rudel sighed. "I can."

"Very good."

"This job that you are doing for the *Oberkomitee*, is it distasteful to you?" Rudel folded the slip of paper Reichmann had given him and tucked it into the pocket with his cigarettes. "By your mood I suspect you share my opinion of them."

"The mission itself is not distasteful," Reichmann said. "But you are correct, I have little use for the *Oberkomitee*."

"Then why?"

"As I said, something of great value was stolen—stolen from the custody of the *Oberkomitee*, but it belongs to us."

"Us?"

"Those of us who believed in the Reich, in the Fuehrer."

Rudel's face registered alarm. "This thing that was taken . . . was it—was it in an underground chamber?"

Reichmann displayed no emotion. "Yes."

"Mein Gott!" Rudel cried. *"Der Fuehrer?"*

"You know of the place then?"

"Yes, I visited there only last year when Skorzeny died. Only a very select few knew it existed." Rudel was terribly agitated. "Stolen? How was it—"

"Strausser believes it was the Jews."

"But how could they have known? No one knew of its existence!"

"It is gone. Someone found it. And the rest—" Reichmann paused "—destroyed."

"Destroyed!"

"Burned and buried by explosives beneath tons of earth."

Rudel squeezed his eyes shut, dropped his fist against the arm of the divan.

"I am to see that it is returned, Herr Colonel. You now understand the importance of this mission. It is not out of loyalty to the *Oberkomitee* that I have offered my services."

Rudel opened his eyes, sat up to the edge of his seat. "You must let me help you, Eduard." A genuine plea. "I will do anything."

"That is why I have come to see you, Herr Colonel. Out of respect. But, you must see, I can only accomplish the objective with the minimum of . . ."

"Hindrances." Rudel nodded. He glanced at his artificial limb. "Yes, I quite understand."

"You are too well known to take an active part. Not even the *Oberkomitee* knows I have come to you."

"Yes, Eduard, you were right to take this course. Whatever I can do, promise that you will call on me."

"There are two important services you can render in addition to the identity papers."

"Anything."

Reichmann reached into his pocket and took out a paper. He unfolded it and handed it to Rudel. It was a detailed sketch.

"I will require a trustworthy artisan who can duplicate this to my specifications."

Rudel studied it a moment. "But this is . . ."

"Yes," Reichmann said.

Rudel nodded, staring at the object on the paper. "I don't understand, Eduard. But I will do what I can."

"I would prefer that the craftsman be German."

"And he shall be," Rudel said. He touched the sketch where the raised surface of the object would be if it were real, then glanced questioningly back at Reichmann. "Why do you want another?"

"Because it is important to me," Reichmann replied, "and my objective. I have worked it all out very carefully. In time, you will understand."

Rudel frowned. "You intend to *use* this as part of a strategy?"

Here Reichmann permitted himself a wry smile. "The duplicate, yes. Do not be distressed. As I said, I have worked it out very carefully."

"May I ask how you intend . . ."

"It concerns my mission, Herr Colonel. It would be best if you did not know the details."

"Yes, I see."

"I will need a name and address of the craftsman who does the work. I will instruct him on the specifications personally. He should also have a knowledge of armaments."

"An armorer *and* a craftsman." Rudel arched his eyebrows. "Your request intrigues me." He held up his hand. "But I will not inquire further. How shall I contact you when I have the names of these technicians?"

"I am at the Sacher. Leave a message for me there with the names. I would like to have them tomorrow."

"Right."

"Herr Colonel, after this visit, I will not see you again. At least not until the mission is completed."

"I understand," said the old warrior.

"Your aid will guarantee my success."

"Do not forget, Eduard, if I may be of further use . . ."

"Rest assured."

"This number," Rudel said, writing it down, "is a call box in the *Stadtpark*. You may call there for me at any time . . . from any call box on the Continent without fear of being traced." He handed it over. "Promise me you will let me help if it becomes necessary."

Reichmann glanced at the six-digit number, then slipped it into his jacket pocket. "Yes, my colonel, if it becomes necessary."

Rudel nodded slowly, satisfied the promise would be kept. "You mentioned two services I could render. What else can I do?"

"A personal favor," Reichmann said. He glanced away from Rudel.

"Anything for the Man of the Reich."

"I have been gone from my homeland for more than thirty years."

"Yes, I am sorry for that, Eduard."

"And Heidelberg, I have not seen it for—" Reichmann paused a moment, cleared his throat. "It has been a long time, Herr Colonel."

"Understandably. You wish a visit."

"To see the old place once again." Reichmann took a breath. "Where I was born, if it was not destroyed in the war, or since."

Rudel shrugged. "Yes, but how can I help?"

"My father, he was a shoemaker. He died when I was nine. Tuberculosis brought on by the mustard gas of the Great War. But my mother. I have not seen her since 1944."

"Of course," Rudel said immediately. "I will have her located."

Reichmann looked up sharply.

"Discreetly," Rudel added quickly. "You may rest easy, if she is alive I—" He stopped suddenly, realizing.

"And if she did not survive—"

"Surely, Eduard, she did!"

"If she has died in all these years," Reichmann continued in a low controlled voice, "I would be eternally grateful to know the place of her burial."

"I promise you!" Rudel said, feeling the heaviness of the moment.

"There are no brothers or sisters, but I did have an uncle. Helmet Bohle. My mother's only brother." Reichmann looked at his hands. "His name may help to find her."

"At once! I will have it done immediately."

Reichmann rose. "Thank you, Herr Colonel."

Rudel pulled himself out of the divan, rested his hand on Reichmann's shoulder. "Good luck to you, Eduard Reichmann. God be with you."

Reichmann shook his hand firmly. "Yes, and to you. *Auf Wiedersehen.*"

He rode the elevator to the street level. The day had faded to dusky twilight, the summer air was full and sweet with the smell of the Vienna Woods to the northwest. It was like the smell of summer when he was a boy. He remembered his early years, in a small, reserved space in his memory, that had not been crowded out by the recollections of war. Reichmann walked along the boulevard to the Hofburg Gate, past the massive statues depicting the labors of Hercules. There was no hurry now. He was going home. A brief respite before his destiny was fulfilled; the tranquil time before the tumult of battle.

He was returning to his homeland—to his Germany—and his thoughts were there. Would it be an encounter of affirmation or confrontation? Had his Lili Marlene lost her soul in the reconstruction like the Japanese? Would he recognize her after a generation since the resuscitation? Reichmann came to the end of the boulevard. He would know soon enough, if it was important to know. It was only important now to go where home had been, to stand on ground that had been once his own. The rest would take care of itself.

A light breeze came up and carried with it the scent of rain in the great forest. There would be a shower tonight. The *Kettenhund* turned up the flap of his collar and started back to the hotel.

It was a longer walk, going back.

16

The hospital was cold. It was the first thing Aaron noticed when he entered the emergency room. All hospitals smell the same, but this one was cold.

"Excuse me, miss?"

The nurse turned. "It's lieutenant," she said, indicating the silver bar on her shoulder.

Aaron nodded impatiently. "I'm looking for Ira Linka. He was brought in here several hours ago."

"Full name?"

Aaron sighed. "Ira Linka."

"No middle initial?" she said dispassionately.

"I don't know! Look, how many Linkas do you have here with three gunshot wounds in the chest?"

"Gunshot wound?" The lieutenant frowned as if she should remember.

"Yes, in the chest," Aaron said a bit rudely. "Transferred from D. C. General early this morning."

The nurse brightened. "Oh, him." She pointed to a corridor. "Down there all the way until you see a sign that says I.C.U."

Aaron hurried down the hall. He found Nickelson reading a book in the waiting lounge.

"Henry."

Nickelson got up. "I was beginning to wonder if I would see you again."

"How is he?" Aaron said quickly.

The big man shrugged. "Four hours in surgery, but he's alive. It was touch and go there for a while. Where have you been, boy?"

"Cops," Aaron said. "We played twenty questions for hours, then all of a sudden this plainclothesman comes in and says I can go. I went back to D. C. General, but they told me he'd been transferred to Walter Reed at 4 A.M. I've been driving around trying to find this place. Whose idea was it to move him here?"

"Mine." A man stood at the door that led to surgery. He was dressed in a green surgical gown, but he didn't look like a doctor.

"Who are you?" asked Aaron.

The man rubbed his eyes. He looked tired, sad. "A friend."

"Friend?"

"Ira Linka's friend," the man said. He took a deep breath and patted his pockets. "Do either of you gentlemen have a smoke? I've been in there since he left surgery."

Aaron said he didn't smoke. "How is Linka?"

"Not good, Mr. Miller. The next forty-eight hours will be critical. For the moment at least, he's alive. If he survives he will have the use of only one lung and one kidney."

"You know my name," Aaron said. "Do I know you?"

"I certainly hope not," he said, grimly amused. "But I am acquainted with your . . . recent line of work. And Lubetkin. And Miss Diels." He nodded toward Henry. "We don't have anything on Mr. Nickelson just yet, but that is being corrected."

"Who are you?" Aaron demanded.

The man held up his palms. "Ira and I worked together. That should be enough." He patted his pockets again, then scanned the lounge for a vending machine. When he didn't find one he glanced back at Aaron. "So, Mr. Miller. You're the one who started all this." It wasn't exactly a question.

"I haven't started anything," Aaron retorted angrily.

"I know about the urn."

"Everyone seems to know about the goddamn thing!"

"Everyone?" The man contemplated it a moment. "Yes, indeed. I should like to speak with you about that, Mr. Miller."

"About what?"

"We are looking for a man. A German. I think you are looking for him, too." He clasped his hands behind his back. "I'd like us to work together . . . now that we don't have the urn. We could be very helpful to you. This man is of extraordinary interest to us, as you know." He'd been looking at the floor, but now his eyes found Aaron's. "He must be found."

"What do you mean 'work together'?"

The man with no name shrugged. "We have sources that could be of great value to your own search."

"Why me?" Aaron looked at Henry, then back.

"I would think that was obvious, Mr. Miller. You know what he looks like. No one else does."

They talked for a long time, in the I.C.U. visitors' lounge. There were just the three of them, though Nickelson had no part in it. When they finished, Aaron and Henry drove to Lubetkin's place in Virginia.

Emma was waiting.

"He's gone, Aaron."

She was on the garden patio, off the library, smoking one of those decorative cigarettes in the shade of a large umbrella table.

"Who's gone?"

"Lubetkin." She'd been sitting there some time. The ashtray was full. When she turned to look at Aaron he could see she'd been crying. "He left early this morning after he heard Linka was out of surgery."

Aaron sighed. "Where . . ."

"Florida by now. He's headed for Argentina. He wouldn't listen to me."

"What!"

"After he heard what happened last night—" she paused as if she couldn't believe it herself, stubbed out the cigarette "—after Ira was shot . . . I guess he felt responsible somehow."

"He can't go down there!" Aaron shouted.

"He did."

"Christ Almighty, I'm supposed to be the rash one here." Aaron glanced at Henry. "We can't let him do it, Henry. Not alone. He'll go straight to the resort. You know what he'll try to do."

The fat man nodded.

"Suicide," Aaron said. "He won't even get close."

"I should make it a double suicide." Henry folded his big arms across his chest.

"Someone needs to follow him, keep him out of trouble." Aaron studied him a moment. "Will you?"

"Because I'm so good at it?"

"Because you're the only one who can," Aaron said.

"And you?"

Aaron inhaled deeply. "You know what I'm going to do. The German. Is your passport current?"

"You know, kid, you already sound like Abe," Henry said with a smile. "Giving orders."

"Will you?"

"Who's going to watch over you?"

"I am, goddamnit," Aaron blustered. "*Will you!*"

The fat man nodded patiently. "I never argue with a Miller."

"What about me?" Emma said. She wiped her eyes. "He brought me here, after all."

"We have work to do."

"We?"

"Linka has a lot of friends," Aaron said. "I met one tonight. We're going to work together to find the Nazi."

"You are?"

"Don't look so surprised."

"But you said—"

"Jesus, will you forget what I said!" He pushed her cigarettes toward her. "Light up, then take a big breath because we're going to be very busy. You're going to help me put a name to a face."

"Me?"

"We'll go back to the files. He's got to be in there. We haven't got much time—now that we don't have the urn."

"What do you mean?"

"We have to beat a deadline." Aaron looked at the date on his watch. "If we don't find the German in less than ten days . . ." He shrugged.

Emma's eyes were dry now. "Somebody dies."

Aaron nodded without looking at her. "Somebody else."

Rafai Jamil made his first call to Paris at noon precisely. The Palestinian was elated at the news.

"And it is safe, Rafai?" the voice from Paris said again.

"Yes, *Yahid*, it is safe. Here with me."

"You are well protected?"

Jamil glanced up at the two bodyguards. The same two who were with him when he took the vessel from the Israeli. Bandages attested to their encounter with the art collector's guard dogs.

"Yes," he said finally, "I have protection."

There were no instructions from the Palestinian except to remain underground, call again tomorrow.

Jamil replaced the receiver as Gaafar, the Sudanese whose face was badly clawed, switched the black-and-white television to a different station. Lloyd Dobyns and Betty Furness of the NBC "Today" show were discussing the events ahead in the day's program of competitions at the Montreal Olympics. There was conjecture about whether the Cuban heavyweight, Teofilo Stevenson, after winning the golf medal in 1972, could repeat his performance and take another gold.

Jamil settled back to watch. There was footage of previous Olympic boxing matches. George Foreman. Joe Frazier. Jimmy Ellis. Muhammad Ali when he was Cassius Clay. Jamil admired a good fight. As he watched he found himself feinting, jabbing with the sweaty figures in the ring. He decided he was going to enjoy this assignment. He wouldn't be cooped up in a tiny hotel room with nothing to occupy the hours. He had the Montreal Olympics on television. The ABC network was going to be broadcasting eighty hours of coverage.

It wouldn't be dull after all, Jamil told himself. He would have the thrill of victory and the agony of defeat right here in his room. He loved competition. And the competition would continue until the day before the deadline the Nazis had set. It was all going to work out beautifully.

Jamil made himself a comfortable place on the divan. The television was reporting now on basketball, another of his favorite sports. Then there was the awarding of the medals— the television reviewed the three American winners of the 200-meter butterfly swimming event. The three youths bowed to receive the medals around their necks, then stood proudly erect on the winners' platform as the gold medalist's national anthem was played. Some day there would be one standing there representing his Palestine. Some day when the fighting ended. That would be a proud day.

He watched the competitions, mesmerized. He would like to meet one of these athletes. Someone who had done well at the international competition among nations. Perhaps, even, a gold medalist.

Strausser burst into Mengele's suite without knocking. He virtually danced about, waving a paper over his head.

"Josef! Josef!" He pounded on the bedroom door. "Up, you lazy dog! I have good news. Wonderful news."

The *Oberkomitee* Direktor ordered coffee from Mengele's house phone. He went to the windows and pulled back the drapes, flooding the room with morning light. The lake below glimmered a vivid blue, its surface smooth, reflecting the snow-capped Andes to the west.

"Josef!"

He pushed open the windows, breathed deeply of the mountain air. After a moment, the bedroom door cracked open.

"Alfred?" Mengele squinted through the opening.

"Josef!" Strausser cried joyously. "Come. I've ordered *Kaffee*."

"You idiot," Mengele said, shielding his eyes as he took a step slowly from behind the door. "Do you know the time?"

"It is a glorious day, Herr Doktor." Strausser inhaled another deep breath at the window. "See for yourself."

"*Wunderbar*," Mengele said sarcastically, holding his head. He sat down on the sofa, his back to the window. "What is it, Strausser?"

"News! Great news for us."

Mengele pulled the hem of his robe over long, skinny legs. "Would it not be good news later, also?"

"A message came," Strausser said, hurrying over. "I wanted to share it with you first, before the others."

"What message?"

"From the Jews."

The Doktor came quickly awake. "The Jews?"

"Yes, yes," Strausser said excitedly. "They promise to cooperate."

"Wait." Mengele went to the bedroom door, peeked in. He closed it quietly, raising a finger to his lips. "A girl from the village. She sleeps."

"Ah," Strausser said, arching his eyebrows. "A good one?"

"Never mind." Mengele frowned. "What do the Jews say?"

Strausser handed him the paper. "They say they will get the urn to us."

Mengele read. "It says we should be patient." He shook his head. "The urn must be returned immediately."

"They are frightened of Reichmann," Strausser said with delight. "He has threatened them. Just as he promised. The Jews are pleading with us not to allow Reichmann to harm anyone."

Mengele studied the paper again. "I don't see anything here that resembles a plea."

"You must read *between* the lines, Josef. The Jews are frightened. We have struck terror into their hearts."

"We?"

"Our instrument. Reichmann."

"Yes," Mengele said, considering it. "Reichmann."

"He went after their ambassador in Spain. The incident was reported in *La Prensa*. His car was destroyed. He was accosted by an unidentified man."

Mengele nodded but said nothing.

"Our plan is working, Josef. We will have *Der Fuehrer* returned."

"But it is not *our* plan, Strausser." Mengele got up, paced back and forth on the polished tiles in his bare feet. "I do not like Reichmann having control like this. He answers to no one."

"But we agreed, Josef."

"Yes."

"And he is doing the job."

Mengele nodded. "Yes." He stopped pacing, faced Strausser. "That worries me."

"It worries you?" Strausser laughed. "Dear Josef, there is nothing—"

"You remember what he said to us," Mengele said grimly. "To the *Oberkomitee*. I do not trust a man who does not trust me."

"Josef, Josef . . ."

"We must consider what is to be done with Reichmann when he returns."

"He will be a hero," Strausser said.

"He will be a threat," Mengele replied.

Strausser shrugged. "Possibly . . ."

"You know I am right." The Doktor stood his ground.

"Yes?"

For a long while Strausser was silent, staring out the window at the snow-capped Tronador. He sighed. "Yes, Josef, I suppose what you say is true."

"Good." Mengele smiled.

"I will have to discuss it with the others. We all must be agreed."

"I already have," Mengele said. "Everyone agrees that once the job is finished Reichmann must be eliminated."

"Everyone?"

"Yes. Mueller was most insistent, as a matter of fact."

"Well, then, there is no need for further discussion. Reichmann dies." Strausser shook his head sorrowfully. "Such a pity, too. He looked so glorious in the uniform."

17

For two days Reichmann waited for the two bogus passports and identity papers. Rudel had supplied him with the names and addresses of two forgers who could be trusted. One was in Vienna in the Ottakring District a few blocks off Universitaetsstrasse. The second was in Graz, 190 kilometers to the south.

Reichmann took a train express and met the man, a former Waffen-SS *Oberscharfuehrer* who'd lost two fingers to frostbite in the winter Russian campaign in forty-two. The man had known only that Reichmann (a name he did not use) was recommended by Rudel. There were no questions except those pertinent to the documents. They'd had lunch together in a garden bistro near a park. They sat away from the other patrons and talked about the war years and the changes since. Reichmann listened because it suited his purpose to understand the changes in Europe in the thirty years since he'd left. They'd gone to his office then, a small bookstore with a printing press in the rear for stationery and piecework to augment his income, though his occasional jobs for the likes of Reichmann made the income from the bulk of his other work tiny by comparison.

Reichmann paid cash. Twenty thousand schillings—$1,200 of his stake from the *Oberkomitee*—and an equal amount when he returned to take possession of the papers. The forger was a likable fellow, perhaps a bit too gregarious, but absolutely dependable. Reichmann tested him several times by asking him what important or unusual requests for illegal documents he had acted on in his career. The forger was polite, but firm. No names were mentioned or alluded to by the man from Graz.

Reichmann left shortly before six and took with him on the train a novel from the forger's bookshop. It was by an American author, about skyjacking at the Atlanta airport, and Reichmann read it with amusement through dinner. He'd always thought the Americans were very clever.

Upon his arrival at the Hotel Sacher, Reichmann found a message waiting. As he read it, his eyes narrowed. He thanked the concierge and slipped the note into his jacket pocket.

He found the row of public telephones in an alcove off the main lobby.

"*Hallo?*"

"It is Reichmann," he said.

"Eduard, I hope you do not mind my leaving the message. I have located your mother." Rudel's voice was slightly tense, slurred, as if he might have been drinking.

"Yes."

"I am sorry, Eduard. It pains me deeply to bear such ill tidings."

"She is dead."

"I am sorry, Eduard. I promise you."

"Where is the grave, Herr Rudel?"

"The family plot," he said. "Heidelberg. Your city."

"The name of the cemetery?" the German asked.

"Odenwald Friedhof."

"Thank you, Herr Rudel. You have been helpful once again."

"Yes, but it is not the main reason that I called, Eduard."
The voice sighed. "It grieves me, my friend. This should not
be . . . not for the most honorable of all the German soldiers.
Not for the Man of the Reich!" There was the sound of a bottle
clinked against glass. Rudel swallowed.

Reichmann was patient. "Yes."

"It is your uncle," Rudel said. "The man Helmet Bohle." He
spoke the name with bitterness. "Your beloved mother's own
brother."

"What of my uncle?"

"A traitor!" Rudel's voice rose, supported, perhaps, by
drink. "A contemptible swine!"

Reichmann was silent, waiting for Rudel's rage to subside.

"Eduard?"

"Yes."

"Forgive me, Eduard. You could not know." He swallowed
again. Reichmann had a picture in his mind of the former
Luftwaffe ace sitting on the flower-print sofa, his artificial leg
propped up on the ottoman, with a bottle of wine and the
telephone. An unforgiving old man who could not reconcile
past and present.

"What has my uncle done?"

"A minor government official," Rudel went on. "From an
office in Ludwigsburg near Stuttgart. Center for the Investiga-
tion of War Crimes." His voice was high, broken. He almost
wept. "A hunter of the SS! Your uncle!"

"I see."

"You cannot go to him for aid. That is why I called. You
must stay away from this Helmet Bohle. I have made inquiries, Eduard. He is worse than a swine—I am sorry to say these
things to you, but they are true. After the war he approached
the Allies like a snake. He was an informer. But worse—he
turned your mother out of his home. His own sister! Because
she would not give them information about her SS son who
had disappeared. It did not matter that she did not know
anything. Her brother did not care. He was a lackey to the
American and British SS hunters. He had your father's
pension—from the first war—he had the pension stopped.
Stopped! There was no money for her. She was treated as a

criminal. Her property was confiscated." Rudel paused to catch his breath, his fury nearly spent. "She died—your mother—the mother of the Reich Man—in a beggars' hospital. Alone. With no—"

"Enough." Reichmann spoke quietly in the darkness of the phone stall. His eyes were closed.

"Eduard, forgive me. I am sorry. Believe me, I—"

"Yes," Reichmann said icily. For several moments neither spoke.

"Eduard?"

"Moment, bitte." Reichmann remembered a time when he'd returned home late from school. He was twelve or thirteen and he'd been practicing the pole vault. His mother had scolded him. She'd kept a vegetable stew warming until the water was gone and all that remained was a pasty mess. Reichmann, the boy, cried. It was the last time he could remember crying. Then she held him. His mother pulled him to her and soothed him, running her delicate fingers through his short blond hair, whispering that the supper did not matter. He would be a great athlete one day. She was proud of her son. His father would have been proud too, she told him. He was a good man and his son would be a good man. The stew did not matter. She cried then. He felt her tears against his cheeks.

Reichmann opened his eyes, waited a moment, then spoke into the telephone. "Thank you, Herr Rudel." His voice was calm, giving away nothing.

"I am sorry, truly," said Rudel. "I had to warn you. Certainly, now, you see you cannot go to Heidelberg."

"But I will," Reichmann said.

"Eduard! Surely you must see—"

"I will visit my mother." Reichmann's voice was hard.

"But—"

"Please do not contact me again, Herr Rudel. It could be dangerous for you as well as for me. Anyway, I will not be staying. Tomorrow I must leave."

"Where will you be?"

The German said nothing.

"Yes, you are right not to answer," Rudel said, after a pause. "If you go to Heidelberg . . . please, my friend, be careful. Do not be foolish."

"I cannot afford to be foolish."

Rudel sighed. "Thank God, you are sensible."

"Yes," Reichmann agreed. "Thank God."

He went to his room and began packing. There were still several errands that needed his attention. There were more things he must accomplish than he'd expected. Heidelberg was an important stop now, but there were other stops to come first. He mustn't rush his own timetable. Rudel was correct. He would not be foolish. The mission had not changed, only an item added.

He wondered how his uncle would react, after all these years. When they met again.

By the end of the fifth day of the Olympic Games in Montreal, the United States was leading in the total number of medals awarded with sixteen. East Germany was second with fourteen and the Soviet Union, third, with seven. The Americans also led with the most gold medals, seven; one ahead of the East Germans and three more than the Russians.

Of course, it is universally understood that there is no official winner of the Olympic Games. Amateurs all, the contestants are brought together every Olympiad—the four-year span between the games—to foster better international understanding through the universal medium of youth's love of athletics.

The most important thing, as the Olympic Creed goes, is not to win but to take part, just as the most important thing in life is not the triumph but the struggle.

The essence of the Games is not to have conquered, but to have fought well.

18

"Good evening, Aaron," the telephone voice said. Nickelson sounded rested, even jolly. "Are you hot on the trail?"

"At the moment, just hot," Aaron said. "You have Lubetkin?"

"A matter of viewpoint," the fat man said. "Who has who, I mean. We're together anyway. A luxurious suite in the Adlernest, number 617. He's paying. Expensive, but the accommodations are magnificent. You should see this lake, Aaron, it's—"

"Spare me the tour, Henry. When are you coming back?"

"That's the sticky part, Aaron."

Aaron sighed.

"But before we get into anything, let me tell you that I'm calling from my room."

"You suspect—"

"Let's just, to be safe, refer to our friends by initials." Henry paused then said, "You never know when a rival industrial concern might eavesdrop on our corporate secrets."

"Right," Aaron said. "I think it is imperative that the head of our company return as soon as possible. As you know, in our business this is not the best season to take a vacation."

"I can't force him to return. Anyway, as much as he blames himself for losing our last big contract, he's reevaluated his purpose for coming down here ... decided against trying something gallant, if you know what I mean. Incidentally, I spotted a few executives of our competition last night. It looks like they brought the whole board of directors down for a holiday. They didn't recognize us, thank God. I didn't think it was a good idea to contact them as long as we have that business deal still pending with one of their subsidiaries. I saw Mr. S. on the balcony of his suite last night. He looked in good health."

"Large entourage?"

"Huge," Henry said. "You'd think they brought their entire legal department with them."

"Where is Mr. L.?"

"Asleep. It's after nine, you know."

Aaron nodded to himself. Even there Lubetkin remained faithful to his schedule. "Try and get back soon. I don't want, ah, our president falling in with the wrong crowd."

"Yes, I understand. Actually, I'm quite enjoying it here. How are you progressing?"

"Slowly, very slowly," Aaron said. "I'll check with you tomorrow or the next day. Just keep him from drinking too much—keep him out of trouble."

"Right."

"And how is our friend?" Nickelson asked.

"Which?"

"Linka."

"Holding," Aaron said. "I'll get back to you, Henry. Take care of that old man."

"Good hunting," Nickelson said. "And look out for yourself."

"Always," Aaron replied. He set the receiver on the cradle and drummed his fingers across the faceplate. The library was quiet except for the rhythmic tick-tock of Lubetkin's grandfather clock in the corner. Aaron disliked solitude, it was an experience he'd recently come to abhor. It forced him to reflect. He thought about Abe. He wished he could close it out of his mind—Abe, the guilt. Aaron shut his eyes and leaned back in the old man's chair. He let the pendulum swing of the clock's measured cadence take hold of his thoughts. For a few minutes, he told himself. *Crowd out Lubetkin . . . Linka . . . Henry . . . Abe . . . How many others to come? For just a few minutes . . .*

Mueller smoked a cigarette as he listened to the tape recording in the small room. He'd played it several times, punching the machine's buttons, listening again. He never spoke. He just sat next to the wooden table. Smoking. Listening.

"*. . . did spot some of our competition last night . . .*"

Fast forward. Stop.

"*. . . brought the whole board of directors down for a holiday . . .*"

Rewind. Stop.

"*. . . something gallant, if you know what I mean.*"

Rewind. Stop.

"*. . . Adlernest, number six-one-seven . . .*"

Fast forward. Stop.

"*. . . Where is Mr. L.? Asleep, it's after . . .*"

Rewind. Stop.

"*. . . you have Lubetkin?—*"

Rewind. Stop.

"*. . . have Lubetkin?—*"

Rewind. Stop.

"*. . . Lubetkin?—*"

Stop.

Mueller extinguished the cigarette under his foot, grinding out the embers on the white vinyl floor. He sat there a long time, his mind occupied with a face.

Emil Lubetkin.

Finally Mueller nodded to himself, drew out a cigarette from his pocket. He lit it, inhaled deeply, sighed. Lubetkin was executed in 1944. Wasn't he? He'd signed the order himself. Mueller shook his head sadly. Another survivor Another old face. Another fanatic seeking vengeance.

Another?

Mueller glanced at the tape recorder.

He'd dealt with them before. He could still.

19

In Innsbruck Reichmann registered at the Hotel Zum Wildenmann as Werner Stolz, a writer from Salzburg. In the lining of his suitcase was his second identity, courtesy of the bookseller in Graz. When he needed to be, Reichmann would be Paul Daimler. Swiss. When he left the Hotel Sacher, Reichmann had also left behind his Reichmann passport. Ashes in a fireplace.

He phoned Munich and spoke briefly, setting an appointment for Saturday. He then made a similar call to Nuremberg. When he was finished, the Reich Man was pleased. Rudel had accommodated him with the names of German craftsmen. The forger in Munich was known to him. Victor Klausner, like himself, had been an SS officer with the *Wiking* Division. Before the war Victor had worked in his father's employ as an apprentice silversmith in Freising. He'd spent six months in a French detention camp after the war awaiting trial for his part in an assault on a village in 1944. Ultimately the charge was dropped—the Allies were after bigger game—and Victor was freed. He settled in Munich, married, saw his daughter develop into a budding concert pianist, and followed his former trade. But Victor did not forget. He did not forget the injustices done him and his countrymen by the avenging victors. If he could save lives, help with escapes, he was more than willing to do his part. After all, he was a *Hauptsturm-fuehrer*. Had been. It made a difference.

Josef Weisse was altogether a different man. This was the name Rudel had given Reichmann. The artisan Reichmann had asked for who was also knowledgeable in armaments. His first reaction was one of surprise when he realized who Rudel had contacted on his behalf. Surprise and pride. Herr Weisse had been a hero even before the war.

As a young pistolsmith engineer, born in Sarajevo, Bosnia, before the Great War obliterated his homeland, Weisse was instrumental in designing the efficient and simple self-loading pistol of .32-inch and 7.63 mm. After the Treaty of Versailles, German and Austrian arms factories were forbidden to manufacture or sell pistols or revolvers of the 9 mm Parabellum type. The treaty was quite specific in its order. The Parabellum pistol—literally, "Pistol for War"—was outlawed for manufacture. Instead, Weisse and a handful of Austrian and German engineers concentrated on the 7.65 mm and 7.63 mm weapons which could be converted to Parabellums with very little difficulty and on short notice by supplying 9 mm barrels and magazines. The Luger was such a weapon—all parts except barrels could be used interchangeably in 7.65 mm and 9 mm types. One of the successful results was the German Mauser 7.63 mm automatic. His efforts were not overlooked in the early years of the Reich.

Reichmann looked forward to their meeting.

Reichmann rented a car and prevailed on the head reception clerk to book him a single room for the weekend, July 24–25, in Munich. The clerk suggested the Koenigshof for it had a private bath with shower.

He had dinner out of his hotel, preferring to find a spot not so heavy with tourists. He ate peacefully and alone and paid cash before he left.

At the bar of a less expensive hotel, on the east side of

Drosselgasse, Reichmann struck up a conversation with a traveling salesman of a well-known athletic shoe manufacturer who was a bit drunk and looking for a girl. Reichmann had studied several of the customers in the place and chosen this one. They were about the same build, about the same in physical features, though the salesman was younger and had the makings of a large belly. They drank together and even sang to the amusement of a tableful of Japanese tourists seated near their booth in the dimly lit lounge. It was nearly midnight when the salesman lost hope and desire of finding a girl, having been drinking with his German friend since before nine. Reichmann had shown repeated interest in the salesman's wares until the man finally invited him up to his room to give him a "complimentary" pair.

They drank for another three quarters of an hour. Finally, the salesman, hopelessly drunk, excused himself to go to the bathroom. He staggered into the bedroom, Reichmann heard the toilet flush, then met the salesman at the bedroom door. With the agility of an expert, Reichmann applied the correct amount of pressure to the back of the salesman's neck and within five seconds he collapsed into Reichmann's arms. He dragged him to the bed and covered him over with the bed sheets. When he awoke in the morning he would have the worst headache of his life, but he would not remember how he'd come by it.

Reichmann closed the door silently and went to the telephone. The switchboard operator was courteous and placed the call from the salesman's room to a resort in Argentina. When Reichmann heard Strausser's voice, he smiled.

"Yes?"

"Herr Strausser, it is der Kettenhund. How are you today?"

"Major?"

"What news of our property?"

"You haven't called in two days. What happened?" The old man's voice was tense.

"I'm calling now," Reichmann said. "I take it the property has not been returned."

"No, but they say it will be."

"So you've heard from them?"

"Yes. The Jews themselves. Prime Minister."

"Excellent," Reichmann said.

"They are searching for you, Major. I think everyone is looking for you now."

"I expect so."

"But there is another worry here," Strausser said. "Two men are with the hotel guests. We monitor all calls to and from the resort. These men talked to the United States. They tried to be clever, but Herr Mueller was not fooled. Obviously, they are Jews. What do you make of it, Major?"

Reichmann was quiet a moment.

"Major?" Strausser said impatiently.

"You are secure there?"

"Yes, perfectly."

"Then do not worry."

"But—"

"Possibly the other side is not convinced of our threat," the blond man in Innsbruck said. "I will remind them again."

"Where are you?"

"You may easily answer that yourself by checking with the operator, Herr Strausser. But I am leaving now, always moving."

"Major, I—"

"You will hear from me again." Reichmann replaced the receiver.

He walked about the room for several minutes, then sat and read a travel brochure from the salesman's suitcase. By 1 A.M., when he left for his own hotel, Reichmann had made some notes, rifled the salesman's things and decided on his next move. Tomorrow—today—he would torment his Israeli pursuers. He must sting them again.

The *Kettenhund* was up by half-past seven. He'd packed, eaten breakfast, checked out of the hotel and was on the *Autobahn* south in his rented car by quarter of nine.

The Porsche handled easily and Reichmann made good time with only a quick stop for customs at the Brenner Pass, then south into Italy's Lombardy Lake country to Trento by ten where he stopped for coffee. The country was beautiful and the greenness of the farmland smelled glorious. Reichmann took his time, stopping once at the northern tip of Lake Garda to remove the Porsche's top. He drove in his shirt-sleeves along the mountain road between the lake and Mount Baldo, enjoying the scenery that had taken the Ice Age thousands of years to create. He made his way south through the lakeside resort towns of Malcesine, San Viglio, Garda and Bardolino and finally to the east to Verona, city of Shakespeare's unfortunate lovers, just before noon.

He entered the city following the Adige Canal and parked near an open-air flower and fruit market that had once been a Roman forum. For an hour he joined a tour group visiting the thirteenth-century Capulet Palace and shared a seat with an Englishman from Bristol who was along especially to see the famous balcony of Juliet's.

By three, Reichmann had made his way back to the cathedral north of the Piazza dei Signori. He encountered a young priest just inside who was helping an old lady to the door. Reichmann carried a small box that contained a windup clock inside his coat. He'd purchased the souvenir at one of the tourist shops along the Piazza Bra. The clock face was mounted into the base of a metal bust of Julius Caesar.

"Signore?" said the priest pleasantly.

Reichmann smiled. "Father, I am . . . I am looking for the bishop."

"His Excellency has just returned from Milan," said the priest. "He is tired and—"

"It is very important," Reichmann said.

"Perhaps I may help you, signore?"

Reichmann kept his head lowered, avoiding the young priest's eyes. "Please, father, my confession . . . I must confess to the bishop."

The priest reached out, touched Reichmann's shoulder. "Confessions are Saturday—"

"Father, please . . ."

Reichmann faltered, nearly fell and the priest held him, supporting him against his body. "My son, I will hear your confession."

"No, please, the bishop."

The priest moved him to a pew and Reichmann collapsed beside the kneeling rail, sobbing. "Please, father, please . . . a terrible thing has happened . . . I am so ashamed . . . I have caused a death . . . I must see the bishop . . ."

From his vantage point Reichmann could see the feet of several people gathering around the priest. The priest whispered quickly, nervously, and the feet began to move away. After a few moments there was another voice.

"My son, please control yourself."

Someone touched his head. "I am Monsignor Luciani. What troubles you so?"

It was a soothing voice. Its owner sat in the pew beside Reichmann. He felt the hand on his head, patting. Gentle.

Reichmann sobbed incoherently. More feet. More whispers. He'd counted less than a dozen people in the church when he entered, mostly women. They seemed to be leaving, ushered out with polite whispers by the men in black.

"What troubles you, my son?" The monsignor's voice again. Less soothing than before. A bit more impatient.

"My confession . . ." Reichmann blurted between sobs. "The bishop . . ."

"I am Monsignor, my son, let me help you."

"The bishop must hear my confession!"

"What is your name, signore?"

Reichmann said nothing.

"Is this the way a man acts in God's holy place? How can we help you if you do not trust his servants?"

"Please . . . let me confess to the bishop . . . only the bishop can hear this terrible guilt. . . ."

Whispers. Someone hurried away.

"Trust in Him. You are among friends."

There was a gentle prodding, someone lifting his arms.

"My confession!" Reichmann cried. "My—"

"Yes, yes, my son."

They had him on his feet. He held his hands over his face, the box under one arm.

"This way, please."

The church was empty except for the priests. They were guiding him toward the side of the church, toward the row of polished wood confessionals.

"Wait here, my son," said Monsignor Luciani. "His Excellency will hear your confession." He closed the door to the box. Between the louvered slats, Reichmann could see the priests move away, gather in small groups and shake their heads. A few smiled. Reichmann opened the box, wound the clock mechanism several times, then replaced it and slid it inside his jacket. He waited several minutes. The priests who had gathered together now had dispersed, returning to their other duties. The cathedral received its worshipers. Monsignor Luciani stood outside the nave of the church, near the confessionals as if his job was to watch over the bishop. Reichmann sat back on the bench. The box was cool and dark. To his right was the mesh screen that separated him from the adjoining box where the bishop would sit. The opening was approximately a foot wide by a foot high. Plenty of room, if he needed it.

A door opened, closed. The small slide gate opened behind the screen mesh.

"I am here, my son." The voice was old, tired.

"Your Excellency?"

"I am here."

Reichmann moved closer to the screen, reached inside his coat for the box. "Bless me, father. I confess. It has been twenty years since my last confession."

Reichmann heard movement from the other box. "So? Twenty years. It is good to have a wandering sheep return to His Almighty protection."

He had the box in his hands. When the lid was off, the clock was loud in its ticking.

"I accuse myself of many sins," Reichmann said. He set the clock on the bench. He wondered if anyone else could hear it, decided it didn't matter. "Your Excellency?"

"Yes, continue, my son."

"I am not of the Catholic faith. But you must hear what I have to say."

For a moment the bishop was silent. "You are not Catholic? But what is—"

"Do you hear the ticking? Do not leave the box or I will explode this bomb I have devised. Many will die in your cathedral."

The bishop was quiet a moment, then, "What do you want?"

"I want you to listen. I want you to deliver a message."

"This is sacrilege!" said the bishop. Through the mesh, Reichmann could see his dark form starting to get up, the door latch creaked.

"Stop!" Reichmann said. "I will kill myself and you and everyone in this church if you open that door!"

The dark figure froze. Slowly the bishop sat back down. The door latch clicked shut.

"Listen closely, your Excellency. There is not time to repeat myself."

"Why do you threaten my church?" the bishop asked.

"Deliver this message," Reichmann said, ignoring the question. "Golda Meir, the old woman, who was a head of state, is not immune from our rage. You have twenty-four hours to remove your people from the resort. Do you understand the message, your Excellency?"

"That is a threat?"

"Exactly."

"Against Madam Golda!"

"I am one of many who will see that she dies if certain things are not done."

"Assassino!"

"You may deliver the message to any government embassy you choose so long as it finds its way to Israel. They will understand."

"Israel?"

Reichmann got up. "I am going, now, your Excellency. Do

not leave your box until you have counted to one hundred. Count very slowly. I will take the bomb, but if you raise an alarm I will explode it in the church or in the street."

"You are an Arab? A terrorist? Why do you do this?"

"I am very sincere, your Excellency. I will sacrifice my life in a moment for the cause I believe in."

"A terrorist! Your soul is—"

"Don't concern yourself about my soul. Just deliver the message." Reichmann turned the door latch. "Start counting."

"Please, you must not—"

"Count!"

There was a long, frightened sigh, then: "*Uno . . . due . . . tre . . .*"

Reichmann picked up the cadence in his head. "*quattro . . .*"

He slid the clock into his jacket, stepped out of the confessional.

"*cinque . . .*"

He returned a priest's smiling bow near the end of the row of pews.

"*sei . . .*"

At the door of the cathedral, he looked back at the confessionals, all the doors of which were still closed, and left.

"*sette . . .*"

By five the German was through Monza on the autobahn and headed north into the torturous and beautiful country of Switzerland's Lepontine Alps. He stopped once for petrol and once, outside Splügen, to raise the top shortly before a rain shower. The Porsche's wipers were beating furiously when he finally pulled up before the Sonnenhof Hotel in Vaduz, near the castle, residence of the Liechtenstein royal family. He dined alone in the hotel restaurant after an hour's warm bath in his room and dawdled a long while over his notes with a bottle of the local red wine to keep him company. It was late when he went to his room, but he'd planned this stop carefully. A day's rest before he set out for Germany. There were busy days ahead. And still a long trip to plan.

It was early Friday, July 23. In nine days or less he would have the prize. In nine days, exactly, he would stun the world.

Strausser, Mueller, Mengele, none of them mattered. The reign of the *Oberkomitee* was nearing its end. They were finished, they just didn't know yet. But they would. Very soon.

Though it was a risk, Reichmann made a call from his room to Vienna. Rudel had been asleep, but after a few moments he was alert, his voice slightly anxious.

"There is a problem, Eduard?"

"No," Reichmann said. "There are a few items I must have that I cannot acquire without inquiries being made. I thought perhaps you . . ."

"Of course, Eduard. What is it you need?"

"A medical supply," Reichmann said. "It may be difficult to obtain."

"Nothing is difficult for my friend."

"Yes, perhaps," Reichmann replied. "Have you pen and paper? It must be exactly as I request."

"A moment." There was a rustling of bed sheets. In a moment he was back. "I'm ready now, Eduard. What is it you need?"

"A chemical. Acetylcholine. A small amount will do. And a *Spritze*."

"Acidal—"

"Acetylcholine," Reichmann repeated. He spelled it out.

"Yes, I have it. Are you ill, Eduard?"

"No, the chemical is not for me. I'd prefer it to be in ampule form, but you may not be fortunate enough to find it in its liquid state. In that case, the powdered chloride will be adequate."

"Powdered chloride form," Rudel said. "I have it. How much do you want?"

"Very little. One gram will do."

"So little?" Rudel replied abruptly. "If it is necessary, I will see you have a boxcar full!"

"No, my colonel." Reichmann was amused by the thought. "A gram is more than you think."

"And where shall I have it delivered? Will you come here?"

"In a few days I will let you know."

"Anything else?"

"Nothing at the moment. Thank you for your help."

"It is I who should thank you, Eduard. Does it go well?"

Reichmann nodded to himself. He remembered the frightened bishop of Verona. "Yes, very well. I must tell you, my colonel, you may be interrogated by those who search for me. I fully expect that you will be."

"They will learn nothing!" Rudel said quickly. "Nothing, my friend, I promise you!"

"Of course," Reichmann replied somberly. "Of course they won't."

20

The work had been tedious to the point of exhaustion. Aaron's education on the Third Reich was expanding by the hour, particularly on the Black Order known infamously as the SS.

For nearly two days Aaron spent every minute in Lubetkin's den reading, studying photographs. Hundreds had turned to thousands. He slept on the sofa when he slept. Emma prepared coffee and they drank it black by the gallon, one cup after another. She really did know what she was doing and Aaron wondered more than once where he'd be now without her.

They'd divided the work into three areas of prime interest: the thirty-nine Waffen-SS divisions from which volunteers were drawn to make up the elite *Kettenhund* Division, the known SS men who'd escaped after the war to South America or the Mideast, and a huge list of men known killed or missing. Despite the Nazi addiction to keeping scrupulous records of every kind, no document was ever found that listed the members of the *Kettenhund* Division. Lubetkin believed, according to his notes, that the Nazis destroyed all papers pertaining to *Die Kettenhunde* during the last days in the Fuehrer's Bunker beneath the Chancellery. The thirty-two-year-old order to destroy the "chain dog papers" made for another obstacle in Aaron's search.

The *Kettenhund* Division, as far as Lubetkin was able to learn, was made up of less than fifty soldiers from the Waffen-SS. Emma had ruled out searching for the assassin through the parent organization, if for no other reason than its sheer size. She made a case for concentrating on the Fifth SS *Panzerdivision-Wiking* where many of the early recruits were selected by Otto Skorzeny himself. By a cross-reference system, Emma would select dossiers on SS men known to have escaped and check it against the list of Viking Division paymaster's roles. Somewhere he was there—the assassin—Emma said. She was convinced. Somewhere.

So Aaron read and studied photographs. It was an amazing story of manipulation and terror, and the SS was a driving force behind it. From a corps of less than three hundred men in 1929 it grew to the size of an army with nearly a quarter of a million troops organized into divisions and regiments whose military component had tattooed under their arms the SS symbol. The Nazis were impressed with tattoos. Aaron had seen one.

A row of numbers on the forearm.

Lubetkin wore it like a badge, lest he ever forget.

So Aaron read and studied. Somewhere he would put a name to a face. It was here.

Somewhere.

The corridor was burning furiously and Aaron was running again; running toward the exit at the far end of the hall. He could feel the heat on his feet. His shoes were burning and the harder he ran, the farther away the door seemed to be. It was as if he were running in place and the long gallery before him was getting longer. He was running from the voices. Voices behind him shouting together above the sounds of the fire in a terrible chant that he could not understand. Aaron could not stop running. He could not turn to face the voices. Huge flags were burning all around him and as they fell from their mountings they turned into dark smoky bats that swooped down at him, pecking at the bundle under his arm. Suddenly the door in front of him exploded, and the walls disappeared and the fire was gone, but he was still running, running across an enormous parade ground lined with thousands of soldiers. Soldiers in brown uniforms with black armbands. Soldiers standing in perfectly aligned ranks. Rows and rows of soldiers calling him, urging him on. Ahead was a large platform with a single figure standing behind a rostrum. The voices were chanting louder and louder and the lines of soldiers were closing in. Aaron's chest was heaving. He could hear them now. "Die! Die!" He clasped his hands over his ears and kept running. When he reached the base of the platform, they were all around him, in perfect rows, hundreds of thousands of them, chanting. He could see their faces. They had the faces of Abe.

Aaron covered his face and screamed.

Emma was at his side when he woke. He'd fallen asleep on the sofa in Lubetkin's library beside a stack of photograph-crammed folders. His shirt was soaked with sweat. He was panting when he opened his eyes. Beads of perspiration stood out on his face.

"Aaron . . . Aaron . . ." Emma was on her knees beside the sofa, dabbing his forehead with a moist towel. "Aaron . . ."

Aaron glanced quickly around the room.

"It's all right now," she said softly. "It's all right, Aaron."

He sat up on one elbow, took a long, deep breath.

"Here, take this." She offered him a glass of bourbon and he gulped it.

"More?"

Aaron shook his head.

"I couldn't wake you," she said. "You were so deep I couldn't—"

"Nightmare," Aaron said finally. He took the towel and wiped his face. "Over now."

"They're never over," she said. "Not those kind."

"Bad dream. That's all."

"You were in that place . . . in your nightmare? Underground." Her eyes sought his.

"It's over, I said." Aaron wiped the coolness of the towel at the back of his neck.

"Abe meant a great deal to you." She sat back on her heels, set the empty bourbon glass on the floor. It wasn't quite a question.

"He was my brother."

"Maybe he meant too much."

He looked at her sharply. "What?"

"I don't think you can accept that he's dead . . . or how he died."

"Look, Emma, I'm tired. This isn't the time—"

"When *is* a good time, Aaron? When someone's done to you what they did to Abe? I don't want to wait till then."

"Let's just drop it, okay? I don't want to talk about it."

"But *I* want to," she said, looking up at him. Tears welled in her eyes. "It's happening to you, Aaron. I've seen this before. The nightmares . . . the hate. You think you can keep something of your brother alive by doing what he did."

Aaron shook his head. "No, that isn't it."

"You think it isn't. But it's guilt that's driving you."

"I have a different stake in this, Emma. It's got nothing to do—"

"Yes it has." A tear ran down her face. "You say it's revenge, but it isn't. It's guilt and vanity and pride. Your brother ran up against a *real* professional and he's dead and you can't accept that. You make it sound like you blame yourself for his dying, but it's really him you blame. You thought Abe was the best at everything and now you're faced with the reality that it wasn't so. You have to finish this confrontation to satisfy your own vanity, to prove to yourself that through you Abe was what you've always thought he was."

"You're talking like a fool," Aaron snapped.

"Abe is dead because he finally met up with the ultimate

combatant with the killing instinct. He played a game until it caught up with him. Only he paid the price and you survived. Isn't that it? It's not revenge that motivates you."

"Shut up."

"Find the German. Prove to yourself you're a better animal, for Abe's sake, the better warrior. Isn't it? It's an adolescent fantasy. Only you don't have the animal need to kill, Aaron. Not yet."

"Shut up, I said!"

"You're *not* your brother. You can't try to finish his life."

"No," Aaron shot back. "And I'm not the celibate Saint Jean-Paul, savior of orphaned girls, either. You can't make me the husband you wish you had, but didn't get. Don't push off your frustrated self-pity on my head. 'Never made any conjugal demands!' Jesus! Who gave whom the cold shoulder in the sack between you two?"

She slapped him hard across the face, rage and terror in her eyes. There was a moment of blazing fury between them, then Emma broke. She slumped against the arm of the sofa sobbing. Aaron watched her triumphantly, chest heaving, daring her to challenge, then he saw himself.

"Oh, Christ." He knelt beside her on the floor. Emma's whole body trembled. Her face was buried in her arms. "Christ . . . Emma . . . I didn't mean . . ." He touched her shoulder. "Emma . . ."

They'd said shattering things to each other. That they might be true wasn't an issue now. She had put into words what he had already sensed. And he had struck back defensively. But his attack was the more devastating. And the truth of that was huddled before him, shuddering, crying out a passion that had never been returned to her. She held a mirror for him to see himself and he'd turned it back on her. Aaron damned Jean-Paul Delouette, but it was an empty damnation. He was responsible now.

Aaron pulled her to him. "Emma . . . I'm sorry, Emma. God, I'm sorry." He rocked her in his arms, her face against his chest. He stroked her hair, smelling her light scent, until her trembling stopped and she was quiet.

"I'm sorry, Emma," he said gently.

"It doesn't matter," she said in a distant voice.

"It does matter." He tilted her head up, wiped the tears. "It matters very much to me."

"We're lonely pathetic people, Aaron. You and me. I . . . I—"

Aaron touched her lips. "Don't talk." He kissed her cheeks. "Don't talk."

She looked into his eyes. "I should not have said those things. I just don't want you to get hurt. Linka was right about that. You can't go searching—"

He kissed her, pulling her to him and Emma's initial hesitancy dissolved and she clung to him hungrily. He gathered her up and set her on the sofa.

"Do you *want* to make love?" she asked.

"Yes."

She kissed him then and said, "So do I."

"Quiet, now," Aaron said, pushing a strand of hair back from her face.

"Aaron . . . I'm sorry—"

"Later." He moved beside her. "We'll apologize later."

The girl brought the pastry Henry had ordered for dessert. Lubetkin was in better spirits than he had been yesterday. He appeared to be less annoyed that Henry was along as bodyguard—at least, politely interested companion—and Henry found that a good sign.

They were in the resort restaurant, beside a window with a breathtaking view of the lake. Below them guests strolled in a garden walkway lined with shrubs and shade trees and fountains and benches. It was an expensive place, but one Henry found exceedingly pleasurable. The pastry was delicious, an ambrosial delight Henry would normally have avoided due to his calorie consciousness. But this was Argentina—a hiding place for sinners—and his doctor would not find him.

"I would not have dreamed there could be a place like this

in South America." Lubetkin was staring at the lake. It seemed to glisten in the afternoon sun, undisturbed as if it were not a lake at all but a great stretch of canvas that some masterful artist had splashed with vivid hues of green and blue.

Henry nodded. "Yes, a magnificent resort." He nearly said hideaway.

"Have you ever been to Europe? The highlands?" Still, the old man did not look away from the window.

"Yes," Henry said. "Zurich. Vienna once. It was my great misfortune that they were only brief stops."

"Bavaria?" Lubetkin's voice revealed an interest that had been absent before when they spoke together. "The Alps?"

"Unfortunately most of my scenic experience there was from the seat of a Boeing 707."

The old man nodded. "That can be beautiful too. This place is much like the Alps. Perhaps more vivid if that is possible." Lubetkin sighed, turned back to Henry as he finished the last of the pastry. "My parents owned a retreat at Garmisch. I learned to ski there as a boy. I remember when the Kreuzeck cableway was built. It's a beautiful area. The Fourth Olympic Winter Games in 1936 were held there. But I enjoyed summers there more. More leisure. The old men of the village smoked their long pipes and wore the traditional Bavarian costumes. In the evenings the village herds were brought down from the mountains and roamed the streets. There was a smell in the evenings . . . sweet . . ." He shook his head. "I cannot describe it to you. This place is much like it. The Eibsee is much like this lake."

"You sound homesick.

"No, it is foolishness." Lubetkin glanced at Henry. "You can be homesick for a place, but not for a time. It is like being nostalgic for one's youth. It is as past as a memory. It is—" Suddenly the old man stopped dead. His mouth was slightly open, trembling, and Henry thought he was suffering a stroke.

"Mr. Lubetkin . . .?"

"Oh, my God!"

"Mr.—"

"It's *him!*" Lubetkin pointed behind Henry. He clutched his arm. "It's him! My God!"

Henry turned to see where the old man was staring. Across the restaurant behind two elderly women in sunglasses stood a tall man in his sixties. He carried a black cane with a silver head. His deep-set eyes scanned the room, and when they fell on Henry's table he smiled.

"He's coming here! Henry, my God . . ."

"Who is he?" Henry was suddenly caught up in the old man's frenzy. "I don't know—"

"Chief of the Gestapo," Lubetkin said. He was breathing heavily as if the air had suddenly gone sour. "*Gruppenfuehrer* . . . Heinrich Mueller!"

"*That's* Mueller?"

But Lubetkin hadn't time to respond. The man with the black cane strode to their table. He walked directly to Lubetkin, ignoring Henry. He planted the cane before him, placed both hands over it and smiled. "Good morning, Emil. I hope you are enjoying yourself."

Lubetkin could barely speak. "You . . .! You're alive!"

"Of course I'm alive. You look well." Mueller glanced up. Henry followed his eyes. Two resort "pages" had taken positions across the room. They were very tall and muscular with blue eyes. Neither smiled.

The fork that had come with the pastry was beside the empty plate and Henry palmed it. He didn't know what else to do.

"I come to the Adlernest not often enough," Mueller said, looking down at Lubetkin. "A beautiful resort, don't you agree, Emil? Like the old country. Truly, is it not, a nest of eagles."

The old man still could not speak.

"Yes, wonderfully peaceful," Henry interjected. He moved his hand into his lap, slid the fork back under the sleeve. He looked up at the man with the cane, smiling. "I'm Henry Nickelson. We were just talking about what a beautiful view—"

"And I am known as Anton Herzog," Mueller said. He did

not look at Henry. He was watching Lubetkin. "I have a rabbit farm in Cordoba. And other interests."

"I know who you are," the old man said defiantly. "Gestapo."

"Yes, well, that was some time ago, Emil. You know we, we thought you . . . forgive me, we thought you died during the war. Funny, isn't it? We are all so durable."

"I'll see you dead." Lubetkin's rage was controlled now, the quiver in his voice gone.

The Gestapo chief shook his head. "Such talk. Old acquaintances such as we are beyond that. The war is over, Emil. The unpleasantness behind us."

"Never!"

"There is nothing you can do here," Mueller said. The smile was fading. His eyes bore into Lubetkin. "You are in my country. I trust you will remember that. You are an old man with foolish notions. Be careful what you say here." Now he turned to Henry. "And you, my friend, be extremely cautious. I do not know you and so you mean nothing to me. My advice, if you value your life, is to replace the utensil you took from the table. *Take* my advice, Mr. Nickelson. You could be dead in less than a minute."

Henry sighed, nodded. "I try not to argue with a persuasive man." He placed his hand carefully on the table, letting the fork slide out.

"Very sensible of you." Mueller turned back to Lubetkin. "I have a question I wish you to answer, Emil. I understand why you are in Bariloche. You and"—he nodded toward Henry— "your companion. Somehow you traced me here . . . perhaps it was an accident, but whatever the reason you are here now. Others have accomplished the same thing. Very few others. On that you should be congratulated. But I can assure you, my friend—"

"Don't call me that!" the old man said quickly.

Mueller shrugged. "Let me assure you that I cannot be extradited and I have not been killed, as you can plainly see. As I said there have been attempts. All failed." He paused to let the words take hold. His eyes never left Lubetkin. "My question is this: Why *are* you here? I mean, surely you don't believe that the two of you—"

"The urn," Lubetkin said firmly.

"What?" Now Mueller was confused.

"I'm here about the urn."

"How could you possibly know—"

"I took it."

"You what!" The Gestapo chief's eyes had lost their confidence. Suddenly Mueller shook his head violently. "*You are not a Jew!*"

"Still, *I* have the urn," Lubetkin said. Henry could see it in the old man's face. Self-confidence born of rage. It was Lubetkin's eyes that bore into Mueller. Strategies reversed in an instant. "I came here to negotiate. You *will* negotiate. With me."

"You don't have it," Mueller hissed. "You couldn't! The Jews took—"

"Shall I tell you where it was? Shall I describe the underground chamber? The mausoleum? The flags, the crypts . . . all of it burned and buried beneath a mountain of earth? Shall I—"

"Enough!"

"I have it, Mueller," Lubetkin said. "And if you don't do exactly what I say—"

"But we have commissioned an agent! A world figure will die if—"

"Listen to me," the old man interrupted. "I have it. I will destroy it. The Jews have nothing to do with the urn. Only me. Your threat means nothing to me. An assassination might sway the Israelis, *if they had the urn*. But they don't, Mueller. I do. Emil Lubetkin. You will do as I say."

Mueller was wild with fear. "What do you want? Money? We have millions."

"I already have all the money I want. An old man does not need more money."

"Then what?"

"Two things."

Mueller's knuckles were white where his hands gripped the

silver head of the cane. He bent forward slightly, his lips taut. "What is it you want?"

"First, call off your chain dog. The assassin must be stopped at once. If anyone dies, Mueller . . ." Lubetkin didn't need to finish the sentence.

"But we cannot stop him unless we have the urn!"

"You brought him into this, you can take him out."

"Impossible! He is . . ." Mueller took a chair from the next table and sat down. "He is uncontrollable. We made an agreement with him. We do not even know who he is after."

"You are in communication with this man?"

"Yes, but only at his convenience. He calls us."

"For a report?"

"Yes . . . about the return of the urn."

"Then tell him you have it."

Mueller shook his head. "You don't understand. He must receive it. It was his idea so that we could not be tricked."

"Then you'd better stop him some other way," Lubetkin said.

"What other way?"

Lubetkin shrugged. "I don't care. Just stop him."

"He'll have to be killed," the Gestapo chief said lowly. "There is no other choice. It was the decision of the *Oberkomitee* that he would ultimately be eliminated anyway."

Lubetkin glanced at Henry. "Their methods haven't changed in all this time."

"What is the second condition?" Mueller asked. "You said you wanted two things in exchange for the urn."

"Yes," Lubetkin said, "it is the most important part." He looked slowly at Henry, then raised his eyes to Mueller. "I want you."

Mueller reeled back. *"What!"*

"Or one of the members of the *Oberkomitee*. Any one. That's the deal. One Nazi in exchange for the Fuehrer's urn. I think it's fair. Actually quite generous considering what is at stake. Don't you?"

Mueller's face reddened, his eyes grew round as if he might

have apoplexy. "You are an insane man, Lubetkin. *Insane!* I could have you killed . . . at this moment!"

"One of you for the urn," Lubetkin said. "A final sacrifice for the Fuehrer. I would think it would be an honor. And I do not think you will kill me, Mueller. Not as long as I have the urn. If any harm comes to me you can guess what will happen."

"Mad," Mueller said. "You are—"

"I am tired of talking," the old man cut in. "Meet with your comrades. Let me know who it will be. I'll be waiting."

Mueller left. Quickly. And with him the pages across the room. When they were gone only Lubetkin and Nickelson remained in the restaurant. The old man looked outdoors. The lake had not changed. Henry touched a napkin to his perspiring forehead.

"That was one hell of a speech," Henry finally said.

"It wasn't a speech, my friend, it was an ultimatum."

"Yes, well, it was an excellent idea but there's one flaw in it."

Lubetkin glanced back at Henry. "Yes?"

"You don't have the goddamn urn!"

"Mueller doesn't know that."

Henry shook his head. "Not now, maybe. What do you think is going to happen to us five minutes after he does find out? You cannot play these people like fools!"

"But they are fools," Lubetkin said. "That's why we'll win."

Henry started to protest, then realized it would do no good. The old man had made up his mind. *Crazy,* he thought. *Maybe Mueller was right.* Henry wiped his forehead again and looked out the window. The lake, the mountains, the beautiful people enjoying the pleasures of wealth, none of it had changed. But the view, somehow, was less magnificent than it had been. And Henry knew why.

Fear.

21

Reichmann left the rented car with the agency in Baden-Baden and took a train to Munich. The temptation was there, when he changed in Stuttgart, to go north to Ludwigsburg and Heidelberg, but his timetable could not allow for detours. The mission, always, came first. He must go to Munich. Then Nuremberg. When the arrangements had been finally settled, then he could go to his uncle. A debt remained unpaid. Before leaving Stuttgart, Reichmann visited the Federal Ministry. He used another name in the Bureau of Health office and his request was dispatched without difficulty after only a few routine questions. He was on his way after less than an hour.

Munich, the capital of Bavaria, had changed a great deal since he'd seen it last. Energetic reconstruction had eliminated the scars of American and British bombings, and the city had recovered much of its prosperity and appearance. From the moment he stepped off the train in the huge Hauptbahnhof, Reichmann felt, finally, at home. This was a German city. Somewhere he could hear a brass marching band. The sound of people talking struck a responsive chord he had secretly hungered for for nearly thirty years. This was not the polyglot chatter of Spanish and Portuguese he'd forced himself to master in the backwaters and jungles of halfbreeds and Indians. This was German; pure, guttural, abrasive.

Reichmann walked half the morning through the streets of the city Hitler had once called his home. On Schleissheimerstrasse he passed the Koenigsplatz and the great arch, Propylaen, the square beyond, where a nearly forgotten time before he'd stood with a hundred thousand others to catch a glimpse of the Fuehrer's motorcade as it passed. He turned down the Briennerstrasse, past the castle-like restaurant brewery Löwenbräuhaus. The city had not changed greatly after all, at least, less than he had expected. It was as if he'd been away but a short while.

When he found the address, a narrow cul-de-sac off Georgenstrasse in the old student district, he felt an inner contentment, even cheerfulness. He was not prepared for what he found there.

The shutters of Josef Weisse's house were closed from the inside. On the door was a black shroud. He rang the buzzer and waited several minutes before pressing it again. When no one answered, he walked to the alley behind the row houses to the rear entrance. Through a window he could see only a short dark hallway lined with several pictures. Reichmann forced the ancient lock with a penknife and quietly let himself in. The place was small, two bedrooms upstairs, one obviously Weisse's, the other a woman's. Weisse's room, the larger of the two, was recently cleaned—scrubbed was more accurate—and bright rectangles in the otherwise faded wallpaper were evidence that picture frames had been recently removed. The bed was stripped, the closets empty.

Downstairs, dishes had been left in the sink of a tiny kitchen. The sitting room was furnished with an odd assortment of old pieces placed to best advantage before a stone fireplace. A grandfather clock beside the front door only partially covered a threadbare patch in a large rug. The place had that musty, slightly stale odor of an old house much used.

In a closet full of overcoats and umbrellas he found framed photographs that he guessed came from the walls of the large bedroom upstairs. They were old photographs of a younger Weisse with other men. Most were collected around a table that displayed different types of hand guns. One was with a German officer and another man Reichmann recognized as Albert Speer, Reich Minister of Armaments and War Production.

Reichmann was in the small study, searching the desk, when he heard a key in the front door. He flattened himself against a bookcase behind the door. Footsteps approached, then turned into the kitchen. He heard water run into the sink, the door to the cupboard open and shut, a chair squeak. For a long while he waited. There was no sound from the kitchen, only the ticking of the large clock in the front of the house. Then there was something. A sound he'd heard before. The low, quiet measure of a woman weeping.

Reichmann's appearance in the doorway startled her. She was sitting at a knife-scarred wooden table, a bottle of brandy and a half-filled glass beside her. She wore the black crepe of a woman in mourning.

"I didn't hear you," she said, quickly wiping her eyes. "I won't be long in finishing the house. I just was gone to mass at Frauenkirche." With an embarrassment born of guilt she took the brandy bottle and set it back in the cupboard.

"Frau Weisse?" Reichmann wasn't sure what to call her.

"Frau Hauptmann," she said awkwardly. "Anna Weisse Hauptmann. Josef Weisse was my father."

"Was?"

"My father died two days ago. Are you . . . I thought you were from the Ministry of Housing."

Weisse dead. Reichmann couldn't believe it. He'd only spoken with him a few days ago. "I'm sorry . . . I . . . we had an appointment today."

"It was very sudden," Anna Weisse Hauptmann said. "A stroke. He was seventy-four years old." She wiped her eyes again, large brown eyes that studied Reichmann. Frau Hauptmann was a slender woman in her forties and her refined good looks could not be diminished by the tears or black funeral clothes.

"I'm sorry," Reichmann found himself saying.

"You're from Vienna?"

"Salzburg," the German said. "My name is Werner Stolz."

"Yes, of course." Josef Weisse's daughter nodded. "I've been expecting you."

"My father received a call from Vienna several days ago. He hadn't worked as a craftsman in years, but whomever he talked to seemed to instill in him a sense of need. I'd like to thank you for that."

They were in the front sitting room. She'd opened the shutters to let in some light. Reichmann sensed it was a sad room for her.

"You do not know who called your father?"

"No. Someone from the war. Someone he held in high regard."

"He was to make something for me," Reichmann said. "The caller in Vienna put me in contact with your father. We thought he was a great man."

Anna acknowledged the tribute with a bow of the head. "In his time he was, yes. Today people forget. He was only an old man." She looked away, taking in with her glance the room as if Reichmann should notice it. "His government service pension allowed him this house until he died. In a few days, I must remove what remained of his life for another old man. The notice came this morning."

"You lived here also?"

"Since 1969. After my divorce. My father needed someone to look after him."

"And now?"

Anna Weisse shrugged. She looked into his eyes. "I am Herr Weisse's daughter. I will finish his work." Reichmann could see her eyes clouding before she looked away. "You may . . . pay me. . . ."

For several moments she was silent. She looked at her

hands, folded in her lap. There was something about this woman that touched Reichmann. He felt her pain. Somehow, he knew, they were alike. She was one of the forgotten generations of Germans—too young to take on the responsibilities of a broken nation, yet too old to harvest a benefit from its reconstruction. Unneeded.

"My father, he started the design," she said, interrupting the quiet.

"Design?"

"The work he was to do for you. It was a challenge he found interesting. Of course, he could not do the work himself. He spoke with a trusted friend who will cast it exactly to your specifications. I thought it a curious request."

Reichmann frowned. "He told you about it?"

"I have worked with my father since I was a little girl, Herr Stolz. I understand my father's feelings and his loyalties. I can finish the work. But I cannot do the casting or set the plastic. What is it for, may I ask?"

Reichmann said, "Surely, if you are aware of the specifications . . ."

"My knowledge of explosives is limited." She raised her eyebrows. "But this . . . this object. It is a bomb?"

"An explosive device, yes," Reichmann said.

"The entire surface to be gold-plated?"

The German nodded.

"But the inscription? Is that correct?"

"Yes, exactly as it is described. That is very important."

She sighed. "What is the purpose of this 'device'?"

"To explode."

"If you want my help . . ."

"Men have died for selfish reasons that I cannot begin to explain," Reichmann said. "Men have died because of a select few who chose to let them die rather than remember their contributions. I do not forget. This device will make the world understand. I cannot tell you more, except that your father understood and was willing to do his part."

"I don't understand. You're going to kill someone . . . more than one? Why?"

"Retribution for inconceivable wrongs."

"My father agreed?"

"His part was to design the instrument."

Anna Weisse was quiet a moment. "My father was a Nazi. A party member. He did not kill Jews or murder innocent women and children in French villages. He was only a Nazi party member. He was not an evil man!" She looked at Reichmann for reassurance. "But they made him out to be evil. They said he designed guns, guns that slaughtered . . ."

"Yes, I know." Reichmann recalled Rudel's information about his uncle. *He was an informer. He turned your mother out of his home. His own sister! She died in a beggars' hospital!* Reichmann returned his gaze to the woman. "Your father was a victim of vicious men."

"For so many years he tried to . . . to . . . I hate them! If I knew who *they* were—"

"I know who they are," Reichmann said. "It's part of the reason I'm here."

She was crying now. Tears of anger and frustration. "I could kill them myself."

"You won't have to." He moved to her, let her cry against his shoulder. "I've already made plans." Reichmann's hard gaze fixed on a picture leaning against the fireplace mantle. It was of Weisse as a young man, like the others had been. He was holding a little girl with large brown eyes. It was a moment in a happier time—a moment that had been forgotten, of a time that had been cursed. Reichmann soothed the little girl in the picture who was now the broken woman crying against him. She was another man's Lili Marlene, another man's hope; and as he thought of it, the words came back to him.

> *Time would come for roll call,*
> *Time for us to part,*
> *Darling I'd caress you;*
> *And press you to my heart . . .*

"The Nazi criminals who abandoned you will pay," he whispered in her hair. "I promise you."

*   *   *

Aaron was scrutinizing photographs in the study before the large french windows at dawn when Henry called. The last three days had been at once feverish, frustrating and sensual. Together they'd gone through the files of the infantry divisions of the Waffen-SS soldiers. She had sorted the files in stacks on the patio and they sat in the shade against the folding glass doors of the study, searching for a face.

Emma would eliminate those photos of SS members who were confirmed dead by cross-checking against other reference files. They'd skipped some altogether where Emma decided the division makeup was unlikely to include their man: the XII Division, *Waffen-Gebirgsdivision der SS-Handschar*, organized in 1943, was made up of Yugoslavs. The XXI, Albanians; the XXVI, Hungarians; the XXVIII, Walloons and Belgians; the XXIX, XXX and XXXI, Russians. They'd left the panzer and mountain divisions and concentrated on the infantry because it was the logical choice. There were so many files.

They'd been at it from dawn to after midnight for three days and found not a face Aaron recognized. They had slept together in her room because it had a balcony with a swing and a view of the garden. Emma would fall asleep curled against him in the cool breeze of the summer night, rocking gently in the swing, lightly in his arms like a child with its father. For Aaron it was the most tranquil time of his life, despite the circumstances. Their alliance had been born of a fiery rage and had moved past the limitations of mutual sympathy. She had said they were lonely pathetic people, survivors fate had marked as its victims. Aaron would hush her with a kiss. They were more than that, he told her. Later, he would carry her to bed and they made love with infinite tenderness and afterward slept exhausted in each other's arms.

Aaron had slipped away early, kissed her gently before he left, made coffee and was buried in the files by first light. Henry's call was a surprise and a relief. Lubetkin was safe for the moment. But there was a new stick in the fire. Henry talked as if he was cupping his hand over the receiver. Aaron could hear the sound of dishes clattering in the background.

"I'm afraid the old man put his foot in it, Aaron."

Aaron held the telephone in the crook of his neck while he sorted a stack of SS dossiers from the Viking Division.

"How so?"

The fat man breathed a long heavy sigh. "I'm not in the room. I'm at a little place about three miles from the resort—across the lake. You and I have a little catch to work out. I had to find a phone I didn't think was bugged. I suspect that's how Mueller got onto us."

"Mueller?"

"Heinrich Mueller, for God's sake, Aaron!" Henry said impatiently. "Chief of Gestapo for the Reich. He's down here with the rest. He visited Lubetkin and me at breakfast."

"What about Lubetkin?"

"He told Mueller he took the urn."

"What!" Aaron dropped the folders and grabbed the phone with a free hand.

"Not only that, he said he *had* the urn and wants a trade—one of the Nazis for the urn and call off the assassin. You'd have been proud of the old man for the look on Mueller's face. I'd have been proud if I wasn't so fucking scared."

"We don't *have* the goddamn urn!"

"Bingo. That's the catch."

"Christ!" Aaron stared out at the garden.

"Lubetkin wants to stonewall it. He thinks he can bluff them into recalling their trigger man."

"What do you think?"

Henry paused. "I wish I was in Poughkeepsie."

"Can you get him out of there?"

"Are you kidding? Lubetkin is the righteous white knight in mortal combat with the Black Order. He's on the side of right. Naturally he can't just put down his lance and go home."

"Naturally," Aaron said bleakly.

"Besides, after this morning's confrontation, the chances of them letting him out of their sight are slim to nonexistent. And as long as I am his sidekick, it puts me in the fishbowl too. Neither one of us is going to be leaving this place anytime soon. I can try, of course, but . . ."

"No," Aaron said, "you'd better stay put."

"I thought you'd say that."

"You're going to have to make them believe we still have the urn."

"As of now, they do. Lubetkin's threatened to have it destroyed if anything happens to him. For the moment we're okay. But not knowing where it is makes me nervous. Very nervous. What's to prevent the PLO from making its own deal with them? That bothers me, and not because of what might happen to the old man. I have a stake in this too. My neck."

"I'm sorry, Henry."

"I guess if I've made it this far," Henry said with an uneasy laugh, "we'll make it. But that doesn't mean you can sit up there on your ass doing nothing. You know what I'm saying?"

"Find the urn," Aaron said.

"That too. But it's this assassin of theirs who's compromising everybody's peace of mind."

"We'll find it."

"You and Emma?"

"She's efficient, Henry." He wanted to say more, explain to Henry who Emma was, that she was more than an orphan and a widow. She was a part of him now. She filled a void. But instead he said, "Emma knows what she's doing."

"She's going to have to be a damn sight better than efficient. Remember, kid, we're all working against a deadline."

"I haven't forgotten," Aaron said. "We just need a little luck."

"Your self-assurance is certainly confidence-inspiring," Henry said. "All right, then. Good luck. Take care."

Aaron nodded to himself. "Sure."

He replaced the receiver as Emma entered the study, wearing a robe. Behind her was the man from the hospital. The man with no name who worked with Ira Linka. Emma's face was pale.

"Emma—"

She moved to Aaron's side. The man stood at the door as if he wasn't sure whether or not to leave.

"He . . . he died." Emma held a hand over her eyes, staring at the floor. "Ira, this morning."

Aaron shook his head, ran his fingers through his hair. "Shit." When he looked up, the man was still standing there, looking uncomfortable. "Is there something else?"

"I'm here because I want to help."

"Help?"

"I'm afraid—" his glance took in both of them—"you're in some danger."

Aaron sighed.

"The people who killed Linka and stole the urn, the Palestinians, they resent your trying to locate this German." He paused to observe Aaron's reaction. "You see, they *want* an assassination. Israel would be blamed. So any threat to this assassination plot they will try to . . . discourage."

"You mean us?" Aaron shook his head. "Christ, if they knew how splendidly we are doing here, they would laugh themselves sick."

"They aren't laughing, Mr. Miller. You'll find that the PLO has an atrophied sense of humor."

"Oh, that's fine," Aaron said. "That's terrific. The PLO thinks *we're* a threat and you offer help. What kind of help can you promise? The same kind you gave Linka?"

"Please, there is no need for that. I told you we could be of very much use to one another. It takes time. But we've developed a positive lead."

"What is that supposed to mean?"

The man with no name glanced at Emma, then at Aaron. "We know who the assassin is."

"He isn't an assassin yet," Aaron said. "Not yet." He studied the man a moment. "Who is he and how did you find him?"

The man took a small envelope from his pocket. "First, we want assurance of your cooperation."

"We? What do you mean, we? You already know I'm looking and you know why."

"Yes, Mr. Miller, but we want him alive."

Aaron said nothing.

"You didn't answer Aaron's question," Emma said from beside Aaron. She held the top of her robe together with one hand. "I think we should know who you represent."

"I think you do know."

"Israel."

"More specifically, the Shin Beth," he said. "My name is Yossi Bar Tov."

"Linka's friend," Aaron said.

"Yes."

"Well, the deal I had with Linka was canceled the night they took the urn. I don't think there's anything we can do for each other, Mr. Bar Tov."

"You underestimate your effectiveness, Mr. Miller."

"No," Aaron said. "I underestimate yours. At least, where I'm concerned."

"I do have some measure of influence in the U.S." Bar Tov offered a slight smile. "It was through my efforts, Mr. Miller, that your detention by the metropolitan police was terminated. Will you cooperate with us? We want to avoid any killing . . . including this man, this chain dog. Israel has by no means lost interest in tracking down those responsible for war crimes against the Jews. But there are so many groups that have been looking for so many years, nearly everyone assumes they are Jews."

"And they aren't?" Aaron said.

"Lubetkin is not. To be sure, a great many are Jewish, but it does not make them Israeli. That is why we must be careful, Mr. Miller. After Eichmann was found, great pressure was brought to bear on my country. Since then we have not gone to extralegal means to locate these Nazi criminals. We have worked within the laws governing international extradition."

"Which explains why you haven't been very successful?" Aaron said.

"True. Several countries do not cooperate. Argentina, for many years, did nothing. Even today Paraguay's dictator, General Stroessner, is friend and protector to many of the most notorious Nazis who hide in South America. And that is one reason why we monitor the activities of several hunter groups. We are well aware of the work done by Miss Diels's organization *Le Trident* in France and have, on occasion, offered our assistance. We have known of Lubetkin's efforts for a great many years. There is a group in Brazil known as The Committee That Never Forgets."

"Herbert Cukurs," Emma said.

Bar Tov nodded. "Yes, the Latvian air force officer who was responsible for the deaths of thirty thousand Jews in Riga. His body was discovered in 1965 in Montevideo in the trunk of a Volkswagen. But his death was not the work of Israelis. That is why I am here, Mr. Miller. Normally, we would stay out of your search. My superiors like to be kept informed about the activities of all such groups as yours, but this time we've run up against something entirely new. The Nazis have made a threat. A threat we cannot ignore. It was our intention to retrieve the urn and return it to these madmen who've commissioned an assassin to back up their threat. We would deal with them later, since they were gracious enough to identify themselves in a telegram. Men we, quite honestly, thought were dead. But our primary aim was to remove the threat—the assassin—by acquiescing to their demand."

"The urn," Aaron said.

"Exactly. Unfortunately, that is now missing. So we must work on two fronts. We must locate the urn or stop the assassin. At the moment we are engaged in a massive search for the men who stole the urn from you."

"And killed Ira," Emma snapped.

Bar Tov sighed. "Yes. Our struggle is not limited to threats from old Nazis."

"So," Aaron said, "you want me to help on the first front. The assassin."

"*Alive*, Mr. Miller." Bar Tov watched Aaron's eyes. "We want him alive. His debriefing could be invaluable to us. You can help us. We can help you. There is only the one stipulation."

"And *if* I find him ... he may make your condition impossible to comply with," Aaron said. "I don't intend to get myself killed on a technicality."

"Of course not. And we may locate the urn before you find

him. But we only ask that you try to work within our stipulation."

Aaron sat down at the desk. On it were strewn hundreds of dossiers. With Emma they might find the German, but not in six days. Aaron glanced up at the Israeli intelligence man. "What you're saying is that you'll give me a name in return for my cooperation, but only on your terms. Right?"

Bar Tov nodded.

Aaron looked at Emma. She shrugged. "There isn't much choice, is there, Aaron?"

Aaron looked at the dossiers, sighed, glanced back at Bar Tov. "Okay, what's his name?"

"You agree, then?"

"Yes, damn it," Aaron said angrily. "What's his name?"

The Israeli handed over the envelope. "Reichmann. Eduard Reichmann is your *Kettenhund*."

Emma sat up quickly. "I know that name. We've seen it here in the files."

"A pure Aryan," Bar Tov said. "Blue-eyed blond. Born in Germany."

"Berlin," Aaron said, studying the contents of the folder. "Six-foot-one. One hundred ninety-seven pounds." He glanced up at Bar Tov. "There's no picture here. How do you know this is him?"

Emma went to the file cabinet, quickly searching through the dossiers of known SS escapees.

"This man left São Paulo six days ago on a new Brazilian passport," Bar Tov said. "Destination Lisbon. Two days later, in Madrid, the Israeli ambassador to Spain was attacked."

"That's all you have to go on?"

"Eduard Reichmann was granted a residence permit by the Immigration Office of the Ministry of the Interior in 1949. He was naturalized in 1955. Many of the SS came to be in South American countries at about that same period. Most were granted residence on the authority of a Vatican passport which was issued to so-called displaced persons. That's how Bormann got there. It was the same with this man."

"Here it is," Emma said, pulling a file from the cabinet. She rushed to the desk, opened it for Aaron. "Eduard Reichmann. *SS-Sturmbannfuehrer.* Waffen-SS. Fifth Panzer Division." She looked up tiredly at Aaron. "The Viking Division. Panzer. I was convinced he was in infantry." She sighed. "Sorry."

Aaron studied the folder. "This shows him joining the unit in 1940. What about before that?"

"The Fifth Panzers was only organized in 1940," Emma said.

"I don't care about that," Aaron said. "There's nothing here about this guy before 1940. I want to know where he's from, what he did, where he went to school. . . ."

"Look here, Aaron." She pointed to another page, paymaster records. "From September 1942 he drew his pay from the quartermaster of the *Reichssicherheitshauptamt*, Section IV. That was Central Security Office. Skorzeny's department. The chain dogs!" Emma looked in his eyes. "It's him, Aaron. It has to be!"

"Is there a picture?"

"I'll know in a minute," she said and dashed to the file containing the photographs.

"There is one curious thing about this man Reichmann," Bar Tov said.

Aaron shook his head. "I think there's probably more than one."

"Did you notice his date of birth?"

Aaron looked back through the pages to the one with vital statistics. The entry marked DOB was 8/1/36.

"Thirty-six?" Miller frowned. "That isn't right. If he was born in 1936 he'd only be four years old when he joined the Waffen-SS. They took children, but that is ridiculous."

"Yes," Bar Tov said with some annoyance. "Obviously a typographical error. But that isn't what I meant. Look at the month and day."

"Eighth month, first day," Aaron said. "Eighth month . . . Jesus!" He looked wide-eyed at Bar Tov.

"August first," said the Israeli. "The deadline."

"He picked his fucking birthday!"

Bar Tov was silent a moment. "I wonder why. This Reichmann is something of a romantic spirit in his own way. He chooses his birthday to kill a world figure. A world he has no stake in. No future. Only revenge. Interesting, I think."

"Maybe to you," Aaron said. He turned to where Emma was ransacking the files. "Is there a photograph?"

She shook her head. "I'm still looking. There are so many— wait!" She pulled a file, spilling photos. "Here!" She brought the folder, dropped the worn photo on the desk. "That's Reichmann!"

He was standing beside a much taller man with a small mustache. Both wore the black uniform of the SS and both wore the Iron Cross medal around their necks. The taller man was Otto Skorzeny. Aaron recognized Reichmann. Younger, of course. But there was no question in his mind. This was the German he'd encountered underground. This was the man who killed Abe. Eduard Reichmann.

"It's him?" Bar Tov asked.

"It's him." Aaron held up the photograph. "A face with a name."

"He's in Europe somewhere." The Israeli moved to the large globe on a pedestal beside the desk. "We've been able to trace him to Vienna, a hotel there. Then we lost him for a while."

"Vienna?"

"Yes. A few days later he showed up in Innsbruck. He made a call to the resort in Argentina. That's how we found him again, tracking back from the overseas call. But he's using a different name. Probably a phony passport."

"What name was he using in Innsbruck?"

Bar Tov shrugged. "We don't know. The call was made from a hotel room registered to a traveling salesman."

"An accomplice?" Emma said.

"No. Reichmann got him drunk and used his phone. He's getting help from someone, but it wasn't the salesman. He's getting papers, a traveling I.D. Someone he knows has connections."

"Who?" Aaron said.

Bar Tov threw up his hands. "We don't know yet. But he

must have made a contact in Vienna. Reichmann disappeared in Vienna. He picked up new papers there."

"So," Aaron said, "I should begin in Vienna."

"We should," Emma corrected. "Europe is my territory. Reichmann isn't the only one with connections. They're my contacts. People who wouldn't trust you." She turned to Bar Tov. "Tell him."

The Israeli nodded. "Miss Diels has many friends, it is true. Normally, I would hesitate to recommend a woman to such danger." To Emma he said quickly, "Forgive me if that smacks of chauvinism. But, Mr. Miller, this is an extraordinary circumstance. I can only welcome any aid that is offered."

"No." Aaron looked sternly at Emma. "You're not going to go anywhere near that guy."

"Don't be gallant, Aaron," she said. "We're a team now."

"It's a team I want to keep intact. I'll go, you knit."

She pulled away from him infuriated. She sat down on the sofa, pulling angrily at the hem of her robe. "I'm going with you, Aaron. Get used to the idea. Wherever you are, I'm going to be there too."

"Look—"

"No," Emma said quietly. "This is more than just a hunt for Abe's killer. It isn't simply your private vendetta. The rest of the world has a life at stake now. Besides, we agreed, Mr. Aaron Kyle Miller. I don't take that kind of agreement lightly. And if you think you're running off without me, then you don't know the stubborn lady you've been screwing for the past three days." She folded her arms. "I'm going and that's it."

Aaron glanced at Bar Tov who looked away sheepishly. "Emma . . ." He moved to the sofa. "Emma, half a dozen people are dead. I don't want you to be the next. I don't want anybody to be next, but you've become very special to me. If something happened to you . . ."

"You're not exactly invincible yourself, you know. I'm taking the same risk, Aaron. Maybe together the odds will be different, but different or not, you're not going without me."

Aaron let out a long, tired sigh. Stubborn wasn't the half of it. Wrong or not, she was coming. He shook his head, half-smiled at her. "Just to set the record straight, we weren't screwing." He saw Bar Tov glance in his direction. "I've always thought that was an entirely inadequate description of lovemaking."

Emma grinned. "I'm in love with a prude."

Aaron turned to the Israeli. "Like I said, we're going to Vienna."

"I can't minimize the danger," Bar Tov said, looking concerned. He began pacing as Linka had. "I wish I could tell you it won't be hazardous. With terrorists involved, as well as this Reichmann—" he glanced at them— "you may be exposing yourselves to great risk."

"So is Reichmann," Aaron said.

"Yes, but he is the professional, isn't he?" Bar Tov waved it off. "But, then, you would go in any case, isn't that true?" He stopped pacing, interested in the answer.

Aaron nodded. "Yes."

The Israeli pulled a cigarette from his pocket and lit it. "Right." He exhaled the first puff in a long sigh of resignation. "There's one more thing. Reichmann has made another threat. In Verona, Italy."

"Another ambassador?" Aaron asked.

"No. He relayed the threat through a bishop this time . . . against Golda Meir."

Emma gasped.

"We think it's a red herring, of course," he continued. "He wouldn't announce it if he really intended to strike at her. But it's a warning. He wants to reinforce the threat by showing us he can hit anyone he chooses," Bar Tov sighed. "He also used the bishop to deliver another message. He thinks Lubetkin and your friend Nickelson are at the eagle's nest because we sent them. He wants them out."

"Then he'll be in for a surprise," Aaron said. "I spoke with Henry. Lubetkin talked to one of the Nazis. Mueller. He told him he still had the urn and wants to make a trade. The urn restored in return for calling off the assassin." He took a deep breath and glanced at Emma. "But the old man didn't stop there. He also wants them to surrender one of their own to him. One of the *Oberkomitee*."

"Fool!" Bar Tov said.

"So you see, I don't think they're going to want Lubetkin to leave anytime soon."

"Of course not." Bar Tov shook his head. "They will never agree! How could he imagine they would even consider it."

"Because, for the moment," Aaron said, "they believe that he has the urn."

"And when they learn otherwise?" Bar Tov asked. "What then?"

"I couldn't say," Aaron said. "I guess the next move is ours."

22

When the *Oberkomitee* met at Heinrich Mueller's request, Strausser listened calmly as the former Gestapo chief in-formed them of his confrontation with Lubetkin. When he finished, Mengele was the most vocal of the group. "Kill the Jew lover," he said over and over.

Helldorf and Gluck were stoically quiet as if the events of the last several days were enough for sane men to endure. Only Westrick turned to Strausser and asked what could be done now.

"If what Mueller says is true, Herr Strausser, then Reich-mann's mission is for nothing," Westrick said. "But how can we bargain with this Lubetkin? Who does he think he is that he can make such demands?"

"He thinks he has us stymied," replied the chairman. "And perhaps he does, at the moment."

"Kill him!" Mengele shouted.

"Yes, we know how you would handle it, Josef." Strausser looked at him coldly. "But it would mean losing forever the symbol of our strength. Your suggestion has merit, but not at the present time." He looked around the circle. "Other suggestions?"

Westrick, Gluck and Helldorf offered only blank expressions.

"What if we go along with his demand?" Mueller seemed amused by something. "What if we tell him we'll do as he says?"

"Preposterous!" said Mengele.

"Impossible!" Gluck added.

"But only if we *say* we will do it," Mueller said. "Once the urn is in our possession . . ."

Strausser raised his eyebrows, nodded. "But we must not forget Reichmann. He would never agree to this."

"Must we tell the major *everything* we do?" Mueller smiled. "Besides, we could use this to excellent advantage. Let Lubetkin eliminate Reichmann for us. As long as the urn is returned, what difference as to the means?"

"But he wants one of us!" Mengele said.

"I was just thinking about that," Mueller said. His smile broadened as he stared at the Doktor.

"You swine!" Mengele shouted. He reached furiously for his cane. "You filthy bastard swine!"

"Don't exercise yourself," Mueller said, quickly rising. "It is only a ploy. We will only let this Lubetkin *think* we are so desperate that we will give up one of our own."

"Then let him think it is you!" Mengele shot back angrily.

Just then the door to the meeting room opened and a messenger slid a small envelope onto a long table nearest Mueller and left.

"Gentlemen, if you please." Strausser rapped the tabletop with his knuckles. "Sit down, sit down."

"But, Alfred, he—"

"Sit *down*, Josef," Strausser said. He looked at Mueller, nodding thoughtfully. "There is something to what you say, Heinrich. But every deal has its area of compromise. Let us say, forgetting the consequences for a moment, that we agree to stop the major from completing his mission. You explained to Lubetkin that we, ourselves, cannot recall Reichmann?"

"Yes," Mueller said. He glanced at the envelope, noticing it was marked for Strausser, and abstractedly held it between his index fingers. "I told him we have absolutely no control over him at this moment."

"I see." Strausser nodded. "But he does not know the identity of the assassin he would have us restrain."

Mueller nodded to himself. He turned the envelope over in his fingers, then laid it on the polished tabletop and casually slid it to Westrick who glanced at the name and pushed it on to Strausser.

"That is correct. I did not tell him it was Reichmann."

"What difference?" Mengele said, suddenly curious.

"This Lubetkin demands two things in return for the safe delivery of our property," Strausser continued. He counted on his fingers. "First, stop the assassin. Second, turn over to him a high-ranking member of the Third Reich." Strausser smiled. "I think there is a way."

"But, Alfred," Westrick said quickly, "we could never agree to his second demand!"

"Perhaps we can." Now Strausser's complacent smile broadened. "Consider this, gentlemen. Consider that we eliminate Reichmann altogether . . . through Lubetkin. Reichmann, the hero of the Reich. The symbol of all that was Aryan. The Fuehrer's personal favorite . . ." He paused a moment. "A member of the *Oberkomitee*. Reichmann, a high-ranking SS officer, delivered, with our compliments." Strausser splayed his fingers out on the table before him. He noticed the envelope, reached for it. "This Nazi hunter Lubetkin does not know who Reichmann is."

"Yet," Mueller added. He smiled. "Yes, a member of the *Oberkomitee*. I like that, Herr Strausser."

"Yes," Mengele joined in. "Reichmann instead of . . . us." The Doktor glanced at the others. Everyone was smiling.

"Two birds with one stone," Mueller said. "Everyone's difficulty is solved. And the urn is returned." He nodded happily. "We *can* cooperate with Lubetkin. We will give him Reichmann, and he will give us the urn."

Strausser's smile disintegrated as he read the contents of

the message in the small envelope. His eyes widened.

"The fool! What is he doing?"

All faces turned to him.

"Alfred," Mueller said anxiously, "what is—"

"Reichmann has made another threat," Strausser blurted.

"Ah, excellent," replied Mengele.

"He threatened Meir, the old woman, but . . . but he assaulted a Catholic bishop with a bomb." Strausser handed the message to Mueller. "What is he doing?"

The room was suddenly full of frightened faces. When Mueller spoke, after he'd studied the message, it was with frustrated rage. "This news cements our resolve, gentlemen," he said grimly. "Reichmann must be stopped, and quickly."

"Exactly so," Mueller replied. "Exactly so."

Their agreement was unanimous.

They drove in Anna's five-year-old Volkswagen. Josef Weisse's daughter took the wheel because Reichmann's forged papers in the name of Werner Stolz did not include a driver's license. The 162-kilometer motorway from Munich to Nuremberg was scenic, though Reichmann catnapped for much of the drive.

They'd spent the previous night together in her room. Their lovemaking had not been something either would long remember for its passion. It was an act born of need and sympathy. Anna had gone to sleep immediately, and Reichmann had lain awake for some time, aware of the night sounds outside, the slight breeze gently stirring the small window's curtains and the warm rhythmic breathing of the sleeping woman against his chest. There had been much to consider.

What to do about Anna, when the time came, was a question he would soon have to resolve. She was a threat and yet not a threat to him. On the one hand, though she had no idea of his plan, she knew more about a critical phase of his scheme than anyone else. In that way, she jeopardized his security. On the other hand, however, she was a guiltless casualty of a violently destructive conflict that he'd had a hand in prosecuting—and losing. It was as if she—like so many others—had suffered in his place. The dilemma was in deciding whether or not to take a chance and let her go. He'd been trained to neutralize all hazards to his strategies, but that was more than thirty years ago when hazards were erected by a well-defined enemy bent on defeating him. Anna was not an enemy. She was little more than a victim. Perhaps that was the answer. Perhaps there was a way to make her innocence work to his advantage. He would prefer that. He didn't want to kill her, but he would if it became necessary—without hesitation. Considering his ultimate goal, anyone was expendable.

"The Frankenstrasse is just ahead," Anna said, interrupting his thoughts. "Do you know the number?"

Reichmann was awake, abstractedly watching the sights of the city as they entered Nuremberg. There had been much reconstruction since he'd last seen it. When Anna spoke, Reichmann sat forward quickly. "Frankenstrasse?"

"Yes." She pointed to the intersection ahead. "The number?"

"It isn't necessary," Reichmann said. "Let me off here. I can find it."

"But I can take you there."

"No." He touched her hand on the steering wheel. "I don't want anyone to see you or the car. Stop at the nearest café. I'll find you."

Anna stopped at the street light and Reichmann got out. He walked three blocks to the address. It was a toy shop—Das Rote Spielzeug. A thin man in his early forties with jet-black hair that Reichmann suspected was dyed greeted him.

"Good morning," the shopkeeper said.

"I am looking for Conrad Lindermann," Reichmann said.

"And you have found him, my friend." The shopkeeper nodded. He turned and gestured to Reichmann to follow him. They went into an office in the rear. Reichmann closed the door as Lindermann snapped on a table lamp on a small desk.

"You have come for the passport?" Lindermann said, lighting a cigarette.

"Yes. Is it ready?"

The shopkeeper shrugged, exhaled loudly. He held his cigarette awkwardly to one side with his elbow bent, like a woman. "I have never met Herr Rudel. They say he has only one leg. Is that so?"

"Yes," Reichmann replied, as if it was a foolish question. "Is the passport in order?"

"Oh, dear me, yes," Lindermann said. He puffed again on the cigarette. "My name was passed to Herr Rudel by a friend whose judgment Rudel trusts implicitly. Anyway, that's what my friend says. We are in a similar line of work, my friend and I." The toymaker smiled. "Actually, it was my brother who my friend trusted so completely. We owned this shop together—we also print calendars"—he nodded to one on the wall— "and I worked with him on these, ah, special printing requests. But, Karl—that was my brother—Karl was killed in a motorcar accident outside Würzburg last October. So you see, there is only one of the Lindermann brothers left."

Reichmann nodded solemnly. His eyes narrowed. "Is that significant, Herr Lindermann?"

"Yes," the thin man replied with a smile. "I am not trustworthy."

"I see."

"Do you?" Lindermann let the ash from his cigarette fall to the floor. "I am not absolutely trustworthy for the ten thousand Deutschemarks that was mentioned concerning this passport. Let me say, the work is done and it is as good a job of faking an official passport as you will find anywhere, but . . . but for an additional sum I could guarantee absolute silence on my part."

Reichmann sighed. He shook his head.

"I am not offended by the word blackmail," said the shopkeeper. "And that is exactly what I propose. People in our line of work tend to be much too sensitive about loyalties. My loyalty is only to myself. You understand that."

"Yes," Reichmann said.

"And don't believe the common misconception that I will not find other work such as this, if you were considering threatening me. I am very good at forging things. Craftsmanship in this business outweighs ethical considerations."

Reichmann pulled a chair over to the desk and sat down. "It is a straightforward proposition, Herr Lindermann." He offered a tentative smile. "How much blackmail money do you want?"

"Ah, a realist. Good." The forger grinned triumphantly. "I would suggest another five-digit figure."

"An additional ten thousand?"

"I was thinking more—"

"Dollars," Reichmann said. "American."

Lindermann couldn't contain his surprise. "Dollars!"

Reichmann stood up. "In total then about thirty-five thousand Deutschemarks. Acceptable?"

The toymaker stubbed out his cigarette with a quick gesture. "Yes, yes. You have it with you?" He almost extended his hand across the desk.

"I can have it in less than an hour," Reichmann said. "I only wonder that if I return you will demand more. Blackmail has a way of escalating."

"Absolutely not, Herr Stolz. You have my word!"

Reichmann shook his head. "Your word? I should like to have more than that. Your friend may feel thirty-five thousand Deutschemarks is not enough. I want assurance that this transaction will be the end of our business. Also, before I leave, I want to see the passport."

Lindermann laughed. "No, Herr Stolz, my friend is not concerned in this. I am too greedy to share the proceeds of my work. You must trust me on that. This transaction is known only to the two of us."

Now Reichmann smiled. "I see. And the passport?"

"I will hand you the passport as you hand me the American dollars. And do not be so foolish as to think I have not protected myself. I have copies of all the papers Rudel sent me. Those I will keep. It is my insurance that you will not cause me any harm."

"Safe in a bank vault?"

"Who trusts banks?" The forger smiled. "I am a craftsman." He gestured around the room with a wave of his arm. "Karl and I, we built this shop. You would not know it, but there are hundreds of hiding places built into these walls and floors. It would take ten men a year to ferret out all my secrets."

"Nonetheless, I must see the passport now."

Lindermann sighed. "You have no alternative than to do as I say. You can trust me in this, Herr Stolz." He patted the locked drawer at the side of the desk. "Your passport is safe. Anyway, you have no choice."

Reichmann got up from his chair. "Unfortunately, I must agree."

"Then you will be getting the money?"

"No," Reichmann said.

"No?"

Reichmann walked to the window behind the desk. A narrow cobblestone alley was littered with trash. He stood there a moment, looking out, then closed the shutters. "You've made it very plain. I have no choice."

The toymaker shook his head, confused. "Then you *will* pay me? I don't understand. I am a busy man, either you pay me or—" Lindermann stopped abruptly when Reichmann turned back toward him. There was a small pistol in his hand.

"You've admitted you cannot be trusted unless it is on your own terms," Reichmann said. "I cannot accept that."

Lindermann offered a nervous laugh. "You should not threaten me. I have taken precautions. My insurance is—"

"Tell me, Herr Lindermann, what good is your insurance if you are dead?"

The thin man licked his lips quickly. "The police . . . I have all the papers from Rudel. The passport would not do you any good. You would be caught."

"Does that give you peace of mind? It is enough to die for?"

"You would be caught!" the toymaker raised his voice unevenly as Reichmann walked nearer. He held the pistol close to the perspiring head. "I think you are *too* greedy. You have no partner. A mistake. If you had an unknown partner, I might be intimidated." Reichmann shook his head wearily.

"Obviously, I am the first customer you have tried this blackmailing scheme on or the others were so incredibly rushed that your demands were not much more than a tiring inconvenience. In any case, it was a mistake that you attempted it with me."

The toymaker was sweating heavily now. Reichmann kept the gun near his right temple. Lindermann could see the tips of the bullets in the cylinder when he glanced up at Reichmann's hand. "But, please . . . I . . ."

"And your third mistake is a very costly one." Reichmann nodded at the walls. "Never, never, if you are a blackmailer, do you let your target know where the incriminating material may be found."

"But—"

"You have gone to a great deal of trouble for nothing." Reichmann smiled grimly. "You do smoke, Herr Lindermann?"

The toymaker nodded.

"Hand me your lighter. Slowly."

Lindermann obeyed and Reichmann struck a flame several times. "You know, smoking is very bad for you. Potentially dangerous." He slid a sheet of paper from the desk, touched the flame to its edge. Lindermann watched nervously as the fire moved up the page.

"Very dangerous for a businessman whose shop is handsomely decorated with such fine mahogany walls," Reichmann said. "There must be many coats of shellac to bring out such a luster. Beautiful but also highly combustible." He let the flaming paper drop into the wastebasket beside the desk.

Lindermann's eyes were on the wastebasket. Flames were building quickly. "Herr Stolz!"

"How long do you suppose it would take to incinerate this shop of yours? Half hour? Quarter hour? Less?" Reichmann gathered more paper from the desk, dropped them in the wastebasket one at a time. Flames leaped higher. "I do not need ten men or a year to find your secrets, Herr Lindermann. I don't need to find anything." With his shoe Reichmann pushed the burning container close to the wall.

The forger's eyes were wide, terrified. "Please . . . please, don't."

"I understand fear. I have always understood what makes men afraid. You might say it's what I do." Reichmann held the pistol, still trained on Lindermann. He pushed the wastebasket against the wall.

"Please!" the forger gasped. "I'll give you the passport!"

"Not enough," Reichmann said.

Above the fire a portion of the highly polished paneling began to darken. The finish blistered, turned black. The room suddenly smelled of smoke and lacquer. Lindermann divided panic glances between Reichmann and the fire. "I'll give you the passport!" he shouted. "What else do you want?"

"Your secrets," Reichmann said. "Everything you received from Rudel."

"Yes, yes." The forger's eyes were on the fire. Flames were starting to lick slowly up the paneling. "Stop it . . . please!"

"The passport first."

Lindermann dug frantically in his pocket, produced a key. He handed it over to Reichmann. "Top drawer! It's there!"

Reichmann opened the drawer. He slid the passport into his pocket. "Now the papers."

"Under the desk," Lindermann said, stuttering over his words. "The floor opens . . . a hidden box . . ."

"Open it." Reichmann stood back, kept the pistol on him.

"The fire! Please . . ."

"Open it!"

Lindermann scrambled quickly to the floor below the desk. He found the place, the hidden latch under the desk. Two boards of the polished oak floor snapped open. In seconds he had a long narrow box on the desk. He ripped at the clasp, watching the fire on the wall glow red as the flames melted shellac and contributed fuel to the spreading flames. The toymaker grabbed the papers inside, held them out to Reichmann. "Here! This is everything! Now, please, stop the fire!"

Reichmann took the papers, glanced over them. When he was satisfied they were complete, he walked carefully to the wastebasket and dropped them inside.

The fire was nearly to the ceiling, spreading out from the corner of the office. Reichmann walked to the door. The smell of smoke was heavy now, the fire larger. "Go on, Herr Lindermann, save your other secrets."

The forger lunged toward the fire, kicking the wastebasket away. With a cushion from a small sofa, he tried to beat out the fire, but only managed to smear the burning shellac on the cushion. The fire was no longer easily contained. He screamed at it, pushing, pulling at decorative panel adornments until a long strip opened. Then Reichmann saw the reason for the forger's panic. Inside the hiding place were bundles of neatly bound cash—Deutschemarks, Swiss francs, English pounds, American dollars—stacked in tall rows inside the false wall. Some of it was already burning.

"Swine!" Lindermann screamed. He threw armloads of money across the room away from the flames. "You are burning my money!"

The blaze had moved across the wall. One of Lindermann's shirtsleeves had caught the sticky fire and he beat it against his side, gasping. Frantically, he glanced around the office. He was standing in the smoke, eyes watering, trying to catch his breath in the heat.

Reichmann opened the door and oxygen from the hall rushed in giving the fire renewed strength. "Good luck, Herr Lindermann."

"No!" The forger dropped an armload of smoldering bills. He raced to the window, pushed open the shutters and gulped for air. When he turned back the room was ablaze. "No! No! Stolz! You . . . you bastard!"

From somewhere at the desk he found a revolver. He raised it, aiming wildly toward the door. "Stolz! Bastard!"

Reichmann fired once quickly. The small caliber bullet ripped through Lindermann's throat, knocking him backward against the wall. For the brief moments before the forger's head lolled to one side, Reichmann was aware that the thin man's eyes were not fixed on his executioner. Instead, Lindermann's last conscious concern was for his money. Burning.

Reichmann let himself out the rear door. In twenty minutes

he was with Anna at a sidewalk café, drinking coffee.

"What is that odor?" She wrinkled her nose. "Your coat . . ." Her look was amused surprise. "You smell like a chimney, Werner. I thought you didn't smoke."

"I don't." Reichmann smiled. "Some of my friends have the habit." He shrugged, finished his coffee. "I think smoking is bad for one's health."

The transatlantic flight from Dulles was only two hours' old and cruising at an altitude around five miles from the ocean when Emma woke up. She'd dozed off against Aaron's shoulder about an hour after takeoff and now, as she tried to refocus her eyes to the dim light in the jet's pressurized cabin, she found herself reclined in the seat with a light blanket across her lap.

She leaned forward to see Aaron studying a map of Europe from the pencil of light over his seat. She yawned and her ears popped. "Aaron . . . what time is it?"

He glanced at her with a warm smile. "Who knows. Sometime between midnight and four. Why don't you try and get some more sleep?"

"What are you doing?"

Aaron folded the map and slid it back into the seat pouch in front of him. "Just looking. You know, I've never been to Europe."

Emma nodded. She adjusted her seat up and rested her head on his shoulder. "Can't sleep?"

"That too, I guess." He reached up and snapped off the light. "This is the first night we've spent together that I've actually been bored." He smiled at her. "Well, perhaps not bored . . . just not otherwise preoccupied."

Seeing him smile stirred an urge in her to be closer to him. She touched the side of his face with her hand, felt the prickly stubble of his blond beard. In so many ways he was still like a little boy. "I wish there were time to take you to all the beautiful cities, Aaron. I would like to show you the new Germany. Paris, Amsterdam, London. . . ." Emma sighed. "You would like it."

"Maybe later."

They were quiet for some time. Emma let her hand slide down to his chest, listened to the steady drone of the engines. She was almost asleep again when Aaron stirred slightly.

"Emma."

"Hmmm?"

"Emma." She could feel the slow, measured beat of his heart beneath her hand. "I want to talk to you a minute."

"Um-hmm."

"About Reichmann."

She opened her eyes and looked up at him warily. "Yes?" Aaron's face was mostly in shadows, but she could see his eyes and the line of his hair against the window.

"I don't know if we will find him or not," he began slowly. "And if we do I don't know exactly what will happen—".

"We'll let Bar Tov handle it," she said quickly. She raised her head to try and see him better. "That's what you promised." She suddenly remembered what Henry had said about men with the killing instinct. *Against a pro?* *He wouldn't last ten seconds.* She wasn't going to let that happen. That's why she was here. She wasn't going to lose Aaron too. "You promised," she said again. "Bar Tov can—"

"Will you just listen!"

Emma took a deep breath. "I'm listening."

"All right, then." He held her hand. "Bar Tov said this could be dangerous. There isn't just Reichmann to contend with. There's also the PLO and God knows what that means. I just don't want you doing something foolish—"

"Me!"

"Yes, you," Aaron said. "If something happens . . . something unexpected—I don't want to have to worry about you."

Emma shook her head. "Spoken like a true chauvinist."

"Emma—"

"If something happens, something unexpected—like what happened in Washington—neither one of us is going to have time to worry. That's why we're working with Bar Tov. Anyway, we're only two people. Chances are someone else will find him or the urn long before we even get a solid lead, even if you do know what he looks like. Every country in Europe is looking for him."

"Our chances are as good as anyone's," Aaron replied firmly. He sounded as if he wanted it that way. "Better."

"We'll see," Emma said. She lay her head back against his shoulder. "We'll see." She held his hand tight. He was slipping away from her. They were taking him away from her. Reichmann was doing it. And Abe. Phantoms that menaced him haunted her. They were driving a wedge between them and she was powerless to stop it. *Someone had to find Reichmann!* Anyone. But soon. Very soon. And not just because of the threat he posed to the Jews or heads of state. Her motive was self-serving, but, then, they owed her that. Her suffering and Aaron's were part of the same struggle. They'd been little more than survivors. Now, with each other's help, they could be more than that. But Reichmann was the key. Everything hinged on ending the threat, on stopping Aaron's *Kettenhund.* Only Reichmann could set Aaron free. Only he could put a ghost finally to rest.

Emma held his hand tight. They *would* find the German. There was nothing else to do.

By late Sunday, with six days of competition remaining in Montreal, the Soviet Union had a decisive lead in the unofficial standing of total Olympic medals with seventy. The United States with fifty-six total medals had done well that day, particularly in the swimming divisions with two golds and two silvers in the men's class and a gold in the women's relay.

Hungary won its third gold medal in the javelin throw, setting a new world record at 310 feet, 4 inches. Sports pundits who covered the event said the twenty-nine-year-old Hungarian was bred for sports. His father was a gold-medal winner in the hammer throw twenty-eight years before at the XIV Olympiad in London. His mother was a national discus champion.

"My father never pushed me to be a hammer thrower," he

told interviewers, smiling at his little joke. He did agree that it was fortunate he could take counsel from his parents' experience. There is no substitute for experience.

Anna Weisse set the telephone back in its place. She rolled over on the bed to her quiet lover. The hotel room was nearly dark in the settling twilight.

"The casting is finished," she said, nestling against his chest. "I can drive to Berlin for it tomorrow."

"We will go together," Reichmann said. "In the morning."

"But you need a green card to cross the frontier and a transit visa at the Berlin entry point."

"I have papers to cross into Berlin."

"But, Werner—"

Reichmann put a finger to her lips. "I have the papers. It is not for you to worry." He stroked her hair, letting strands of it slip through his fingers, and they were quiet a few minutes.

"Werner, I—I don't want you to think I am a silly, sentimental woman." She took his hand and held his knuckles against her face, touching them to her lips affectionately. "I do not even know you and . . . and already I am afraid for you. Is it so important, this thing you will do?"

"Yes," Reichmann murmured. "Very important."

"Then . . ." She sighed next to him in the failing light and he could feel the whisper of her breath on his bare chest. "If there is time, in the morning, before we leave, I would like to light a candle and say a—"

"You are Catholic?" Reichmann interrupted.

Anna raised her head suddenly and looked at him apprehensively. "I . . . I—" Her eyes were wide with bewilderment as if she didn't know whether to lie or tell the truth. It was plain she didn't want to trouble him, even with this small trifle. "I was," she said hesitantly, then, as if to explain, "but it has been years since I was at mass."

"When I met you in Munich," Reichmann said, "you had just returned from mass."

"For my father," she said quickly. "Before that it was—"

"Years?"

"Yes. I. . . . I haven't been a very good Catholic."

Reichmann remembered the fear in the bishop's voice in Verona. He thought it amusing that he'd used nearly the same words to get close to His Eminence and wondered if there was such a thing as a bad Catholic.

"You aren't angry, Werner?" Anna said.

"That you're Catholic? No."

"Then . . . you don't mind? I mean, about the candle."

"You would say a prayer for me?"

"Of course."

"Why?"

"Because . . . because I want you to be safe. I want—"

"I am perfectly safe," Reichmann said. "Your saints cannot help me."

"Do you not believe in God, Werner?"

"I believe in myself. I believe in destiny. These saints of yours—in a thousand years, how many people lit candles to them? Is the world safer because of them? How many people have they saved from being killed? How many wars have they stopped?"

"It is an act of faith, Wer—"

"My old schoolteacher lived in Hamburg," Reichmann began. "He was a Catholic too. In the spring of 1943 I wrote him and told him he should take his family out and go to Berlin. I told him the Americans and British would surely be bombing the city soon. He wrote back and told me it would not happen. He said the bombers would not come to destroy such a beautiful city as Hamburg. He was praying, he said, for his beloved city. In August I was there. There was no more Hamburg. In a few days the Americans had bombed it into a blazing mass of ruins. A city of a million people. Eight hundred thousand homeless. Seventy-thousand dead. My old schoolteacher and his family—gone. All gone. So, do not tell me about faith. Your saints, your Pope, your cardinals—they can do nothing. The so-called Holy City in Italy and its Holy Father are no more blessed or pure than any other. Your Pope—how is he any more a saintly figure than a cobbler if they are both still only men? Is he immune to sickness or failing health? Can he stop wars? How does he justify a merciful, Almighty Being when the world around him is starving? Is he head of the Church because he *believes* in it more than any other? How does one man believe more than another? How do you measure faith? Tell me, Anna, what good it does. Tell me."

She didn't reply immediately. For several minutes she lay very still beside him. Finally she said, "I think I will go to church tomorrow."

"You haven't been listening to me," Reichmann said.

"Yes, I have listened." Anna's voice was no more than a whisper. "I think I cannot say anything to change your mind."

"And you will pray for me anyway?" Reichmann retorted.

"For you, yes," she said. "And for me."

Anna was asleep when Reichmann slipped out of the room. By the light of the desk lamp, he pawed through his bag until he found the stationery. It was letterhead paper of the major athletic shoe manufacturer that he'd taken from the sales-man's suitcase in Innsbruck. And the message he wrote to Hans-Ulrich Rudel in Vienna was brief: A name and general delivery address at the post office in a small German town. Rudel would be amused by the irony. A letter postmarked in Germany from a British footwear company to a man with only one foot.

Reichmann deposited the envelope in the mail slot, switched off the lamp and slid quietly into bed beside Anna without disturbing her. He lay there for several minutes, staring up into the darkness. Rudel would carry through on his end of the arrangement, Reichmann was confident. All the loose ends were being neatly tied up. And Anna was one he would not worry about after tonight. She was more than a simple pawn in his scheme now. He'd realized how incredi-bly useful she could be to him. Unless he'd made a drastic miscalculation, she would fit perfectly into his scheme. It meant she would be an instrument of justice against those who had made her suffer, even if she didn't know it. It also meant—and Reichmann was relieved of this most of all—that he would not have to kill her.

Anna rolled against him, draping an arm across his chest. Reichmann pulled the bedcovers up around her shoulders and kissed her softly on the neck. Sleep well, my Anna. My Lili of the lamplight. My Lili Marlene.

When sleep came, it was with the knowledge and peace of mind that all was going well. The *Kettenhund* held his woman close to him and slept fitfully. A chain dog does not make miscalculations.

23

Vienna's Schwechat Airport was crowded. Emma held Aaron's arm, and together they found their way to the courtesy counter where the overhead voice paging Mr. Aaron Miller requested him to take a call.

"I'm Aaron Miller," Miller said to the uniformed clerk at the desk. "You have a call for me?"

The clerk nodded to a tall red-haired man with a newspaper folded neatly under his arm.

"Julian Hirsch," the man said, extending a hand. He smiled at Emma. "Welcome to Austria. I've been waiting since nine. Thought you were coming on the TWA breakfast flight from Zurich." He glanced quickly at his watch. "I have a car outside."

Aaron nodded without smiling. "I didn't know we were being met."

"Bar Tov," the tall man said as if the name should explain everything. "There have been new developments while you and Miss Diels were on your way here. I've taken the liberty of reserving two rooms for you at the Hotel Carlton. Your bags will be delivered straightaway." He motioned toward the exit.

"What developments?" Aaron said.

Hirsch handed over the newspaper. "Late edition from London. Note the bulletin in the lower right corner." Aaron held the page so Emma could see the news brief. "A man was killed last night on the northeast lawn in front of the White House," Hirsch said. "There are people all over the world getting very jumpy because of your Nazi friend." He nodded toward the exit. "Shall we go? There are people to see."

A man with an umbrella, standing beside the newsstand, watched them leave. The tiny shutters of the miniature camera flicked half a dozen times. He waked quickly to the row of telephone stands and made a local call.

The American had arrived.

Yes, he was being followed. The film would leave immediately.

The dark-eyed photographer hung up and lost himself in the airport crowd. It had been a short conversation and entirely in Arabic.

Chester M. Plummer, Jr., a black thirty-year-old Washington taxi driver, was shot once in the chest by a White House security guard after ignoring repeated commands to halt. He'd climbed over a six-foot spiked fence near the northeast gate where a group of women was marching in an all-night vigil for the Equal Rights Amendment. He'd tripped the automatic intruder sensors on the lawn that turned on floodlights. When shot he was wielding a length of pipe.

"Jesus, what was he doing there?" Aaron asked, glancing up from the paper in his lap. They were in a limousine, Emma between Aaron and Hirsch in the rear compartment.

"Nobody seems to know," Hirsch said. "He couldn't have timed his rashness any more poorly. The White House knows about Reichmann. No one is taking the slightest chance. I think this illustrates the nervous mood everyone is in."

"Christ!" Aaron shook his head, glanced back at the newspaper.

"You've talked to Mr. Bar Tov?" Emma leaned forward to see the red-haired man who worked for the Israeli agent.

"This morning. And he, in turn, has spoken with your friend Henry Nickelson."

"And?" Aaron said.

"The Germans at Bariloche have offered a deal." Hirsch raised his eyebrows as if such deals were always suspect. "They say for the safe return of their urn they will, one, help us in tracking down this would-be assassin, and, two, give up one of their own. That is to say, one of the members of the *Oberkomitee*."

"They agreed to that!" Aaron shook his head. "I don't believe it."

Emma nodded. "Neither do I."

"It's a very curious arrangement," Hirsch said. "The member they are willing to sacrifice is Reichmann himself. Two for one in other words."

"Reichmann, part of the *Oberkomitee*?" Emma was shaking her head furiously. "Now I really don't believe it. First of all that group is all businemen, so-called . . . Mengele, Strausser, Mueller. Reichmann was—is—a soldier. They're turning on Reichmann. They think they can get their precious urn back without using him and they're cutting him off as the price."

"Don't forget, Emma darling, they think we have the urn." Aaron sighed, turned to Hirsch. "They say they're going to help us? How? Reichmann hasn't told them who he's going after, where he is, nobody knows what name he's using. . . . I'd like to know just how it is they expect to be of any goddamn help to us!"

Hirsch smiled glibly. "They gave us a name. Just a name. You see, we know Reichmann came to Vienna. But he disappeared here. Someone is giving him false papers, helping him with contacts in Europe. We think his target is also in Europe somewhere and—"

"What name?" Aaron interrupted.

"They seemed convinced it is who Reichmann would turn to for aid," Hirsch went on. "He lives in Vienna. He was a national war hero in Germany and after the war he engineered an escape organization called The Spider to get wanted Nazi SS off the Continent."

"Rudel!" Emma said. "Hans-Ulrich Rudel."

"Yes," Hirsch said, surprised. "You know him?"

"He ran as a candidate for the neo-Nazi German Reich party in 1953." Emma glanced at Aaron. "Unsuccessfully. Rudel is an unreconstructed nationalist. A die-hard military man." She nodded at Hirsch. "He *would* help Reichmann!"

"Yes." Hirsch pressed his fingers together slowly, nodding. "Bar Tov thinks so too. The question is, will he help us?"

Aaron had been staring at the newspaper. He folded it, slid it between the seats. "Why don't we ask him," he said quietly, "before someone dies on someone else's lawn."

The french doors to the balcony of the Palestinian's suite were ajar, admitting a cool breeze that accompanied the pounding rain from yet another summer storm. But the breeze and the rain had escaped his notice as he sat brooding behind a Victorian desk, his concentration on the messenger who stood before him nervously twisting a finger in the seam of his Bedouin gown.

"There is no mistake?" asked the Palestinian, his fierce eyes glaring at the messenger.

"No, *Yahid*. No mistake."

The Palestinian rose suddenly, angrily. The messenger cowered, stepped back to let him pass. For several minutes the Palestinian paced the room, his sandals slapping the polished floor. Finally he stopped and turned quickly to the terrified messenger. "The Austrian capital, Rashid?"

Rashid jumped. "Yes, effendi."

"And these friends of the Jews are close to the quarry?" The Palestinian clapped his hands together and the messenger jumped again. "We must not allow it," said the Palestinian. "We must discourage this search!"

"Yes, effendi."

"I want—Allah demands—that the German soldier from the southern America not be interrupted in his mission!" He stared at Rashid. "My meaning is clear?"

The messenger nodded exuberantly.

"Then do not stand there," commanded the Palestinian. "See to it!"

Rashid bowed deeply from the waist. "By the grace of Allah, effendi." He stepped backward toward the door, bowing effusively. "Yes, effendi. Immediately, effendi."

When the Bedouin was gone, the Palestinian returned to his high-back chair behind the secretary. For several moments he scrutinized the photographs Rashid had brought of the couple who arrived in Vienna earlier in the day. The resolution was grainy due to the fast film and the minimum F stop, but the subjects were clearly recognizable. Two men shaking hands, and an attractive woman beside them. Below the figures and written in a bold hand were the names. Miller, Diels, Jew.

With a large pen the Palestinian circled the head of one of them over and over until the paper wore thin. "The German soldier will not be restrained," he said almost inaudibly. Emma's head separated from the photograph under pressure from the pencil. "I promise it."

The next morning Reichmann had a breakfast of black bread and ersatz coffee while Anna checked out of the Bamberg Hotel and had the car filled with petrol. He waited while she climbed the hill to St. Michael's Cathedral, former Benedictine monastery, to light her candles.

Anna drove and they passed without incident through the East German entry point near Hof. In Berlin, Reichmann took the wheel and Anna guided him to the residence of Walter Moltke in central Tiergarten near the zoo.

Anna made the introductions and Moltke offered tea and gingerbread.

"My most sincere sympathy, Anna, for the unexpected passing of your father." Moltke was not quite so tall as Reichmann and had blond hair and fair complexion, but, again, not quite so blond or fair as Reichmann, considering the years that separated their ages. Moltke looked less than forty. He reminded Reichmann of a Gestapo man he'd once met in North Africa who wore a pince-nez. Moltke looked like a man who avoided trouble, a man who was studious and more imaginative than clever. He was, Reichmann thought, probably a good craftsman.

"I am deeply sorry," the Berliner went on. "Your father was an artist as a technician and as a man. I will miss him, Anna."

"Thank you, Walter," Anna Weisse said. She spoke quickly as if it was too painful or a bitter embarrassment in Reichmann's presence to linger on the death of the late Josef Weisse, old man, old German, forgotten follower. "I think Werner would like to complete the business of this meeting. We can talk on a more personal basis . . . another time, if you don't mind."

"Of course." Moltke nodded politely and turned his attention to Reichmann. "Herr Stolz," he said, "you will be proud of my workmanship. It is exactly—"

Reichmann held up his hand. He glanced at Anna. "More tea?" His eyes indicated his cup which was still nearly full. "I've let it get cold," he said pleasantly.

"Oh, let me," Moltke said, moving forward.

Reichmann's sudden cold stare stopped him. "Let Anna." He held out the cup and saucer to her and smiled. "Please?"

She looked at Moltke, then Reichmann. She nodded, got up from her chair. "Yes, Werner."

When they were alone, the man called Stolz turned his glance back to the Berliner. "You were saying about the workmanship, Herr Moltke?"

The craftsman hesitated a moment. "Yes . . . it is exactly as you requested. Exact to each detail. Herr Weisse was very specific that it should be so." He moved to a leaded-glass cabinet surrounded by bookshelves, unlatched the clasp and opened it. Two of the shelves had been removed and the interior lined with a red velvet fabric. Mounted in the center was the source of his pride. "To your satisfaction, Herr Stolz?"

Reichmann was amazed at its beauty. The gold surface shone with as much luster as the original. The inscription exactly the same. Reichmann moved beside Moltke. "Very impressive, Herr Moltke. Your reputation as a craftsman is richly deserved. Very impressive."

"Thank you. The specifications were . . . well, unique."

Reichmann touched the curved surface. "And the weight?"

"My instructions were not to exceed the difference of twenty-five percent more than the original. I am pleased to say it does not exceed more than twenty-three percent."

"Very good."

"Some weight was saved in using a synthetic alloy for the gold plating. The entire body is a molded plastic with a point detonator charge affixed to a hollow vacuum interior for purposes of stability. My instructions did not indicate how long before its use or what temperatures it may be subjected to. Thus the vacuum consideration. Pressure, that is, forces such as those exerted in change of altitude do not make for a dangerous stability problem, within reason, of course. Change of atmospheric conditions above eighty thousand feet or below one hundred and twenty fathoms would be critical. As for transporting it, I have constructed a handsome case. It may be moved about as it normally might be, but . . ."

"But don't drop it," Reichmann said.

"Exactly, Herr Stolz." Moltke smiled. "The resulting impact from a fall no higher than"—the Berliner glanced quickly around the room to a side table, pointed it out— "there. A fall from a distance of approximately one meter will crush the detonator."

Reichmann noted it, nodded. "I see. And the killing radius of the explosive?"

Moltke shrugged. "In such matters, I must tell you, I am not an expert. But considering the amount and weight of the composition, I would be safe in estimating anyone within five meters of the detonation point would not survive the blast."

Reichmann surveyed the room. "Then anyone in this room, if it were to explode now, would die. Would you agree?"

"No question," Moltke said with an acknowledging nod. "We would both be killed." He smiled because Reichmann was smiling. "Absolutely, no doubt."

"Excellent."

"I hope you don't require a demonstration," Moltke said. "There was time to build only one."

The man they called Stolz shook his head. He stared at the finely crafted bomb. "Just one." He smiled at his joke. "I suspect one will be enough."

They spent the rest of the day walking, Reichmann pointing out landmarks he remembered and Anna trying to keep it all straight on a city map she purchased at a druggist's. Just west and slightly north of the Charlottenburg Castle, Anna stopped, tugging at Reichmann's arm.

"Werner, we have walked miles," she said, breathing heavily. "It's late, shouldn't we—"

"It isn't much farther." Reichmann started on, his blue eyes scanning ahead.

"But—what are you looking for?"

Reichmann stopped when he saw the bell tower and the Marathon Gate. "There," he said pointing with his arm.

"The stadium?" Anna said, panting.

"The Olympics," Reichmann said. "I was here before."

She followed him to the stadium entrance, unsure of his preoccupation.

"The *Maifeld* was there," Reichmann said, indicating with a sweeping gesture the area opposite the wide entrance. "There were enormous flags hanging here"—he nodded at the walls— "and here. The Fuehrer came this way." He walked into the stadium, Anna following. "The athletes entered from the tunnel. All the track and field events were held here except the marathon run."

Anna touched his arm. "You were an athlete in the Olympics?" She glanced around at the huge empty stadium. "Here?"

Reichmann looked down at her, his blue eyes clear. "The eleventh Olympiad. Nineteen thirty-six."

"That's amazing, Werner." Reichmann moved off down the cinder track, Anna ran to catch up. "It's amazing. I never thought—"

"The one hundred meter- and two hundred-meter dashes were started here," Reichmann said, standing on the spot. "I saw the American Negro Owens win his semifinal heat." He looked up at the top of the stadium where empty flagpoles were stationed. "I remember in the finals it was cold, but it did not rain that day, I was in the infield. I came to watch the finals in the one hundred meter and I had a bag of peanuts. When the gun sounded, I dropped the empty bag and I remember, it just dropped. Straight down. After Owens had won they said his time did not count as a new world record because there was a following wind." Reichmann smiled, shook his head. "Even the photographs showed the flags as stationary."

"You were a runner?" Anna's excitement was reflected in her eyes. "What was your event?"

Reichmann took her by the arm. "Come, let me show you." They walked down the track and he pointed out places and recounted names that Anna had never heard until he stopped and pointed to the area of private boxes. "The Fuehrer sat there with Goering and Goebbels."

"Hitler?"

"Yes, in a brown uniform."

"The Nazis were everywhere," Anna said bitterly. She looked away. "I don't want to think about them enjoying themselves while . . ." She shook her head, looked up at Reichmann. "Tell me about your event."

"The throwing events were in the infield; javelin, discus and hammer. Willi Schroder, the great discus man—a great German—was my friend. He helped me with my style and—"

"A field event!" Anna clasped her hands together. "Were you good? Did you win anything? Did you place? Of course you did! Tell me, Werner. How good were you?"

Reichmann looked out over the field. "Good? I am a German. It meant something then. I beat Schroder and Dunn. I beat the Italian, Oberweger. I beat them all."

Anna's breath caught in her throat. "You won? *You won!*"

"The gold medal," Reichmann said.

"Werner!" She threw her arms around him. "A celebrity! I

can't believe I am sleeping with a famous Olympian. I want to buy a book about the Olympics. They are everywhere now with the Olympics in Montreal. I want to see your name."

Reichmann shook his head solemnly. "No, Anna."

"But—"

"My name is not Stolz. I am not a writer from Austria."

"I don't understand, Wer— What is your name?"

"I am called Reichmann. Eduard Reichmann."

"Reichmann?"

He took her arm and they walked toward the infield. "I'll be leaving soon. There are things I must do. I don't know when I'll be home again."

"Home?" Anna stopped.

"With you," Reichmann said. "I'd like that."

"I don't understand, Werner. Eduard? What am I to call you?"

"Werner will do. Names mean nothing. I will have a new one when I return. But we are Werner and Anna. Today. Forever."

She shook her head trying to understand. "But—where are you going? What is this thing you—"

He touched her lips with a finger. "It isn't for you to worry," he said. "You must let me go without questions."

"Werner, please . . ." She turned to him, held both his hands in her own. "You must tell me something!"

"I was once the best in the world," he said, staring deeply into her face. "Here. At this place. But it was a long time ago. I don't compete in games anymore. A time may come when I can explain it to you so that you will understand. Can you wait?"

Anna was silent a long while. She stared at his hands in hers. When she looked up there were tears in her eyes. "I am forty-three years old. My husband left me because I was not—" she paused, took a breath "—not a, a, good woman for sex. I was not pretty, even then. I was a good *Hausfrau* for my father, but he is gone. I was Josef Weisse's daughter which was not a good thing to be. I . . . I . . ." She looked away a moment. "I am a lonely woman and I wish to be loved." Anna turned her eyes back to his. "Can you love me, Eduard Reichmann?" Her face was a portrait of terrible sadness.

Reichmann had seen that face before. When he was much younger. From another woman in another time who wiped his tears with the hem of an apron.

Reichmann wiped the wetness from her eyes with his thumbs. "Yes, Anna. I can love you."

"Then you must trust me. I promise you I will not interfere. Tell me—"

"I was SS." Reichmann held her face between his large hands. "I was specially trained to do very dangerous work and I killed many, many soldiers."

Anna's eyes opened wide. "SS!"

"For more than thirty years I have lived in South America. I escaped with Bormann and Mengele and Mueller and—"

"No!" She tried to pull away, but he would not let her go. "Listen to what I say!"

Anna closed her eyes tightly against the tears. "Not you . . . SS!"

"The high committee of the surviving Nazi hierarchy came to me—*me!*—because I have special qualifications. Listen to me! And I *will* do it." She was crying uncontrollably, flailing her arms. But Reichmann held her. "Listen! You wanted this, now listen! I trust you, Anna." He let her go and she collapsed on the grass of the infield. "You must hear me."

Anna crawled to her knees. Her face was puffy. She rubbed her temples where Reichmann had held her. "You were SS . . .?"

"I was not Himmler. I was not a Gestapo. I was not a butcher in the *Totenkopfverbaende* at Auschwitz!"

"Then why did you run away?"

"Are you a fool? All members of the SS were declared war criminals."

"The SS *were* criminals!" she shouted. "I know what they did! My father was accused too. War crimes. Crimes against humanity . . ."

"I was a German officer," Reichmann said. "I fought for my country and my Fuehrer. Did you ever see Dresden? Have you ever seen a sky black with bombers? The rubble with its dead after an Allied raid? Do not speak to me of war crimes."

Anna shook her head and covered her face with her hands. "I . . . I don't want to see. I don't!"

Reichmann reached for her hand. "Anna."

She said nothing.

"Anna." He touched her and she looked up. "I will come back for you."

Anna Weisse nodded.

"Will you come with me when I return?"

"Where must you go? What do you owe those, those Nazis!"

"I owe them nothing," Reichmann said. "It is they who owe me."

"But what you are going to do—it means killing?"

Reichmann inhaled a short breath. "Yes, but I will do it in any case. Will you wait for me then?"

She bowed her head. She was quiet a long time. Finally, she said, "Yes," but she did not look up.

24

"I do not know this man Eduard Reichmann."

Hans-Ulrich Rudel was seated in his favorite spot on the faded divan, near the telephone. Across from him Emma Diels sat with a coffee cup and saucer and munched politely on a fruit strudel. Aaron stood at the side of Emma's chair, hands clasped behind him, staring wearily at the floor as if it were infinitely more interesting than the rubbish he was hearing.

"I believe I met him once—twice, perhaps—during the war," Rudel was saying, "but that was a very long time ago. It would not surprise me to hear that he was killed during that winter of the counteroffensive. So many of our German soldiers were, you see."

"He wasn't killed," Aaron said without looking up.

Rudel shrugged. "Possibly not, but you search for a man who has not been seen or heard from in nearly thirty years. And a soldier?" He shrugged again.

"Major Eduard Reichmann of the Waffen-SS was not killed in the war and he has not died since." Aaron glanced up, grasping the back of Emma's chair. "I know it and you know it. Let's not continue this charade, Colonel Rudel."

Rudel shook his head like a man thoroughly bored with repeating the same answer to a tiresome query. "I must insist, I know nothing whatever about this Reichmann. How often must I tell you, Herr Miller? I admit I have maintained correspondences with many of my fellow officers and subordinates—even Nazis are permitted to have friends after so long a time. But I cannot be accountable for every German soldier who served with the Wehrmacht." Rudel paused to light a cigarette and Aaron returned his stare to the floor with an impatient shake of his head.

"Perhaps you should contact the HIAG—the Mutual Help Association. It is a welfare organization for former Waffen-SS personnel. I believe it is at Ludenscheid in Westphalia."

"Reichmann hasn't lived in Germany for thirty years," Aaron retorted hotly. "He wasn't *just a soldier*. He was a *Kettenhund*, like Skorzeny. And he's back at his old trade. He's hunting, only now he's after bigger game." Aaron looked up red-faced and angry. "But, then, you know all that, don't you, Herr Colonel? One way or another I'm going to stop him and you're going to help me!"

"It will do you no good to threaten me," Rudel said in a low, measured tone. "No good at all." He stubbed out his cigarette. "I think, perhaps, now you should leave. I have cooperated with you, answered your questions. I have nothing more to say." He started to get up from the divan when Emma raised her hand.

"Wait, please." She turned quickly to Aaron. "Aaron, this isn't the way."

"Christ! Don't *you* start!"

"We don't *know* that Reichmann came here."

"What?"

"Well, do we?"

"He's lying through his teeth," Aaron said.

She glared at him. "When we're thrown out of here, when we read in next week's newspaper who Reichmann's victim is . . . won't that be a fat lot of satisfaction to gloat over." Emma turned back to face Rudel. "I don't think you realize the situation—how drastic it is, Colonel Rudel. May I call you that?"

Rudel nodded. "What drastic situation?"

"We know about the *Oberkomitee*, Colonel. Reichmann was sent by them. He was here in Vienna only a few days ago. We *know* that."

Rudel shrugged as if none of it meant anything to him. Aaron noted a flicker of concern in his eyes, but it passed quickly. He'd been this way before.

"Miss Diels, must I say it again? I don't—"

"Is the urn so important that someone will die in place of its return?"

"Urn?" Rudel's gaze communicated nothing.

Emma studied him a moment then turned to Aaron. "Maybe . . ." She shook her head sadly. "Maybe we're wrong. It may only have been coincidence." She raised an eyebrow at Aaron. "Do you see what you've done, Aaron? You and Lubetkin. Why did you go to Paraguay? This is your fault, you know."

"Me!" Suddenly Aaron was on the defensive. Emma's turnabout caught him off guard. The idea was to interrogate the old man, not waste time fixing blame. Aaron stared at her with a bewildered look that turned quickly angry. "Why me!"

Emma avoided his eyes, she turned back to face Rudel. "Because," she said, holding Rudel's glance, "you stole the urn in the first place."

Her ploy had worked and Aaron understood it only when he saw the change of expression on the face of their host. Rudel's eyes widened. His fists clenched as if reacting to a threat. His eyes jerked up to see Aaron, instantly enraged, like a man faced by a lying accuser.

"You took *der Fuehrer's* urn!" The old man trembled with rage. "You destroyed the *Reichsgrabgewoelbe!*"

Emma nodded with a grim smile. "Yes, this man. And I can promise you, Colonel Rudel, unless you cooperate, we will melt down that precious article into eyeglass frames and trinkets for market in Tel Aviv and Jerusalem."

"You stole *der Fuehrer!*" the old man screamed madly at Aaron.

"And you can have him back," Aaron replied. "For a price."

Emma leaned forward, catching his attention. "Tell us about Reichmann," she said. "We must stop Reichmann."

Rudel blinked, anxiously rubbed a hand across his face. "I cannot tell you about Reichmann."

He seemed to look smaller, sitting in the corner of the divan, Aaron thought. He was vulnerable now as all old men are vulerable when their security is undone. "He was here then?" Aaron said.

"I cannot tell you about Reichmann." Rudel looked at his hands. "We are bound by trust."

"Trust?"

"I have pledged my word . . . I . . ."

"Reichmann trusted Strausser and the others," Aaron said. "Now they want to make a new deal—Reichmann's life for the urn."

Rudel glanced furtively up at Aaron. "It does not surprise me so much. They are not men of honor. They are not men like Reichmann. They are scum." He exhaled a long sigh. "Eduard knew that too. He is no fool. You should not underestimate him. You made a mistake if you believe he trusted Strausser. Reichmann is a cunning and resourceful foe." Rudel shook his head sorrowfully. "I cannot tell you about Reichmann because I know nothing of his plan."

"He came to you for help?"

"For papers," said the old man. "Identity papers and passport documents. I know nothing more than that."

"It's enough," Aaron said. "What name is he using?"

Rudel shrugged. "I supplied him only with the names of technicians who specialize in false identities. He said he would require three identities."

"Three?"

"Eduard Reichmann is a cautious man in his work."

"I want those names," Aaron said.

"If he has a reason to return to his homeland after so long a time, I think you will not find him, whatever his purpose."

"His purpose," Emma said quickly, "is to assassinate a head of state. Revenge. Stupid, childish revenge."

"No," Rudel said. "Not at all, Not to him. Reichmann is not an ordinary man driven by ordinary motives. If you find him you will learn that."

"Just give me the passport dealers," Aaron said. "I'll worry about the rest. And let me remind you that your involvement up to this point is conspiracy to commit murder . . ." Aaron started to count on his fingers but Rudel waved him off.

"You needn't bother with all that. It means nothing to me. I will give you the names only because I know it will do you no good."

"We're talking about saving a life," Emma said quietly. "Does that mean anything to you?"

"What it means to me is not important, Miss Diels. You say the *Oberkomitee* has doublecrossed Reichmann." He paused, offered a weak smile. "They are the fools." To Aaron he said, "And you, Herr Miller, you have unleashed a fury that will not be contained. Reichmann does not care about the *Oberkomitee*, unless I have grossly misjudged his intentions, and I think I have not. You would know that if you understood Reichmann. His allegiance was always, from the very beginning, to the Fuehrer. Why, you will discover for yourself. But I will tell you this, Reichmann *believed* in the Fuehrer. More than any of us. He was Hitler's . . . creation. And now, after two generations, that faith is not diminished. But the roles are reversed. The Fuehrer—his honor, at least— needs him. Reichmann and no other. You see, it makes no difference what the *Oberkomitee* says or does anymore. If Reichmann is after the urn, then he will have it. If he intends to strike at a head of government, then it is his way of apportioning punishment. It is *his* crusade now, not the Straussers in Brazil. And he will be victorious because it is his due." Rudel lay back on the divan. He was obviously tired but his stance suggested an odd capacity to recoil from pressure or shock like a resilient prizefighter.

"The names," Aaron repeated coldly. "Tell me who the forgers are, their addresses."

Rudel nodded his head slowly. "Of course." He brought a pad to his lap and took a pen from the stand near the telephone. As he wrote, Rudel asked, "I am curious. I assume a deadline has been set. Do you mind telling me when? With so many terrorist acts these days, it would be interesting to note which death to attribute to Reichmann."

Aaron shook his head in disgust and said nothing.

"This coming Sunday," Emma replied.

Rudel nodded. He handed the pad with the names over to her. "Only four days? You think you will find Eduard Reichmann in four days?" He shook his head. "You will need much more than a list of names."

"We'll do it," Aaron said. "We're all going to celebrate his birthday with a bang."

Rudel tugged one of his earlobes. "Birthday?"

"It's the day he set as the deadline," Emma said, reaching for her handbag. She tore the top page off the pad and placed it inside the purse. "Sunday, August first."

Suddenly, Rudel smiled like a man who'd just been provided the answer to a devilishly ingenious puzzle. "Ah, yes," he said, grinning and nodding as if at a private joke. "Indeed, yes. Sunday *is* Eduard Reichmann's birthday."

From the belltower of a nearby church, chimes toned the passing of another hour. Vienna was always a precise city.

Anna did all the driving. From Berlin to Hamburg, some three hundred kilometers, she did not speak and Reichmann did not encourage her. He'd been sullen and tense since the previous afternoon's confrontation in the stadium. He had not slept well and they had not made love. Anna was afraid to speak, unsure of what to say, frightened of provoking a scene. Reichmann, from nearly the moment he settled himself in the Volkswagen, occupied himself with a road directory, a gazette of departure and arrival times of federal express trains and a KLM schedule of Continental flights.

She followed the autobahn into the city and, on Reichmann's instructions, parked at a large car park near the Kunsthalle Museum of Art. With his two bags, Reichmann walked Anna to a park bench in the public gardens.

"Go back to Munich," he said, setting the bags down. "The Koenigshof." He handed her an envelope secured with an elastic band. "A room is reserved in the name of Stolz, one with a pleasant view. I'll find you there."

Anna looked at the envelope. "Money?"

"Our nest egg," he said. "In a week I'll join you and we'll go wherever you like."

"And if you do not come?"

Reichmann looked away impatiently.

"Yes, all right," she said. "In a week . . . at the Koenigshof." Reichmann nodded and she took his hand in both of hers. "It is so important . . . Werner . . ." Anna paused, took a breath, searched his face for sympathy. "I could—I would not be trouble. . . ." She glanced down at his hand. "I could . . . go with you."

"No."

"But—"

"No!"

"Is it so dangerous, Werner?"

Reichmann withdrew his hand. He glanced back over his shoulder as if concerned someone might be watching. "It isn't for you to worry," he said quietly.

"But I do worry!" she blurted.

Reichmann said nothing. He stared at her and she tried to avoid his blue eyes. "I'm afraid. It's dangerous, I know it is! I—If you are hurt or . . ." Anna shook her head, afraid to admit an alternative. ". . . if something happened, I would not know. At least, tell me where you are going . . . a city . . . something! Please, Werner!"

"It isn't for you to worry," he said again. Reichmann touched her hair and, without smiling, took her hand. "I must go now."

"Yes." She would not cry. She held him tightly for several moments, then he took his bags and she did not kiss him good-bye.

Anna Weisse sat stiffly at the bench and watched him walk down the tree-lined sidewalk. From behind her came the scream of a railway train noisily decelerating into the central *Bahnhof* station, and it suddenly occurred to her where he was headed. Far down the sidewalk, Reichmann stopped for a group of children as they emptied out of a bus and scrambled toward the entrance of the Kunsthalle. He turned and looked back and Anna offered a timid wave, but he did not see her or declined to acknowledge.

For several minutes Anna did not move. Another train came into the station, interrupting her thoughts. She would drive back to Munich this afternoon. Perhaps she would stop in Kassel. She had an aunt in Kassel. . . . Frau Grass, on Tischbeinstrasse. Perhaps they could visit the Löwenburg Castle. Late eighteenth-century architecture, a fantasy in the Romantic manner, with a valuable collection of arms and armor . . .

The strident shrill of another train's braking action abruptly jolted her upright. She looked to see the huge black diesel engine screech toward the Hackmannplatz overpass, sounding its arrival with a burst of its whistle.

He can't go like this! He can't leave me with nothing! Suddenly Anna was on her feet, walking quickly down the sidewalk. She would be satisfied if she knew at least where he was going. Only that. She passed the park beyond the museum. The *Hauptbahnhof* was a huge station a city block square. The ticket booths were on the far north side. Anna Weisse stuffed the envelope full of money into her handbag. Then she ran.

"Oh, yes, fräulein," said the clerk behind the iron-barred ticket counter, "the tall blond one with the bags. Your husband?"

Anna had been to three windows before she found the clerk who'd waited on Reichmann. "Yes, yes . . . he forgot something. I must catch him before—"

"Benelux express to Amsterdam," said the clerk, holding his finger at a spot midway down the list of the departure schedule.

"Which platform?" Anna glanced frantically in the direction where a train was pulling out.

The clerk looked over the top of his glasses. "I am sorry, Fräulein . . ."

"Which platform!"

"The express left just two minutes ago."

"No!" Anna screamed. She could hold back the tears no longer.

"Fraulein . . . please . . ."

"Amsterdam, you said?"

The clerk hesitated, slightly flustered, as if he wasn't prepared to handle a woman on the brink of hysteria. "Perhaps . . . perhaps this was not your husband."

Anna shook her head, wiping at the tears. "I'm sorry. It's— you're sure it was Amsterdam?"

"Oh, yes," the clerk said, visibly relieved to see she was regaining control. "He also inquired after a KLM flight schedule for Rome, but I had to—"

"Rome!"

The man behind the iron bars nodded, as reassuring as possible. "Shall I make you a ticket for the next express?"

Anna bowed her head. She was aware of the line of people behind her at the booth, then pulled her handbag slowly from the counter. "No," she said without looking up. "Thank you for your trouble."

"The next one leaves in an hour," the clerk offered helpfully as she started away.

"Italy isn't so far," she said. "It isn't far at all."

"Pardon?" said the clerk.

She glanced up. "Nothing," she said. "It isn't for me to worry."

Reichmann watched her leave the station from beside a row of lockers on the second level overlooking the central lobby. He watched her bump slowly, dazedly through the crowd and out the large entrance, then moved to a window beside a vending machine and watched as she continued up the walkway toward the Kunsthalle and the car park beyond. He watched her until she was gone. Anna Weisse. His Lili.

Reichmann didn't need the twenty thousand Deutschemarks and he was convinced they would let her keep it. They wouldn't want the money. They would question her and they would believe her because she believed herself. It was something Reichmann had learned and remembered from the war. An effective deception perfected by the British. It had fooled Rommel until it was too late to act decisively. Now it would fool them. Rome was the illusion, the ruse; and they would believe it just as the High Command had believed in Calais.

Anna Weisse was the innocent victim. Reichmann understood that. He had used her and he was sorry for that, but the fact did not overly concern him. What was important was the final objective. If the means, however unpleasant, delivered results, then the responsibility of a good tactician was to exploit every available aid.

Anna Weisse lent credibility to the fraud. He stood at the window awhile longer. *Perhaps,* he thought, *she will use the money wisely.*

Reichmann visited the men's toilet and once inside the privacy of a stall, extracted the fake red Austrian passport and carefully ripped out the first page along the seam. He tore the page with the photograph into small pieces and flushed them down the commode. Before leaving the rest room, he washed his hands and with the paper towel he'd used to dry he crumpled the passport book and dropped it in the refuse bin. Even if it were found, the identity page was missing.

The *Kettenhund,* now a Swiss merchant from Geneva, followed the flow of traffic down the escalator. He stopped and bought a news magazine and made his way to a row of counters. He cashed in his Amsterdam ticket, then stood in line at the next purchasing window.

All his preparations had been completed. There was nothing more to do but wait. There was one other plane to catch, but there was still plenty of time. He'd call Strausser, too. Reichmann looked forward to that. In the meantime, he had one last item of business to look after. It had been on his mind since Vienna. And he'd saved it till now.

When the tall blond man reached the front of the line, he folded his magazine and slid it under one arm. "Destination, *mein Herr?*" asked the ticket clerk perfunctorily.

"Heidelberg," Reichmann said. "First class, *bitte.*"

25

Juantoreno had won the 400-meter gold medal which made the Cuban the first athlete in history to take both the 400- and 800-meter runs in the modern Olympic Games. And television commentators around the world spread the news.

In a Vienna hotel, Aaron Miller scribbled notes as fast as Emma Diels could relate them to him from her source on the telephone. In the background, from the small television beside a balcony window, a sports broadcaster droned on low volume. Had they been listening, they would have been aware that West Germany's Guido Kratschmer led the decathlon competition after five events, eighteen points ahead of the Russian Avilov and thirty-five points ahead of the American Bruce Jenner. No one knew it was significant.

"Yes, right," Emma said into the telephone. She was sitting on the bed in Aaron's room, balancing a cup of coffee on her knee and trying to talk and drink at the same time. "Thank you, Richard."

As she hung up Aaron said, "Now we're getting somewhere." He rubbed his hands together, looking at the notes.

"I told you my contacts were valuable." She nodded at the phone, took a long sip of coffee. "Richard has friends with the Maupintour agency who have access to the reservations computers." She poured more coffee from the pot on the nightstand. "We get a name from the man in Vienna, Richard's friends plug it into their electronic marvel and voilà!"

"Werner Stolz," Aaron said, checking the sheet of notes. "Stayed at the Maria Theresia one night—last Thursday the twenty-second—made two calls. One to Munich, one to Nuremberg. Made a reservation for the weekend at the Koenigshof in Munich and the next morning rented a car."

"I'll bet you a doughnut the call to Nuremberg was to a passport forger." Emma pointed to the second name on the list Rudel had made. "Conrad Lindermann."

"We'll find out," Aaron said. He glanced back at his notes. "Reichmann's been moving around a lot. He was at the Sonnenhof Hotel in Vaduz, Leichtenstein, Friday and turned in the rental at Baden-Baden Saturday morning."

"Heading for Munich?"

"Got to be. But what is in Munich? So far, we know he's been to see two passport counterfeiters . . . Vienna and Graz. The last one is in Nuremberg. So why Munich?"

"At least we know two of the names he's using," Emma said. "Stolz and . . ." She looked at Rudel's list. "Paul Daimler from Switzerland."

"What bothers me is we haven't heard from him since Baden-Baden. That was five days ago. If he's using the Swiss identity, he hasn't made it known."

"Not necessarily," Emma said. "This information from Richard is only good if he checks in at a hotel or rents an automobile or tries to fly. Something on paper. Reservations. But if he stays with a friend or travels by rail we don't have any way to know."

Aaron frowned. "There's another possibility. He may have dumped the Stolz I.D. He may not have started to use the Swiss passport yet." He swore.

"The third set of papers?" Emma said.

"Maybe he already has the new papers from the guy in Nuremberg. It's been five days. If Reichmann is using those papers he could be out of Germany."

"He could be out of Europe," Emma corrected.

Aaron went quickly to the closet for his coat. "Start calling your friends, my love. Get people moving in Munich and Nuremberg."

"Where are you going?"

"Hirsch," Aaron said. "He's checking with Bar Tov. I want to know what he has, if anything. And see about a charter plane. If we have to leave I don't want to wait around for trains or TWA."

"They're expensive, Aaron, and we won't find anything on this short notice leaving the Continent."

"If he's left Europe we're in big trouble anyway. His target is here—Germany, France, England—here. It has to be."

Emma shrugged as if they had to believe something. "Right." She kissed his cheek. "Bring more coffee, will you, darling?"

Aaron took the lift to Stevens' floor. He knocked, but Hirsch did not reply. He waited several minutes, then took the elevator to the lobby. At the front desk Aaron asked if Hirsch had left any messages.

"Messages?" the deskman repeated pleasantly. "No, Herr Miller. But Herr Hirsch has not left."

"I was just at his room," Aaron said impatiently. "He doesn't answer."

"But . . ." The deskman raised his hand, whispered to the switchboard operator. He turned back smiling. "Ah, the gentleman's phone is in use."

"Now?"

"Yes, Herr Miller. For some time."

"Well, cut in then, will you?" Aaron moved to the house phone.

The smiling deskman seemed at first embarrassed, then confused. "I'm sorry, sir, I cannot break into a conversation." He hesitated, looking at the switchboard girl. She nodded at him, whispered something. When he glanced back at Aaron, the deskman looked confused. "There is no one there."

"He's not talking to anyone?"

"No, sir."

"The phone's off the hook," Aaron said quickly.

"Perhaps the gentleman is sleeping and does not wish to be disturbed." A polite smile followed.

Aaron stared at the glowing switchboard light beside room number 306. Hirsch wasn't supposed to be sleeping. Bar Tov's people didn't sleep. But there was another possibility. He remembered Linka. "Do you have a passkey?"

The hotel clerk raised an eyebrow. "Pardon?"

"Passkey!" Aaron banged a fist on the counter. "Do you have a passkey?"

"Herr Miller, I cannot—"

"Where's the house detective?"

The clerk faltered, surprised at the sudden outburst. "We . . . do not employ—"

"Come with me," Aaron commanded. He grasped the man by the sleeve and motioned with his head. "Get the passkey and come with me!"

"But . . ."

"Schnell!"

The elevator wouldn't move fast enough. At Hirsch's door, the clerk paused to knock.

"Open it."

"But, mein Herr, only if there is an emergency . . ."

"Christ, yes," Aaron shouted.

He fumbled with the keys. The lock clicked open and Aaron burst into an empty room. Hirsch's suitcase was neatly folded open on the luggage stand. There was a suit in the closet. The telephone was on the bed, its receiver off the cradle, and beside it, scattered across the bedspread, were pages from a notebook.

"Hirsch?"

"There is no one here, mein Herr." The desk clerk was still at the door, bracing it open with his foot as if trespassing was less objectionable if everyone could see it. "There is no emergency. You are mistaken."

Miller went to the phone, listened. Nothing.

"You must leave at once," said the man.

"He wasn't suppose to leave," Aaron said. He saw the light under the door to the bath. When he started toward it, the clerk headed him off.

"You must come with me to the manager," the man said, embarrassed.

"Check in there."

"No." Now he was getting angry. There would be enough explaining as it was for letting this man talk him into openig the door.

"Look . . . he may be sick. Just check. Then I'll go."

The man wasn't convinced, but he wasn't not convinced. He motioned Aaron to stand aside. "Herr Hirsch?" He tapped politely on the door. "Herr Hirsch?" With the trepidation of a timid cat burglar, he eased the handle down and pushed gently on the door. "Herr—" Suddenly, he froze rock still. "*Ach, du liebe Gott!*" He stepped back reflexively, banging against the door. "*Liebe Gott!*"

Aaron bolted by him. He knew instantly what he'd find, but not what he'd see. "Oh, Jesus!" Aaron looked quickly away, revolted, helplessly enraged.

Hirsch lay in the bathtub. From the look of it, it hadn't been much of a fight. One arm was bent crazily back at the shoulder hanging over the edge, the other floated beside him in the pink soapy water where his death struggle had produced grotesque rosy bubbles. Hirsch's throat had been laid open jaggedly as if by a very sharp instrument used several times and hurriedly. His head rested back over the edge of the tub, eyes horribly wide, mouth gaping.

"Jesus!" Aaron pushed by the man in the doorway with his hand over his mouth and ran to the phone. He banged on the disconnect button for the operator. The pages of Hirsch's notes were in front of him. Lists, check marks beside names, doodlings, scribblings by a man patiently jotting down leads. Aaron scanned one of the pages. Something caught his eye. A name beside a city.

"Yes, sir?" The operator's voice was warm and polite.

"Get me—"

The explosion blasted ceiling plaster like tiny bullets all over the room in a violent shower of debris. The concussion shattered the overhead chandelier, blew the plastic paintings off the wall, disintegrated the windows.

Aaron covered his head beside the bed until the rain of ceiling plaster was over. For perhaps fifteen seconds, the immediate aftermath of the detonation was total silence. Then he heard people stumbling out of rooms, crying, angry voices, confusion. The automatic sprinkler system in the corridor spurted to life. Aaron sat up from the floor. He made a stupid attempt to raise the operator again but the line was dead. Then he realized where the explosion had originated. The blast had been from the floor above. His floor. Where Emma was.

Emma! Aaron ran like a crazy man, knocking people aside, galloping up the stairs. The fourth-floor corridor was filled with dazed guests trying to get out. The ruptured sprinkler system was spewing water everywhere. Smoke was billowing from his room.

What used to be a room. The door was gone and what remained was a jagged hole in the wall. Inside, a portion of the carpet was burning. Nearly nothing was still intact. Aaron pushed against the splintered remains of a wall stud where the closet had been and a section of the ceiling collapsed. He looked out at the gaping breach where the balcony doors had been and saw the people standing in the street, mouths open on upturned faces.

"Emma?" Aaron stumbled through the rubble. "Emma . . . *Emma!*"

The man with the knife seemed to come from nowhere. Aaron heard the sound of glass crunch underfoot and turned quickly toward the door leading to Emma's room. He was a scrawny, haggard man in a long slick raincoat whose eyes were as black as his hair. He came through the door quickly as if he had been surprised and he held the knife in his bony fist, blade down, like he meant to stab a piece of meat with a fork.

When he lunged, he raised the knife high in the air.

It was as if Henry had sent a target for Aaron to practice on. There wasn't time to explain. He was holding the blade wrong from start to finish. *Never, never handle a knife like a ripper unless you are cutting carpet. A slasher gives away balance, eye contact and initiative for one overhead thrust. The Jack the Ripper approach is based on the theory that the victim will reel back or simply freeze with terror. He will not expect you to attack.*

Aaron attacked. Henry would not have called his awkward lunge forward very coordinated, but, then, Henry had never actually tried to open his head with a six-inch blade. Aaron thrust himself forward, stepping inside the radius of the swing, both arms straight at the elbow, wrists rigid, fingers extended and locked. The slasher's momentum carried him into Aaron's killing blow. The full impact of their collision came at a point just below the man's Adam's apple, in the soft fleshy part of the neck with a nearly inaudible snap as Aaron's unflexing fingers crushed the trachea, larynx and two cervical vertebrae.

The whole encounter had taken less than five seconds, yet in that span Aaron had lost consciousness of the shambles of the room, the fire, the people in the hall, even Emma. There was only he and the man with the knife. When it was over the sounds and feeling of fear rushed back to him. No words had passed between them, but there was no mistaking that the man on the glass-covered floor was dead and Aaron was not. *Every man has asked himself if he could kill another even in self-defense. Few ever are put to the test. You will be. It will be a surprisingly short, brutal struggle and when it's over you'll know, one way or another. There is no other way.*

Aaron knelt down and picked up the knife. He suddenly realized it probably was the death weapon used on Hirsch. He hurriedly searched the body. There was no identification, but the lining of the raincoat had a large empty pouch and a smaller one filled with blasting caps. The dead man was the bomber. The others, if there were any, had left him to mop up; finish off him or Emma, Aaron figured. They must have passed each other on the elevators when Aaron went to the lobby. No wonder he looked so surprised to find Aaron unharmed. But how long had he been here before Aaron arrived? Had he found . . .

Aaron was on his feet instantly. *"Emma? Emma!"*

There was a groan. Then, "Aaron . . . here, Aaron . . ."

He followed the voice into the adjoining room. The force of the blast had been concentrated in Aaron's room, near the door, and the old solid walls separating his room from Emma's had absorbed most of the impact of the explosion, but it was still a shambles. Broken glass crunched under his feet as he searched. He found her on the floor in the dressing room between the bathroom and the bedroom.

"Emma." He knelt beside her, quickly checking for injuries. "Are you all right?" Aaron held her face in his hands.

She shook her head, slightly dazed. "Of course, I'm not all right, but nothing's broken." She rubbed her arm. "I fell on my elbow. What happened?"

"Somebody bombed my room." He helped her up. "Can you walk?"

"What do you mean, somebody?"

"In there." Aaron nodded toward the remains of his room. "He's dead." He looked into her eyes. "I killed a man, Emma, the way Henry taught me. It was easy."

Emma touched his face with her fingers, lightly at the temples. "You're . . . not hurt?"

He shook his head. "No. Bar Tov said we were in danger. He wasn't kidding." Aaron brushed her hair back from her face. "What were you doing in here? I mean, I thought you were in my room—"

"Coffee," Emma said. She smiled weakly.

"What?"

"Too much coffee I should say." Emma nodded toward the bathroom. "Fortunately I chose the room with the loo."

Aaron closed his eyes, sighed.

"I was washing my face and I heard glass break on your side. I started to see what it was . . . this is as far as I got."

Aaron nodded. "You feel like traveling?"

"You think I want to stay here?"

"Hirsch is dead," Aaron said.

"Oh, God!"

"Our terrorist friends really don't want us around."

"You sure it was them?" Emma said quickly.

"It wasn't the bellboy."

"I mean Reichmann, maybe—"

"Reichmann? Christ, Emma, Reichmann doesn't care about us, if he even knows we're looking for him."

"But—"

"*Everybody* is looking for Reichmann. Why should he suddenly focus attention on himself by striking at us? His scheme is to keep everyone guessing. He's gone to a lot of trouble to guarantee that. He doesn't have time to stop and play with us. And the reason is he isn't worried. He doesn't think he *can* be stopped."

"I'm beginning to wonder if we can."

"Well, I'm not." Aaron brushed the chalky dust from his coatsleeves. "We're leaving for Munich as soon as we can get out of here."

"Munich? What makes you think we'll be any better off—"

"Hirsch found it," Aaron said. "In his notes. He just didn't know he discovered anything."

"And what's that?"

Aaron pulled the crumpled sheet of notes from his pocket. "This. Hirsch was following up the telephone leads, among other things. The call to Munich, the one Reichmann made from his hotel in Innsbruck. It was to Josef Weisse."

"So?"

"Jesus, Emma, you're supposed to be the Nazi expert here!"

"Please excuse my ignorance." She sounded hurt. "Who is Josef Weisse?"

"I remembered the name from Lubetkin's files. He was something like a hero to the Germans between the wars. A gunsmith. An armorer. He designed the Luger or something revolutionary like that. Hitler gave him the Iron Cross. That's who Reichmann was going to see in Munich. Not a forger, a gunsmith."

"To buy a gun?"

"To procure a weapon perhaps," Aaron replied. "There's a difference. Weisse is a specialist. Reichmann is getting only the best. It might be anything."

"A rifle? Sniper scope?"

"Anything," Aaron said.

The caretaker of the Odenwald cemetery, Gustav Bredow, was a small benign man with thinning hair and glasses. The second son of an Austrian caretaker, he was the last of four generations of burial stewards and took seriously his task as overseer and custodian of the final resting place and its grounds. If he was dismayed that he represented the end of the line of his family's metier owing to his own bachelorhood, it was a quiet internal grief as if a man of his station and responsibility should set the example, even if it was to himself. So when he met with the man whose special request required Gustav Bredow's attention, he was understanding and especially kind because the man seemed embarrassed and somehow uneasy with the encounter.

"Yours is not an unusual request, mein Herr," Bredow said in his most reassuring voice. They were sitting at a concrete slab table in a small garden shaded from the late morning sun but not its heat. He dabbed demurely at the line of perspiration along his upper lip with a linen kerchief. "A transfer is not so uncommon. It can be easily arranged."

The man in the gray suit nodded but said nothing. The caretaker suspected that his reticence was self-consciousness. Generally, large men frightened him, that is, men with a certain restrained calmness about them, and this one undeniably had that quality of menace in his eyes, in his quiet manner. The difference was this man had come to him for help, hat in hand, so to speak, greatly humbled by his request. It was a mood the Bredow family had prided itself in managing as if bereavement was an exacting enterprise.

The caretaker adjusted his spectacles as he glanced at the application before him. "It says here you wish to have the late departed moved to Ehrenfriedhof." He bowed his head to see over the glasses. "A military cemetery. You understand arrangements must be made and permission granted?"

"Yes," the blond man across from Bredow replied courteously. "I have authorization from the federal ministry and certificates establishing military service." He pushed an envelope over the concrete surface. "My father died as a result of an infirmity received in the battle of Ypres, October 1917. Mustard gas. He was a sergeant in the 16th Bavarian Reserve Infantry Regiment."

"I see." The caretaker nodded sympathetically. "And you wish your mother to take her place beside him?"

"At Ehrenfriedhof, yes."

"A transit burial permit is required. . . ." Bredow dabbed again at his lip and once quickly across his forehead. "But that is a small matter. You indicate here that no ceremony is necessary."

"No. Is it customary?"

The caretaker shrugged. "Sometimes . . . but usually only when the most recently deceased is joined by the earlier departed in a transfer for a double service. It is an arrangement most common when a husband predeceases the wife and ceremonies for both are held at the final resting place of the wife."

"That won't be required in this instance. My mother died in 1945." He looked squarely at Bredow, and the caretaker was struck by the compelling coldness in his voice. "She hasn't any friends who would attend that sort of service."

A quick gust caught the application and Bredow slapped it down before it could get away. "You've left the date of the transfer open," he said, sliding to one side a bit to move out of a patch of sunlight. "Is there a time you'd like us to set it?"

"Next week or the week after. There is one other arrangement I have to negotiate. My brother. It requires another exhumation and transfer, but I believe we can settle on a date here at your convenience."

"Will you be attending the burial?" asked the caretaker.

"No. I was told by the federal ministry that only the signature of next of kin is necessary for exhumation and reburial."

"And the transit permit," Bredow offered politely.

"Yes."

"I assume your brother also had a war service record."

The man only nodded and Bredow felt immediately embarrassed for raising the question. "I mean, Ehrenfriedhof is strictly a military cemetery," he said to explain his prying. "Except for spouses . . . that is, ah, wives . . ."

"Wehrmacht," the man said. "He was with the Afrika Korps. Killed in action in Libya, 1942. I have only recently found his grave. I want to bring the family back together." He offered what Bredow considered an amused look. "Ehrenfriedhof has assured me of their willingness to receive his remains."

"Of course," the caretaker said quickly, touching the white linen again above his mouth. "Your signature is all I must have along with an identity card as proof of kinship for the transfer arrangements of your dearly beloved mother."

"I would like also a new coffin, Herr Bredow."

The caretaker nodded. "It is part of our service."

"Your very finest," said the man insistently. "Expense is not a consideration."

"A most commendable gesture." Bredow felt a sudden need to express his compassion to this quiet man with the pale blue eyes. "There is a quite lovely interment facility here in Heidelberg with a selection of quality—"

"I prefer to let you handle such details personally, Herr Bredow, if you agree, of course."

Bredow nodded graciously. "Yes, I understand and I would be pleased to help in any way. I will make a selection of dignity and grace."

The man stood up between Bredow and the sun. He placed another envelope before the bespectacled caretaker. "Will five thousand Deutschemarks cover all the arrangements?"

"Five thousand?" Bredow exclaimed. He shook his head vigorously. "No, no . . . it is too much. More than twice the—"

"Please accept it with my good intentions. I value your

judgment most highly, and since I cannot be present to look after the arrangements I trust it is payment enough for your time."

"But, mein Herr—"

"Please," the man said.

Bredow started to object but thought better of it. "You may be sure the arrangements will see my personal attention."

"Thank you." The man glanced out at the landscaped grounds. "If you do not mind, I would like to take a few moments . . ." He turned back to Bredow. "I will join you later and we can finish the business."

He hadn't waited for a response from the caretaker, but just turned and walked away, leaving Bredow with the formal application and the envelope of money.

Reichmann stood a very long while at his mother's grave.

26

Aaron knocked at the door several times and got no response. The shutters on the windows were closed tight. A house couldn't look more deserted.

"Are you sure this is the right address?"

Emma took the notepad from her purse. "Fifty-eight Luisenstrasse Platz," she said. "This is Josef Weisse's home."

Aaron knocked again, louder, with the same result. From a second-floor window of the neighboring address a woman dressed in a housecoat raised the sash and stuck her head out.

"*Neimand zu Hause,*" she said. Aaron heard a baby crying.

"We're looking for Herr Weisse," he said quickly in German before she withdrew from the opening. "Herr Josef Weisse."

"Weisse?" She held a diaper by the upper corners and folded it lengthwise.

"Yes, do you know where he is, please?"

"*Ja, freilich,*" she said, nodding confidently. "*Herr Weisse ist am Freitag gestorben.*" She slammed the window shut and disappeared.

"Dead?"

"Reichmann was here all right," Emma said cynically. "He's not leaving anyone behind to spin any tales when he goes. You still think he didn't have something to do with Stevens' death?"

Aaron sighed. "No."

"No! Aaron, Weisse is dead!"

"Yes, since Friday. Didn't you hear her?" Aaron nodded toward the second-floor window. "Friday. Reichmann couldn't have been here Friday. He was in Verona intimidating a bishop. Saturday morning he turned in his rented car in Baden-Baden. Weisse is dead, but Reichmann didn't kill him."

"Who did?"

"Who? Jesus, Emma, I wish I had your cheerful outlook. People do still die in their sleep. They call it natural causes." He turned, started down the walk. "C'mon."

"Where now?"

"Someone around here must have known him. Let's find out who."

No one was home at the first door they tried. Or the next. The third was a young housewife who kept children in her home for working parents. Finally, at a house across the cobblestone street, they found a man who knew Weisse.

"Yes, I was acquainted with Josef," the old man said. He smoked a long pipe and the smell seemed to have been absorbed into the faded wallpaper of his small parlor. His name was Graf and he wore corduroy trousers with wide colorful suspenders. "Does he owe you money?"

"No," Aaron said. "We're trying to locate someone who probably came to see him Saturday."

"He owed me money," the old man said. He shrugged. "But not so much. We played some chess in the park on Domplatz. That was before they took all the benches." He nodded at the window. "Children. Too many children."

"You knew him well?" Emma said.

"We walked together sometimes," Graf sighed. "But not since a year ago. Josef was sick this last year." He pointed to his chest. "Here." Then to his head. "And, I think, here. The little ones, they cry, and too much. Always they are at it. Over there—" he stuck the pipe out at the window"—Frau Berchtold. Her little one is worst of all. It is not good for old men to hear always the crying, *ja?*"

"About Herr Weisse," Aaron said.

He nodded. *"Ja*, dead. Too bad. Buried Saturday. He owed me some money, too." The old man grunted, shook his head.

"Did you see anyone come round Saturday?" Aaron said. "To see Weisse."

"No."

"You're sure? Not a tall man with blond hair?"

Graf took a long puff on his pipe and exhaled a rank cloud of smoke toward Emma. He seemed to be taken with her.

"I'm not here on Saturdays," he replied to Aaron, but his eyes were on Emma. "I go to Friesing with my son-in-law on Saturdays to visit the grandchildren."

"Swell," Aaron said. He started to leave. "Thank you, Herr Graf."

"Did you know how he died?" Emma asked.

"An attack of the heart." Graf smiled at her around the pipe. He didn't have any teeth. "I heard he collapsed in the parlor. A long time he was there before Anna found him. I think he was dead anyway, before then. Josef was very old."

"Anna?" Emma glanced quickly at Aaron. "Who is Anna?"

"Anna," the old man said as if everyone knew her. "Josef's daughter." He shook his head. "Not so pretty like you. Sad, too, she was married but he left her. But Anna was a good woman, she took care of Josef. A good housekeeper. No children."

"She lived there?" Aaron said.

"Yes."

"Where is she now?"

Graf shrugged. "Gone. We are mostly pensioners here, except the *Wohlfahrt* fraus . . . and the little ones. Josef lived here on a pension like me. When he died they asked Anna to move." He nodded sadly. "Poor Anna."

"How can we find her?" Emma said.

"I do not know. Monday, when I returned from Friesing,

the house was being closed. Anna and her friend were leaving—"

"What friend?" Aaron asked quickly. "Was it a man?"

The old man Graf sucked thoughtfully on his pipe. "You are sure Josef does not owe you money?"

"Was it a man?" Aaron repeated impatiently, "with blond hair?"

"He was sitting in the autocar," Graf said, slightly startled. "I did not notice if—"

"Reichmann." Aaron said. "Has to be. No wonder he hasn't turned up. He's traveling with the girl."

Emma made a face. "You think he got what he was after?"

"Maybe . . ."

The old man pointed the pipe at Emma, waving it back and forth in the air to draw her attention. "*Fräulein, fräulein* . . . is it Anna that owes him money?" He nodded at Aaron. "Anna?"

"No, Herr Graf. What kind of autocar does Anna own?"

"Volkswagen," he said uncertainly. "A gray Volkswagen. But I do not know where she could be."

"That's all right," Aaron said. He took Emma by the arm. "You've been a big help. Thanks."

Graf stood in his doorway and watched them hurry down the narrow street. He was not so old he couldn't appreciate a pretty young fräulein and this one was pleasant to look at. Much prettier than Anna. Younger. She had a nice bounce about her, the way she tried to keep up with the young man. The old man sighed. He took the pipe from his mouth and knocked the bowl against the palm of his hand, emptying tobacco cinders on the walk. "Anna won't have any money," he said with a sad shake of the head. When he heard baby Berchtold across the way crying, the old man retreated back to the quiet of his own room. Children were not meant to be heard on Luisenstrasse Platz.

Aaron drummed his fingers on the tabletop. He hadn't touched the coffee. Emma had made several calls at a coin box and they had waited nearly an hour at a street café on

Sonnenstrasse near the Sendlinger Gate. When the man came, Aaron was singularly unimpressed. His name was Jacques Crevecoeur. He was short, very short, with gray close-cropped hair, bushy eyebrows and a large nose. If he was two feet taller he might have been mistaken as a blood relative of Charles de Gaulle. To make matters worse, Emma called him *le Souris*—the mouse—a nickname he'd acquired during the war as a member of the Resistance. Crevecoeur seemed very jolly at the moment, a mood Aaron did not share. The Mouse ordered coffee and the attendant brought Aaron another cup as well. When they were alone, Crevecoeur slid his chair nearer Emma and leaned forward as if he had something of importance to relate. Aaron doubted it. The Frenchman, in his wide-collar shirt that opened in a deep vee exposing tufts of gray hair on his chest, did not strike an image in his mind of a man who successfully hunted Nazis.

"So now to business," Crevecoeur said, the lines in his face relaxing. "Weisse had no connection with anyone of interest to us that we know of."

"You're talking about Nazis, right?" Aaron said.

"SS and Gestapo." Crevecoeur's smile returned. "Monsieur Weisse's death would not be of significance to your pursuit of the SS Reichmann except that there has been another death, *mon ami*." The Mouse sipped his coffee and Aaron noticed his hands. They were extremely large for such a small man and scarred. "A toymaker in Nuremberg died suddenly in a fire at his shop a few days ago. Only it was not a fire that caused his death, it was a bullet in the neck. He was not simply a maker of toys, you see. He was also a counterfeiter of documents."

"Lindermann?" Miller said quickly.

Crevecoeur nodded. "*Oui, monsieur.*"

"When, Jacques?" Emma said. "When was he killed? What day?"

"Monday last," replied the Frenchman. "Only three days ago."

"The son of a bitch is cutting off our leads."

"The counterfeiter Lindermann was not a great loss,"

Crevecoeur said. "It will be one less technician available to other Nazis on our list."

"I don't give a damn about your list." Aaron said. "I want Reichmann."

"As we all do," Crevecoeur said with a patient nod. He held his cup in both hands and now set it back in its saucer. "I have given my life to finding these SS barbarians."

"I'm sure God will reward such dedication," Aaron answered. "But the only satisfaction that interests me is getting Reichmann. Just him. You can have the rest."

Crevecoeur looked at Emma.

"It's a personal vendetta with Aaron," Emma said. She shrugged. "That's what he wants to believe."

The Mouse pursed his lips, glanced back at Aaron. "You are Jewish?"

"No, Jacques," Emma said quickly. "This man found the urn. The Hitler urn."

"And two Jews have already died because of it," Aaron said. "I owe it to a lot of people to find Reichmann. The list is getting longer."

The Frenchman sat back in his chair. "Perhaps your dedication, too, monsieur, will have its reward."

"I thought these friends of yours were going to help us," Aaron said to Emma.

She nodded. "Jacques, what about Weisse's daughter?"

"Her whereabouts are unknown to us at the moment. . . ."

"Oh, that's good," Aaron said. "That's terrific." He faced Emma. " 'Don't worry, Aaron, I have contacts in Europe. We'll find Reichmann.' You said that."

"We will, Aaron," she said defensively. "Just—"

"S'il vous plaît." Crevecoeur raised his palms as if he were a referee. "The woman Anna Weisse registered at a hotel in Nuremberg as Frau Anna Hauptmann, traveling with her husband. Also in Bamberg. Herr Hauptmann signed nothing. He was not seen by the concierge of either hotel." Crevecoeur placed both hands together on the table. "It is not uncommon for a woman previously married to use her married name for a discreet rendezvous with l'ami de coeur."

"With what?" Aaron said.

"Her lover," Emma replied.

"Reichmann," The Mouse added. "We believe they are traveling together, *oui?*" Aaron nodded reluctantly. "Frau Hauptmann was charged with one telephone toll. To Berlin. To the home of a Monsieur W. Moltke. Monsieur Moltke is a metallurgist."

Emma stared at Aaron who gazed pensively somewhere across the room. For several moments he was silent, then he said, "It isn't a rifle or anything like that."

Emma frowned. "Then what?"

To Crevecoeur, Aaron said, "You don't know where the Weisse woman is now?"

"No, monsieur," he said, shaking his head. "They left Berlin."

"If we find the girl we find Reichmann," Emma said, staring at Aaron. "Right?"

Aaron said nothing. He stared past them across the room.

"Monsieur Miller?"

"I think Reichmann was surprised—as surprised as we were—that Josef Weisse died." Aaron glanced at Emma. "Weisse was a very old man. A specialist in his day, but still the best. What if Reichmann wanted something unique? An assassin needs a weapon. Weisse was a gunsmith. But what if . . . what if Weisse farmed out the job to someone else?"

"Moltke?"

"Why not? Weisse was pretty old. Either he figured he couldn't do the work himself or he needed collaboration." Aaron swore to himself and slapped a hand on the table.

"What?" Emma said.

"An armorer and a metal craftsman." Aaron said. "Christ, he isn't going to shoot anybody at all! He doesn't even have to be at the place."

Suddenly Crevecoeur understood. *"Mon Dieu!"*

"What!" Emma said frantically. "What are you talking about?"

"A bomb," Aaron said soberly. "Some sort of bomb."

"Oh, no!"

"Finding Reichmann isn't the primary concern anymore."
Miller rubbed his forehead. He glanced up at Crevecoeur. "Do
you see?"

The Mouse sighed. "*Oui, monsieur.*"

"He's changed the focus of the chase and the son of a bitch
knows it." Aaron made his hands into fists, alternately
squeezing one, then the other. "Rudel must have known. No
wonder he was so cooperative . . . giving us those names. He
said we wouldn't find Reichmann. He may be right."

Emma was shaking her head. "I don't understand, Aaron. If
we find him, why—"

"Because, love," Aaron interrupted, "a bomb does not
need someone to aim it or squeeze a trigger. The moment
Reichmann left Berlin with his precision gadget everything
changed. If he travels to London or Cairo or New York or Paris
or Tokyo or . . . anywhere, it doesn't mean a thing if he left it
in the Parliament building at Brussels. You see, he knows he's
being chased. So what better way to throw off the scent than
by changing the game. And he has the whole world as a
playground. Every city he goes to, every street is important
now."

"What now?" Emma asked patiently. "What do we do
now?"

"We go with the best lead we have," Aaron said. He looked
at Crevecoeur. "The girl. We have to find the girl. Anna
Weisse."

The Duke of Württemberg in the early eighteenth century,
dreaming of another Versailles, built an immense baroque
castle which was the beginning of Ludwigsburg, a town with
unimaginative straight streets where tourists today are more
drawn to its park than its castle. The town is not so much an
attraction in itself as it is a rest stop between the red wine
vineyards of Heilbronn in the Neckar Valley basin and the
garden city of Stuttgart. It was here in 1958, near the
Märchengarten, that the Ludwigsburg Center for the Inves-

tigation of Nazi War Crimes began its existence in a drab three-story gray stone building that earlier had served as a bookbinding warehouse.

Reichmann arrived by train, had an early brunch and phoned the local exchange where he was told that there was no such listing for the Center and had never been one. On further inquiry, Reichmann learned that the Bonn government had delegated the judicial handling of war criminals to the eleven states which together constitute the Federal Republic. Stuttgart, the capital of the state of Baden-Württemberg, had not prosecuted a case of importance in more than ten years. And the Center had ceased to function as a vigorous investigative agent even earlier. Only after several more calls did he locate a former *Verwaltungsbeamte* who had served with the Center in the late fifties. He knew the man Reichmann was looking for. He knew where he lived.

Reichmann's next stop was the general delivery window of the post office where he received a small packet secured with string. He sat in a park to unwrap it. Rudel had been generous. The cardboard container held three plastic ampules of a clear liquid substance, each labeled *Achtung! Acetylcholine 10 ccm*, each marked with the manufacturer's name stamped near the end. Wrapped carefully in several rolls of tissue was a new ten-*Kubikzentimeter* glass syringe, its plunger and chassis still packed with cotton. There were also three sizes of needles. The good colonel had left nothing to chance.

Reichmann replaced the items in the container and slipped it into his coat pocket. It was time to visit Uncle Helmut.

The house was designed after a variation of the Alemannian style, typical of the Black Forest region. Built on a slope, its wood-shingled high pitch roof slanted gently to the second-floor stables, then out and down nearly to the stone foundation. There was not another house within half a mile. As Reichmann walked up the path he noticed the corral of goats farther up the slope and a woman toiling on her knees in a vegetable garden.

"*Guten Tag*," Reichmann said, bowing slightly. "Is this Herr Bohle's house?"

She was in her late fifties, her face and hands brown and cracked by the sun. "Bohle's house?" She pulled herself up by a long-handled hoe. "Is that what he's telling them now?" She shook her head in disgust. "He has a room here. Room and board for the work he does, which is more than generous on our part."

"Is he here now?"

"*Ja*, the beer hall is not open yet." She nodded toward the trees farther up the slope. "He's supposed to be mending the fence. That way."

"Alone?" Reichmann said. "Herr Bohle lives here alone?"

"This isn't a hotel."

"What about his wife?"

"Ha! Wife, you say?" She laughed, leaning against the hoe. "Not since three years that my husband hired him. Not that one. Too mean to have a wife. Though I've heard he has a nose for the pretties when he isn't full of the *dunkles Bier*."

Reichmann nodded. He looked up toward the line of trees. "That way?"

"*Ja*. You are a friend of his?"

"From a long time ago," Reichmann replied.

He found him asleep against a tree; a tall man who'd grown fat in the belly. Bohle had his shirt off and his skin was white below the neck. He was much like Reichmann had expected except he'd grown a small mustache. Reichmann nudged him with his shoe and the man came awake with a start.

"Hey, there!" Bohle was on his feet immediately, though slightly groggy, and Reichmann noticed a small metal flask beside the tree trunk. "What's the idea?"

Reichmann gestured with his head back toward the house. "The woman said you were up here . . . working."

"So?" Bohle saw Reichmann glance at the flask and quickly grabbed it and stuffed it in his back pocket. He moved to a coil of wire fence and the ax beside it buried in a stump. "I do my work, not that that old cow and her husband pay me enough." He squinted at Reichmann as if he might be familiar. "What do you want?"

"Some of your time," Reichmann said. "Just talk."

Bohle canted his head. "Talk?"

"Unless you are too busy."

"I don't talk much to strangers."

"You will to me," Reichmann said.

Bohle looked surprised. He pulled the ax from the stump with one hand, held it near the end as if it were a club. "I asked you what you want. What do you want?"

"Retribution," Reichmann said.

"What?"

Reichmann dropped his hands to his sides. "Don't you remember me, Uncle Helmet?"

For the briefest moment Bohle stood there frowning, then his eyes grew very round. "You." It was an awkward, stupid lunge that Bohle made. He raised the ax too high, his feet too close together, so that when he swung he was not in a position to recover quickly. Reichmann used the flat of his hand and his knee in a rapid combination of blows that left Bohle gasping for breath on his back. He'd dropped the ax and Reichmann stooped to pick it up.

"No!" Bohle scrambled for it too late. He caught the flat side of the ax in the mouth and a moment later Reichmann swung the blunt end down in one savage thrust that broke bone just below the kneecap. Blood and broken teeth choked off Bohle's scream.

"You remember me now, do you, Uncle Helmet?" Reichmann knelt down beside the man whose mouth and chin were a bloody mess. He set the ax on Bohle's chest. "I want to be sure you know who I am. I want to be sure of that."

Bohle made some sound of pain. He raised his head slightly and reached for his broken leg.

"You mustn't concern yourself about the leg," Reichmann said. "It's quite a nasty break. But the severity of the pain will subside shortly . . . shock. It's nature's way."

"I . . . thought you . . . were dead . . ." Streaks of blood ran from the corners of Bohle's mouth down his neck. He had difficulty talking through the pain. "I . . . thought . . ."

"And I was for a time," Reichmann replied. He extracted the container from his jacket pocket and set the items from it out in front of him where Bohle could see. "Now I have returned."

"Wh—Why?" His eyes were round with terror as he watched Reichmann unfold the paper, insert the plunger in the syringe chassis. "What are you going to . . ." Bohle rolled his head over a bit, spit blood and broken teeth. "What is that!"

Reichmann chose one of the needles and secured its twist lock mechanism to the syringe. "Some tools."

"Tools?" Bohle tried to move but the blade of the axe was against his throat. "What do you want with me? What are you going to do?"

Reichmann inserted the needle into one of the plastic ampules and drew back the plunger, filling the syringe.

"What are you doing?" Bohle cried.

"You'll see," Reichmann said. "The pain in your leg has lessened, yes?"

Bohle nodded. "Some . . . very little . . . it hurts . . ."

"You'll forget the pain in the leg soon." Reichmann held the syringe up and with his thumb pressed the plunger until the needle squirted a short arc of the liquid. "You killed my mother," Reichmann said calmly without looking at his uncle. He unscrewed the top of the alcohol bottle and touched a cotton ball to it.

"No! No, I didn't!"

"You took her house and you said she did things she did not do."

"It isn't true!" Bohle screamed. "It's a lie!"

"I think it is true," Reichmann said. "You were responsible for her death." He held the syringe like an eager dentist over a terrified patient, casually but with studied purpose.

Suddenly Bohle's face grew angry. "She was a German. Her duty was to cooperate with the Allies."

"Like you?"

"I only wanted to know where you were . . . a reward was offered for—" Bohle stopped quickly. "I mean . . ."

"Yes, I know what you mean, Uncle."

"But it was thirty years ago!"

"You were responsible for her death." Reichmann swabbed a patch on Bohle's shoulder.

"What are you going to do?"

"I am going to be responsible for yours."

"No!" Bohle raised a fist, but the needle was already in the fleshy muscle. Reichmann pressed slightly on the plunger and extracted the needle. The injection produced instant results. Bohle screamed. The muscle in his arm convulsed. For nearly a full minute the spasm continued. The pain, Reichmann had been told, was excruciating. When the pain subsided, Bohle stopped screaming. His face was sweaty and caked with blood around the mouth. His eyes were wild.

"I told you you'd forget about the leg," Reichmann said.

"Please . . . oh, God, please . . . don't kill me. . . please . . ."

"Did my mother plead with you, Uncle? Did she tell you she didn't know if I was alive or dead?"

"My arm," Bohle cried. He clutched the shoulder. "It's paralyzed! What have you done!"

"Your information to the Allies injured many people. Information that was untrue. You testified against many Germans after the war. Mostly women. Why did you do that, my uncle?"

"You're mad!" Bohle gasped. "Insane! Why have you come back?"

Reichmann held the syringe up.

"No! Please!"

"I have seen transcripts of your testimony," Reichmann went on. "I have seen your lies." With one hand the Man of the Reich swabbed the cotton ball across Bohle's right chest and jabbed the needle under the skin. Bohle flailed out with his good arm, then he grabbed at his chest. His legs extended straight out and there was a violent convulsion in his chest. The scream brought more blood from his mouth in a misty spray. When the spasm dissipated, Bohle's eyes were glazed.

"I don't think your heart will take much more," Reichmann said with a sigh.

"Please . . . oh, my God, please . . . no more . . . no more! . . ." Bohle was crying, tears running down his blood-streaked face.

"There were so many you falsely witnessed against. So many. But the others I cannot avenge with great emotion. Only one." Reichmann leaned down near Bohle's ear. "You know her, my uncle. My mother. I want you to remember her now. As I do." Reichmann wiped a sleeve across his face.

"Oh, please . . . no more . . . don't . . . kill . . . me . . ."

"But I am the evil Nazi murderer of innocent women and children," Reichmann retorted. "You testified to it. You spoke against your sister as a sympathizer and abettor of Nazi criminals in hiding."

"She is dead." Bohle cried. "I . . . I cannot help that. She is dead thirty years. Have mercy . . . dear God, please! . . . It is all over . . . don't kill me . . ."

"It will never be over until we are all dead," Reichmann said. "The Jews do not forget or forgive the Mengeles and Bormanns and Straussers. It will never be. Should I forgive you, my uncle?"

"No! . . . please, no . . ."

"You see, it is a habit of humanity to suspend charity for the dignity of mankind. Brutality is an honorable test of civilization. Without infamy there is no measure of virtue. It is what sets us aside from the lesser primates. So I must be hunted to stroke the conscience of morality and you must die to preserve the cycle." Reichmann looked at Bohle who was sobbing. "I think it is too much for you to grasp at one sitting, Uncle." Reichmann swabbed the large blue vein in his arm.

"No! please . . . Georg, no more! . . ."

"This is the last, I promise."

"I don't want to die!"

Reichmann stared at him for several moments. "I wanted to give you great pain, Uncle Helmet. I wanted very much to see you die slowly. With very great pain. But I've changed my mind. It is only important now that you die. This will be quick and you will be conscious of only one violent thrust."

"Please . . ."

"I might have used potassium chloride," Reichmann said casually, "or sulphuric acid from an automobile battery, but neither is entirely untraceable." Reichmann held the syringe for Bohle to see. "Acetylcholine is naturally manufactured in the nervous system. It is a muscle stimulant or depressant, depending on the muscle. In its concentrated form, as you have observed, it produces extraordinary convulsions. Injected into the bloodstream it has exactly the same effect on the heart—function ceases immediately—but it breaks down in less than a minute so you will seem to have suffered a massive heart attack." Reichmann glanced at his leg. "Brought on by this accident."

Bohle dropped his head back on the ground. His whimpering was less than it had been. Reichmann slid the needle into the vein. Suddenly Bohle's head was up, eyes wide, staring helplessly at the syringe.

"Ahhhh! Ahhhh!"

"This is exactly how I shall remember you." Reichmann pressed the plunger to the stop. "Good-bye, Uncle Helmet."

27

By the start of the fourteenth day of the Olympics in
Montreal, the Soviet Union had taken a dramatic lead in the
total accumulation of medals. The Soviets had swept the
hammer throw awards, West Germany's dressage team won
the gold medal in the two-day equestrian competition and the
Americans pinned their hopes on Bruce Jenner to break the
Munich Olympic record in the decathlon.

The eyes of the world were fixed on Montreal via satellite.
Scattered attention was paid in these final days of the games
to the significance of Argentina's "annihilation of subversive
delinquents," the Christian-Moslem slaughtering in Lebanon,
the battle for the United States presidency or the reign of
terror by a vengeful Ugandan dictator.

For centuries the Olympic Games were the great peaceful
festivals, revered by the Greeks both religiously and athlet-
ically, held on a wide meadow on the north bank of the
Alpheus. Hostilities between neighboring towns and states
and other unpleasantnesses were suspended for their duration. But time and Telstar have witnessed the coming of the

modern era where nations replace city-states, rewards replace olive wreaths, cities bid to be Olympia and competitors endorse breakfast cereals.

The Games were a worldwide spectacle. International rivalry in sports, envisioned by Baron de Coubertin, would promote international amity in broader fields. Others saw a different purpose. Reichmann was one of them.

Elbert Schiller was a young man Reichmann guessed to be in his mid-twenties who lived alone on the outskirts of Stuttgart. He was a frail boy, no more than a hundred and twenty pounds, with an angular face and pale complexion. His apartment was practically bare—more office than residence, with a desk and small file cabinet and sofa in the living room. Around the room on metal stands and stacked one on top of another were radios—short-wave radios of every type and description.

Reichmann held out an advertisement torn from a newspaper. "I came about this ad," he said, glancing around the room. "You have quite a collection here, Herr Schiller."

The boy smiled. "A hobby. I do a little repair work too, nothing complicated . . . change crystals mostly. What you see here"—he gestured at the radios with a thin hand—"these mostly belong to customers." He looked back at Reichmann. "What were you interested in?"

"For my nephew," Reichmann said. "He recently got his license and I thought, perhaps, for his birthday . . ."

"A key rig?"

"No, voice."

The boy nodded. "It's all used, the equipment, you understand. I cannot offer a warranty which is why I advertise in the personals, but I can assure you everything I sell may be returned if you are not satisfied."

"It needn't be anything elaborate," Reichmann said. "A small portable transceiver would be fine."

Schiller walked to a metal table. "In the amateur range I have this Eddystone and a Scholenkamp and a Trio UHF single side band. Actually, the Eddystone model here isn't made to be portable. Did you want fixed crystal or tunable frequency?"

"Multifrequency range in the twenty-meter band."

The boy raised an eyebrow. "Ah, you are familiar, then, with this equipment?"

Reichmann smiled. "Not so much as my nephew."

He chose an older model modified AM modulator that was a reconditioned military surplus item over Schiller's recommendation for an FM model. In thirty years a great deal had happened to advance the science of short-wave communication. There were satellites now and computers to boost radio signals. But there was also a more sophisticated and highly efficient method of tracking down the source of such transmissions. The old-fashioned AM model was less likely than something modern to be triangulated through frequency scanners that might be searching for him. It was a risk, but the chances of being detected were diminished. It was important, Reichmann realized, that at this point in his plan he not give away his position on the Continent when he again contacted Strausser. By now, the world would be searching for him. He must be scrupulously careful.

Reichmann purchased several meters of insulated copper lamp cord and, with the radio in a canvas haversack, made his way by taxi to a tavern on the edge of the forest on the city's northwest side. He hiked deep into the woods to a spot high enough to serve his purpose and still be comfortably isolated. Then he returned to the tavern. For an hour he drank beer and made conversation with the barmaid. Eventually, he excused himself to visit the men's room and slipped out the back door. The tavern's proprietor was out of the city, Reichmann had learned, thanks to the talkative barmaid. He parked his truck in a shed behind the inn. He forced the lock and in five minutes was on his way back into the woods carrying a grimy truck battery.

By splitting the lamp cord to a premeasured length and fastening it V-fashion to tree branches, the radio leads could be attached at the point of the V and the wire extended out along a general northwest-southeast axis. Reichmann then constructed a crude but efficient directional antenna. With a pair of short pieces left from the cord, he connected the battery to the radio. Then he plugged the microphone and headset which he'd also bought from Schiller into the set and switched on the power.

Reichmann steeled himself to the knowledge that he would be here for several hours, familiarizing himself with the set. He would first listen, tune several frequencies, but not transmit. There was much to remember, much to learn. And there was still the problem of contacting the resort while avoiding the channels guarded by Strausser's elaborate communications center, but Reichmann had taken the time in São Paulo to learn which frequencies in this band the Adlernest monitored. There were long hours ahead. He settled against a tree and began ranging up from twenty-one megacycles. . . .

"Hello, hello . . . I can't hear you! Are you still there?" Strausser was sitting in the communications room. Beside him the technician adjusted the short-wave receiver. Strausser tapped on the earpiece of the headset with his knuckle and cursed the technician for losing the signal. "Hello? Reichmann?"

"I am here, Herr Strausser." Reichmann's voice came through clearly above the static.

"Can you hear me?" Strausser asked, clutching the headset with both hands. He motioned with his head and the technician left. A moment later Mengele and Mueller were standing beside him. "Do you hear me all right?"

"Yes, I hear you. How is the *Oberkomitee* this morning!"

"It's 4 A.M. here!" Strausser glanced up angrily at Mengele who was dressed haphazardly in pajamas and a red silk robe. Mueller yawned. No one seemed pleased about the hour. "You haven't called us in days!"

"I'm calling now," Reichmann said.

"Yes, well, can't you use a telephone?"

"No."

Strausser adjusted the headset again. "Major—This is an open transmission. Anybody could hear!"

"I prefer the short wave. My position is harder to trace on the short wave."

Strausser gripped the stem of the microphone. "I want to talk to you about that, Major Reichmann."

"Yes, I expect you do."

"Where is he?" Mengele demanded.

"Get back!" Strausser told the Doktor. He reached for the audio switch on the receiver and flipped it so Mengele and Mueller could hear. He held the microphone for himself. "Major Reichmann, we have made contact with those who took the urn."

Mengele and Mueller stared anxiously at the radio speaker. For several moments there was no response, just the crackle of radio speaker. Then the speaker said, "Good."

"We want you to return immediately," Strausser said. "It is the decision of the *Oberkomitee* that you come back. A gesture of good faith on our part." Mengele glanced over to Strausser, nodded his approval.

"When it is safe, when I have seen it," the voice from the speaker said. "That is the plan we all agreed to."

"Yes, yes," Strausser said impatiently. "But we've changed it—the plan. You are to return immediately."

"Sorry."

Strausser licked his lips before he pressed the microphone key. "What do you mean, sorry?"

"I mean no," Reichmann said.

"You don't understand." Strausser scooted his seat closer to the table, leaning nearer the microphone as if it helped him communicate better. "The Jews did not take it. The Jews are not responsible for the destruction of the Chancellery. It was *ein Amerikaner.*"

They all stared at the speaker for several moments but Reichmann said nothing.

"Did you hear, Major?"

"Yes."

"Then you must return at once."

"It changes nothing," the voice from the speaker remarked calmly. "The rules are the same no matter who is responsible." The speaker was silent briefly. "I will continue the mission as planned."

"No!" Strausser shouted. "You are not to continue. I command you to return. The *Oberkomitee* demands it. It is an order."

"I no longer take orders, Herr Strausser."

Mueller wrenched the microphone from Strausser. His chair fell over backward as he stood, pushing Mengele aside. "You are a *Schutzstaffel*, Major—an SS—you will follow orders!"

"Herr Mueller," Reichmann offered with pleasant recognition, "good morning."

"You are a German soldier," the Gestapo chief bellowed. "You will do as we, the *Oberkomitee*, command!"

"I will do what I set out to do. Nothing less."

"You threatened the bishop," Mueller said, quickly moving on. "You cannot make threats against the Catholics. Do you hear? Leave the Catholics alone. Understand me, Major."

"The bishop was my messenger," Reichmann said. "I did not harm him."

"But you threatened him," Mueller shouted. "You threatened him and his church with a bomb. We do not threaten Catholics. Do you hear me? Do not antagonize the Catholic Church."

"Is it so important, these Catholics?" said Reichmann. He sounded amused.

Mueller waved a fist in the air. "You . . . you have no authority!"

"I am my authority, Herr Mueller," the *Kettenhund* replied coldly.

"And the Jew in Vienna?" Mueller said. "There was nothing about killing in this assignment. We have been forced to alter the terms of the release of the urn because of your recklessness."

Mengele smiled, turned quickly to Mueller. "That's good, Heinrich," he whispered. "Very good."

The radio was silent again. Then: "What Jew?"

"The Israeli," Mueller said, full of himself. "Do you think we would not know? With the American, Miller, and the West German woman. We do not condone such tactics. Your plan was only to threaten the Jews, not garrote them in their bath. If you cannot keep ahead of the pursuit without attacking them, then you are not much of a *Kettenhund.*"

"I see," the voice said after a pause.

Mueller smiled. Strausser and Mengele smiled. "Then we can expect to see you soon? No later than twenty-four hours?"

"I am signing off now, gentlemen," Reichmann said.

"When can we expect you?" Mueller repeated. He waited, clicked the microphone key as if it were a telephone. "When are you coming? . . . Hello? . . . Reichmann? . . . hello, hello . . . Reichmann . . . Reichmann? . . ."

But the line was dead.

Their leads went nowhere. Aaron had checked what must have been every hotel and inn between Frankfurt and Munich. Crevecoeur took the north, Kiel and Hamburg to Hanover; Emma checked Münster to Saarbrucken.

Nothing. The odds hadn't been good when they started, a stark fact Aaron became more aware of by the hour. The girl had simply disappeared just as Reichmann had. The likelihood that Reichmann had killed her too was beginning to loom high on Aaron's dwindling list of possibilities.

Emma hung up the phone. They were in a small office Crevecoeur had found for them on the third floor of a women's clothing factory that overlooked an uninviting view of the Isar. "That was Richard," she said wearily. "Six Weisses and fourteen Hauptmanns in Cologne in the last two days. All on holiday. None was our girl."

Aaron stared at a rack of Heinrici dresses, nodded.

"You know, Aaron, what if she never left East Germany?"

"Your friend Jacques said she did."

"Then maybe she went to France. Or Austria."

"Maybe she's dead," Aaron said. "On a boxcar to Flensburg."

"Are you giving up?"

Aaron rubbed his eyes with the back of his hands. "The day after tomorrow is Sunday. Even if we'd found her yesterday, we'd still have to know where Reichmann had been. If she knew." He shook his head. "I don't know, Emma." He got up and stood at the window.

"I thought you were so hot to find the man who killed—"

"Look," Aaron snapped, "I'm not in the mood, okay?"

"I told you at the beginning this was discouraging work," she retorted. "We'll find him. And the bomb."

"Before it goes off?"

Emma sighed. "Yes," she said unconvincingly. The telephone rang.

Emma sprang to it. Aaron continued to stare outside.

"Yes? . . . Jacques, hello."

Aaron glanced over to her indifferently. "Tell him our fabulous news from Richard."

She waved him off, switched the phone to her other ear. "Yes, Jacques . . . you did. Where?" Emma nodded her head vigorously toward Aaron. "I can't believe it!"

"Believe what?" Aaron said. He moved away from the window.

"You're sure! . . . Oh, my God, I can't believe it!"

"Believe what!" Aaron demanded.

"Yes, Jacques." She scribbled down an address that Aaron tried to read, but couldn't. "We're on our way. Thank you, Jacques, I love you!" Emma dropped the receiver back on its hook and jumped up from her place. "You won't believe it!"

"What?"

"Weisse's wife's sister lives in Kassel. Ulrike Grass, a widow."

"How exciting."

"Her niece was there," Emma said. "Frau Hauptmann. Our Anna."

"Was?"

"She left this morning." Emma offered a smile. "She's coming to Munich. To us." Emma stuffed the address in her purse. "Well, get your coat on, love. She's going to the Koenigshof . . . Reichmann made a reservation there, remember?"

"She's alone?"

"Only until we get there," Emma said. "Coming?"

Anna Weisse Hauptmann signed the registry in her own name. The desk clerk had accepted her explanation with an easy smile, that she was taking Werner Stolz's suite and that he would arrive within a few days. He seemed very polite, asked no questions and even escorted her to the lift.

Anna found them waiting in the living room of the suite. A woman and three men.

"Good morning," said the man rising from his seat. "I am Inspector Kurt Olbricht of the Federal Ministry of State." He gestured with a wide sweep of his arm acknowledging the others. "We have been waiting for you, Fräulein Weisse."

Olbricht was Crevecoeur's idea, Aaron learned after the fact. The whole world was now involved in the manhunt for Reichmann and since he was, after all, a German citizen originally and an alleged criminal of the Third Reich, the Federal Republic of Germany had a vested interest in finding him. That's the way Olbricht explained himself. An *official* interest. Aaron didn't like him from the beginning.

"So, you see, Fräulein Weisse, the man Werner Stolz is not an Austrian from Salzburg," Olbricht was saying. "The man is a known SS officer wanted by the German Federal Republic for questioning. His real name is Eduard Reichmann. There is much evidence to believe that he is in Germany to do harm to someone of major importance."

Aaron had not taken his eyes off her in the twenty minutes it took Olbricht to explain why she was of such interest to the government of West Germany. She sat impassively in the corner of the divan next to Emma with her hands folded in her lap, head bowed, staring despondently at the floor. She clutched a colorful pamphlet rolled between her hands and she would glance at it from time to time hopelessly as if the scourge of her despair was not Olbricht and his meddling questions, but contained in the pamphlet's pages. Several times when Olbricht put a question to her she would respond with a nod or shake of the head. She had the self-confidence of an amateur thief, rightfully convicted, awaiting judgment.

"Any information you can provide us, Fräulein Weisse, about this man would go well for you." It was Olbricht's way of cuing her to speak.

"Am I under arrest, Herr Olbricht?" She did not look up.

It was a point Olbricht had never clarified. Aaron glanced at the inspector.

"Arrest?" He said it impatiently, as if considerations of legality were only secondarily important. "No, no, I am interested in information that will lead to the location of Reichmann. You were with him last, Fräulein Weisse."

"Hauptmann," she said, looking up for the first time. "I am Frau Anna Hauptmann."

"Yes, of course," he said, nodding testily. "You drove Reichmann out of East Germany . . . from Berlin."

"Yes."

"Where?"

"I don't know where he is," Anna said softly.

"When did you last see him?"

She glanced pleadingly at the other faces, held on Aaron's. "I don't know where he is."

Olbricht shook his head. "Please, answer the question. When you left Berlin, where did you take this man?"

"We drove to . . . to Hamburg."

"Hamburg," Olbricht said again, raising his eyebrows. "And after that?"

"I . . . I don't know."

"I must impress upon you, Frau Hauptmann. It is urgent that we find this SS fugitive, Anna. He is a dangerous man."

"He did not harm me," she said in a low voice. "I do not

think he would really harm anyone." She looked at Emma, then Aaron.

"He's already killed a man in Nuremberg," Aaron said. "A shopkeeper who also forged illegal identity papers."

"No!"

"Yes."

Olbricht raised his hand to bring her attention back to the official interrogator. He shot a disapproving glance at Aaron. "If you please, Herr Miller." He looked back at Anna. "We are also investigating a homicide in Nuremberg. You were with this man in Nuremberg?"

"Yes, but—"

"You must understand, Anna, the gravity here." Olbricht continued, "A threat has been made by this man, Reichmann. He has promised to assassinate someone of international importance."

"Who?" Anna stared at the inspector with alarm.

He shrugged. "We do not know. Perhaps the Israeli prime minister. Perhaps in France, the president or—"

"No!" she cried. "He would not . . ."

"Where is he now?" Olbricht said again. "Were you to meet him here . . . later?"

"He would not!" She said quickly. Aaron believed she was trying to convince herself.

"Yes, he will," Aaron interrupted. "He will unless we stop him. We have to stop him."

"Please, Herr Miller—"

"You want to kill him!" Anna cried. "You—all of you—you will kill him!"

"No, Anna," Olbricht said, trying to restore order. He attempted to smile, to reassure her, but it wasn't working.

"Yes," Aaron said. "Unless Reichmann is stopped, he will be killed." He waved off Olbricht's objection. "He intends to murder and he will unless we can head him off. You can help us. You can stop a killing. Perhaps only you. There is a very short time left. You can stop it." Aaron paused to let it sink in. "Where is Eduard Reichmann?"

"I . . ." She suddenly shook her head. "What will happen

to him?" Anna ignored Olbricht now. She stared at Aaron.

For a long moment Aaron said nothing. "That is not my decision to make."

Anna glanced quickly at Emma and Crevecoeur, but neither spoke. Then she bowed her head, stared at her hands. "He . . . he took a train in Hamburg."

"Where?" Olbricht said.

"He would not tell me," Anna whispered. Her eyes glistened with tears. She was looking at the pamphlet. "Too late," she said. "I followed him, but he was gone. I was too late to see him."

Olbricht exhaled a long sigh and leaned back in his chair. Aaron continued to study her. Tears dropped on the sleeve of her dress.

"You know, don't you?" Aaron said softly. "You know where he is?"

"He said we could go away together." She closed her eyes.

"Where?" Aaron prodded gently. "We can save a life, Anna. You and I."

"Amsterdam," she said after a moment. "Then Italy . . . Rome." Anna Weisse Hauptmann wiped at the tears with the palm of her hand. She looked at Aaron. "He *will* do this thing. I *must* stop him, yes?"

Aaron nodded.

Anna's eyes went back to the pamphlet. "He lied to me," she said softly. "He said he trusted me but he lied. I would have done anything for him . . . for Werner. But he lied."

Aaron watched her turn to a place in the pamphlet. It was a book of Olympic records.

She shook her head slowly, staring at a place on the page. "He said he won a gold medal." Anna looked at Aaron tearfully. "But his name is not here. Why did he lie? It was all a lie, to love me?"

"I don't know," Aaron said, bowing his head. He could feel her pain.

She looked quickly to Olbricht. "He will not kill the prime minister," she said with determination. "And not the French president."

"No?" Olbricht answered stupidly.

"He does not like the Church," she replied, taking a deep breath. "He has told me many times—this man Reichmann. He does not like the Holy Father."

Aaron glanced at Emma. She returned his stare blankly, then suddenly she understood. "Oh, dear God! A head of state!"

"Sovereign head of the Vatican," Aaron said soberly. "Leader of the largest following in the world. Prince of the Apostles . . . Supreme Pontiff of the Universal Church . . ." He ran a hand through his hair. "The Pope."

Crevecoeur, the Mouse, slapped his hands together as if to pray, touched his fingertips to his lips. "*Mon Dieu*, of course!" He turned quickly to Aaron. "Sunday . . . Sunday evening the Holy Father will deliver a short message from the balcony of the papal residence . . . in celebration of brotherly love for the Olympics."

"Oh, Jesus!" Aaron exclaimed. "St. Peter's Square. Reichmann's going to be in St. Peter's Square."

"With ten thousand other people," Emma added.

"Then we've got him," Aaron said triumphantly. "We won't let the Pope give the blessing. At least, not from the balcony where Reichmann can get to him." He glanced at Emma. "We've got him," Aaron said again.

Reichmann dialed the number from a call box at Echterdingen Airport. It rang several times.

"*Hallo?*"

Reichmann heard the voices of children in the background. "Is this the *Stadtpark* in Vienna?"

"*Ja, hier ist der Stadtpark.*"

"*Herr Rudel, bitte,*" Reichmann said.

"*Herr Rudel?*" There was a long pause, then: "Call back. One hour. *Ja?*"

"*Ja.*"

*　　*　　*

Hans-Ulrich Rudel stumped back and forth before the call box. The sky had been threatening rain all morning and he wore a light jacket with the collar turned up and a hat. The minutes moved slowly on his watch and he checked it again when the phone rang.

"*Hallo?*"

"Good morning, my colonel," Reichmann said.

"Eduard. I hoped it would be you."

"Time is short," the voice said. "I have some questions."

"About the American?"

"He came to see you."

"Yes," Rudel said quickly. "And a German woman. Emma Diels. They are searching for you, Eduard."

"Everyone is."

"The American—Aaron Miller—he destroyed the Chancellery. It was he who took the urn."

Reichmann was silent a moment. "Then it is true."

"I . . ." Rudel took a breath. "I told them about the identity papers."

"Yes, I know. Was a man with them killed? A Jew?"

"Why, yes," Rudel answered surprised. "You know about it?"

"Strausser told me."

"You must not trust him, Eduard. The *Oberkomitee* has betrayed you. The American told me. That much from him I believe." Rudel flattened a paper against the window of the call box. "I have looked into this, my friend. The Jew who was killed."

"Mengele thinks I was responsible," said Reichmann. "He is mistaken."

"He is a fool," Rudel snapped. "Even I know you were not responsible." He stared at the paper. "It made me wonder who else is interested. Who else would want to keep the American from finding you?"

"Yes, I have given it some thought, my colonel. If this American took the urn as he says, then why does he chase over Europe for me? Perhaps he did take it. But it would be a simple matter for him to turn it over. Simple, unless he does not have it anymore."

Rudel nodded excitedly. "Exactly, Eduard."

"And if this American does not possess the urn, then who does? I have given it much attention, Herr Rudel. I believe an enemy of the Jews has stolen it from him. I believe some group of Arabs . . ."

"A Palestinian group, perhaps," Rudel said, pleased with himself.

"Possibly, yes." Reichmann paused. "There are several such organizations. I am calling to ask for another favor, Herr Rudel."

He smiled. "Yes, as I said, I hoped you would, Eduard. I have already made some inquiries." Rudel nodded emphatically to himself. "My influence is surprising sometimes. Did you know, for example, that the headquarters of a group of Palestinians is located in Paris?"

"If it was the right group," Reichmann said.

"It is the right one," Rudel replied confidently. "It is the one that controls the urn."

Reichmann was silent.

"Did you hear, Eduard?"

"Yes," Reichmann finally said. "Then I must go to Paris."

"No!" Rudel adjusted his grip on the receiver. "Do not bother with Paris."

"No?"

"Did I not offer my help, Eduard? Did I not offer every aid available to me to help you?" Rudel nodded to himself. "Yes! And now I can contribute something you alone could not discover."

"The urn," Reichmann said, "is it not in Paris?"

"No, my friend. I have acquaintances, shall I say, at the Postes, Télégraphes et Téléphones. Acquaintances who have solved a great riddle without knowing it."

"Yes?"

"Every day at noon—the busiest hour of the day—a call is received by this organization. A transatlantic call of short duration. Since I had made my inquiries known to my acquaintances concerning this group, they looked into these curious calls. The upshot is, Eduard, that the caller made only two brief statements. 'All is well' and 'the vessel is safe.' The vessel can be nothing else but the urn."

"I see," Reichmann said. "And where do these calls originate?"

"New York City," said Rudel proudly. "The phone number of a hotel." He read from the paper. "West Forty-fourth Street. Number forty-four. It is called the Royalton." He slid the paper in his jacket. "Tell me you approve, my friend. It will be reward enough."

"You found the urn," Reichmann said. "I cannot express my thanks adequately, my colonel."

"Bring it home," Rudel said softly. "To its proper place. Bring it home to Germany."

"Yes," the telephone voice said certainly. "I have already ordered it."

The door to Henry's bedroom burst open with a crash. Henry was on his back reading. There was pitiful little time to reach for the .38 under a pillow. He didn't. The room filled instantly with half a dozen men—pages—blonds all, dressed in their hotel blazers and light turtlenecks that did little to disguise their brawn. Henry unconsciously pulled the bedclothes over his chest.

"Somebody lose the badminton birdie?" Henry was answered with cold stares. "Any of you fat-headed monkeys *sprechen Englisch*?"

Strausser hurried into the room with Mengele close behind. "Get up, Mr. Nickelson. Get up now!"

"It's too late," Henry said. "The redcoats are already here."

"Do as you are told, Nickelson," Mengele retorted.

Henry shrugged. "I really had expected something a little more imaginative," he said, sitting up. "Do I get a last cigarette or choice of blindfolds?"

"Dress yourself," Strausser ordered. "Quickly," he added.

Henry got to his feet. He felt impossibly silly, facing the new order of jackboot supermen in his striped pajama bottoms. "What's it to be?" Henry said wearily. "A one-way boat ride on the lake or an unfortunate climbing accident?"

Strausser shook his head impatiently. "We are not going to kill you, Mr. Nickelson. You are leaving. You are joining your friends. Miller and the girl."

"What?"

"You must hurry. A helicopter is waiting to take you to Osorno . . . across the Andes." Strausser barked an order in German and two of the pages moved quickly to the closet and brought Henry a suit. Another found his shoes beside the bed.

"I don't know anyone in Chile," Henry said as he was helped roughly into his trousers.

"A plane is waiting," Strausser said. "You will leave immediately for Munich. You will be there by noon tomorrow."

"Munich?" Henry repeated dully. "Germany?"

"Dress quickly!"

"Look, I must have missed something. I thought we were indefinite guests here."

"Lubetkin stays. Only you are leaving."

Henry nodded bewilderedly. "I don't mean to sound ungracious, but what the hell's going on?"

"You will deliver some sensitive information to your friends," Strausser said. "We have made a decision. Reichmann must be stopped at once."

"I thought that was the general consensus."

Strausser shook his head like a man who'd led a desperate charge against the enemy only to find his men still hiding in the trenches behind him. "Reichmann has betrayed us. He will not listen. He intends to carry out the assassination."

"Without the urn?"

"He is insane!" Mengele said.

Strausser pointed a finger at Henry as if he were charging a jury. "Reichmann must be stopped. He must not kill the Pope."

"The Pope?" Henry froze, holding one sock over his foot.

"We have only just learned it ourselves," Strausser said. "Reichmann, the fool, actually means to do it. He must be stopped or we are ruined."

"You are?"

"They will think we are responsible." Strausser was terribly upset. Henry tied his shoes. He wasn't in much of a compassionate mood just now. "They will think he is acting as our instrument . . . carrying out our orders. He is not. Do you understand? We cannot control him."

"What do you think I can do?" Henry was fully dressed now, though it was not a suit he'd have chosen himself.

Strausser nodded to Mengele who left the room a moment, then returned with a worn brown leather valise. Strausser took it and handed it over to Henry. "This contains *Sturmbannfuehrer* Reichmann's complete dossier. It is contained in a larger body of information we do not have time to separate." Strausser's hard look commanded Henry's undivided attention. "No one else must see the contents. No one."

"Why not?"

"We find ourselves in an untenable position, Mr. Nickelson. Reichmann threatens our very existence. Each one of us . . . each one of the *Oberkomitee* came to be here through documents provided by the Vatican, a sovereign state. Reichmann as well. The state of Vatican City, it may surprise you, issued hundreds of identity certificates through the Refugee Bureau to many of us as stateless persons. Naturally, we did not use our true names, but in a real sense you may say the Catholic Church saved us in our hour of need after the war. Something the Holy See today finds too embarrassing to acknowledge—revealing as it does their predecessor's indiscriminate generosity."

"That's supposed to be important?"

"Only as background," Strausser said. "In those early years after the war, Martin Bormann found himself the treasurer of a great deal of wealth with few places in which to invest it. You may have heard the *Reichsleiter* called many things, but he was a brilliant financier. Herr Bormann studied world financial operations for months, investigating everything. If not for the Church's unwitting aid in Bormann's own escape, he might not ever have considered developing certain financial ties."

"With the Vatican?" Henry exclaimed.

"Its secular administration," Strausser said.

"The banks," Mengele explained.

Strausser nodded. "Vatican City as a national interest imposes no income tax; there is no restriction of import or export of funds. The banking operations and expenditures are guarded with the utmost secrecy. So Herr Bormann needed only to devise a scheme whereby he could secure Vatican City citizenship and deposit the bulk of the Reich treasury."

Henry stared at the two with measured awe. "You mean . . . you *bank* . . . at the Vatican!"

"Millions," Mengele said vaingloriously. "A wide range of diversified interests."

"I don't get it," Henry said. "What can Reichmann do about it?"

Strausser tapped the valise Henry held in his hands. "At the beginning, when we trusted Reichmann to carry out our plan—"

"I was against it from the beginning," Mengele said, shaking his cane.

"—we made available to him any information he requested, so as to help   —The urn was most precious to us. We would do anything to have it back."

Henry nodded.

"And part of the briefing was a detailed account of our banking procedure. You see, twice annually a member of the *Oberkomitee* visits a financial organization in Vatican City for an accounting, using an alias, of course. This information was given freely to Reichmann, at his request." Strausser rubbed a hand across his face. "We had no idea he planned to use it this way."

"What way?"

"The names!" Strausser shouted desperately. "The passport identities of all our aliases as Vatican City citizens. How do you think Reichmann will gain entrance to the Vatican? He has already obtained false passports. Do you think a man who traffics in fake identity papers will have the slightest trouble duplicating Vatican documents?"

"I see your problem." Henry pursed his lips. "Reichmann,

by infiltrating the Vatican palace as one of you to get to the Pope, would expose you for who you really are." He glanced at Strausser. "Then what would happen?"

"Confiscation," Strausser replied solemnly. "Total and unequivocal confiscation of the entire fortune. We would be wiped out. You see, we have no way to protest."

"Reichmann must be stopped," Mengele ranted.

"And in here?" Henry indicated the valise.

"Our Vatican papers. Reichmann will choose one of the aliases. You can see, Mr. Nickelson, we could not risk sending the information over the telephone. We have decided to trust this delivery to your care."

"It doesn't appear you have much choice," Henry said.

"Reichmann himself used those same words." Strausser's expression made it plain he wasn't about to be burned twice. "But it is you who will acquiesce. No one other than yourself and Miller will read the contents here." He indicated the valise. "And you will return it to me personally. You have until Sunday."

"What makes you think I'm coming back?"

"The old man," Strausser said. "Lubetkin . . . he is a concern to you? He will wait here with us for your return."

Henry took a deep breath, let it out slowly. "Right."

"It is time for you to go, Mr. Nickelson."

"There's just one other thing," Henry said, realizing the obvious, "as long as we are being so frank."

Strausser raised an eyebrow. "Yes?"

"The urn. The reason for all this craziness. What about the urn?"

"Oh, yes, the urn." The head of the *Oberkomitee* nodded as if he was saddened by the reminder. "When one is reduced to basics, one forgets the luxuries. We are struggling for survival here, Mr. Nickelson. Our financial base is at stake. Unpleasant as it is, we must face the reality of our dilemma. And as with all such quandaries, an unpleasant decision must be made." Strausser glanced at Mengele who nodded his agreement. "We have made that momentous decision. The fate of *der Fuehrer's* urn has taken a secondary importance in our point of view. Priorities change, Mr. Nickelson."

Mengele was suddenly amused. "It is an irony, is it not, Nickelson; no one really wants it for its own value."

"Someone does," Henry said.

Mengele's face went blank. Mengele the thinker. "Oh?"

"The only man who has nothing to gain by it," Henry replied. "Your chain dog—Reichmann."

28

The hour was well past midnight before Aaron got word. Emma had fallen asleep on the sofa and came awake quickly when Aaron answered the knock. Inspector Olbricht had with him a rather thin priest with high cheekbones who looked as weary as Olbricht. The priest's name was Keppler from the Church of Our Lady, a secretary to the Archbishop of Munich. Aaron transferred a tray of empty coffee cups from a chair and offered it to the priest.

Aaron was too restless to sit. When Olbricht found himself a comfortable place, Aaron said, "Well?"

Olbricht exhaled an official melancholy sigh. "Father Keppler will explain."

The priest's eyes flickered nervously around the room, avoiding Aaron.

"Well, Father?"

"The Holy Father's message will not be canceled," he said almost apologetically. "He will address the public from the balcony of the papal residence at 10 P.M. Sunday . . . following evening mass."

Aaron stared at the priest, incredulous. "But, that's . . ." He glanced at Olbricht. The inspector responded with a reluctant nod.

"That's—they *didn't* cancel it?" Aaron's stare locked on the priest. "You mean the Pope is going ahead with this, this blessing!"

"It is not a blessing," said the priest quickly. "His Holiness had long ago decided to deliver a public message. The Olympic Games in Montreal end Sunday and as a gesture to acknowledge the spirit and international brotherhood promoted by the Olympics in the interest of world peace, the Holy Father—"

"He's going to get his holy ass blown to kingdom come," Aaron retorted.

"Look here now, Miller," Olbricht said gruffly, "no need for that kind of talk."

"Don't you people know about Reichmann?" Aaron watched Keppler. "Do you think he's bluffing?"

The priest shook his head. "It is a serious dilemma."

"Serious?" Aaron looked at Emma. "*Serious!* Reichmann is going to assassinate the Pope and all they can do is shake their clerical heads. . . ."

Olbricht started to object but Keppler raised a hand. "This was the decision of the Holy Father himself. Let me say, Mr. Miller, that this is not the first time His Holiness has been threatened, and undoubtedly it will not be the last."

"We'll know about that shortly after ten on Sunday, won't we?"

"Please understand," the priest said. "If the Holy Father was intimidated in this way to cancel, then a precedent would be set that others might attempt to exploit." He shook his head again. "No, Mr. Miller, the Supreme Pontiff of the Roman Catholic Church will not yield to threats."

"And Reichmann?" Aaron said. "What about him?"

"The Vatican employs a regular army of more than one hundred Swiss Guards. It has been an adequate security force in the past. With God's help it will be enough."

"Yes, well, I don't want to be disrespectful, but if you don't mind I'd like to be around myself."

The priest looked to Olbricht. "Your *help* won't be necessary," said the inspector. "The German and Italian governments have already moved into action. Interpol is involved. Every border crossing to Italy, every airport, every tourist and businessman is being scrutinized."

"Oh, that's good," Aaron said sarcastically. "That's great. He's probably already in the country, but you're going to make sure he doesn't get out, right?"

"The Rome police have also been alerted," Olbricht said patiently. "In addition to the three public entrances to the Vatican, officers are being placed at each of the three private entrances. If Reichmann attempts to get through he will be apprehended."

"You're sure?"

Keppler answered. "What else can be done, Mr. Miller?"

"Change the Pope's mind," Aaron said. "You know, it isn't just the Pope who's involved here. That's his choice. But how many hundreds of people who *don't* know there is going to be an assassination are you taking responsibility for? Reichmann isn't going to shoot or stab him or anything quite so personal. He will use explosives, Father. You or somebody might remind His Holiness of that."

"Somebody already has."

Neither Olbricht nor the priest had spoken. Aaron followed their stare and turned back quickly toward the door. Yossi Bar Tov was standing in the light shadows of the alcove, a summer jacket folded neatly over one arm.

"Bar Tov?" Aaron said dully. "What are you doing here?"

Bar Tov paused to light himself a cigarette. "Taking over the hunt," the Israeli said.

"What the hell do you mean you're taking over?"

Father Keppler had left, the position of the Church having been charted. Olbricht remained in his comfortable chair, reading quietly over the papers Bar Tov had handed him.

"You've done a job most any competent policeman could do," Bar Tov said. "But now you must let the professionals finish the work."

"Professionals?"

"My men," Bar Tov replied casually. "We have a mop-up team. It's only a question of time now. Once we know who Reichmann is after and where he will strike, his mystery evaporates. He is only a terrorist now and we are very good at rounding up terrorists."

Emma shook her head bewilderedly. "But, Aaron . . . you said you needed Aaron . . . and me. Aaron can identify him."

"Not necessary," Bar Tov said with a slight wave of the hand. "Actually, it was only important if we could not discover his victim. As long as Aaron was determined to get into this search, I thought it best if we worked together."

"You mean so you could keep tabs on me," Aaron responded angrily.

Bar Tov nodded.

"And me?" Emma sat up straight on the sofa.

"As I said before, my dear, you have certain contacts that were helpful in many ways. But now your work is done."

"That's what you think," Aaron said.

"Yes, it is." Bar Tov glanced at Olbricht who was now finished with the papers. "Inspector? Would you officially inform Mr. Miller that he is leaving the Federal Republic of Germany."

"Damn right, I'm leaving! I'm going to Italy and there's not a goddamn thing you can do about it!"

"Sorry to disappoint you." Bar Tov held the cigarette to his mouth, inhaled slowly, his eyes on the German. "Inspector?"

Olbricht's pale frown changed to consternation. He held his hands out above his lap, palms up, as if he were beseeching. "Herr Miller . . ." He glanced at the papers for guidance. "You are under arrest."

"What?"

"The government of the United States has requested that you be extradited immediately." Olbricht wiped his forehead with a large handkerchief. "Violation of passport regulations, material witness to homicide, smuggling, interstate flight, attempted kidnapping . . ." He looked up at Aaron. "These charges . . . they are true?"

"No doubt they will be cleared up as soon as Aaron meets with the U.S. attorney," Bar Tov said. "In the meantime I'm afraid you'll have to postpone your visit to Italy, Aaron." The Israeli stubbed out the cigarette. "I really don't need you in Rome . . . underfoot."

"It's a sham!" Aaron exploded. "That's just bullshit to keep me from finding Reichmann. You can't do that! Those charges—" Aaron waved angrily at the papers. "It's bullshit!"

"Oh, they're authentic," Bar Tov said. "Just a few questions in Washington and I'm sure you'll have it straightened out. But you *are* going home. Told you I had a measure of influence with your government."

"You arresting her too?" Aaron nodded at Emma.

"Emma? Whatever for?" Bar Tov shook his head. "However, if Miss Diels wants to travel to Rome, she may find some difficulty in passing through customs. Probably just red tape."

"You think you've got it all covered, don't you?" Aaron said.

Bar Tov smiled. "Yes, as a matter of fact."

"How did you manage all this? I mean, who the hell do you think you are?"

"I told you when we first met, Aaron, that there are several questions we would like to put to Reichmann. And if you had your way that would not be possible. This seemed an expedient precaution." Bar Tov took off his glasses, polished them absently with the hem of his tie. "Also, this hunt for Reichmann has taken on international dimensions. Your government, my government, everyone concerned wants it wrapped up with a minimum of publicity, which means none at all."

"So I get shackled in leg irons and shipped back to the good old U.S. of A. while you and your crowd snatch Reichmann?"

"Nothing so dramatic as all that. You'll be escorted to a plane this morning and leave for Washington International where you'll be met and interviewed. Nothing painful in that, eh?"

"What about Emma?"

"Yes," Emma said. "What about Miss Diels?"

"As far as I'm concerned, you're free to leave." Bar Tov raised a finger. "However, you will find that Monsieur Crevecoeur and several other of your associates have reluctantly agreed to cooperate with us in this matter. I should not try to follow along on the hunt for Reichmann as it will prove frustrating for you."

"Bastard!"

The Israeli shrugged. "I wish you would not take this personally. I like you—both of you. Sincerely, I do. But you are, forgive me, amateurs. Please let us finish this business our own way. Yes?"

Aaron said nothing.

"You'd better find him," Emma said. "You'd better find Reichmann."

"Put it out of your mind," Bar Tov said confidently. "The *Kettenhund* is in Rome or will be soon. We *will* find him. No harm will come to the Pope. I assure you that Eduard Reichmann is only a few hours away from the net."

At that moment in New York, a tall blond traveler stood at the reception desk of a small hotel. He'd deplaned only three quarters of an hour earlier at John F. Kennedy International Airport. He carried only two pieces of luggage. One was a Samsonite two-suiter and the other a small black bag, like doctors use.

29

The televised Olympics had been a wonderful show and Rafai Jamil had watched every minute. Bruce Jenner, the American, had just won the decathlon and title to "the world's greatest athlete." He had seen Juantorena, the quiet Cuban, set world records in the 800-and 400-meter races. He suffered through the gymnastics and the broadcasters' antics revering the fourteen-year-old Rumanian girl and rooted the South Korean women's volleyball team to a bronze medal.

But his happiest moments were with the fighters and Jamil could not help himself: He applauded the American team. Five of the nine had made it to the finals. Tomorrow he would watch the Americans. Saturday, the day of the finals.

It all had been just what was promised. Jamil shared in the thrill of victory. Only once had he nearly forgotten to make his scheduled call to the Palestinian. It had been in the tight basketball competition between the Soviets and Yugoslavia.

At the beginning, Jamil's two companions had not demonstrated any interest in the Games; being too occupied with salving their wounds from the guard dogs that had attacked them. But Gaafar, the Sudanese, had slowly warmed to the competition if for no other reason than it was the only entertainment available in the heat of summer cooped up in a small hotel room. El Shaibi, the Bedouin, could not be enticed away from the solitude of his room. For hours he would sit at the window and watch nothing more dramatic than the pedestrians below and the traffic light at the corner. The dogs had hurt his pride the most. His face and arms bore the marks of his humiliation.

On the floor in an empty closet, wrapped in a sheet and knotted at the ends, was the object that had brought them together in a mission none of them had thought carefully through. Not that it mattered. The object meant nothing to them. If ever they had been aware of its notability, it had been forgotten in the preoccupation with the Games or the scrutiny of pretty young jaywalkers.

Emma stood at one of the windows in the blue concourse of the Munich-Riem Airport and watched the Lufthansa jet streak down the concrete and lift gracefully off the runway. It hadn't been much of a good-bye. Aaron was escorted to the plane by two *Polizisten* who had nodded their impatient consent when she insisted on coming along. He had not spoken a dozen words in the car, opting instead to stare forlornly out the window. He had surprised her at the last moment before boarding when he took her hand, then kissed her. The old college try is what they'd given it, he said. "Rah-rah." She'd felt awkward and embarrassed having it end this way and if Aaron had given the slightest encouragement, she would have been on the plane with him. But the moment, if there'd been one, had passed and she was left to the role of bystander.

The lighted digital clock above the concourse tolled the time with an electric flick as she moved toward the lobby. Emma might not have seen him if not for the clock. Not that he wasn't easy to pick out of a crowd anyway, but the slight distraction of the chronometer's changing minute card attracted her glance in that direction. She stopped still in stunned surprise. He'd just walked through from the red concourse and was making an inquiry at the information desk, nervously holding a small briefcase under one arm.

Henry Nickelson.

Emma caught up with him halfway across the lobby. She touched his arm and he nearly bowled her over he turned so fast. "Henry? My God, it *is* you."

"Jesus, you scared me half—" Henry stopped, looked at her queerly. "Emma?"

"How did you get here!"

"There isn't time to explain." He glanced around expectantly. "Where's Aaron?"

"He's gone."

"Gone?"

"I just watched his plane take off," Emma said.

"Where?"

"They know where Reichmann is. They don't want us underfoot." Emma shook her head hopelessly. "Bar Tov arranged for Aaron to be extradited back to Washington so he wouldn't be in Rome for the final showdown. That's where Reichmann is . . . Rome."

Henry pulled her by the arm to an empty telephone booth. "You know about Rome? The Pope?"

"Yes, but how did *you* know? And for God's sake, Henry, what are you doing here?"

"The *Oberkomitee* is in a panic over the coming exploits of their unchained chain dog. They sent me with the goods to head him off."

"Bar Tov's already—"

"Where is Bar Tov?" Henry said quickly.

"Rome—or will be soon. He left this morning. I think the whole world will be waiting for Reichmann when he shows up at Vatican City."

"No." Henry shook his head. "They've got it wrong."

"Who has?"

"Bar Tov . . . whoever thinks Reichmann is after the Pope."

Emma frowned. "He isn't?"

"I've just spent fourteen hours over the Atlantic Ocean with this." Henry held up the valise. "It's Reichmann's file. The *Kettenhund* file. It has his entire life history. I've been reading nothing else. His real name isn't even Reichmann."

Emma stared blankly at the briefcase. "If he isn't after the Pope . . ." She shook her head. "Henry, he has to be. It all points to Rome. Everyone is waiting there."

"Then everyone is wrong."

"That's easy for you to say, Henry. You didn't talk to Anna."

Nickelson frowned.

"Anna Weisse," Emma continued. "She helped Reichmann—took him to Berlin where he picked up a bomb specially made for his target, the Pope."

"No," Henry said. "It isn't the Pope."

"Look, Henry, don't shake your head at me. She was meeting him after he did his job. She wasn't lying, Henry. I believe her."

"This girl, this Anna Weisse . . . she said he was going to Rome?"

"Yes! Damnit, you weren't there, Henry. You didn't see her."

Henry glanced at his watch. "Probably why I wasn't taken in. We have to get Aaron. *And* Bar Tov." He looked down the row of airline counters. "Aaron's flight, was it direct to Washington?"

"Lufthansa to Frankfurt," Emma said. "Then Pan Am nonstop. Why do you insist that Reichmann isn't going where we think he's going?"

"Because of his record." The big man tapped a finger along the side of the briefcase. "Reichmann got straight A's in deception in the Wehrmacht. He was chief of staff of *Kettenhunde* counterintelligence. Every operation he ever planned was distinguished by its brilliant duplicity."

"Meaning?"

"The ruse, my dear Emma. The ruse." Henry wedged himself into the telephone booth. "I think our friend has taken you all in by one of his disinformation shenanigans. He *wants* you to think he's going to Rome. Reichmann was the prototype Aryan, did you know? They called him the Man of the Reich. With an understanding of his background, I think we can run him down now. He thinks he is Hitler's avenging angel." Henry counted out his change.

"Who are you calling?"

"Strausser gave me some very interesting material here along with Reichmann's file. I want to share it."

Emma stared at him several moments. "What about Aaron?"

"What about him?"

"We have to get him back . . . we have to—"

"Back? Good lord, no. Didn't you say Bar Tov had him deported?"

"Extradited," she said impatiently. "To keep him out of their hair. I told you."

"Yes, well, I think Bar Tov has done Aaron a service; the wrong instinct but the right move. We are leaving for Washington ourselves . . . as soon as I make some calls."

"Henry, for God's sake—" Emma stopped herself. It only just occurred to her. "If . . . if Reichmann isn't going to assassinate the Pope then who *is* he after?"

"Killing the Pope would only give us another martyr. Reichmann knows that. He's after something more. Chaos. Political chaos."

"Who?" Emma demanded.

"You haven't been reading the papers, Emma," Henry said. "The biggest show in town comes every four years and the world watches with nervous anticipation . . . when the Americans elect a new President. Would you like to guess when the Republican party convention begins?"

Emma's eyes opened wide. "Oh my God."

"Wouldn't that be a bicentennial surprise."

30

The Saturday-morning children's television fare was not a great source of amusement to Rafai Jamil, though Gaafar found it endlessly entertaining, especially enjoying the Road Runner Show, wincing delightedly beneath the bandages that crisscrossed his wounded face. Jamil had been restless the entire morning. The Olympic coverage would begin at noon and Jim McKay, the ABC anchorman, had promised in a 9 A.M. station break between the Pink Panther and Scooby-Doo that highlights of the boxing competition would be featured first, plus an "Up Close and Personal" interview with the fearless Spinks brothers. Jamil paced anxiously back and forth to the gleeful chortles from the Sudanese. Mercifully, according to *TV Guide*, which was never out of reach, there was only the adventures of Fat Albert that remained to be suffered through.

The timid knock at the door was a welcome diversion. Though the maid had been instructed to leave the bed sheets outside, she insisted on handing them over personally as if she was exclusively responsible for their accounting. Jamil was surprised, when he cracked the door, that it was not the tired-faced woman. It was a tall man, blond, and he carried a small black bag.

Jamil touched the knife concealed inside his *aba'a* robe. "What do you want?"

"Excuse me . . . ah, Mr. Jay-mill?" He glanced nervously at a clipboard.

"What do you want?" Jamil repeated fiercely.

"Excuse me, sir, I . . . I am Dr. Ernst Schmidt," the man said, fidgeting uneasily with the clipboard. "From the New York State Department of Health."

"I am not sick." Jamil started to close the door.

The man in the hall shook his head, trying to smile. "Oh, no, sir." He wiped his forehead with a handkerchief. "Um, I want . . . I mean, the registrar at the front desk said there were three gentlemen here of . . . of . . . that is, foreign nationals."

Jamil scowled.

"We are—that is, the New York State Department of Health is working with the U.S. Public Health Service," he went on quickly. "A survey, you see."

"What for?"

The man called Dr. Schmidt glanced self-consciously up the corridor and wet his lips. "Actually, you see, it's about this, this so-called Legionnaires' Disease." His voice was very low. "You may have read about it, Mr. Jay-mill."

"The fever?" Jamil said. "The fever on the news?"

"Yes, that's it," the doctor said brightly.

"People have died from this fever. Why have you come to me?"

The doctor raised a hand. "Now, you needn't be alarmed, Mr. Jay-mill. Really. We don't want to create unnecessary concern, but we are, um, interviewing persons like yourself who have recently come to this country from abroad."

Jamil looked at him suspiciously. "You think maybe we have this fever?"

"No, no, of course not." The doctor dabbed at his forehead again. "But, you see, it has us in a bit of a quandary, Mr. Jay-mill. It may be a virus introduced by someone from your part of the world. Quite innocently," he added. "We'd just like you to come down to our clinic some time convenient in the next—"

"No!" Jamil said quickly.

"Excuse me?"

"We do not leave this room."

"It would be just for a brief examination, perhaps a vaccination . . ."

"No."

The doctor sighed nervously. He tried to smile again. "Forgive me, truly, sir," he said, "but the federal authorities have been rather insistent with us. You see, personally I don't see the sense of it what with all the visitors here in New York, but unless you make an appointment . . ." He sighed again, avoiding Jamil's eyes, and shook his head as if it all were a sad state of affairs.

"Yes? Unless what?"

"Believe me, Mr. Jay-mill, the state of New York is not responsible for this threat of police action. . . ."

"Police?" Jamil's eyes narrowed.

"I'm sorry, sir. We have been instructed to report anyone who does not voluntarily submit to an examination."

"I do not want the police here," Jamil said angrily.

"Oh, no, sir. We are totally agreed there, sir. Foolishness, that's what—"

"You are a doctor?"

The blond man looked up sharply. "Oh, yes, Mr. Jay-mill. Twelve years' practice at St. Mary's and another—"

Jamil waved him off. "You can make this examination yourself? Now?"

The doctor smiled. "Why, yes, I can."

Jamil closed the door, slipped off the security chain and opened it again. "Come."

The *Kettenhund* examined them each in their turn. Jamil first, because he was the leader. Then Gaafar. El Shaibi, largest of the three, was sullen and bad tempered about being touched near the face, but Jamil barked a command and the Bedouin reluctantly acquiesced. Stripped to the waist, they sat on the sofa together like three adolescent girls in puberty, self-conscious yet curious. Reichmann thumped their chests, peered into their eyes and inspected their tongues with careful diligence.

"You really should have someone look at those scratches," he said, nodding at Gaafar and El Shaibi. "Change the bandages, you know."

"Yes, later," Jamil said from his place on the end. "You are finished?"

"Very soon now," Reichmann said. He went to his bag and took out a syringe.

The Bedouin's eyes opened wide. He said something excitedly to Jamil.

"What is that?" Jamil demanded quickly.

Reichmann held the syringe up, drawing liquid from a small ampule. "The vaccination." He smiled. "Just a little shot in the arm."

"I do not want this vaccination."

"But, Mr. Jay-mill, I thought I explained all that. It's part of the examination. Antivirus is all. You aren't really afraid of the little shot now, are you?"

"Him." Jamil nodded to the giant Bedouin. "He does not like the shots."

"It's nothing," Reichman said with a shrug. "A prick."

Jamil spoke rapidly to El Shaibi, but he would not be convinced. They raised their voices. Jamil won. "If it is necessary so that the police are not involved, we will have the vaccinations," he said to Reichmann, but stared at the big man who glared at the floor.

"Very good," Reichmann said. "Might as well start with you."

"What is this antivirus?" Jamil's eyes were on the needle as Reichmann moved to him.

"Acetylcholine," as a matter of fact." Reichmann saturated a cotton swab with alcohol. "Now, if you gentlemen will hold out your right arms."

He instructed Jamil, and the others followed his lead. Each was to press the thumb of the left hand deep into the crook of the right arm, arresting circulation of the radical vein and allowing it to "show itself." Reichmann explained carefully each step as he went along. He swabbed a patch of alcohol across each of the exposed forearms. By slowly releasing pressure on the vein, thirty to forty seconds after the injection, the antitoxins in the serum would be less likely to burn. Releasing pressure quickly, he explained, would mean an immediate discharge of the antivirus into the bloodstream which would result in a slightly uncomfortable burning sensation. Reichmann smiled reassuringly his best family-doctor smile and slid the needle expertly into Jamil's forearm.

Reichmann's ruse worked—the absurd notion that slowly releasing pressure to the vein would prevent the burning sensation bought him the time to make all three injections. He could not have afforded simply to burst into the room shooting. One gunman against three, even with the advantage of surprise and using a silencer, was not acceptable odds. He still had to find the urn and there was no guarantee someone, perhaps a policeman, would not get to the scene before he'd left with what he came for. Besides, a gun battle meant press coverage. Publicity he didn't need. So, he struck on a quieter more cerebral approach.

It was working. He extracted the needle from Jamil's forearm, wiped it with the alcohol swab and moved to Gaafar. Jamil held his thumb in position obediently, watching curiously as Reichmann eased the needle beneath the skin along the blue line that was the vein of the Sudanese. There would be no problem with Gaafar; he clutched the joint of his elbow with such intensity his knuckles were white. He was not going to be burned, this one.

Technically, if not medically, Reichmann had executed the two men with their arms upraised like questioning school-children as he moved to the last of his victims—El Shaibi, the huge brooding Bedouin. He had not been reassured by Reichmann's soothing words. He did not like the needle.

Reichmann wiped the needle once more with the alcohol swab. "Last one."

But the Bedouin pulled back as Reichmann leaned forward. He growled something to Jamil.

"He doesn't like the needle," Jamil said. The dead man not dead nodded at his own arm. "He wants a different needle. He says Gaafar has contaminated it." Jamil shrugged. "Bedouins."

Reichmann held the alcoholic swab for El Shaibi to see. "Sterilized, you see . . . not to worry." Reichmann moved in. It was a mistake and he realized it too late. The Bedouin reared back, then pushed himself forward and up. He was on his feet before Reichmann could react.

"No, wait . . ."

El Shaibi grumbled angrily at Reichmann, pointing to the needle, then to the small black bag. The shouting match began. Jamil was quickly up, then Gaafar, waving his arms like a toreador. When he saw Jamil release his arm, Reichmann lunged toward the Bedouin with the needle. The death clock had started. The big Bedouin pushed Reichmann away as if he were a leper and he fell backward over the coffee table, crashing breakfast dishes. The quarrel was over before it began.

Gaafar screamed first.

The effect of the chemical as it raced through the bloodstream to the body's primary muscular organ was like a massive heart attack. Gaafar clutched his chest and went down heavily. Jamil's death scream caught El Shaibi with his mouth open, stunned to silence. Jamil tore at his *aba'a* robe for the knife, his eyes wild on Reichmann. His last coordinated movement was one faltering step forward, then his eyeballs rolled back and he collapsed awkwardly like an unstrung marionette.

For several moments, nothing happened. Reichmann lay sprawled on his back, the syringe in one hand, shaking off the dizziness from striking his head on the floor. The Bedouin stared wide-eyed around the room. At Gaafar who'd fallen back against the sofa, eyes up and open. At Jamil. At Reichmann, and the needle. Then the Bedouin looked down at his arm which he still held like a dullard in the thumb-over-vein pressure position. Realization dawned slowly.

"*Hatelak*," he screamed. He went after Reichmann like a mad bull. "*Hatelak!*"

Reichmann was nearly to his knees when the huge Arab's fist crashed down on his back, slamming him back to the floor. A kick in the kidneys doubled him up and another glancing blow on the side of his head nearly blinded him, but he managed to roll. The Arab was using the heel of his bare foot as a weapon. He could kill with one stomping stroke and Reichmann scrambled desperately to keep him away from his head. He tried to knock the Arab's support leg from under him but it was like kicking a tree trunk, and he was hit again in the side. When the Bedouin raised his heel once more, Reichmann feinted with his head to one side and lunged. El Shaibi's heel slammed like a hammer blow against Reichmann's shoulder, but he'd grabbed hold of the mammoth leg and with all his strength heaved up and back. They fell over together, toppling across Jamil's legs. Reichmann had held onto the syringe and now he jabbed it blindly over his head. The needle struck the Arab in the groin and Reichmann thrust the plunger home. He pulled it out and stabbed again and again. In the stomach. In the thigh. In the diaphragm. When he rammed it into the hip, the needle struck bone and broke.

Reichmann rolled on his back, panting and stunned. But El Shaibi was not finished. Through pain that would be unendurable to any other man, the huge Arab rose up like a mountain and crashed down on his assailant. His massive hands were on Reichmann's throat, slowly squeezing his thumbs into the soft hollow of the neck. His putrid breath was hot in Reichmann's face. The German groped frantically on the floor beside him, his fingers searching wildly for the syringe. The needle was there. It had to be there! The vise at his neck was closing. Reichmann's fingers found the syringe. He jabbed it with a roundhouse swing that punctured the Arab's neck at the base of the skull. The broken needle point carved a jagged wound across the vertebrae but Reichmann hadn't the strength to depress the plunger. He jammed the needle deeper as the darkness of unconsciousness began to engulf him. Suddenly, the fingers at his throat slackened, released their hold and fell away. The Bedouin's eyes blinked, then took on a dull, drunken stare as his head lolled, there was a sickening, racking intake of breath, and he collapsed, his face sliding down Reichmann's chest.

Reichmann rolled on his side. For several minutes he lay there, between the bodies of El Shaibi and Rafai Jamil, sucking heavily for air. Across the room the television silently extolled the virtues of a toilet tissue.

Reichmann's coat and shirt were folded over the bar of the shower curtain. He was on his knees before the bathroom sink, splashing water on his head and neck. The Arab had hurt him. His left side and shoulders were sore and bruised, but nothing was broken. He stood up to inspect himself in the mirror. No visible marks except a lump behind his ear and a redness at the throat. He splashed his face again, resting his arms on the sink. The Bedouin had nearly killed him. Let it be a lesson, he told himself. Thirty years ago he would have handled himself better. Today he'd been lucky.

He rested for several minutes, sitting on the edge of the bathtub, a towel draped over his head. Fifteen minutes later the *Kettenhund* was dressed. He found the sheet-wrapped object in a closet and he sat with it in his arms in an overstuffed chair beside the television. The gold surface of the urn gleamed brightly. It was more beautiful than he had imagined. And it was his now. His alone.

The television made note of the time and Reichmann glanced at his watch. It was noon, time to make a call.

The voice from Paris was gruff, impatient. "Yes, what is it?"

Reichmann spoke slowly. "All is well. The vessel is safe."

"Rafai?"

"No."

"Who is this?" The Palestinian in Paris demanded.

Reichmann smiled. "The urn is in good hands, effendi."

"Who—"

"*Auf Wiedersehen, mein Herr,*" said the *Kettenhund* before he severed the connection.

*   *   *

The Man of the Reich had a busy afternoon ahead. He would visit the city morgue and a south Manhattan mortuary. It promised to be an afternoon of much paperwork.

By 10 P.M. the groundwork would be finished. At 10:10 he would leave John F. Kennedy International Airport. Not a long flight. Tomorrow was Sunday. He would rest. Then he would celebrate. The world would remember this Sunday. It would remember his birthday.

The television was still playing when he left. Jim McKay had kept his promise. Highlights of the boxing competition reverified that Sugar Ray Leonard and the other semifinalists on the American team had fought their way to the finals and a chance to win the gold. The "Up Close and Personal" interview with the Spinks brothers had a special note of sentimentality as their mother had been flown to Montreal from her home in a St. Louis housing project through the financing of an anonymous donor.

It was a show Jamil would have found interesting.

CLOSING CEREMONIES

31

His name was Fisher, a middle-aged man with curly brown hair and an eye for clothes. He drove an official government sedan and, Aaron thought, talked rather too much. He also took Aaron's passport at the airport.

"How did you first come to be interested in National Socialist history?" Fisher asked from the bar of his Georgetown apartment.

There was no end to the man's ridiculous questions. And it had been going on this way for hours. Fisher was first in the line of greeters when Aaron got off the Pan Am jet at Washington National. The weather, the flight, the current exchange rate in Munich, Fisher inquired about everything except Reichmann as if it was a taboo topic. In his office, a cubicle really, on the third floor of the Department of Justice Building and the furthest door from the elevator, Fisher did mention something offhandedly about the unfortunate business of extraditing American citizens, then quickly went on to explain that Miller had not been actually, *officially*, extradited. It was a voluntary thing, Fisher said, to answer a few questions. After all, hadn't the government paid his ticket?

Aaron demanded to be charged with something or allowed to leave. He demanded his passport be returned. He demanded that he be allowed to fly to Rome. But Fisher only shrugged. Unfortunately, there had been a misunderstanding. The passport had been revoked, invalidated, and that could not be changed on a weekend. Fisher apologized. Aaron would be issued a new passport "the very first thing Monday." It was all extremely regrettable, Fisher had said in his easy Washington manner. All very unfortunate. All bullshit. Bar Tov had influential friends.

Fisher poured another Scotch and soda for himself and climbed back on the bar stool across from Aaron. It was nearly midnight and in the last eight hours—ten?—Aaron felt he had learned more about William J.(for James) Fisher than even his ex-wife back in Ohio whose complicated hysterectomy in '73 that cost him two grand had ever cared to know. He'd been a marshal (United States Marshal, Division I, District of Columbia) for twelve years and Aaron was the ninth case he'd been associated with under the Witness Security Program (though Aaron's situation was rather stretching a point, he thought, but then they were all a little eccentric in the W.S.P.).

Fisher had had six drinks by Aaron's count; two extra dry martinis before dinner at San Souci, one after, and now he was working on this third Scotch.

"I never got into the war," Fisher was saying. "Sophomore at Buckeye State when Roosevelt sat down with Stalin at Potsdam to divide up Europe. Never paid much attention to the National Socialist movement. You must be quite an authority on the Nazis." Fisher sipped his drink, looking over the rim of his glass as if to grant Aaron a chance to talk. There had been few such intermissions.

"I'm not an authority," Aaron said dryly.

"Oh? I had the impression you were."

"No." Aaron ran his finger around the edge of his glass. "I'm only interested in one man who happened to be an SS major."

Fisher nodded. "The one in Rome?" His response was surprising because it was the first acknowledgment Fisher had made that Reichmann existed.

"That's right. You know about him?"

Fisher shrugged. "Not really. Just that he's a Nazi and you were looking for him."

"And now I'm not."

"And now you're not." Fisher nodded. He swallowed more Scotch. "They'll find him. Don't worry about that."

"Who's worried?" Aaron smiled wryly. "You're a terrific baby-sitter."

The telephone woke him. Aaron rolled over groggily on the bed and was distantly aware of Fisher's voice in the next room. He lay there for several moments trying to make out Fisher's end of the conversation, but couldn't. The clock on the bedstand put the time at just after 3 A.M. Aaron got up to get himself a drink of water. He'd been dreaming about the former Mrs. Fisher laid up in an Ohio hospital, counting out two thousand one-dollar bills.

"Aaron?" Fisher was standing in a robe in the middle of the living room with the telephone and a cigarette.

"Water," Aaron said. He moved sleepily toward the kitchen.

"You'd better put on some coffee," said the barefooted United States marshal, cupping the receiver. "Company's coming."

Aaron stopped. "At three in the morning?"

"The Secret Service never sleeps." Fisher took a long deep sigh. "They're bringing some friends of yours."

"I don't have any friends at this time of night."

Fisher listened to the receiver for a moment, glanced up at Aaron. "This guy says to remind you it's Sunday. Time to put on your party hat." The marshal frowned, shrugged. "Someone's having a birthday?"

*   *   *

If Aaron was surprised to see Emma, he was astonished to find Henry with her. Three Secret Service agents had escorted them. The leader of this blurry-eyed group was a round-faced man named Bickham (*senior* agent Bickham) who kept a pair of aviator sunglasses handy in the breast pocket of his conservatively cut suit coat.

Henry and Emma quickly went through their story. Reichmann was not in Rome, was never going to Rome. Bar Tov had it wrong. He'd followed where Reichmann had led him, which was away from the real target.

"So who is the real target?" Aaron asked.

"The President," Bickham replied. "But we've canceled all his engagements today. He's spending a quiet day at home. He's not even going to church this morning."

"You're sure it's the President?"

"Without a doubt." Bickham looked up to one of the other Secret Service men and was handed a manila envelope. He opened it and passed three photographs to Aaron. "Recognize any of these men?"

Aaron didn't know the first picture. The second was Rafai Jamil. "This one," he said quickly. "This is the guy outside Henry's place." Aaron glanced up at Henry. "The one who shot Linka."

Henry nodded.

Aaron studied the photo again. "He looks dead."

"He is dead," Bickham said. "They're all dead. The maid found them last night. A hotel in New York."

"Reichmann," Henry said. "They had the urn. Now he has it."

"Reichmann's in New York?"

"Was." Henry nodded at the photographs. "Yesterday."

"How did he get here with nobody knowing?"

"We think he's traveling under the name of Kruuze," Bickham said. "According to Nickelson here, it's his real name. Georg Kruuze."

Aaron leaned back in his chair. "Does Bar Tov know yet?"

"I talked to him before Emma and I left Munich," Henry said. "He knows. He just doesn't believe it. Bar Tov is convinced Reichmann is in Rome. He thinks *we're* following the wild hare."

"A belief that the United States Secret Service does not share," Bickham added. "Bar Tov doesn't know about the Arabs, yet."

"If Reichmann has the urn," Aaron said, "then . . . isn't that what he wanted? He'll go home now. Right? He's got what he was after."

"We are not taking a chance that he won't go ahead," Bickham said.

"Besides," Henry added, "Reichmann isn't working for Strausser anymore. I don't think he really ever was. He doesn't care about the Nazis. He doesn't respect them or trust them. There is only one man in the world worthy to keep it."

"Reichmann?" Aaron said. "Himself?"

"Who else?" Henry frowned. "I've been reading the *Kettenhund* file. Something about this man bothers me. He's committed himself to this plan. He's dedicated to it. A man like Reichmann does not easily pull back from such a grandiose scheme. I think he's decided that having the urn isn't enough. Someone has to pay for his trouble. An American took the urn. An American will suffer for the sacrilege."

Aaron looked at Bickham. "Well? Reichmann can't very well walk into the White House. Today's the day he'll make his try."

"There won't be any public tours today. There won't be anyone except White House security on the grounds. He can't get in."

"And if he wasn't planning to get in?"

"The only activity Reichmann could possible count on that is part of the President's Sunday routine is church," Bickham said. "Whenever Mr. Ford is staying at the White House on Sunday, he and his wife attend St. John's." The Secret Service man took a breath. "He won't today, but two of our people will. The whole place is being searched right now. If your Nazi friend tries anything, we'll have him."

"That's what Bar Tov said about Rome." Everyone looked at Emma. She had been quiet nearly the whole time, glancing through Henry's file on Reichmann. She didn't look up when she said it.

"Bar Tov was wrong," Bickham said confidently.

"It all makes sense," she said, turning the pages of the file slowly. "Reichmann was in New York. He promised to assassinate"—she raised an eyebrow—"try to assassinate, a head of state. The only head of state of any great consequence we have is the President. That makes sense. It's logical." She stopped turning pages. She slid one of the sheets of Reichmann's file out of its paper clip. "Maybe I'm just too tired or too dumb to see it, but there's an inconsistency here I don't understand. Maybe someone else can explain it."

"What inconsistency?" Aaron said.

"His name," Emma said. "Reichmann changed his name, I mean his alias. He's traveling as Georg Kruuze." She shook her head. "Except he is Georg Kruuze." She stared at Aaron. "Why did he do that, Aaron? He had forged passports and identity papers. He could have been anyone he wanted to be, but he chose to be Georg Kruuze. Why?"

Bickham looked impatiently at the ceiling. "What difference does it make who he says he is?"

Aaron shook his head blankly.

"I think there is a reason," Emma said earnestly. "I think it's important. We might find the answer in Lubetkin's library." She held Aaron's stare. "Who is Georg Kruuze?"

Aaron nodded at the *Kettenhund* file she held in her lap. "It doesn't say there?"

"This is *Reichmann's* file," she said. "There is only this legal document that attests to an official change of name and some vital statistics. Georg Kruuze changed his name to Eduard Reichmann."

Aaron shook his head. "So what?"

"Maybe I'm crazy," she said. "We've been chasing this SS assassin before he could blow somebody up . . . he set his own deadline . . . August first. Today. His birthday."

"So?"

Emma handed Aaron the page she had taken out of the folder. "This. The legal name change form."

Aaron scanned quickly over the page. He nodded, not knowing what he was supposed to see. "Yeah, that's what it is, all right."

"This isn't his birthday, Aaron," Emma said. "Georg Kruuze was born May 17, 1920." She stared at Aaron for an explanation. "So, who is Georg Kruuze?"

32

They drove to Lubetkin's house. Aaron and Emma started immediately on the old man's files. Indexes of names. Henry began a series of transatlantic calls. He used the only clue they had. Georg Kruuze. He started with registry of births in Heidelberg, where Kruuze was born.

Emma searched the dossiers on political activists, a set of nine volumes, hampered by the inconvenience that the names were not in alphabetical order. Lubetkin's primary interest had not been in political personalities during the formative years of the Third Reich, though he discarded nothing, so this set of volumes had not been painstakingly organized as the others had been. Aaron worked on the military and SS files. They were more neatly arranged. Names crossindexed and alphabetized. But no Kruuze.

Emma had wasted nearly an hour on one false lead. An Alfred Kruuze, Catholic, who was a speechwriter for the former Chancellor Franz von Papen when he was ambassador to Vienna, turned out not to have any connection with Georg Kruuze. There was simply no Georg Kruuze to be found. The name did not appear on any list index. As far as Lubetkin was concerned, he had done nothing significant politically or militarily with the Third Reich to warrant any interest whatever. Aaron and Emma had exhausted themselves searching for a name that might as well not have existed. By 10 A.M. they had searched every index and turned up nothing.

By eleven, Henry had made his last transatlantic call. He was successful where the others were not because he spoke with those who knew Georg Kruuze. The key to knowing the enigma that was the Man of the Reich was buried in the psyche of a sixteen-year-old German youth. On the strength of an old man's recollection of a boy, Henry had assembled the final pieces of a puzzle that described a man's life spirit. What he found was both unexpected and frightening.

Aaron was still at the desk, rummaging through an un-marked box of Lubetkin's notes, when Henry entered the library. Emma was smoking a cigarette at the window, staring drearily outside. Neither had to say that he hadn't found anything.

Henry moved to the desk, cleared off a section and set down three brandy glasses. He poured from a cut crystal decanter he'd brought with him.

"I'd like to offer you two a drink," he said. "Even if it's not the right time of day."

Aaron shook his head. "Not now, Henry. I haven't eaten."

"Eat later. Reichmann will wait."

"Wait?"

The fat man nodded. "We have a little time. I think you should know who Reichmann is before you kill him."

Aaron and Emma exchanged puzzled glances.

"Emma was right, you see," Henry went on. "There *is* something important about Reichmann's true identity. When you understand Kruuze, you'll understand Reichmann. We've missed what was right in front of us all along."

"You mean you actually got something out of those calls to Germany?" Emma looked surprised. "On Georg Kruuze?"

"Georg Kruuze doesn't exist," Henry said. "No, that's not quite right . . . he ceased to exist on August first, forty years ago. Until today he has been the Reich Man."

Aaron sighed. "Henry—friend—you're not making any sense."

"I know where Reichmann is." He took a sip of brandy. "It isn't Washington, D.C., or Rome. I also know, well, I'm pretty sure, who he intends to punish. Not a President, not the Pope, not a prime minister."

"Jesus, Henry," Aaron exclaimed, "are you going to tell us or do we sit here like fools and applaud."

"Take a drink." Henry offered a glass to Emma. "I want you to hear this astonishing story. How a shy, fatherless schoolboy became a Nazi superman."

"From the planet Krypton, right?"

"Please, Aaron," Emma said. "Go on, Henry, I'm listening."

"This is important, Aaron, and you'll see why in a moment. First, Georg Kruuze was an only child. His father was a soldier in World War I who, when Georg was still a youngster, died of complications from mustard-gas poisoning. Hitler's father also died when he was young. The similarities in their lives are quite important. Georg was raised by a tender and loving mother who he reveres to this day. Hitler, in his youth, was surrounded by women . . . sisters and his mother who he never forgot."

"Fascinating," Aaron said.

"Isn't it," Henry replied. "But there's more. Both Hitler and Kruuze demonstrated a natural talent when they were boys. Hitler could draw. But Kruuze was a gifted athlete. Hitler's dream of becoming an artist or architect ended in bitter disappointment. Kruuze reached the pinnacle. When he was sixteen he won a gold medal in the Berlin Olympic Games."

"Reichmann?" Aaron said quickly. "A gold medal?"

"No, no, Aaron." Henry held up his index finger as if to allow him to speak. "Kruuze. Georg Kruuze won the gold. And not just *a* gold medal. The first one . . . on the first day. That's important. Hitler received him personally in his box. It was quite an honor to be hailed by the Fuehrer himself for our Georg Kruuze. Can you imagine? It was a personal triumph for the boy, but it was something of a spiritual triumph for Hitler. The invincible Reich was real and here was the proof. Georg Kruuze."

Aaron nodded but said nothing. Henry was building to something and he would not be rushed. Aaron sipped the brandy and tried to be patient.

"Hardly a household name, Georg Kruuze," Henry continued. "But Hitler was intoxicated with fantasy visions of victory. The Berlin Olympics were to be his showcase to the world of the new Germany. The more he learned about this young hinterland Aryan, the more he identified with him. Kruuze was the future. He was the new Reich as Hitler saw it—young, strong, determined, ambitious. . . . The boy was everything the Fuehrer aspired to be. So to guarantee it, in the Fuehrer's mind, he made this boy the personification of the indomitable Reich. A turn of fate had a hand in the Fuehrer's given name. He was a Schicklgruber turned Hitler. Now he could return the favor. So from that day the boy was no longer Georg Kruuze. He was the Reich Man. Conceived, born and delivered by the supreme judge of the German people . . . in the city that would one day be the capital of the world . . . on the first day of August . . . opening day of the eleventh Olympiad—"

Henry stared at Aaron, waiting.

"Jee-sus Christ." Aaron finally said in a voice that was barely a whisper. "The Olympics. The fucking Olympics!"

"It is Reichmann's birthday," Emma said. "Today really is his birthday."

"It's much more than that, I think," Henry added. "Forty years ago the Olympics began on August first. Through a coincidence of time, this Olympiad ends on August first. Reichmann must see it as the hand of fate at work. It is an important date to him because it was the one and only time he ever met Hitler."

"Reichmann is in Montreal!" Aaron looked quickly at

Emma. "Right now he's in Montreal . . . with a bomb!"

Emma turned to Henry. "You said you knew who his victim was."

"Yes, I believe I do," said the fat man. "And when he'll strike. But let me test my theory."

"Henry, for Chrissake—"

"If we come to the same conclusion, then—"

"Okay." Aaron nodded impatiently. "Okay, go on."

"It's occurred to me to reason why Reichmann would go ahead with the assassination if he already has the urn," Henry began. "My first thought was simply revenge. Adolf Hitler saw a piece of himself in Reichmann, and Reichmann tried to live up to the image, but there isn't a Reich anymore. It's gone. Hitler's gone. But that isn't good enough. Thanks to Strausser and the others, the Fuehrer lives in Reichmann. Hitler *is* Reichmann."

"Henry," Aaron moaned, "c'mon."

"Bear with me, please. Reichmann has the opportunity to repay his debt to the Fuehrer by a punishing act. And what better stage than the Olympics as the whole world watches? There is also an interesting thing about ages that I discovered while I was looking at Reichmann's real date of birth. Reichmann is fifty-six, even if he doesn't look it. Hitler died May 1, 1945. He was fifty-six. I doubt that fact has escaped him."

"So?"

"Anyone so deeply involved in role-playing as Reichmann is could take the part over completely."

"He'd have to be crazy."

Henry shrugged. "Reichmann may be stepping in where his Fuehrer left off."

"I just want to know who he wants to kill, Henry," Aaron said. "I don't follow all this psychological bullshit."

"All right, Aaron." Henry downed the rest of his brandy. "Considering Reichmann's identification with Hitler, especially his great affection for his mother—"

"His mother?"

"Yes, didn't I tell you? As a matter of fact, according to the Heidelberg *Staatsdienstbüro*, he visited her grave and made arrangements to have her moved to the military cemetery with his father. A dutiful and loyal son."

"Touching." Aaron's patience was nearly exhausted. "Who, Henry?"

"The obvious choice," Henry said. "At least obvious to me. To a man in that state of mind? A man who regards his mother with the highest reverence? Any mother?" Henry set down his glass. "Conversely, who could he hurt that, in his mind anyway, would be a shattering blow? A mother. A sovereign mother . . . a royal matriarch . . . revered by the world . . ."

Emma blanched. "Oh, my God!"

". . . who opened the Olympics the first day and will close them tonight."

"The Queen." Aaron nodded finally, staring at Emma. "Elizabeth of England."

"We've got to tell Bickham." Emma started toward the phone. "We have to tell them where to find him."

"I already have," Henry said somberly. "Twenty minutes ago."

"Thank—"

"Not that it did any good," he added quickly.

Aaron's eyes narrowed. "What do you mean? You told him, didn't you?"

"Oh, yes, I did that. But the Secret Service seems to have a sour attitude to our tips lately."

"What?"

"The church," Henry said unhappily. "St. John's church was staked out by every Secret Service agent in Washington and every off-duty cop by Bickham's description. Nothing happened. No bombing. No gun play. No Reichmann. The Secret Service does not like to look foolish. . . ."

"Shit!" Aaron said.

"And they are not going to compound that error in judgment by passing on this new ludicrous fantasy—that's what he called it, a ludicrous fantasy—to the Canadian authorities. As a matter of fact, they now have revised their appraisal of the matter and concur with Bar Tov's conclusion that Reichmann is in Rome."

"They're crazy!"

Henry sighed. "Well, they certainly think somebody is. Bickham told me what to do with my tip. A crude fellow, Bickham."

"If the Secret Service won't do anything—"

"Nor the FBI," Henry said. "There's only us. Three fruitcakes nobody is going to take seriously."

Aaron went immediately to the phone book. "Damn if they won't. There are going to be a lot of red faces around the Vatican when no one shows up to do away with His Holiness."

"But his speech isn't until ten tonight," Emma said. "The Olympics will be over."

"You're still thinking Munich time." Aaron ran his finger down the list of airlines. "Rome is six hours later than Montreal. Ten P.M. in Rome is 4 P.M. here." He began to dial. "We're going to be in the Olympic stadium this afternoon."

"And find Reichmann in the middle of seventy thousand people?"

"Right," Aaron said. "This is my second chance, if I don't blow it. I *will* get him this time. If ever there was truth in the notion of destiny—"

"Destiny!" Emma's eyes widened. "That's something Reichmann would say!"

"Is it?" Aaron smiled. "You know, I believe he would."

Emma glanced at Henry. The fat man shrugged helplessly. She looked at Aaron again. "Then you go get him, Aaron. Fulfill your destiny. Avenge your big brother's murder. Be your big brother." She shook her head. "But do it alone. This is where I quit."

Aaron held the phone to his ear. The airline reservations clerk was on the line.

"What?"

"I'm not going to fight them anymore," Emma said. "Just . . . just do whatever you want." There were tears in her eyes. She stared at him hopelessly for several seconds, then ran out to the patio and across the terrace to a wooden bench in the garden.

Aaron replaced the receiver. He looked at Henry in stunned silence. "What the hell did I do?"

"For a bright boy," Henry said, "you're pretty stupid."

"Henry, for God's sake—"

"She's in love with Aaron Miller." The fat man's look was hard. He spoke as if he was talking about someone else. "She tried to explain it to me on the plane over here. I didn't understand . . . until now."

"Well, then," Aaron retorted, "maybe you should explain it to me."

"You want to be something you can't ever be. I suppose we all try it once in our lives, that kind of role-playing. But we usually stop before it hurts us. You're very close to the edge, kid. You and Reichmann. In some frightening aspects, you two are very nearly twins. Emma doesn't want to be around for the final explosion."

"What kind of bullshit are you spouting now?"

"You're trying so hard to be *like* Abe that—" Henry shook his head "—you almost *are* him." He nodded toward the garden. "That's what frightens her. Let me tell you something, kid. I knew Abe better than you did."

"Oh, Jesus—"

"Better than you," Henry repeated grimly. "He wasn't that great. He wasn't my big brother, either. But I didn't have to look up to him as though he were on a goddamn pedestal. I knew him for what he was. He was a guy with a kid brother who worshiped him. But he was also cynical and pitiless and cruel and other things you never saw. He was a lot like Reichmann."

"You're crazy!" Aaron shouted.

"No, I'm telling you the truth. Abe was just a guy with warts and bad habits like the rest of us. He wasn't even especially bright, just good at what he did. He finally ran into somebody who was a little better. And now he's dead." Henry looked deep into Aaron's eyes. "He was just a guy, kid. Let go of him."

Aaron tried to blink the stinging tears out of his eyes. "Why are you doing this?"

"Because it's time for you to grow up. Because you're the only one who can stop Reichmann now and you can't afford any illusions. Reichmann has convinced himself he is the reincarnated soul and symbol of his Fuehrer's dream because he doesn't have any other choice. You do. You're just Aaron Miller, the man who's going to stop an assassin. If Reichmann's made any mistake, it's that he is living out his fantasy. You don't have to."

Aaron nodded without looking at his brother's friend. He moved to the partially opened glass-paned doors and stared out at the garden. Emma was still sitting on the bench crying. He remembered their first night together, her vulnerability. *We are pieces of each other*, she'd said in Munich. *Pieces.* He remembered the shattered look on the face of Anna Weisse when she realized Reichmann was never coming back. *You can't afford any illusions.* Aaron shut his eyes tight. *I'm telling you the truth. Abe was just a guy. Let go of him. Let go?* Aaron pinched his eyes with his fingers, stared out at the lonely figure on the bench.

Without turning, Aaron Miller said to Henry, "Call the airline. Get us on the next flight to Montreal . . . the three of us." Then he went out in the garden to Emma.

33

Emil Lubetkin sat in the main lobby with most of the other guests. It had happened so fast, whatever it was, that no one was sure what the confusion was all about. Federal police escorted all the hotel guests to the lobby from their rooms, the grounds, the golf course, the cruise boat, everywhere.

Guests were segregated from resort employees. Jeeps were parked on the lawn. A large contingent of militiamen with automatic weapons searched the rooms. More were outside. An Argentine army major gave orders.

With nothing else to do but wait for an explanation, the mass of guests gradually broke into groups of common languages. Of the total number Lubetkin guessed to be about two hundred, less than forty were Americans. The longer they waited, the more terrified some of the women became of the grim-faced men who stood about in doorways with their guns slung low on shoulder straps. Some cried. Oddly, though he'd never been on a ship, Lubetkin felt it was all much like the controlled panic of a luxury liner with no lifeboats, about to sink.

A man with a bullhorn, the Argentine major, walked to the center of the second-floor balcony and spoke Spanish to the entire group in the lobby. His voice was calm and reassuring as he spoke, and Lubetkin noticed several of the women in another cluster of guests sigh gratefully and cross themselves.

The major finished and handed the bullhorn over to another officer of less rank and stature.

"Ladies and gentlemen," boomed the voice of the little man. "Please, not to be alarmed. There is no danger to your persons. The military junta of the Republic of Argentina has declared a temporary period of martial law. There is no danger. Please prepare, all persons who are not citizens of the Republic of Argentina, to have your passports inspected. *Gracias.*"

Lubetkin left his group, moving as fast as he could to the militiaman at the door where the Americans were being processed.

"I have to see the man in charge," he said quickly.

"*No comprendo.*"

"Please!" Lubetkin pointed to the door. "*Importante . . . rapido!*"

"*No—*"

The old man pushed past him and burst into the office. "*Importante! Importante!*"

The Argentine army major was sitting at the desk, across from him a tall woman Lubetkin had seen before in the restaurant. The major was holding a passport.

"I must talk to someone in charge! *Importante!*" Lubetkin turned to the woman. "Do any of these people speak English?"

"I speak," the major said. He waved away the guard who had taken Lubetkin's arm. "What is it, señor?"

Lubetkin licked his lips nervously. "I want to report a guest . . . ah, there are some people here you must arrest!"

"Yes, señor?" The major sat back in the reclining chair, a pencil between his index fingers.

"Please, you have to find them quickly!"

"What people, *por favor?*" The major smiled knowingly at the woman as if to show his patience with eccentric American tourists.

"I don't know what the others are calling themselves," Lubetkin said meekly, "but one calls himself Herzog. It isn't his real name, he—"

The major sat up instantly in his chair. He dropped the pencil, his dark eyes narrowed, locked on Lubetkin now. "You know this man? This Herzog?"

"I . . . I know his real name isn't Herzog."

The major rose, ignoring the woman and her passport, and came around the desk. "You will come with me please, señor." He led Lubetkin to an adjacent office where the old man waited for several minutes. When the Argentine returned he asked, "Who is Anton Herzog?"

"He's a Nazi war criminal," Lubetkin said. "His name is Heinrich Mueller. He ran the Gestapo."

The major nodded. "Please, señor." He pointed through the window at a jeep with driver. "To see my general. *Si?*"

The ride took less than an hour with a driver who thought he was Mario Andretti. They stopped at a dusty little village full of militiamen and chickens. The general's name was Martinez Alfredo de Sodre. He wore a neatly trimmed mustache and had a half-moon-shaped scar across the bridge of his nose. He spoke English very well. With the general was a dark-haired man in civilian dress who sat quietly in a chair across the room, his hands folded carefully in his lap as if posing for a portrait. He watched Lubetkin and his eyes communicated an uneasiness as if he was unsure himself why he was here. Sad eyes, Lubetkin thought.

Nearly another hour passed before De Sodre finished his questions and Lubetkin got to some of his own.

"This area is heavy with the Montoneros," the general was saying. "Peronist guerrillas."

"You think the resort hotel at Bariloche kept revolutionaries?"

De Sodre gave a quick jerk of the head. "No."

"Look, General, you may not know who Heinrich Mueller is but—"

"Yes, we know him. And Alfred Strausser and Josef Mengele. They are the Nazis." He studied Lubetkin a moment. "You are . . . a Jew?"

"No, but my reasons for finding those men are just as valid. They were staying at the resort, General. You must help me. We must arrest them."

General de Sodre glanced at the man with the sad eyes, then: "I cannot."

"Please . . ."

"I cannot," the Argentine repeated. He looked pleadingly toward the man in the chair. "Father?"

The man who had sat so quietly unfolded his hands, got up, nodded. "Yes." He walked to the tiny wooden table beside Lubetkin. "Thank you, General de Sodre."

The general shook Lubetkin's hand, a bit formally, and executed a polite military bow. Then he pulled his dusty cap down over his head and left the hut.

"A troubled man, señor," said the man before Lubetkin. "As we are all troubled men in these disturbing times."

Lubetkin glanced at him queerly.

"Excuse me, Señor Lubetkin. Let me introduce myself." He stood erect. "I am Monsignor Pedro Cabellero, domestic prelate to His Eminence Avela, Cardinal Valdivia, Archbishop of Buenos Aires, Archdiocese of the Roman Catholic Church." He extended his hand. "Welcome to Argentina."

"Please excuse me," the monsignor was saying. He'd pulled a chair nearer to Lubetkin. "In view of the circumstances, His Eminence suggested I not wear my vestments."

"What circumstances?" Lubetkin said.

The Catholic sighed. "This situation with the Germans. I cannot offer details, but the Church is . . . is involved to a certain degree here. It is an unusual involvement, señor. It is why I cannot officially represent the Church."

The old man shook his head. "I don't understand, Monsignor. I only want the Nazis arrested. They are monstrous criminals who—"

"There will be no arrests," said the priest sadly.

Lubetkin squeezed his eyes together. "But the general! Surely he—"

"The general is a military man who must follow the directions of his superiors, however distasteful they may be to him personally."

Lubetkin swore loudly, bitterly.

"Do not blame the general, señor. He searches for the Montoneros. There was evidence the Peronist guerrillas were in this area; that they were receiving financial support from certain associates of the old Peron regime."

"Strausser," Lubetkin said. "And the others."

The monsignor nodded.

"So they paid off the military to keep themselves safe." The old man nodded. "They have the money for it. I can understand that. But what is your interest? I don't see—"

Monsignor Pedro Cabellero held up his hand. "And I cannot explain it, señor. There are even aspects that are still unclear to me. I can only say the Church was instrumental in uncovering a vast financial empire operated by these men which was invested in certain Vatican institutions."

"Money?" Lubetkin looked into the Catholic's face. "Nazi money?"

The monsignor nodded with a sadness born of guilt. "It is no one's money now. That is, the initial investment was effected under false pretense. As a result, the Prefecture of Economic Affairs has ordered that all financial ties and obligations be dissolved."

"Dissolved?"

"Confiscated," the monsignor said. "It is a condition of Vatican banking procedures. The Church has assumed control of the entire investment portfolio."

"But . . . how . . ."

"As liaison to the Third Prefecture, the Office for the Protection of the Holy Word, I am authorized only to say, señor, that the Vatican was innocently party to a serious pecuniary subterfuge which had gone undetected for more than a generation. That situation has now been corrected."

"*You seized the Reich fortune?*"

The monsignor avoided the old man's eyes. "I cannot say more."

Lubetkin closed his eyes and shook his head hopelessly. "So they're gone again. Gone." He made a fist and held it against his forehead.

"I did not say that, señor."

Lubetkin glanced quickly up. "But—"

The monsignor got up from his chair. He gestured toward the door. "Please come. I will show you."

Lubetkin followed him out into the sunlight. They walked across the village square to where the general was standing beside a tent. The plainclothes priest nodded and the general pulled back the flap.

"Inside, please."

There were three wooden tables. The old man squinted to adjust his eyes after being in the bright sun. The tent was full of flies. Each table supported a blanket-covered corpse. Lubetkin's heart caught in his throat.

"You can identify these bodies please, señor?" the general said.

For several seconds the old man could only stare at the flies.

"Señor?"

Lubetkin moved to the first table. He lifted the end of the blanket. He went to the next table and the next. The face of the last body was badly bloodied, but he knew it. He recognized all of them.

"Señor Lubetkin?"

The old man took a long breath. He pointed to the first table. "Otto Gluck. That one is Walter Helldorf. The fat one is Gerhard Westrick . . . my God, what did you do to his face!"

"We found these bodies, señor," De Sodre answered, slightly antagonized. "The wounds were self-inflicted."

"Suicides?"

"You are sure of the identities?"

"Yes, positive," Lubetkin said. "I don't understand. Why did they . . ."

"They have no money," the priest said from behind him. "The Church has confiscated the entire fortune."

Lubetkin stared at the three corpses. "What about the others? Mueller or Mengele is more important than all of these. And Strausser?"

The man with the scar shook his head. "Gone."

"Gone!"

"Disappeared, señor. But there is no place for them to go."

"I'll find them," the old man said almost to himself. "I will find them!"

"I think you will go home now," De Sodre said. "You will go back to the United States."

"No . . . I—" Lubetkin touched one of the tables, scattering a handful of flies. "I'm so close to them now!"

"You will please go home," Monsignor Cabellero repeated softly. "The general will hunt the Montoneros, and the Nazis will have no money." He led the old man gently by the arm to the front of the tent. "God will do the rest."

34

Aaron and Emma stepped off the Eastern Airline flight at Montreal's Dorval Airport at exactly 3:15 P.M. with Henry close behind. Twenty-five minutes later they were standing before a Sergeant Pitt, Royal Canadian Police, at Station Four security on the ground floor of the white stone Olympic Stadium.

"Chief Inspector Liddell has the stadium security," the burly sergeant was saying. "I wouldn't be worrying about the safety of Her Majesty. We have the situation well in hand, thank you, suh."

"I'm sure you do, Sergeant," Aaron said. "All the same I'd like to see Mr. Liddell."

"Sorry, sir, the chief inspector is quite a busy man," Sergeant Pitt offered dryly. "Olympics, you know."

Aaron had promised himself he would not tell another person "You don't understand." Instead, he asked, "To whom do I report an attempt on the life of one of the dignitaries in attendance tonight?"

"That would fall into my purview also, sir."

336

Aaron glanced at Emma forlornly. Henry sighed.

"There is a man somewhere here at the stadium with a bomb," Aaron said.

"Is there now?" Sergeant Pitt clasped his hands together on the desk.

"Yes!"

"You know who this man is, do you, sir?"

"He's probably using the name Kruuze. Georg Kruuze."

"Using, sir?"

"He's a Nazi!" Emma blurted. "Eduard Reichmann . . . an assassin!" She looked at Aaron in time to see him wince. "I mean . . ."

"A Nazi," the sergeant said, nodding. "Here." He nodded again. "I see."

"Look, we're not weirdos, Sergeant," Aaron said quickly. "There is a man here with a bomb. Good God, how many reports do you get that—"

Sergeant Pitt held out a handful of papers. "In two weeks, sir, nine reports of a man with a bomb. Actually, one of those was of a man with a mortar shell hidden under his coat. Fifteen or sixteen snipers have been reported." The Royal Police sergeant sighed. "We get them all here, sir; robberies, pickpockets, assaults, attempted rapes, solicitations . . . but you're the first with a Nazi assassin."

"Jesus."

"If you'd like to make out a formal complaint, sir . . ." He pushed a form across the desk.

"No, thanks," Aaron said. "We'll just sit here and wait. Your chief inspector Liddell will be getting a call shortly." He looked at his watch. "Just tell him I'm here. Aaron Miller. The guy chasing the Nazi."

Reichmann had been watching the coverage by the Canadian Broadcasting Company. The grand prix team jumping first round was nearly ended. The equestrian competition, traditionally the closing event of the Olympic Games, would begin its second and final round at 5 P.M., in less than an hour.

Reichmann would be at the stadium by six. The formal closing of the twenty-second Olympiad would begin precisely at nine.

The arrangements had been made. The phone call from São Paulo twelve days earlier had insured the success of his mission once he arrived at the Olympic Stadium. There would be no problem with police. Getting *into* the stadium was a *fait accompli*. Getting out was even less a concern. If not for the efforts of a single body of men, none of it would have been possible. The help of the International Olympic Committee was immeasurable. Another group of old men, with an eye for tradition.

Reichmann went to his suitcase and laid out his wardrobe; red blazer, black slacks, gold turtleneck. He unwrapped the box and tissue that held the gold object designed and engineered by German craftsmen. He tested the clasps of its gold-plated chain to be sure it could be easily and quickly uncoupled.

The strategy phase was over now. The trap was baited and set. Only the interval between plan and execution remained. It was the most critical period and Reichmann had witnessed the collapse of other men's preparations during this pause when reflection and reexamination by timid and vacillating officers had combined to ruin a sound operation. But it would not be that way with this operation, just as it had never happened with him before. Reichmann had thought through his plan deliberately, considered every detail. At a time when other men might be tense and anxious about the outcome, Reichmann waited with calm anticipation. He was eager for the task, yet at peace with himself with the steady confidence of a man who knew what he was about.

The waiting was nearly over. Only a few hours more.

With quiet resolution, Reichmann dressed. The challenge was ahead.

"Take heed that ye do not your alms before men . . .

therefore when thou doest thine alms, do not sound a trumpet before thee . . . but when thou doest alms, let not thy left hand know what thy right hand doeth: That thine alms may be in secret, and thy Father which seeth in secret himself shall reward thee openly."

The Pope had spoken.

If Bar Tov heard the Pope's message, he did not listen. St. Peter's Square was filled with people. The Pope's message was brief, as promised. His Holiness then retired.

There was no sudden explosion to excite the night air. No wailing. No screams of terror. There was none because Reichmann was not there to start it. Bar Tov didn't understand. If Reichmann wasn't in Rome and he wasn't in Washington, where in holy hell was he?

St. Peter's Square was empty before the last of the plainclothesmen left. The six Vatican gates were locked and watched over by a doubling of the Swiss Guard from within and patrolled by a special detachment of Italian police from without. The Israeli was taking no risk, though it was a futile effort now and he knew it. Most of the Western world was slipping away from Reichmann's threat with each tick of the clock. Soon, all Europe would be beyond Reichmann's deadline. Like the steady tide of the march of time, August second was gradually moving to the west.

Toward the Olympics, Bar Tov learned shortly.

Where Reichmann was.

Waiting.

As if following the advice of the Pope's message, the Olympic authorities knew little if anything of the machinations of their security services. And as is the usual way of these cooperative efforts, the reverse was also true. It was the concern of the Olympic committees that their own be protected against another disaster such as Munich in 1972. Likewise, it was the highest priority to the security services that the Olympic participants, their functionaries and guests be protected. The two entities were like ships passing, with each interested only that they did not collide.

It was a subtlety of purpose that did not escape Reichmann's notice. Not that the vast security force was not diligent, but all such bodies the world over have the same weakness in common. It was a weakness Reichmann had prodded before. Successfully. The crucial point of his discovery was elementary. In a long and desperate hunt, the safest place for the fox is not in the bush, but with the hounds.

"Ah, yes, Mr. Kruuze," said the portly representative of the I.O.C., "I spoke with you on the phone a couple of weeks ago." He shook Reichmann's hand energetically. "I'm certainly glad you could make it to Montreal."

"It's an honor to be here, I'm sure."

"Have you been enjoying the Games, sir?"

"Very much," Reichmann said. "Am I late?"

"Oh, not at all. Not at all." The man was still pumping the *Kettenhund*'s hand, smiling all the while. "It was a tiny bit of trouble when you called—" now he laughed to himself, shaking his head "—actually, no trouble at all. None a-tall! The day we can't find a spot for one of our illustrious gold medal winners in the parade of nations will be a sad day for these Olympic games, right?"

The man obviously was an American. He wore a string tie and a Rotary Club medal in the lapel of his blue Olympic Committee blazer. Distinctions of affluence. His chubby pink cheeks were lined from too often smiling and he smelled heavily of Mennen Skin Bracer.

"I appreciate your efforts to let me walk with my countrymen," Reichmann offered humbly. "This chance may never come again."

"Our pleasure, I assure you, Mr. Kruuze. It's an honorable and long-standing tradition that former medal winners make that proud walk with the youth of today." The jolly little American patted Reichmann's shoulder where the day before El Shaibi's heel had left a dark blue bruise the size of a fist. Reichmann flinched slightly and smiled. "I see you've found your clothes to match the West German team's colors." He stepped back to admire. "You'll fit right in, now how about that!"

"They are proper, my clothes?"

"Absolutely." The little man attached the official Olympic identification to Reichmann's lapel. "Now you're complete. You don't want to lose that, Mr. Kruuze. You couldn't buy one of these tags. You could call it your license to march." He laughed again.

"Does it begin soon?" Reichmann asked.

"Pretty soon . . . another hour, maybe. They'll be clearing away the obstacles from the jumping competition anytime now." He glanced across Reichmann's chest, then looked back, suddenly absorbed. "Say, is that—" He touched the lapel of Reichmann's jacket to see the thing that was partially hidden under it. "Is that your medal?"

The man called Kruuze unbuttoned his blazer so the chubby little American could see the medal that hung around his neck from a gold chain. "Yes, it is mine."

"Jeez . . . I've never seen a thirty-six gold." He ran his fingers over the raised face of the gold-plated bomb. "You must be awful proud of this."

"I am," Reichmann said. "Awfully."

"We have been aware of the threat posed by this man Reichmann for several days. It isn't as if we aren't prepared, you know." Chief Inspector Liddell pointed to a stadium layout hung on a large board behind his desk, a separate diagram of each of the three tiers.

Liddell was a man besieged by crisis since before the Games had started. As head of stadium security, his first and most bothersome worry was providing iron-tight security to a $700-million sports complex that was only 85 percent complete. Forty police officers patrolled the top of the massive structure with instructions that absolutely no one could approach the oval opening over the playing field. Though spectators went through airport-model security booths on entering the stadium, each night the stadium was inspected by bomb-detection crews. Every day rest rooms were examined. Every day concessionaires' wares were audited. It had been a trying two weeks. The job had called for a man with the patience of Job and the dedication of a fanatic. Liddell had been that man for more than fourteen days. His capacity for perseverance stretched to the ragged limit. Now, with merely hours to go, he faced the challenge of his career—a madman and a bomb. The threat was no longer implied. The call from Ottawa relaying a message from Rome had made that clear.

Aaron surveyed the stadium plans, noting the several entrances. "You can believe that Reichmann has figured a way to get in with his bomb. He may be in."

"We are already checking people with packages," Liddell said. "Because this is the last night and because of the large turnout of VIPs, the security here even now is extraordinary. Even if we knew Reichmann was coming a month ago, we could not make security more vigorous, Mr. Miller."

"Well, he's here, Chief Inspector," Emma said. "And he has a bomb. That's certain. Reichmann has not turned back and he won't because he is driven by a sense of duty and honor. You might as well accept the fact that he's here, somewhere. So don't waste time trying to keep him out. We have to find him inside."

"I don't know what he looks like," Liddell said hopelessly. "My men do not know. The best I can do is to keep a sharp eye out for anyone answering his description, which won't be easy in a crowd of seventy thousand jubilant spectators. Of course, the Queen is protected against anyone with a gun. No one can get near her."

"Reichmann has used forged papers," Aaron said. "He may have some identity cards we don't know about . . . a policeman or security guard."

Liddell pointed to the map. "You see those pins? Yellow, blue, red and green pins? They represent two thousand men. Every man represented by a color knows personally every other man of the same color. The color sectors are so arranged so that no officer of one color is in the zone of another color. If Reichmann was to disguise himself as a police officer, he would be spotted immediately. The idea was not initiated particularly for Reichmann's benefit—there have been other threats of violence at the Olympics—but it will do. As an added measure of precaution, today at noon every officer was issued a special badge. If that is his plan, then we will have him."

Aaron nodded without smiling. "And the press?"

"Everyone inside the stadium, except spectators, will be wearing an identification badge. Camera operators, photographers, reporters . . . everyone, including the athletes. We have gone to the extreme measure of forbidding admittance to anyone of the press who has not covered some event inside the stadium before or who cannot be vouched for personally by a police officer or another certified press organization. Other than that I don't know what we can do except cancel the closing ceremonies, which isn't in anybody's power to do."

"And the final ceremony begins when?" Henry asked.

Liddell turned to the clock on the wall. "A little more than three and a half hours from now. Immediately after the parade of nations, Her Majesty will mount the rostrum and declare the Games officially closed, the flame will be extinguished, cannons will fire, the orchestra will play, and it's over."

"Cannons?" Aaron repeated.

"Mostly noise. We're watching that too. It's the traditional end to every Olympics."

"Noise and confusion," Aaron said. "People running and screaming, acting crazy."

"Celebration." Liddell shrugged.

"That's when he'll make his move." Aaron clasped his hands together. "When everybody is running in the aisles and cheering like lunatics. That's what Reichmann will be waiting for."

The chief inspector nodded at the map without looking at

it. "Do you know that the city of Montreal has spent one hundred million dollars for security of these Olympics alone? Sixteen thousand men in this police force . . . it is the largest armed body of men assembled by this country since World War Two. We have every conceivable police aid . . . dogs, computers, instant satellite communications with nearly any nation on earth, and still . . ." Liddell shook his head disgustedly.

"He hasn't done it yet, if that's what you're thinking," Aaron offered.

"I met Jesse Owens this morning." Liddell smiled wearily. "It was the high point of my day. It reminded me that the next time I see him, in the parade of nations, I'll be soon going home. Now I wonder."

For several moments no one spoke.

"You know, Mr. Miller, tonight the VIP section will be chock full." Liddell pointed out the place on the stadium diagram. "Here. Prince Philip, his three sons. Princess Anne. The Grand Duke and Grand Duchess of Luxembourg. The Prince and Princess of Liechtenstein. Prince Bertil of Sweden. Prince and Princess Takeda of Japan. Prince Gholam of Iran." He sucked in his breath. "Chock full. And that's just the royal VIPs. The Prime Minister and Mrs. Trudeau. The Quebec premier . . . he certainly picked the night for it, didn't he, this Reichmann?"

"Look, Chief Inspector, I know it's a slim proposition, but if I can spot him—"

"There are sixty thousand seats!" Liddell cried. "Another fourteen thousand standees. That many people do not turn and smile when you snap your fingers."

"No, but—"

"Wait!" Henry suddenly stood up from his chair. "Of course. Aaron can recognize him, but he won't have to gallop all over the stadium to do it. You'll pick him out from the back of a truck," Henry said. "ABC is televising this little celebration to the world. The control center in one of those trailers must have dozens of monitors. We'll put Reichmann on television."

Aaron was momentarily awestruck. He glanced at Emma. "The man's a raving genius. Television!"

"Only if it works," Henry said.

"It has to, Mr. Nickelson," answered the chief inspector. "There's precious little else."

"There's nothing *else*," Emma warned gently. "Nothing at all."

35

Roone Arledge, executive producer of the American Broadcasting Company's Olympic coverage, brought thirty commentators and an army of nearly five hundred directors, cameramen and technicians to Montreal. The $35-million gamble turned into an overnight bonanza with the network receiving almost 50 percent of the American television audience every evening.

"Rooney's Regulars" served up the Olympics to a hungry audience with technical support provided by a fleet of communications trailers. Twenty-five color cameras including five mobile units and ten backpack "minicams" broadcast the Games from twenty-four locations. The control center, a prefabricated and soundproof television headquarters, contained a pair of full-sized studios and two control rooms with the capacity to monitor thirty-two cameras simultaneously.

In addition to the ABC coverage, CBC, in conjunction with the Canadian Olympic Radio-TV Organization, employed 104 cameras to simulcast twelve signals via three satellites to broadcasters from seventy countries.

346

For the final ceremonies of the 1976 Olympics the hectic pace of fourteen consecutive days' broadcasting had slowed to an anticlimactic tempo. All but the three stadium cameras and a pair of minicams were packed up for the drive back to the United States. Control-room activity lessened and the tension translated into weariness. With only a few hours remaining of the Olympian extravaganza, the great machine was winding itself down. A power supply tractor-trailer had already left for New York. Out-of-work cameramen and technicians sat with the crowd to watch the wrap-up of the Games or slept in campers before the big move home.

David Michaels, assistant director for the second crew that covered the stadium infield events, was sitting back in a swivel chair with his feet on a VTR box watching a panel of monitors and sipping an Uncola when the trailer door swung open. He craned his head around and was surprised to see two men and a woman climbing inside.

"Hey, you can't come in here."

The first man in held up his lapel badge. "Son, I'm Chief Inspector Liddell, stadium security chief. I want you to crank this place up. We're going to be using some of your equipment."

Michaels got the word from his second unit director who got the word from the assistant producer who got the word from the main man in the central control booth. The word was cooperate.

Michaels started calling. In ten minutes the backup trailer control center was alive with activity. But instead of a hookup for a direct feed to network control in New York, this operation was to be strictly local. And secret. There would be no commentators. No broadcast. Though Michaels didn't know, the intended audience of this hurried production of ten minicams was only one man. Michaels met him briefly between calls. His name was Aaron Miller.

Liddell hovered over a small table with a plan of the stadium, Aaron beside him, Michaels looking on.

"We only have ten of these mini things," the chief inspector said.

"Minicams," Michaels helped. "ESGs . . . backpack power sources."

"Right." Liddell pointed to an area of the stadium plan. "This, Mr. Miller, is the critical area. I'm putting three cameras in here . . . your Mr. Nickelson and Miss Diels because they're more likely to know who to look for, and my Sergeant Pitt because I want someone out there that I know personally. The rest will be Michaels' people because we don't have the time to instruct a lot of policemen in the art of photography." The chief inspector nodded to himself. "Right. Now, two of Michaels' cameramen will be on the second tier between rows forty and forty-nine; two more on the third tier here and here; one each on the opposite ends of the stadium; and one roving on the infield. I'm gambling that we can forget about the far side of the complex. Our man wouldn't do much good over there if he's carryng what you say."

Miller nodded.

Michaels frowned at the diagram. "That . . . say, isn't that the VIP section?"

"It is," Liddell said. "Now, it's important, Mr. Michaels, that we have instant communications with each one of these cameras."

"You will. They all have headphones. Everyone's on the same line direct to me here in the control wagon." Michaels turned to the stacked rows of monitors. "We'll get everything they transmit on those two top rows there."

"Good." Liddell put his hands on his hips. "Is there anything else?"

"Well, sir . . ." The assistant director scratched his head. "This is going to cost *somebody* a lot of coins. All ten minicams? The other control center has five cameras already working inside. Do you really need all these angles?"

"Angles?" Chief Inspector Liddell said.

"Yes, sir. That many operators are going to get in each other's way shooting down like that."

Aaron shook his head. "We're not shooting down. We're shooting up . . . at the crowd."

"At the crowd?" Michaels repeated with astonishment. "Ten minicams? But the action's on the track, not in the stands."

"Let's just say we're trying to keep the action on the track," Aaron said.

Michaels shrugged. "I hope you know what you're doing."

"So do I," Aaron nodded. "More than you know."

The senior cameraman on the stadium second unit gave a five-minute crash course in the operation of the Electronic Sports Gatherer. He skipped over the technical aspects of adjustment. Here is the power switch. This is the monitor screen. That is the zoom control. Don't pan too fast or the image will blur.

Emma caught on quickly. Henry's initial difficulty was fitting into the backpack while Sergeant Pitt was distressed that due to the headset he could not wear his hat, a breach of the Royal Canadian Police dress code.

"The communications will be simple," instructed the veteran camerman. "Your mikes will be open which means you don't have to press anything to be heard in the control room. Just talk. You'll all be talking and hearing each other if you're not careful. So the rule is no talking unless you're called by control. Every operator has a number corresponding to the monitor in the control trailer. Miss Diels is camera one. Mr. Nickelson is two. Mr. Pitt—"

"Sergeant Pitt, sir," corrected the policeman.

"Sergeant Pitt is camera three. The other minis are four through ten. All you have to remember is to move slowly and don't interrupt the controller."

Following the briefing, Emma went to the communications trailer, pushed her way through the policemen where Liddell was giving hurried instructions. She found Aaron alone at a corner desk in the darkened trailer, brooding over a map of the stadium.

"We'll find him, Aaron," she said quietly.

He looked up. "You look like something out of Star Trek," he said, nodding at her gear.

"There isn't much time left, Aaron." She touched his hand. "Whatever happens—" she hesitated, shrugged.

"It will be over," Aaron said. "One way or another. After tonight it will all be over." He held her hand in both of his. "The hating ends."

"And mine. I'm not going back to it, Aaron." Emma held him with her eyes a long moment. "Jean-Paul is dead. Abe is dead. My debt has been paid in full. What about yours?"

"Done," he said. "Finished."

"I love you, Aaron. I want you to know, I mean, I want to say it again." She paused a moment, then added, "Don't worry, I'm not going to cry."

"No regrets?"

"No regrets."

Aaron nodded to himself, smiled at her. "We'll make one hell of a pair, you and me. The stubborn one and the unemployed."

"Be careful, Aaron." She tried to smile. "Please?"

"Piece of cake," Aaron Kyle Miller said. He kissed her, then watched her from the door of the trailer as she left, moving with Henry and the other cameramen until she was out of sight, swallowed up in the crowd of people moving into the gate of the stadium's huge ramp.

An hour before the formal closing, the stadium was filled to capacity. The mood was electric. The crowd was poised to celebrate the end in a burst of jubilation. Obstacles for the jumping competition had been cleared away from the soggy turf of the infield where rain yesterday and last night had soaked the huge playing field. But tonight was clear and the massive oval opening in the roof yawned at a sky full of stars.

Twenty minutes before the closing ceremony, the VIP

section began to fill up behind the red-carpeted wooden box that had been built at the rostrum for the many celebrated speakers who would address the crowd. Directly across the stadium was the orchestra that had been serenading the spectators for nearly two hours. With the coming of the visiting monarchs to their special seats, the orchestra surged into selections of stirring music.

Below the stands at the west end of the stadium, an army of athletes moved into place to begin their farewell march. Nine thousand competitors. Security agents moved through the mass of winners and losers, oblivious to the difference, checking identification badges.

Reichmann was there. From deep in the tunnel, he could see a part of the playing field, the tiers of flag-waving spectators; he could hear the orchestra. He was one face in thousands. Only a few minutes more. The *Kettenhund* held tightly the gold medal that hung from his neck.

Soon now. Very soon.

Aaron's eyes were glued to the five monitors along the top row. With Michaels on one side, giving camera instructions, and Liddell on the other, helplessly looking on, Aaron scrutinized each monitor as it panned slowly across the rows of faces. He could hear the crowd and the orchestra through his headset.

"Steady, camera two," Michaels monotoned calmly into his face mike. "Take your time. Slow and easy. That's it." His stare moved from the second monitor to the next in line. "Okay, camera three. Begin pan. Start with the lady on the aisle . . . that's it. Pull back a bit. Good. Not too fast now."

They worked out a routine. Each camera panned three rows at a time continuously until Aaron signaled to move along. Then they would move up three rows and start again. The two cameras at the end of the stadium picked up those spectators in the aisles and at the rear of the first tier who moved about. The roving infield camera concentrated primarily on the rostrum area and anyone moving there.

But the process was slow and Aaron knew it. There were more than twenty thousand people in this area they were covering. In half an hour they'd scanned about four or six thousand faces. It wasn't working.

"Pan faster," Aaron said. "We're wasting time."

Emma finished another row, moved up the aisle and started panning more faces. The minicam's power source on her back was beginning to be a maxiweight.

Michaels' voice crackled through the headphones. "Pull back, camera one. You're too tight. Back on the zoom. That's it. Hold. Good, now begin pan."

Emma panned. The camera was taking its toll on her shoulder. She was standing in the aisle on the east side of the VIP section when the rippling of applause started. Two men came to the middle of the special section. The music stopped. The applause was louder now, all around. There was more movement in the center of the VIP area. The loudspeakers made the announcement. People began to stand, applauding, waving flags.

"Ladies and gentlemen, the Queen."

"Can you hear, Aaron?" Emma said into her mike. "It's starting?"

"I hear."

"Keep panning," Michaels' voice prodded.

"We aren't going to find him like this," she pleaded. She glanced across the sea of faces to where Henry was standing with his camera in the aisle on the far side of the VIP section. "Henry?"

She saw him shake his head. On the headphones his voice said patiently, "Can't give it up now, Emma."

"But . . ."

"C'mon, Em," Aaron chided. "He may be right in front of you."

Emma glanced back fearfully at the rows of VIPs, then adjusted the minicam on her shoulder, looked into the monitor screen.

"Steady, camera one. Keep panning, please."

"What do we do if you spot him, Aaron?" she said in a controlled tone.

Liddell answered. "My people are standing by, Miss Diels."

They'd better be quick, Emma told herself. From the corner of her eye she caught a glimpse of two figures entering the VIP box.

The Queen of England, of the United Kingdom of Great Britain and Northern Ireland, of the Commonwealth of Nations, entered on the arm of her husband, Prince Philip, Duke of Edinburgh, and nodded graciously at the cheering throngs of well-wishers as the orchestra struck up "God Save the Queen."

The procession of athletes began.

They marched out of the tunnel four abreast on the deep reddish brown eight-lane track, Greece first, past the reviewing stand. Then, in alphabetical order, the other nations followed. Algeria's twenty-eight competitors. The Australians in their bright yellow blazers. Barbados next, in aquamarine. Bermuda in light blue. It was a spectacle of color. Long straight rows of athletes, marching to the cadence of shrilling music, followed the narrow lanes of the track around the 220 curve, down the back straightaway and then into the infield like some magnificent multicolored snake with no end.

As each nation passed in review, the huge scoreboard flashed the country's name in French, as Quebec Province is bilingual. Espagne dipped her colors. There was a loud roar from the American spectators as the Etats-Unis team, with its legion of 474 Olympians, marched out.

In the tunnel, Reichmann heard the roar.

"You are nervous, mein Herr?"

Reichmann turned to see one of the West German swimmers; a young man, blond, standing beside him in the line.

The Man of the Reich shrugged.

"I am . . . a little," said the swimmer. He wasn't wearing a medal. "So many people watching us."

"It will pass," Reichmann said. "We are only two in the midst of thousands."

The boy nodded. "Do you think they will notice us on the television at home?"

"What city are you from?"

"Dortmund, Westphalia."

Reichmann looked down the tunnel toward the stadium. "Yes, I think so," he said. "I think they will notice us tonight."

The parade guide blew his whistle and the procession of athletes moved up to fill the place as another country marched out into the glare.

"There is the American team," Chief Inspector Liddell said. He was watching another monitor on the board which was receiving the network Canadian broadcast.

Aaron continued to scan the faces on Michaels' monitors. "Great."

"And there is Jesse Owens," the chief inspector said wearily.

"Jesse Owens, good." Aaron repeated.

"A great athlete," Liddell said. "A great man."

"Right."

"You don't agree?"

"If Jesse Owens could pick Reichmann out of this crowd I'd kiss his feet. They were both at the thirty-six Olympics." Aaron's eyes darted from one monitor to another. So many faces. The frustration was beginning to show. Several times he reprimanded Michaels because a particular camera was moving too slow. Or too fast. The parade went on. Five minutes.

Ten minutes.

Fifteen. And still nothing. There wasn't much time left. The parade of nations would be ending soon. The Queen would be calling for the extinguishing of the Olympic flame. Where was Reichmann?

Camera six panned across a row of dark faces. There was something nagging at Aaron. Something about those faces.

"You said Owens was in the parade?" Aaron asked.

Liddell nodded. "Yes, marching with the American team."

"But he didn't compete."

"He did in 1936," the polceman said. "It's an Olympic tradition. Former medal winners are invited to march with the new champions in the closing parade of nations. It's . . ."

Suddenly Aaron turned away from the monitors. Liddell blinked at the screen, looked at Aaron. For an interminable moment, the two men stared blankly at each other.

"Jesus Christ!" Aaron breathed. "The parade! Reichmann's on the field."

Aaron grabbed Michaels by the shirt. "Turn them around!" He pointed wildly at the monitors. "Turn them around."

The assistant director shook his head, pulled the head-phones down. "What?"

"Reichmann . . . he's not in the crowd, he's in the parade!"

"What?" Michaels screwed up his face. "What are you talking about?"

Aaron grabbed a pair of headphones on the console. "Emma? Henry? Listen, everybody with a camera. Turn around! Focus on the athletes. Reichmann is with the marchers. He's down on the field."

Aaron spun back to see the monitors. The ten screens jerked quickly around, blurring faces and lights in a long sweeping motion, then settled on several different angles of marchers.

"Keep it on the athletes in the parade," Aaron shouted. "Wait." He looked quickly over to Liddell, cupping his hand over the mike. "What country is passing now?"

The police inspector leaned down to see the Canadian network broadcast. He looked back at Aaron. "Suisse—the scoreboard says. Switzerland."

"Switzerland?" Aaron pulled his hand off the mike. "Reichmann hasn't come out of the tunnel yet. Henry, Emma, keep watching for him."

"We don't know him." Emma said.

"You know enough about him to recognize him now."

Aaron ripped off the headphones. "He's still in the tunnel, Inspector. West Germany hasn't started its march. I'm going down there. C'mon!"

They bolted out the door, Aaron first, and hit the pavement running. The tunnel entrance was a hundred yards away and one floor down.

The delegation of athletes from Sweden had just left the mouth of the tunnel. What Aaron had not realized in the excitement of the moment was the Olympic nomenclature of listing nations. In the case of Germany, since 1949, being politically and physically divided, the handy reference was East and West. Officially, the Bonn government is the Federal Republic of Germany, but in Quebec it was République Fédérale d'Allemagne.

The West German team had already left the tunnel. As Aaron and Liddell raced down the entrance ramp into the rear of the tunnel, Reichmann was already past the reviewing stand, headed into the soft green turf of an already crowded infield.

36

Inspector Liddell, his face red and sweaty, gasped for breath, leaning with his hands against the cool cement of the tunnel wall. Aaron came trotting back to the exhausted policeman after a hurried conference with the parade guide.

"I am not in shape for this kind of exercise," Liddell wheezed, trying to get his breath back.

"They're out on the field," Aaron said. "The West Germans have already left."

Liddell straightened up, turning around with his back against the wall for support. "Then we mst go get him. I will send my men out onto the field—"

"Now! He's already out there, Inspector."

"Exactly so. And we know he is wearing the identification badge of Georg Kruuze." The policeman signaled to an officer with a walkie-talkie on his belt. "I will send my men—"

"Wait, Liddell. If you send an army of police out there now he'll know it's not to check library cards. Reichmann is no fool. You'll only force him to do something desperate." Aaron pointed toward the field. "Look out there, Inspector. Thousands of athletes from all over the world. Do you want to take a chance with their lives? A man with a bomb?"

"I did not see a bomb."

"A man could carry *two* grenades in his coat pockets."

Liddell shook his head. "Not through *this* security, Mr. Miller."

"All right, all right," Aaron said impatiently. "The fact remains that Reichmann has been searched for by every police force in the world. He's outsmarted them all. He's been in hiding until right now. But he is here—out there—at this moment. Do you really think he *doesn't* have a weapon?"

Liddell wiped his forehead with a handkerchief. "What would you have me do, Mr. Miller?"

"We have to get to him," Aaron said. He glanced up at the parade guide when he heard the whistle. Another country marched out onto the field. There were only a few teams left. "Reichmann worked this whole thing out beforehand. The entire security system in this stadium is working *with* him now. He knows nobody can get out there. He's safe to do what he came here to do with the Royal Canadian Police to protect him. The police are guarding the athletes and the VIPs from the crowd. *But nobody is protecting the crowd—or the Queen—from the athletes!*"

"If you have a suggestion," Liddell snapped, "then give it quickly."

"Take off your coat, Inspector." Aaron unbuttoned his own. "Even if you could sneak your policemen in, you don't have time anymore."

"What are you doing?"

"Turnabout is fair play," Aaron said, tossing his jacket aside. "We're going to get Reichmann. Just you and me."

Aaron was wrong. Emma had known it for five minutes as she scanned the faces of the athletes standing in the infield, zooming in and out on individuals as they waited patiently for the ceremony to end. She could not know absolutely which one was Reichmann. The picture she saw of him in his

SS uniform was thirty years old, when he was a young man. The task was more difficult when in her mind's eye she tried to imagine an older man as she panned across so many faces. And they were not all young men, which surprised her. The lean countenance of the classic white male athlete—strong, jutting chin, straight nose, high cheekbones—was a common trait of nearly all the tanned faces. Athletes look alike, at least, she was beginning to see, when you are trying to pick out one from among so many.

Emma jumped when she felt the hand on her shoulder. She turned to find Henry panting beside her, his minicam sagging heavily under one arm. He'd taken off his headphones and reached down and slid hers off too.

"You won't be needing them," Henry said.

"But—"

"It's occurred to me that even if we spotted Reichmann down there it wouldn't do us much good."

"What?"

Henry jerked his thumb toward the green uniformed mounties that surrounded the tiers of spectators. "You think they're going to rush into nine thousand Olympic athletes because we tell them to?"

"But Inspector Liddell—"

"Chief Inspector Liddell isn't going to lead a charge of Canadian mounties into that crowd on the infield." Henry nodded toward the track. "Have you noticed the procession, Emma. The last team is marching out before the reviewing stand."

Emma twisted around to see.

"Canada," Henry said over her shoulder. "The host country of the Olympics is always last."

"My God, Henry, it's nearly over. The Queen will be getting up to give the closing speech. Where is Aaron?"

"I hope he's marching after the *Kettenhund*," Henry said. "Use your camera. Look down there in the Canadian delegation. Go on, take a look."

Emma obeyed. She scanned across the ranks of Canadian marchers. Suddenly she stopped, moved back, zoomed in.

Aaron was in the fourth row near the end. He was wearing the blue blazer and slacks of some Canadian athlete. Beside him, in a pair of slacks that was too short and a blazer that barely covered his stomach, was Chief Inspector Liddell of the Royal Canadian Police.

"What are they doing out there!" Emma yelled, looking over the camera. "What is *Aaron* doing out there!" She shot a terrified glance at Henry. "My God, Henry. We can't let him—"

"We can't stop him, Emma," said the fat man helplessly. "Whatever happens now, Aaron's on his own."

Lord Killanin of Ireland, president of the International Olympic Committee, moved toward the rostrum as the last strains of "O, Canada" died away.

The president began his introduction and acknowledgment of special guests as Aaron scanned across the heads around him. The West German delegation was positioned nearly in the middle of the field, directly in front of the red-carpeted wooden speakers' platform. Flashbulbs were exploding all over the stadium and Aaron's vision was momentarily blinded by them. He shut his eyes and saw a dozen red flashes surrounded by darkness, like little red suns; brilliant red disks. Suddenly, Aaron opened his eyes and glanced frantically around him. The medal winners, like proud fathers, were wearing their gleaming awards from ribbons around their necks. Olympic medals.

Disks.

Aaron grabbed Liddell's coatsleeve. "Christ, I just figured out what Reichmann's going to do!"

One of the Canadian cyclists turned around. "Shhh."

"Look at them. They're all wearing their medals. Reichmann's wearing his."

The policeman stared back blankly. "Yes?"

"It's the bomb!"

Several heads turned toward Aaron, faces frowning. "Quiet, *please*."

"You said yourself the man's not an idiot," Liddell whispered. "He's not going to dash out in the middle of a speech and run towards the platform."

"Reichmann's not going to run anywhere." Aaron stepped back from his place in the ranks, with Liddell by the arm. He pointed to a medal around the neck of a youth who was amazed at the sudden disrespectful breach of etiquette. "Eduard Reichmann won the gold medal for the discus! He doesn't need to get close to the platform—he's well within range from out here. *He's going to throw it!*"

The policeman studied the medal briefly. "Oh, my." He looked at Aaron grimly. "We mustn't let him do *that*."

Another voice in the row whispered loudly, "Stop talking, the Queen is about to speak."

The two men looked up toward the platform.

Her Majesty moved forward to the rostrum. She smiled at Lord Killanin, then looked out over the field of Olympians. "May the flame of these Olympic Games be now unlit."

Aaron was running between the rows of athletes from Finland, past startled faces. Liddell was behind the delegation from Italy, pumping his arms to match the rhythm of his strides. The West German group was just ahead of Aaron now and he could see Liddell puffing around the front rank of Mexicans. In the narrow space that separated West Germany from Rumania, Aaron skipped to a stop and nearly tripped, his eyes racing over the mass of faces; searching, rejecting. The West German team was one of the largest to compete, not as large as the Russian team or the American team, but an assemblage of more than three hundred competitors. On the playing infield, in long even ranks of red blazers, the youth of the modern Germany stretched some twenty rows across and fifteen deep.

Aaron started in the middle, because that's where he was standing, and began to walk toward the front row, as slowly as he dared, inspecting every face, only an instant on each, flicking his glance nervously from one to the next and to the next and to the next . . .

*   *   *

The light of the Olympic flame was extinguished.

The great stadium was quiet as death as seventy thousand people held their breath in anticipation of the final pronouncement when they would explode with jubilation.

His eyes raised to the wooden box, Reichmann watched the Queen with unfeigned interest as his fingers moved surely to the clasps of the medal. He'd computed the distance to be not more than forty meters. An easy throw. He had rehearsed this moment a thousand times. Ten thousand times. At forty meters a schoolboy could do it. One step, turn, pivot, release. An effortless motion.

The Man of the Reich unfastened the first clasp of the gold chain.

". . . may the youth of all countries display cheerfulness and concord so that the Olympic torch will be carried on with ever greater eagerness, ever greater courage . . ."

The *Kettenhund* unfastened the second clasp of the gold chain.

". . . and honor for the good of humanity throughout the ages . . ."

He slid the round medal into his right hand, into the crook of his fingers at the first and second joint. It had a good weight, the feel was exactly right. Reichmann's hard blue eyes were on the Queen as she slowly began to raise her hands.

One step, turn, pivot, release.

". . . until once again the youth of the world is called upon four years hence in Moscow . . ."

Her Majesty's arms were up, nearly outstretched.

". . . there to celebrate with us the Games of the Twenty-second Olympiad . . ."

The Fuehrer's own chain dog stepped out from the row of athletes. The challenge was here. The moment was now. He planted his left foot in the classic tradition toward a pose as ancient as the memory of Coroebus of Elis.

One step . . .

37

Aaron was sweating like crazy.

Somewhere back in the rows of Germans he could see Liddell, wandering between the ranks. Not that it mattered. There was only one man who could pick Reichmann out of this crowd. And he's doing a lousy job of it, Aaron thought.

He was moving backward, letting the rows of faces pass in front of him. When he nearly tripped, Aaron looked behind him each time he stepped back. The Queen was wrapping it up now. He wiped his face with the sleeve of his blazer. The place was still as a tomb. When he stepped back again, looking around so not to trip, Aaron saw the movement. Someone was moving! Not someone, a man. With blond hair. Short cut. Aaron blinked. From the corner of his eye, he saw the figure at the rostrum raise her hands.

". . . there to celebrate with us the Games of the . . ."

The man was moving out of the ranks! At the end of the row, one file up, on the other side of the delegation.

He was twenty yards away and Aaron was running, ripping divots in the soft grass, bumping people aside as he careened like a wild man toward the tall blond man who'd just set his foot and was turning down, shifting his weight, twisting his body lower, arm rigid behind him, coiling his strength for a throw. Aaron could hear the squish-squish as his feet pounded the mucky turf and the echoing words of England's second Elizabeth as she spoke from the platform. Her voice came from a dream, far away, the slow cadence of her delivery keeping him from racing faster.

Ten yards.

Aaron could see the gold surface of the medal between the man's fingers. Reichmann was at the bottom of his turn.

". . . of the Twenty-second Olympiad . . ."

Two strides, seven to go. Reichmann was coming up, pivoting, unleashing his power in a violent orchestration of balance and coordination.

". . . I declare these Games officially closed."

With his last ounce of strength, Aaron screamed and lunged.

"REICHMANN!"

He hit the German in mid-pivot at full speed exactly in the chest. At the instant of collision, as the impact grunted out their breaths and they were two bodies falling, the stadium exploded with the tremendous reverberation of seventy thousand fans and nine thousand athletes' triumphant demonstration of joy. In half a moment the dignified serenity was shattered by an eruption of jubilant madness. The spectators went crazy with noise, cheering wildly, setting off balloons, chanting victoriously, while the rank and file of perfectly aligned nations on the field broke and were instantly intermingled in a huge mosaic of colors.

Chain dog and stalker crashed to the turf in the same moment. Aaron was on his back in the wet grass; Reichmann, on his side. The impact had knocked them back from each other, neither aware if he had done his job.

As a platoon of dancers reeled above him, Reichmann turned dazedly back toward the rostrum. Aaron followed his glance.

The Queen was leaving. Prince Philip was at her side, their

personal bodyguards huddled in close to them as a mass of spectators crowded the fringes of the VIP section, cheering her, waving flags.

The rostrum was intact. There had been no explosion.

Yet Reichmann had not missed. He just hadn't thrown. The German pushed himself up unsteadily on his hands, stunned at the realization. His eyes searched around him until they found Aaron. For several seconds he could only stare. All around, the Olympic competitors danced to the Indian folk music of the stadium orchestra.

Aaron tried to smile.

Reichmann stared. His senses returned, the blue eyes seeing, calculating.

"Miller."

It was not a question or an exclamation. Just a statement of recognition. Reichmann nodded solemnly, his eyes finding something, coming back to Aaron, and suddenly Aaron knew it wasn't over. Reichmann reached into the pocket of his red blazer.

Aaron hesitated too long. He didn't see the medal until it was too late to move quickly. It was stuck in the muddy grass, on its edge, between them, but nearer Reichmann. It should be over now! He glanced up at the royal box. The Queen had not left. She was standing with the Prime Minister, near the VIP entrance, arm in arm with her husband, chatting. *Chatting!*

It should be over now! Jesus, it should be!

Aaron lunged for the medal, but Reichmann was there first. He had something in his hand, jabbing. A pin or needle, for God's sake. It should be over now, he kept telling himself. The blond German kept poking at him with the needle. Reichmann had the medal now and the Queen hadn't left. Aaron saw Liddell searching, but in the confusion, walking away. For some crazy reason nobody sees what's happening here. This maniac was trying to jab a needle in him and nobody was doing anything but dancing around like happy lunatics. Over the orchestra music, a cannon boomed. And another. Aaron could see a mountie leaning against the barricade near the track, tapping his foot, smiling, nodding to the music.

Reichmann went left with one hand, Aaron covered, and the needle punched through his sleeve into the shoulder. Suddenly, Aaron's right shoulder was ablaze with pain. He dropped to his knees. It felt as if something had suddenly crushed his entire right side into a tiny ball and set it on fire.

Then he was alone. Reichmann was up, walking quickly to the track. Now he was on the track, walking toward the raised platform of the VIP section. Aaron saw the Queen. She was moving slowly into the exit. *Reichmann was going to do it!*

Aaron clutched his paralyzed arm and staggered to his feet. *It should be over now!*

He was running again. Why was *he* always running? Reichmann was across the track, moving closer to the railing of the lower tier. Aaron was trying to move faster, commanding his legs. Reichmann hadn't looked around. He was taking the medal out of his pocket, bringing it up in front of him.

It should be over now!

Aaron stumbled into the German from behind, with less force than before, but using his good shoulder like a battering ram, his tired legs churning, slamming Reichmann under the platform, ripping through the Olympic bunting that hung from the lower tier. With Aaron shoving at the German's back, they fell over a rolled tarpaulin in the darkness beneath the superstructure of the stadium. Reichmann protected the medal against his chest. He hit the muddy ground on his shoulder and rolled paratrooper-style back to his feet. Aaron wasn't nearly so coordinated. He fell spread-eagled on his face in the mud, gasping from the pain in his shoulder.

Aaron pushed himself on his side, his chest heaving from the exertion, holding the aching shoulder. He looked up at Reichmann.

"It's over," he said against the pain. "It's all over, Georg Kruuze."

Reichmann's cold eyes communicated a look of begrudging respect. He raised his head as if to nod. There was an instant of professional esteem as between two wounded veteran gladiators who understood the game.

"Yes," Reichmann said. He brought the Berlin gold medal

up in his hand. "Over for my little friend Georg."

They saw them coming at the same time. Liddell and five or six soldiers, carrying stubby, short-barreled machine guns, were running toward them from the infield and Emma was with them.

"It ends," Reichmann said simply. It wasn't an apology. He glanced indifferently at the men running toward them. "Now you will see me home, Miller." He started to turn toward the soldiers, raising the medal bomb above his head. "Ehrenfriedhof. Near Heidelberg."

Aaron reached out as if to stop him. But there wasn't time. There wasn't time to tell him that he was only an amateur. Or about Abe.

Before the first bullet struck him, the German swung his outstretched hand hard against his chest, detonating the gold medal. Fragments of shrapnel that were not absorbed in Reichmann's body ricocheted harmlessly into the soggy ground. The explosion propelled him backward like a straw doll, his body splashing into a puddle, one leg twisted awkwardly over the other. The slightly sweet smell of death rose with the body steam of the corpse beside Aaron in the mud.

Police and soldiers with their guns swarmed under the platform, but it was over.

The chase was finished.

Aaron lay on his side staring at the dead man's face until Emma came, crying. But it was over.

The birthday party was over.

It was not a very expensive marker Aaron had chosen.

There were just the name, dates and a short inscription.

He had made all the arrangements himself and Emma was with him at the cemetery. And Henry.

It was Henry who'd retraced Reichmann's movements in New York to the mortuary and discovered the air transfer order of one plain coffin to Ehrenfriedhof. A coffin with a gold crematory urn inside. Aaron was the only claimant to step forward for the body of the German in Montreal. He and Emma accompanied it on the flight from Canada to Germany.

They were waiting for the priest when the large black car pulled up abruptly outside. An old man climbed out from the rear door. Lubetkin.

"I came as soon as I got your telegram, Aaron," the old man said. He unfolded the yellow paper. "We're burying Kruuze on the tenth," Lubetkin read. "Ehrenfriedhof Cemetery, outside Heidelberg. Come if you like." The old German looked up at Aaron. "I don't hear from you in weeks and suddenly a telegram to attend a funeral?"

"You came," Aaron said.

"Yes, of course I came. Four thousand miles I came." He glanced around past Emma and Henry. "Where is it?"

"I sent you the telegram because I thought you'd like to be here for the end. We're burying it today. It's all over."

Lubetkin nodded impatiently. "Yes, yes, I know all that. Reichmann's dead. But what about the urn?" He lowered his voice. "What have you done with the urn?"

Aaron's glance touched Emma a moment and Henry. He looked into the old man's eyes. "The war is over now. All finished. That's why I asked you to come. Did you find Strausser? Mengele or Mueller?"

"No. They totally disappeared. I think they're dead." Lubetkin sighed. "At least I'm satisfied they're dead. There's nothing for them to return to. If they're not dead, they might as well be. The Church has all their money."

"Then you've won," Aaron said. "It's all finished."

"Not at all, my boy," Lubetkin smiled slightly. "There's still the urn. I want to have it . . . like a memento. A trophy of our victory."

"And put it in a special place where we can all look at it?"

"Of course. A museum, perhaps, or some sort of—"

"Shrine?"

The old man suddenly made a face. "No. Not like that. I didn't mean that." He looked at the others. "Where is it?"

"You can't have it," Emma said. "Nobody can."

"Look, Aaron, Emma . . ." He looked at their empty faces and suddenly he was angry. "I have a great deal of money. I'll buy it. I'll give you—"

"I destroyed it," Aaron said. "I melted it down. There isn't an urn anymore."

"Mmm-melted?" Lubetkin stammered. He touched a frail finger to his lips. "But . . . but the contents, you didn't—"

"Scattered to the four winds from a rampart of the Heidelberg Castle."

"Oh God, you didn't!"

"I told you, it's over now." Aaron turned to the polished wood casket on a portable metal frame "We're burying the very last vestiges of the indomitable thousand-year Reich today. The chase is over, Emil. If you can see that, maybe others will."

"But the urn. You didn't really—"

Aaron pointed to the casket. "Judge for yourself."

The old man glanced at it, then again closely. His eyes widened.

"Aaron!"

"The old Reich and the new have been defeated," Aaron said.

Lubetkin moved quickly to the casket. He wouldn't take his eyes off it. "How could you do this?"

"Because it's over," Aaron said. "Today we finish it and it's done for all time."

Lubetkin reached out a trembling hand to touch the inlaid gold band that circled the casket—melted gold recast from an urn. Tears filled his eyes as the memories came flooding back to him. Buchenwald. Sachsenhausen. The faces of those lost. Here was the symbol of all that he loved and hated of a nation that existed only as a memory. The old man touched the gold band.

"Done for all time," he said. He raised his gray, tired eyes to Aaron. "For all time?"

Aaron nodded. Then a priest came for them.

Georg Kruuze was buried beside his mother. The stone was engraved simply, "Devoted son," with the dates of his life.

MAY 17, 1920–AUGUST 1, 1936

Four persons attended the brief service. After a priest had read the short passages and ended with a prayer, the ceremony was finally, quietly, closed.